3.50

SWEEPING DRAMA, FLAMING RAPTURE!

In one year, Katherine Lawrence blossomed from a backwoods country girl into a brilliant young actress. But international stardom wasn't enough. Greedy for life, she played just as many parts off the stage as on—with as many men . . .

NICHOLAS VAN DYNE—The vagabond aristocrat, lured from her intoxicating embrace to the gold fields of Brazil . . . SASHA DESCHAMP— Half-gypsy, half-noble, he brought Katherine back from the brink of despair . . . TERRY O'NEILL—A fiery Irish actor, his genius spurred her career—his loving almost destroyed her . . . J. CARLYLE WHARTON—A Southern gentleman, Katherine was his last hope, as he was hers . . .

THE DARKER SIDE OF LOVE

INTRIGUE AND ROMANCE IN THE BRIGHTLY COLORED WORLD OF THE VICTORIAN THEATRE

Also by Anna James

from Jove Books

SWEET LOVE, BITTER LOVE

THE DARKER SIDE OF LOVE

ANNA JAMES

J

A JOVE BOOK

Printed in the United States of America

First Jove edition published September 1979

10 9 8 7 6 5 4 3 2 1

Jove books are published by Jove Publications, Inc.,
200 Madison Avenue, New York, NY 10016

THE
DARKER SIDE
OF LOVE

OVERTURE

France, August 1876

The moon, full and bright, sneaked quietly behind a cloud. The dogs began to bark. A baby cried. Through the night air came the strains of a plaintive violin. It was late summer in the South of France, and the Rom were here. The gypsy caravans were arrayed in a loose circle, far off the main road that winds through the Loire Valley north toward Orleans. The last embers of a fire flickered in the inky darkness left by the disappearing moon. Now and then a dark shape was outlined against the candlelight of an open wagon door.

Moving abruptly from the shadows, like a shadow herself, a slim figure appeared. Her full skirts swirled about her ankles as she began to move to the music of the solitary violin. She lifted her arms above her head and bent like a young sapling blown in the breeze. Her thick hair hung to her shoulders, and as she turned in a slow circle, it fell upon her face like a dark waterfall.

Seemingly alone, yet watched by many eyes, she took up the accelerated tempo of the music. At that moment the moon rode out of the clouds, illuminating her swaying figure with a ghostly iridescence. The tempo of the violin quickened and her body answered its passion, her hips swaying sensuously, her hands spontaneously outlining the curves of her breasts, her waist, her hips. Her soft leather boots were like magic, so lightly did they touch the ground. She gave herself to the music as if to an unseen lover, possessed by it, tormented by it. At last the violin reached a crescendo of finality, and she fell exhausted and trembling to the ground, her head lowered.

The night air was full of silence, and then she felt a soft touch on her hair.

"Katerina, you dance like a *gitana*. No one would guess you are not one of us."

It was the *vataf*, Josef, and he spoke softly in French as he helped the girl to her feet. Still holding onto her hand, he led her around the circle of applauding Rom as the music began once more, and one by one, the men and women started to dance.

Far into the night the music and the dancing continued, and Katerina joined in with as much vitality as the others; she was not one of them, not a *gitana*, but seeing her among them, a stranger could not have guessed.

Morning in the gypsy encampment came in a leisurely fashion. The Rom did not keep time in the usual way but awoke as nature intended, going about their tasks at their own pace, with no clocks to guide or to impede them. But this morning, when Katerina opened her eyes, all was still quiet, and the sweet, heady smell of brewing coffee had not yet invaded the camp. She dressed quickly, gathered a soft towel and a bar of fragrant soap, and headed toward the creekbed at the edge of the clearing. She had learned that she must bathe downstream, away from the drinking water, and that the men and women never bathed near each other.

The sun was just beginning to creep over the treetops as she made her way toward her bathing spot, but perspiration was already gathering on her forehead, and tiny insects had begun to buzz about her face. She rounded the bend that led to a secluded pool formed by large boulders protruding from the stream. She hung her clothes on a bush, carefully put her boots high on a rock, and waded into the water, moving slowly at first, until she became used to the chill against her skin. Then on lathering herself, luxuriating in her outdoor the fresh, clear air and lit by the rising sun. Finally, deep breath, she submerged and rinsed the soap from her hair.

When the bath was completed, she drifted to the edge of the stream and reached for her towel. It was not on the bush. What had happened to it, she wondered. Then she saw him, standing under the low-hanging branches of a tree, with the towel held casually in his hand. He smiled but said nothing. She stood hesitating, not knowing whether to return to the water or move to retrieve her towel. He had seen her nakedness—covering herself now would accomplish nothing—and so she advanced toward him.

Josef smiled upon the beauty of the girl. Her rich brown hair hung wetly to her shoulders, partially obscuring the small, heart-shaped face. She reached to brush back a strand of hair, thus revealing a wide, perfectly formed mouth. Her eyes, large and doe-brown, were startled but flashed as much with temptation as with fear, and the proud chin was still held high. He did not ask who this girl was. She had come among them, and they had accepted her. He did not suspect, nor did any of the tribe, that she was not Katerina at all, but Katherine Lawrence, the startling young American actress who had captured the heart of the public in her own country and abroad. He did not know why she was here in France, in this tiny camp of the Rom, her skin darkened by the sun until, with her dark hair and eyes, she looked as if she had been born among them. He did

not know what had brought her to his people at the
height of her career. He did not know, but he suspected
it had been an unusually long journey. And so it had
been.

New York City, November 1875

The theater lay in darkness except for a few gaslights
that flickered at the foot of the stage upon which the
girl sat in a straight-backed chair, alone. In a side aisle
near the corner of the proscenium, four people were
gathered, forming a shadowy tableau: a tall man beside a
much shorter one and, standing somewhat apart, an attractive couple whose bearing was decidedly theatrical.
The tall man moved up the aisle and then turned, one
hand resting on the back of a house seat, to face the
stage. He was sturdily built and impeccably clad in a
pale gray suit and vest and a soft Eton collar, with a
cravat barely a half-shade darker than the vest. He
wore his well-fitting clothes with an unconsciously elegant air, but although thoroughly at ease, he did not
seem to belong to the musty world of this dark, empty
theater, nor did he appear to be impressed by its magic.
He was joined almost immediately by the shorter man,
who was dressed in a rumpled plaid suit and spoke rapidly while wiping his brow with a crumpled handker-

chief. It was a reflexive gesture, for the theater itself was cold.

The girl on stage, the object of everyone's attention, remained quietly seated behind the dim flames of the footlights, her dark eyes fixed on the tall man as if, from the distance of forty feet or more, she could pick up his words.

He spoke impatiently. "I don't understand your logic at all, Lester. The girl has no experience worth considering, and although God knows she is beautiful enough, I still can't imagine you would want to take such a chance."

Lester Markan, owner of the 14th Street Theater, wiped his forehead again.

"It's this way, Nick. I trust the Piersons. They've been with the company a long time. Hell, they're the mainstays of the Markan Tours, you know that. They wouldn't be pushing the girl if they didn't think she had talent. And I heard her read, Nick. She's good, very good." Lester gestured to the couple who had remained standing in the shadows near the stage. "Glenna and William would never have brought the girl to New York if they didn't think she could make it."

"Where did they find her?"

"Oh, some two-bit town in the Carolinas—"

"Deaton, South Carolina, in fact, Nick," William Pierson answered, as he and his wife moved up the aisle. "Our ingenue ran off with a carpetbagger, and Katherine appeared at just the right moment. Her accent was godawful, but she had a natural talent, and Glenna has been working with her."

"Holy Jesus." Nick Van Dyne shook his head. "I'll never understand this business. God knows why I trust Lester with my money, but I do."

"And we've made a big profit for you these last years," Lester said in his most authoritative voice—the voice of the impresario of Markan Tours and its resident theater. He pocketed his handkerchief confidently.

"I can't complain, Lester, but when there are so many experienced actresses in New York—"

"Like Edwina Ramsay," Lester responded. The Piersons did not enter into this phase of the conversation, but they had obviously heard it all before. "Now, Edwina is a beautiful woman and a fine actress, but she's over thirty, and even though she's your current—that is, a close friend—she's not, let's face it, an ingenue. Besides, Nick, I thought we agreed never to mix business and pleasure." He paused for a reaction, but the twinkle in Nicholas Van Dyne's eyes was so quick that Lester missed it as he went on, "Now this little girl—look at that face, such freshness—"

"Lester, Lester, did I even mention Edwina?" Lester looked up, trying to remember just how this whole conversation had begun. "No, I did not; *you* mentioned her." Nick grinned, revealing the slightest dimple in either cheek, almost at the corners of his mouth. "But, of course, I was going to bring up her name." The Piersons had to smile then, as Lester brought out his handkerchief once more. "After all, I am seeing her this evening, and she'll certainly ask! But as for the hiring, you've always had the last word, and with Glenna and William's approval, hell, you can choose anyone you wish, even this little—"

"No. You're my partner, Nick, and I want you to approve our choice. Just talk to her. You'll see."

Nick stole a glance at the Piersons before he said softly to Lester, "Are you sure *you* aren't mixing business and pleasure?"

Lester Markan ignored his friend's question and moved down the aisle to the stage-left steps. Katherine rose from her chair as he and the others crossed to center stage.

"Miss Lawrence, may I present Mr. Nicholas Van Dyne? Nick, this is Miss Katherine Lawrence."

"How do you do, Mr. Van Dyne."

Her voice was soft and husky, only slightly accented. Almost honeyed, he thought involuntarily. And she was as beautiful close up as she had seemed from a distance. Nick knew from experience that this was rarely the case. Her eyes were so large that they almost dominated her face, but the other features could not be dominated, so nearly perfect were they. Her nose was small, tilted slightly at the end, and it wrinkled in a beguiling way when she smiled. He wondered if that occurred naturally, but remembered immediately that she was an actress and had no doubt spent hours of practice before the mirror. Lord knows, he had seen enough such women not to be fooled by this one.

She spoke again, looking now at Lester Markan with those dark eyes. "I'm so grateful for the part in your troupe, Mr. Markan."

Lester shuffled uneasily. "Well, Miss Lawrence, that's what I wanted Nick to talk to you about. You see, he's my partner and—"

"Mr. Van Dyne does not approve?" Her lips remained parted after the question was asked.

Another trick of the trade, Nick thought, and very effective with that wide mouth, its line so deeply etched that it was all Nick could do to resist bending down to kiss the parted lips.

But that was hardly Nick Van Dyne's style. "I don't know you, Miss Lawrence, and am therefore not yet in a position to approve or disapprove."

"Are you in the theater, Mr. Van Dyne? A director? An actor?" She drew herself up to her full five feet two inches, tilting her head back to look into Nick's face.

"No, I operate the business, not the theatrical side, and in that capacity, I haven't yet found it necessary to reach into the backwater South for an untried commodity."

There was clearly a sexual overtone in the remark that the girl did not miss. And yet Nick was teasing now; his mind was already made up. But Lester and the Piersons did not know that, and they seemed uneasy as the little episode between these two played on.

"Perhaps, then, Mr. Van Dyne, I could audition for you." She paused effectively. "So I would no longer be 'untried.' "

"But you just read for me, Miss Lawrence; there's no need—" Lester began, but he was silenced quickly by looks from both protaganists. They were, for all practical purposes, the only two people in the theater at this moment.

As Nick descended the steps to take a seat in the front row, he turned and looked at her again quickly. She was not toying with him, as he had been with her. She was no tease. The girl was serious, and under her spirited response there was none of the hardness he had seen so often in other actresses. Nick settled into his seat, wondering to himself, as many would do after him, how much of what he saw was the woman and how much was the actress. What elements had combined to shape her, this beautiful Katherine Lawrence?

ACT I

"Speak the speech, I pray you, as I pronounced it to you, trippingly on the tongue . . ."

Hamlet, Act 3, Scene 2.

Chapter 1

I remember the first day I discovered the world of play-acting. I was six years old, and there was a terrible war raging about me. Even now, if I close my eyes, I can hear the roar of cannon, the crackle of rifle fire, as the Yankees wrought devastation everywhere, terrifying those left behind—the aged, the children, the women whose men were fighting on other battlefields. We were a house of women then: my brother's wife, Laurel Ann, her baby daughter, Courtney, and myself. That spring afternoon, I stood beside the road watching a long line of soldiers march by, and I played my first role. The sullen face I had worn since the Yankees had first appeared was lit up as if by magic as I turned my prettiest smile on the last soldier in the formation. And for this smile I was rewarded with a sack of hard candy which I clutched greedily to my skinny chest as I made my way back to the house. I soon learned that a pretty song was worth a precious bag of sugar or salt.

I hated those crude-talking men who ranged over our

land, yet I learned to dissemble and act and turn the situation to my advantage, at least during those most terrible months when our need was greatest. At least until the day my smile of thanks was returned with a soldier's hug, and I felt something thick and hard pushing against my stomach. When I moved away, I saw the throbbing bulge in his trousers. And I ran. I didn't tell Laurel Ann, but she knew, and I was never allowed to stand by the road again.

But my play-acting had another purpose. Life on a farm in the South, even after my brother's return in 1865, was difficult, often painful. Day after day we worked in the fields, plowing, planting, hoeing, harvesting cotton, trying desperately to bring a new crop to life after four fallow years. Reality was not pleasant. So I pretended. I pretended I was a princess who had come in disguise to visit the poor of her kingdom. I made up long scenarios for my fantasy and so staved off the heat of summer, the aching muscles, the hunger that accompanies reality. What had begun as an escape was soon a way of life, and I had become an actress. I grew to womanhood with a commitment to my dream, a dream for which I was well suited. I had never lacked self-discipline. My mind was quick, and I could memorize whole speeches after one reading. My ability to mimic amused my school friends and amazed my teachers. I was also pretty; I had only to look in the mirror to see that for myself. My dark hair and eyes set me apart from my blonde, blue-eyed playmates. "A fly in buttermilk," Laurel Ann always said when she saw me returning from school surrounded by towheaded friends. I felt exotic and foreign, and I knew the boys—even the men—found me attractive. I pranced like a filly under their gaze, not unaware of the feelings I provoked, but ignoring their meaning. It was not the approval of one man I sought, but the applause of many. At eighteen I had gone as far as I could go in my own training, and I knew the time had come for me to look beyond my home to the place where my dream must carry me.

"Katherine! Get on in here now. Supper's almost ready and the table's not even set."

"I'll be right there, Laurel Ann," I called from the back porch where I sat on Mama's old rocker, the well-worn book open in my lap. I closed my eyes tightly, memorizing yet another line, envisioning myself as Ophelia as she becomes consumed by confusion that borders on madness. I was sure I could capture her feeling as she spoke, "There's rosemary, that's for remembrance; pray, love, remember . . ."

"Katherine Sloane Lawrence," Laurel Ann called again, using my full name to show she meant business.

I reluctantly put the old volume of Shakespeare aside to join her in the large kitchen that served as dining room also, our more formal dining room having long since been turned over to Laurel Ann's loom and needlework. My brother's wife was a gentle woman, but sometimes she just couldn't seem to resist chiding me, however gently. "Katherine, I don't want to fuss, you understand that, because you always carry your load, but someday, honey, you're going to have to get your nose out of those play books and start paying some serious attention to things that matter. Just last night, Jamie was saying—"

"Jamie's my brother, not my father." I took the heavy earthenware plates from the cupboard and set six places at the table.

"Well, he's the head of the house, anyway, and you're his responsibility."

"No, Laurel Ann, *you're* his responsibility, you and the children. I'm just his sister. I have my own life."

"Then you'd better start paying some serious attention to those young men who come calling, if you're planning to make a home of your own."

I folded the linen napkins instinctively as I looked at her across the long room. "I didn't say a home, I said a life."

"It's all the same." Laurel Ann began moving the platters of food from the stove to the kitchen table. "Go on now, and wash up. I'll ring the bell for the others."

I sighed audibly as I moved down the hall and climbed the stairs to my room. How could I say to Laurel Ann, who was so kind and good, that I would rather die than live in Deaton all my life? It was right for her, but not for me. I knew there was more to life than the town of Deaton, and I would have it. Laurel Ann often told me I was too greedy for life—that I wanted everything, and that nobody could have everything. But I could. And I would. Somehow. Looking out the window, I saw Laurel Ann wipe her hands on her apron before she stepped up to the huge bell that summoned the family to meals. It rang out through the late afternoon air, three loud peals that flushed the birds skyward and sent the squirrels scampering to the treetops. Two rings were for emergencies—I had heard those often enough, and closed my ears against the memory. But I couldn't remember ever hearing just one ring—that had been to summon the Negroes from the fields in the long-ago days before the war, when I was just a baby.

I was a child of my parents' old age. After Jamie was born came another boy, Andrew, who lived just a year before succumbing to scarlet fever; and then the twins, both stillborn. For years the doctor had told Mother she was too frail, too weak to have another child, but she wanted a little girl, and at last she got her wish. She lived just long enough to see me. Jamie was twenty when I was born, and that same year he married Laurel Ann and brought her to live with us.

The echo of the bell still hung in the air as I washed and dried my hands before going down to join the others at dinner. Apparently, Laurel Ann was still harping on my future. I entered the room to hear nine-year-old John saying, "Well, some day she's going to be a famous stage actress, right on the stage."

"Where else would she be a stage actress, in the hayloft?" asked Phillip. He was twelve now and going through a very smart-alecky period.

"She isn't going to be a stage actress anywhere," my brother said as I took my place at the table.

I looked at him sharply but didn't answer. Once I had hoped he might help me and encourage me in my dream, but after many tearful scenes, I had learned better. His world was a tangible one, a world he could touch, a world his hands could become calloused on: the world of the plow, the hoe, the milkpail. Maybe his dream had already come true—his and Laurel Ann's—come true in the land they had brought back to life, in the three children they had reared and the warm home that now, at last, had good food on the table, not just the sweet potatoes and turnip greens of wartime. The years had been hard, but Jamie and Laurel Ann had never lost hope, and what's more, they had never lost their sense of humor.

I heard Jamie's laughter now, as he said, "Remember the time you put on *Sleeping Beauty* in the shed and the curtain collapsed on the Princess?"

"That was *Rapunzel*," I corrected him.

"Who could ever keep up with which one you were putting on?" Phillip asked.

"Not 'putting on,'" I admonished again, "staging."

"And starring in," Courtney added without a trace of jealousy. She was just two years younger than I, but as long as her costumes were pretty, she had never cared which part she played. Besides I had usually played the male parts since John was only a baby and Phillip could never remember his lines.

"My favorite," Laurel Ann spoke up, captured by the mood, "was *Rumpelstiltskin*."

"Was that the one where Phillip wet his pants?" Courtney asked unabashedly.

Phillip, just about to bite into a drumstick, looked up in horror. "I did not!"

"Yes, you did. You only had one line, and you were so scared you forgot what it was, and you—"

"Phillip was only four or five then," I laughed. "I guess I began too soon trying to make an actor of him."

We were all laughing now, and the meal ended pleas-

antly, as it so often did these days. Times had changed,
but one thing would not, could not change, and that was
Jamie's attitude toward my career. My childish antics
had amused him, but the idea of my leaving home to
pursue a career was preposterous and could not be con-
doned. Jamie, whose coloring was as dark as mine,
glowered like a thundercloud when he became angry.
None of us liked to cross him, but I knew that soon I
must, for my will was as strong as his.

Our Sassy arrived early the next morning. She had
been with us since the days of slavery, and although
most of her family had left for the North after the war,
Sassy had stayed, and she still came in to help with the
housework. After she gave me a hug, she told me to
scoot off and let her finish the morning dishes.

Eager for some time to myself, I picked up a book
and walked down the hall to the front porch. The day
was warm, but the sun was not yet high, and I stood for
a moment looking out across the broad front yard to the
long row of magnolia trees which bordered the lane
leading to our house—named *Magnolias* by my father
when he had built it over forty years ago, before he and
Mother were married. It was a rambling two-story
house with large, airy rooms and high ceilings. Mother
had papered most of the walls, but the living room had
been painted a very pale yellow. The floors were all oak
except for the kitchen and back porch, which had cool
stone floors worn smooth over the years. Long before I
was born, a high rock wall had been built beside the
road and along the perimeter of the yard, surrounding
the house and adding a feeling of security and privacy.
Later, Papa put a cannery out back, and farther down
the hill beyond the wall were the barns and other out-
buildings, including the shed where I had produced my
plays.

Father had died in a prison camp during the last year
of the war, but Jamie survived and came home to fight
the battle of Reconstruction.

I should have loved what we had all brought back to

life, but having so long ago tried to escape its sadness by burying myself in my own imaginary world, I no longer thought of my home at all; or if I did, it was only as a place from which I would go to find my own life, my life in the theater.

I moved across the yard to the hemp hammock that hung between two fat live oaks. How old these trees were no one knew, but their girth was such that it had taken yards of rope to tie the hammock to them. I fell into the hammock, letting it swing for a while before I lay back and opened my book, a new one I had ordered from New York after months of saving up and, of course, without Jamie's knowledge. The old Shakespeare had been Papa's, so Jamie could hardly begrudge me that, but I knew he'd have a fit if he found out I had used precious funds to send off for a book. Especially this one, *Memoirs of Mrs. Siddons,* by the English actress who had long been my idol. I forced myself to read slowly, lingering over each page just as, when a child, I had lingered over each sweet, savory bite of a rare piece of candy, sucking slowly rather than chewing, dreading the moment when it would be finished. In the same way, I savored the book with a glorious gluttony, not knowing then that I would reread it many times and that it would travel halfway around the world with me.

The air was heavy, and no breeze stirred. Just as I was considering a move to the old rocker on the cool back porch, a familiar voice called out from down the lane, "Katie! Katie!" There was no mistaking the high-pitched squeal of my best friend, Thelma Cooper. "Katie, you'll never believe it!" Thelma pushed through the gate and almost flew across the lawn, tendrils of golden hair falling from her pompadour and curling about her flushed face. In her hand she clutched a piece of paper, which she waved wildly in my face. "They're coming! Look! Look!"

"Stop jumping so, Thelma. What in the world is it?"

I managed to grab the flyer from her hand and read the bold black type aloud: " *'Markan Touring Theatrical Company. William Pierson—Glenna Nelson.'* Oh,

my Lord, Thelma. They're in Deaton, and for a whole
week. They're doing—oh—*Rip Van Winkle*." I tried to
hide my disappointment, wishing the choice were more
to my liking. "Oh, who cares which play. This is real
theater."

"I know, I know! But who is William Pierson? Who
is Glenna—"

"They're very famous actor-managers from New
York. Oh, Thelma—" I let out a wail. "How can I ever
get to see it? Look, it costs thirty-five cents, and I don't
have a nickel to my name. Jamie will never give me the
money to go to a play. Damnation!"

"Katherine, you mustn't say that."

"I know, I'll go straight to hell, but who cares? I certainly don't, not if I can't see this play." Thelma joined
me in the hammock, which swayed erratically as she
bounced about. After a moment I shouted out, "David
Goodwin!"

"David?"

"Yes, he keeps calling, almost every day. He's invited
me to the church picnic. I've already said no, but I'll
just tell him I've changed my mind. We'll go to the
theater instead."

"Do you think he'll do it?"

"There's not the slightest little doubt in my mind," I
said in my most Southern accent, looking at Thelma
with lowered eyes and quivering lashes.

Thelma squealed again. "Katie, you *are* an actress."

"Well, I must say it is handy to be able to 'put on'
once in a while, but you do the same thing every time
Marshall Hammond comes around."

"I never!"

" 'Course you do. That's not acting, that's just being
a girl, that's just doing what Laurel Ann is always after
me to do—bat my eyes, look pretty, and sound helpless."

But I was not a flirt. I never had been, in spite of
Laurel Ann's prodding. I saved my acting for the stage.
It was true that, as a child, I had created a world of
make-believe in which to hide, but even then I knew the

difference between acting and reality, and as I grew older I could see clearly—more clearly, perhaps, than those whose lives had not begun as mine had—the fine line that separated reality from make-believe.

But David Goodwin was another thing. I needed him, because I knew that somehow I must see this play, even though it was only *Rip Van Winkle*—hardly a serious Shakespearean drama—but it was real theater. Oh, we'd had circuses and other traveling shows in Deaton, South Carolina, the small town where, the year before, I had graduated from school; where, for three years running, I had captured the declamation prize; and where I had annually played Gabriel, the Messenger Angel, in the church pageant. But never in all my life had I seen a professional play.

I accepted David's invitation to the church social that Saturday, and, with hardly any effort, convinced him that we would have much more fun if we went alone—just us two—to see *Rip Van Winkle*.

The play was performed on a makeshift stage at the old warehouse by the river, the largest building in Deaton, with the audience sitting on a variety of hard-backed chairs, on boxes, or even standing in the back of the "theater."

The scenery didn't quite fit in the area that served as a stage; there weren't enough gas lamps to give adequate light; the curtain hung slightly askew and didn't close completely. But I was transported out of myself into the world of the long ago Catskills, the world of Rip and his friends. I had read the play at the library a number of times, as I had read all the popular plays, whether they were favorites or not, and I had considered it a silly theater piece until tonight when it came to life. Peggie Dale played the ingenue, and before the evening was over, I decided to learn those lines. It was a part I would love to play and, who knew, perhaps one day I would.

David was particularly talkative on the ride home and didn't seem to notice that I spoke not a word.

Somehow, I just couldn't, nor could I bear to invite him
in for lemonade. He spoke of seeing me the next day,
and I mumbled an answer. Finally, he left.

During the hard years when Laurel Ann was beset by
the problems of day-to-day existence, I recall her saying
after one especially trying experience, "I just didn't
sleep a wink all night." I had laughed to myself at that,
sure she was just talking nonsense—how could anyone
lie in bed all night without sleeping? Well, I didn't sleep
that night, the night I saw my first real play. I lay
awake until dawn, reliving every scene, every line, every
nuance. I knew I must see it again, I must meet the
cast. And I would.

At noon the following day, I walked up the steps of
the Cleveland House quickly; if I didn't hurry, I was
afraid I might turn back. My stomach began a slow rise
upwards to my throat, and I felt as if I were getting
ready for a performance myself, which in fact I was: I
was getting ready to play a very important scene, but I
did not know my lines. I was about to meet Glenna Nelson, but I had no idea what I would say. I had rehearsed a dozen speeches in my mind. None of them
seemed right, and in the end—as always—I played myself.

Miss Nelson was sitting on the side porch of the hotel, her slim figure erect, her jet black hair piled high. I
stopped for a moment to take a deep breath before approaching her. I had sent a note asking if I might call at
twelve o'clock. Then I had waited until late morning to
have the note delivered, so that she wouldn't have a
chance to turn me down, but as I moved to meet her, I
could see in her dark violet eyes that she welcomed me.

That day and every day during the week's tour, I sat
beside Glenna Nelson at the Cleveland House, and we
spent half an hour, sometimes longer, talking about the
theater. I listened like a pupil to her stories, her advice,
her wisdom. Looking back, I expect that she welcomed
the interlude as much as I, for tours can be lonely as

well as tiring, and often the fresh face and spirit of an unassuming young person can be a delight.

On the last night, Glenna's husband, William Pierson, allowed me to watch the play from the wings, as long as I was careful not to get underfoot. Having assured him that I would make myself invisible, I stood mesmerized as the speeches drifted toward me like the scent of the sweetest-smelling flowers.

An older, well-known actor named Eugene Fitch brought the character of Rip to life. Glenna and William played the second lead couple with Peggie Dale and Drew Dowd as the young lovers. It was Peggie's role that had captured my imagination on opening night, and which I had learned by heart in less than a morning's time, lying in the hammock while Laurel Ann and Sassy were out shopping.

Too soon, the play was over and I went home to confront Jamie. After fumbling with excuses that he knew were not true (I had never mastered the art of lying to my brother), I told him where I had been and listened patiently as he scolded me for my hopeless dreams, for acting like a silly schoolgirl. "You're grown now, Katherine, and it's time you put this nonsense behind you. I don't expect this sort of behavior to happen again." I didn't answer as I climbed the stairs, for I had already decided that I would slip away from church in the morning to get to the hotel in time to tell the actors goodbye.

But when I arrived the next day, there was no sign of the cast, and for a terrible moment I feared they had already left. I rushed past the desk clerk and climbed the stairs to find Glenna's door open and everything in complete disarray. Peggie Dale had run off after the final curtain with a carpetbagger whom she had met in Columbia two weeks before.

William and Glenna paid little attention to me as they reviewed the choices open to the company. "Could you play Lowena?" William asked his wife.

"I don't see how; she's practically a child in the first act. No, we'll just have to go through the repertory and find a play with fewer female roles, one where I can pass for the ingenue, either that or cancel the remainder of the tour."

"I can do Peggie's role," I said.

Glenna did not hear me, or appeared not to. "Oh, William, do you remember that little comedy about the Revolution—what was it called—*Love in '76?*"

"My dear, we haven't done that in years. No one has."

"Yes, but if I recall, there were only two major women's roles."

"I can play Lowena," I said again, more loudly.

For the first time, they stopped to look at me, both with expressions of disbelief—William's bemused, Glenna's more serious. "Katherine," she said sweetly, "we've talked often these past days about your ambitions, but, my dear, you have virtually no training, not to mention the fact that you'd have to learn the part—"

"I've already learned the part." Looks of disbelief passed between them once more. "I liked it and thought it might be a good part to know. I've learned lots of parts—Ophelia, Leady Teazle—"

They both began to laugh. I controlled my tears, thinking they were laughing at me.

"Well," William said finally, "we certainly won't be doing *Hamlet* or *The School for Scandal* on this tour, but since you know the part—" I caught my breath— "we could give it a try. It's certainly better than cancelling, and the role is not large." He paused thoughtfully. "The accent's going to be a big problem."

"Oh, I've been training my voice for years. I'm a good mimic, really I am." I delivered one of the lines in my most Dutch voice. They laughed again, and again I despaired.

"No, dear," William said, bringing his laughter under control, "we'll just have to try it straight—no accent at all. I don't believe you're quite at the point in your career to do more than eliminate as much of the South as possible from your voice. Come, let's read through it now, and we'll see."

I tried to control my panic as William handed me Peggie's playbook. My voice "training" had amounted to listening more than speaking, since, from early childhood, I had trailed after newcomers to Deaton, hanging on each word, memorizing pronunciation and speech patterns. Afterwards, I would stand in front of the mirror in my room, repeating entire speeches with a pencil clamped between my teeth. Somewhere I had read that that was a sure way to perfect enunciation! I sighed deeply. For now, I would simply have to do the best I could.

When the reading was over, Glenna and William moved aside to discuss the verdict. Perhaps desperation won out over reason, because they agreed to take me on. Since I knew my family was still at church, I had the Piersons drive me to Magnolias. They came in with me and waited in the parlor. I ran upstairs and threw all my clothes into my trunk while Sassy screamed, "You can't do this! It'll kill Miz Laurel Ann. And Mister Jamie, he'll kill *you*!"

I was screaming now, too. "I don't care. This is my only chance to get out of here, and no one will spoil it for me. No one! I'm going to act!" What the Piersons thought of my display, which was clearly audible throughout the house, I did not know. But as they helped load my belongings for the ride back to the hotel, I sensed a feeling of uneasiness over how Jamie might react to my flight. About this, I was able to reassure them. My brother would never do anything to cause embarrassment to the family. He would put out the story that I was in Charleston visiting relatives, and then he'd sit back and wait for my return and my admission of failure. Well, I wouldn't come back, and I wouldn't fail.

At the age of six, when I learned of the world of make-believe and decided to become an actress, I did not know what an actress was; as I grew up and began to study seriously on my own, I thought I knew. But not until my tour began did I finally learn just what it meant to be an actress: it meant weeks of travel over rough roads in weather that was either stiflingly hot or torrentially wet; it meant nights spent in shabby, impersonal hotel rooms; and it meant days of work and evenings of performing—often before rude, unappreciative audiences. And I loved it. I loved it from the first moment I stepped into the carriage and we headed for the next stop on the Markan tour—Charlotte, North Carolina.

As soon as we had arrived and unpacked the scenery, costumes, and props, we went immediately into rehearsal, specially called because there was now a new player in the troupe—one who had never performed on the professional stage, in this or any other play. The cast was very patient as William blocked out each move for me, making marks on the floorboards in chalk, from my first entrance through each of my scenes. We did the run-through in street clothes, not stopping to take time with costumes and makeup. I had learned my lines and felt that I understood the character I would play and could bring her to life, and with William's help I memorized the technical aspects of the role. In one day, that was all we could do. We hoped it would be enough.

And for Charlotte audiences, it was. The play was well-received, and although I was not singled out, neither was I booed!

William's first words as he entered the dressing room Glenna and I shared were kind. "You did a very adequate job with your interpretation. You didn't miss a line, nor did you step on anyone else's lines—and that, as you will learn, can make an actress the lifelong friend of her company."

I smiled my thanks to his reflection in the mirror before which I sat, spreading cream over my face to remove the greasepaint.

"Unfortunately, adequacy is not enough," he added in a voice that was light yet serious.

I turned then to look at him, and to my surprise, he laughed.

"Tuck a towel into your collar, my dear, or you'll have cream all over yourself."

I did as I was told, still waiting for him to continue.

"For the next few weeks, we will be playing Southern towns, and if this one is an example, they will not be offended by your untrained voice—"

"But Glenna and I are working on my accent. I'm getting better, aren't I, Glenna?"

Glenna had stepped out of her costume and into a soft cotton robe. The air in the tiny dressing room we shared was close and sticky. She had pinned up her long black hair, and now she wiped her damp neck with the corner of a makeup towel.

"You're coming along very nicely, Katherine, and learning fast."

"However," William went on, "this is a Markan tour, and with each stop as we approach New York, the play should improve significantly. I expect each player to be as perfectly tuned as the most mellow violin. Because you joined us late, Katherine, we should ask less of you, but because you show signs of becoming a fine actress, we will ask more."

That was all there was to it. I would practice during every waking hour that we weren't performing, working not only to eliminate my accent but to enunicate so that I could project my voice without straining it.

Soon something began to happen that I had never dreamed possible. I was able to say a line softly, almost in a whisper, and William, seated in the last row of the theater, was able to hear every word. And then something else happened, considerably less thrilling—I became so hoarse that I was forced to travel from town to town laden with fresh lemons and jars of honey! Before each performance, Glenna patiently rubbed my chest with camphor. In time, my voice grew used to the nightly trials I put it through, and the camphor was at last packed away. I survived. We all did—but barely—

and the few days of rest after two weeks in Virginia
were as welcome as the long sleep Rip himself took on
the hillside nightly.

During the interlude, William let up on me enough to
suggest that for a day or two I forget the play and relax.
And so, when Drew Dowd asked me to take a walk
through Charlottesville with him, I accepted. We had
been together on the stage every night, he as my sweet-
heart, Gustave, but once the curtain descended, we saw
little of each other until it rose again the following evening. Occasionally he had asked me to join him for a
meal, but I had declined unless there was a special reason for us to work together on a change in stage business. But this time, I joined him for a long walk through
town and out to the University of Virginia, with its lush
campus surrounded by the serpentine wall that had
been designed by Thomas Jefferson.

The day was unusually pleasant for late summer in
Virginia, and we sat together under a tree just outside
the curving wall, talking.

Sometime during that afternoon, I stretched, leaned
back against the tree, closed my eyes, and decided to
fall in love with Drew Dowd.

Within me, I heard a tiny voice say that an actress
should keep her personal and stage lives separate. But
another, clearer voice answered that every actress must
enrich her life's experience and thus lend dimension to
her performance. After all, I had experienced suffering
during those terrible years at Magnolias when war
raged. I had been infatuated, from time to time, during
the courting days when young men came to call. I had
felt frustration at being held back from my dream, and
happiness at last on the tour. Surely, love was next.

I was convinced that I understood that emotion—it
was what Juliet felt for Romeo, Isolde for Tristan, and,
even in our own play, Lowena for her dear Gustave.
And it was more than a mere meeting of the heart—it
was ecstasy. I was eighteen now; the time was ripe.

Having made the decision to fall in love with Drew, I
began to endow him with all manner of special, even

astonishing, characteristics. Nor did I have to use much imagination, for not only was he a particularly good actor, he was also handsome and slim, with merry blue eyes and a rich speaking voice that filled me with awe both on the stage and in our private conversations when he spoke of the theater—and later on, of love.

Since it was still summer recess, very few students were on campus, so Drew and I decided to take a long stroll back, meandering down the brick paths that led from building to building through the University. We laughed and talked and shared secrets about ourselves and our childhoods. I told him of the way I had used play-acting to endure the aftermath of war, and Drew confided a secret of his own.

"I changed my name, you know."

"You didn't!"

"Yes. It used to be—Horace."

I laughed along with him. "Horace Dowd! That would look awful on the playbills."

"I thought so too, so I began searching for a better first name, oh, a long time ago, when I was just a boy."

Although Drew was three or four years older than I, he seemed a boy still, but of course I did not say that.

"Drew is a fine old theater name," he continued, "and I thought it sounded just right. Drew Dowd. The two sort of go together, don't you think?"

"Yes, I do. And one day, when you're famous, that name will be on everyone's lips."

Having begun to talk of ourselves, we continued happily, the words tumbling out as we discussed our goals and our backgrounds, which, we found, were strikingly similar, both of us having fought family disapproval to finally get on the stage. Most actors in America in the 1870s, Drew told me, came from theater families— many from abroad, where their parents had been "strolling players." He told me that Eugene Fitch had actually been born backstage, at a theater in Bristol, England.

"It's also said that he inherited his flamboyant father's love of drink as well as of the stage!"

I laughed, remembering some evenings when Eugene's performance had been a little more ribald than necessary, but the audiences loved him, and fortunately, extra drunkenness hardly detracted from Rip's own character.

"The man's a marvelous actor," Drew added, "and he never forgets a line or throws anyone off with a wrong cue. Nothing else matters."

His blue eyes were serious, and I knew just how he felt, for I felt the same way.

"I wonder if William and Glenna come from acting families too?" I said.

We had worked together constantly, but I had never felt close enough to the Piersons to speak personally, although they, of necessity, knew all about me.

"William does, I know," Drew answered. "In fact, I once saw his father on the stage—years ago, in California. I was just a boy, but I sneaked away to see *King Lear*."

My breath caught at that, for I had never seen a Shakespearean play, although I had read *Lear* many times.

"He was very old even then," Drew went on, "but he was wonderful in the part. He looked much like William—tall and thin, with silvery hair."

"I'd love to play Cordelia."

"Let's do it some day, Katherine. I'll be Lear."

I laughed. "But Drew, you're much too young to be my father."

"Don't you know I'm going to be a great character actor? I plan to play Lear by the time I'm thirty."

We laughed together, but we were serious, and we believed totally in ourselves. Continuing our walk, we passed through the campus and came within view of the James River. Far in the distance, we could see fine homes rising above the bluffs across the water, with beautifully manicured boxwood hedges leading for what seemed miles up to the columned brick houses. I sighed and took Drew's offered hand, walking beside him back to our hotel in silence. The day was cool, but his hand felt damp in mine—a not entirely pleasant sensation. I tried not to notice; after all, I was about to fall in love.

Two days later we headed North—eight more cities to play before reaching New York and the end of the tour. The first ones were smaller, borderline towns that could be considered "Southern" and therefore, according to William, amiable to my accent, but the final four were "Yankee"—two of them quite large: Harrisburg and Trenton. But that was still over a month away, and I put my fears of audience rejection aside as I concentrated on the play—and on my rapidly developing passion for Drew.

One night before the performance, he came into my dressing room to wish me luck, something he had never done before. Glenna and William had not yet arrived since there was still an hour before curtain. I asked Drew to join me for a few minutes before I began my makeup. I could tell something was on his mind as he paced around the small room, unable to come to rest.

Finally he stopped behind my chair and grinned boyishly at me in the mirror, his blue eyes bright.

"Kate, I think my chance may have come. I've been approached by theatrical agents!"

I had no idea what this meant, but, of course, was eager to hear.

"They were in the audience a few nights back, and came to talk to me about going West. California is booming with theaters, almost rivaling New York. Lots of actors are working there—even Edwin Booth."

Suddenly, I panicked. He couldn't leave the troupe, not before my plan was accomplished!

"Oh, but Drew, Mr. Booth is already such a star actor that he can play anywhere and people will flock to see him. Besides, he started out in California."

"Yes, but so did I, and I'll certainly want to return there. I'm just not sure whether the time is right. Perhaps I should wait and give them my answer at the end of the tour."

His eyes met mine briefly before turning away in thought. "They'll wait until then, and I may even be able to hold them off longer. If I could get in one or two more good parts—"

He looked at me again, and this time his gaze did not turn away. "Besides, I don't want to leave you, Katherine."

Before I knew it, he had bent over to kiss me, his lips warm on mine.

Quickly, he pulled back, apologizing. "Do forgive me, it's just that you're so beautiful. I couldn't help it."

I tried to act affronted. "Well, it mustn't happen again. Promise, now." Inside I was secretly pleased.

"I promise."

About that time, Glenna came into the dressing room, and Drew made a swift, if fumbling, departure. As the door closed behind him, Glenna looked at me rather sternly, I thought, with her violet eyes, but said nothing.

After that night, everything happened so quickly that I was never able to put the events in sequence, never able to remember what town we were playing when he kissed me again—more than once—in spite of his promise; or in what hotel hallway we stood when he first held me tight, our bodies pressed together in the dark. But I remember vividly the feelings that stirred within me when he first touched my bare skin, his hand awkwardly caressing my breast, fingering the tender, oh, so tender nipple, causing a moan to escape my lips. We were standing just outside the door to my room, and I moved back slightly, trembling. Then he suddenly withdrew his hand, kissed me hastily on the cheek, and moved down the hall without even saying goodnight.

I undressed in wonderment, not even bothering to light the lamp but dropping my clothes in a pile, slipping into my gown and sinking onto the bed. The touch of Drew's fingers was in my memory now, yet I felt it still, his hand upon my breast. But it was not his hand—it was my own. I sat up abruptly. I had touched myself and caused that same feeling, the deep, dark feeling of longing.

This was not my first such sensation, only the most vivid one. Often, as I grew to womanhood under Jamie's strict supervision, one of the boys who called to take me riding or to sit beside me in the parlor had aroused feelings which I sensed were desire, but which I refused to acknowledge, channeling all my desires then in one direction only—toward the stage. Nothing, nothing, must interfere, and especially not some hometown boy with a freckled nose and slicked-down hair, spouting words of adoration.

My passion was for the stage, and it was physical itself, one that gave me a sense of excitement that was almost sexual, had I but stopped then to think of it.

But when Drew had held me, a wick of passion had been lit; when his lips crushed against mine and his hand found my naked skin, the blaze began to erupt. And then he had left me, but the longing continued to smolder, leaving me confused, not knowing when the explosion would come and what form it would take. I only knew I was ready—ready for Drew to light that fire within me, light it this time until it blazed fully and sent a bombardment of glorious colors exploding inside my very being. I knew it would be a wonderful experience—my first love.

I removed my hand from my breast, not shamefully, for I had never felt shame, but with the determination that my first great excitement must come with a man— with Drew, whom I would love.

The next day was Sunday, a day when I usually slept late to rest up from the week's performances. But the sun had not yet risen when I sat bolt-upright in bed, the knowledge pounding within me that this day was to be the one for which I had so yearned.

As if in conspiracy with my own plans, there was a soft knock at my door. Drew stood before me, dressed for riding—a pleasure most of the cast liked to enjoy on our days off. Today Drew wanted us to leave early, escaping the others. I was agreeable, and happy to see that whatever had caused him to leave me so abruptly the night before must not have been my fault. Possibly he had been as confused as I. But whatever the reason, he seemed himself again this morning, and I eagerly dressed for our ride.

The morning was brisk and clear, a nip of autumn in the air as the pale sun lit the sky pinkly. Our mounts were skittish, ready for their first run of the day, and we both felt that same daring as we spurred them on, faster and faster along the well-worn bridle trail, over the crest of a hill and down the other side, flying now, letting the horses have their heads, the cool air whipping our faces as we challenged them on, neck and neck. I refused to ride sidesaddle, but rode as I had as a girl, headlong, helter-skelter, daringly.

Against the wind I heard Drew yell, "The tree yonder—I'll race you for it."

"What's the wager?" I shouted back, digging my spurs deeply into my horse's flanks.

His eyes shone as he looked over at me. "The winner takes all!"

With that, he inched ahead. Urge as I would, my mount simply did not have the stamina to meet the challenge. I fell behind as Drew pulled up beside the tree, his horse rearing and pawing the air, so abruptly did he stop. I cantered on past the tree, reining in more gently. When I turned to meet him, Drew had already dismounted and his horse was tethered beside him, blowing heavily.

He helped me down, and we collapsed on a bed of bright leaves, laughing.

"All of what?" I managed to ask, my breath still coming in gasps.

"All of you."

I laughed again, but he did not.

"I want you, Katherine. Last night—I might as well admit, I'm not very experienced, and I was afraid of what might happen, of what I might do."

I looked up at him questioningly. Perhaps if he knew my own inexperience, it would soothe him. "Drew, I've never—"

"I know," he answered. He seemed to hesitate, to draw away from what I had been waiting for.

No, I thought to myself, it must be now. I moved closer to him, my face near his, our lips almost touching.

Suddenly, he took me in his arms, kissing me roughly as he pulled my jacket open and fumbled with the buttons of my riding shirt. I felt a moment of panic, but it was too late. I had wanted it to happen slowly, lovingly, but Drew did not seem able to stop himself now, as he tore at my clothes until, somehow, his bare skin was on mine. I felt him, hot and damp, pushing against me. The tender beginning that I had experienced the night before was replaced by panic, a tightening of all my muscles, as I found myself fighting against his desire.

Then he was inside me. Could this be what I had longed for, this terrible thing, this pulsating rod tearing through me, plunging deeper and deeper until I feared it would rip me apart? I was afraid the agony would never end; I was afraid I would die.

Then suddenly, miraculously, it was over. With a moan, Drew fell against me, his face wet on my neck, his breathing harsh in my ear. That's when the tears came, tears of disappointment, of confusion. I tried to stop them, but it was useless.

He heard my sobs and took my face in his hands, gently now. "Oh, Kate, I love you, please don't cry, don't—hate me."

"I don't hate you," I said through my sobs. "It's just—"

"I know. I know. It was wrong. I never meant it to happen like this, but I couldn't stop myself. The only women I've known have been—Kate, I've never done it with a girl like you, but next time—"

I didn't want to hear about next time, because there would not be a next time. If this was what it was like to be with a man, I wanted no part of it. I had imagined beauty, magic, some other feeling I couldn't even name, but not this, not this.

I managed, in my humiliation, to straighten my clothes, to wipe away the blood. Somehow we got back to the stables, left our horses, and returned to the hotel, but I did not speak again, nor did Drew.

Later in the day he came to my room to talk, to explain what had happened, but I couldn't make myself listen. I didn't want to think about it. It was over and done, and as far as I was concerned, we would just have to return to our old relationship, being together only on the stage. But there would be no more talk of love, and as for passion, if that was what had passed between us, I was disgusted by it. There was anger within me now, but at the same time there was shame—not shame because of what we had done, but because I had been as much at fault as Drew. I knew this, and he did not. He was blaming himself, and that wasn't fair. So I confessed my secret, confessed that I had wanted to know passion and love, and had chosen him to lead me to those feelings.

"I wanted to know all about what happens between a man and a woman. There are feelings in me that are so confusing. I wanted to understand. I know now how wrong it was to use you to find love—when it wasn't there."

He didn't answer, and I poured out my other secret fear: "I don't think I will ever feel love or be able to give myself to a man. Maybe I was born to realize only one dream—that of being an actress."

Here Drew stopped me. "Kate, you're beautiful, and you do have feelings. I wanted you to love me, but you'll find someone else, I know you will."

"Perhaps." I didn't believe his words and wondered if he believed them himself.

When we reached Baltimore, Drew accepted the California offer and left the company as soon as William had replaced him with another player from Markan's in New York. Drew was a fine actor, and he had his future to think about. I knew he felt stiffled with our troupe now, unable to perform at his best because of me. After several days of rehearsal with his replacement, Drew took his leave quietly one morning, not stopping at my room to say goodbye. Later that day, I was given a note which he had left for me at the hotel desk:

Kate,
Please don't despair, and never let what happened between us turn you against the man you will someday love. You will love, and deeply, I'm sure. Until then, there is a great career ahead of you. I wish you well in all you do, and I believe we will meet again as friends.

                                                    Drew

Chapter 2

Love—if such an emotion would ever come to me—could wait. What I had tasted of it I had found wanting, and I felt no desire but to concentrate all my energies into my acting. Like a sponge, I began to soak up not just my lines but the whole atmosphere of the theater. I learned to do my own makeup, applying the paint and powder with a touch that was at once theatrical and natural. I reworked the costumes Peggie had left behind to add style to the wardrobe and, I hoped, to Lowena's character.

Glenna did not speak of Drew to me, but she seemed to sense the relief I felt when he left. She once again took me under her wing to work on the many rough edges that remained.

"You have a natural grace, Katherine, especially when you move on the stage. That is very important, of course, but what we must now add is grace in repose." She caught my frown and went on, "For a girl with the beauty you possess, it is not difficult to transfer it to the

47

stage in your movements. But to stand or sit quietly with such beauty is another thing, which many actresses never learn. We must fill in your stage presence with a fine brush. Do you understand?"

I believed I did.

When we reached Trenton, I waited in the wings on opening night with a confidence that almost equaled my fear. For the fear was always there, would always be there. Without it, Glenna had once assured me, I would not be a true actress.

"No actress ever stands waiting to go on without at least a momentary feeling that her voice will not sustain, her lines will not come, the curtain will collapse on her head."

I laughed at that, remembering my *Rapunzel* of long ago. But tonight I was ready—ready to face a large, more sophisticated audience, to face a Yankee town.

Of course, my entrance was not greeted by applause, which always greeted the Piersons and Mr. Fitch. I was not known. But I played the show that night as I never had before, and when at last I rushed into old Rip's arms, sobbing "Father!" there were tears in my own eyes, but from the audience there was not a sound. Something in me panicked. They did not like me, I thought, but then I remembered that Sarah Siddons had said that silence could sometimes be more flattering than applause. As the curtain fell and we took our bows, I hoped she was right, for, though I had never been hailed by thundering applause, neither had I ever encountered total silence!

In confusion I left the stage, only to be greeted by hugs, kisses, and praise from everyone, even the stagehands.

William shook my hand politely, but his thin face was lit with a smile. "Remember, Katherine, the critics might not have been as awed as the audience."

"But if they were," Glenna continued, her lovely face flushed with excitement, "you may have had your first taste of success."

I went back to the hotel with the others, all laughing and chattering while I remained in a daze.

It was not until the next morning that I finally realized what had happened. The press was overwhelming in its praise of the show, one critic saying that he had never witnessed a more delightful rendition of *Rip Van Winkle* and adding that, "Katherine Lawrence, in the role of Rowena, adds dimension to the part as no other actress this critic has seen. She is a new star on the horizon."

I read and reread that sentence, thrilled but still somehow unbelieving. I had played the part many times, and although last night had seemed different, I had not realized how much I had improved along the way with the Pierson's help. They cautioned me not to let this one taste of flattery go to my head, adding that Trenton was hardly a theater capital. More time and work were needed before I would be ready to tackle the stoic, stone-faced audiences of Boston and New York, audiences who dared an actress to show star quality.

But their caution was unnecessary. I knew I had done well, and I was glad to be praised for my work; I also knew that this was only the beginning, and if I were to sustain, to improve, to become the fine actress I dreamed of becoming, I could not do so with pride as my companion.

We finished our two weeks in Trenton, closed the play on Saturday night, and left the following morning for New York, where I was to be the Pierson's guest at their town house on East Seventeenth Street. Glenna wrote Jamie about this arrangement, and he seemed appeased. The Piersons planned to take a repertory company of three plays on tour after New Year's—an exciting tour commencing the first day of 1876, and playing at least a month in Philadelphia just prior to the Centennial Exhibition. Lester Markan was already assembling a cast and preparing rehearsal schedules. William and Glenna found it necessary to assure me again and again that Mr. Markan would approve my inclusion in the tour—at least in lesser parts.

But in spite of their kind words and the Trenton reviews—which I had clipped and sent to Laurel Ann and Jamie—I was filled with apprehension. I envisioned Mr. Markan as a formidable monster whom I would have to confront with only my voice as a weapon—a voice he was sure to find "regional" and unacceptable.

We took the train to New York, leaving the stagehands behind with the property manager and lighting expert to pack up and follow, later in the week, by coach.

That night, as we sped through cold November fog, I had a terrible dream about Mr. Markan, one which frightened me so that I actually awakened in a sweat. He had appeared in the form of Simon Legree, brandishing a whip, his eyes red and beady, foam gathering in the corners of his mouth. I hovered before him, hysterically repeating my lines, but never satisfying him, as the whip came down upon my bare shoulders again and again, stinging me with an agony not physical but verbal—the pain and agony of criticism.

When we arrived in New York, the fog had not lifted and, in fact, was now mixed with a light, cold drizzle that made it impossible for me to see anything of the city as we drove in a closed carriage from the station to Seventeenth Street. The very next day, I was to audition for Lester Markan. Long after Glenna and William had retired—having told me that I was letter perfect and not to worry—I stayed up, going over and over my lines, adding different nuances, unusual pauses, and new breathing patterns I had not tried before. Finally I awakened Glenna and insisted that she listen once more. I knew how tired she was from the trip and the months of playing; I knew that she wanted to rest in her own bed at last, but I couldn't stop myself from dragging her back into the parlor to hear my recital one final time. She was only half awake, but she came to life very quickly somewhere in the middle of the reading.

"No, Katherine, that isn't the right feeling at all. You

had it earlier; what in the world have you been doing?"

I tried to explain that I wanted to try another interpretation, something more exciting.

"Katherine, we have two months before the new tour. Worry about those changes during rehearsal, if you must. But for your audition, read it as you have been, just as you did in Trenton. After all, dear girl, it is a light play and simply doesn't lend itself to such dramatic style."

"But I want to overwhelm him, to make him realize the depth of my interpretation."

She finally convinced me there wasn't that much depth in Lowena to realize, adding that I had a long career ahead of me, during which I could play many powerful parts, but this was not one of them, and if I wanted the tour, I should simply read as before. Having exacted a promise to that effect from me, she led me to the guest room and would not leave until I had gotten into bed and the lamp was extinguished.

The fog had disappeared the next morning, and in its place, a bright autumn sun shone on the city of New York as we left for the three-block walk to the 14th Street Theater. As nervous as I was, I could not ignore my surroundings. The streets were filled with delivery vans, pushcarts, carriages, and people. Never had I see so many people, their voices filling the air with accents and, indeed, languages foreign to my ear—languages of the opera, German and Italian, which hung in the air as musically as an opera itself.

The 14th Street Theater occupied its own narrow building, and although the facade was not grand, I was duly impressed, for it was the first New York theater I had ever seen. I sighed deeply. This was it, the ultimate. We entered through the stage door and climbed narrow iron stairs that led directly into the wings. The theater was dark except for one or two gaslights that illuminated the lone figure of Lester Markan. Seeing him, I breathed a sigh of relief; he was hardly a Simon Legree, nor was he even particularly prepossessing. He was a rather small, balding man with a jolly face, constantly mopping his brow with a wrinkled handkerchief. After introductions were exchanged, he and the Piersons left me alone on the stage to recite the part, and I delivered my lines just as Glenna had insisted, with feeling but without fire. Apparently she had been right, for Mr. Markan was full of compliments as he beckoned for me to take a seat in the chair upstage. Someone had just come into the theater through the front foyer, and Lester went up the aisle to greet him.

To say that my first glimpse of Nicholas Van Dyne was an exciting one would be incorrect, although, looking back, I have an impression of handsome elegance. However, I doubt if I was able, at first sight, to make out his features at all in the darkened theater. I do remember that we had a rather unpleasant encounter, after which I insisted on auditioning for him also, having learned that he was a major stockholder in the company. I'm sure William and Glenna cringed when I announced that I would play the death scene from *Romeo and Juliet.* But the latecomer had so raised my ire that I was determined to make him sit up and take notice, and I knew that if I simply recited a dull speech from *Rip,* the effect would not be what I wanted. I wanted to bring the man down, to make him see that I was, in fact, an actress and not some little girl from the provinces with more ambition than talent.

The scene was short but ripe with meaning, and I delivered the last lines in hardly more than a whisper: "O happy dagger! This is thy sheath. There rest, and let me die . . ." Then I knelt quietly, my head lowered, waiting for the verdict.

It came quickly. Pulling his coat over his shoulders, Nick Van Dyne moved toward me.

"I apologize, Miss Lawrence. You were exceptional. We shall be honored to have you in the company, and if there is anything I can do to help you, please don't hesitate to call on me." He extended his hand.

"You are much too kind, Mr. Van Dyne." My tone of voice belied the cordiality of the words as I took his hand but ignored his offer. He flushed slightly and then shrugged.

"Oh, Nick, we're going out for dinner tonight—somewhere special to celebrate." That was William, always benevolent. "Please join us."

"Another time, Will, thanks. I have a previous appointment." He turned and made his way back up the aisle. I knew I had been rude. I knew I would have to apologize to Glenna and William later, but now I could not resist one last barb. I raised my voice just enough to reach the departing figure and said, "Well, the South may have lost the war, but we can still win an occasional battle."

Mr. Markan and the Piersons chuckled merrily. I knew my voice had carried far enough; he had heard me, as I had meant him to. I was part of the theater now, and needed to prove my talent only to myself—certainly not to Mr. Nicholas Van Dyne.

Time blurred as the difficult job of putting together a three-play tour began. Mr. Markan, unlike some producers, preferred to rehearse one play at a time, and *Rip* was perfected quickly since most of the cast remained the same, and the sets were ready except for a few minor repairs and a little brightening. I was handy with a paintbrush and found myself working happily backstage during the long intervals when I was not on.

Sets were available, too, for the second play, *The Octoroon*, which had been chosen with an eye toward the Centennial. My part was important—that of Zoe, the young girl in love with one man and desired by another. It was typical melodrama, but I didn't care since, at the end, I would die by my own hand in my lover's arms—an actress's dream!

We were well into rehearsals for *The Octoroon* before the third play was finally chosen. Rumors were flying backstage that it would be a departure for the company—a Shakespearean comedy—but no one was less concerned than I. Whatever the choice, my part would be of little significance. I was not ready for

Shakespeare. At night, Glenna and William either sent
me home in a hansom cab while they stayed to confer
with Mr. Markan, or he returned with us for late supper
at the Seventeenth Street house. The discussions were
heated and prolonged, and I usually excused myself and
went to bed to be ready for the next day's rehearsals of
The Octoroon.

The decision was finally made one night when we received word from Clara Montrose's producer that she
could be released to travel with Markan Tours.

Throwing stacks of scripts aside, Mr. Markan announced, in a voice full of relief and finality: "*As You
Like It*, with Clara as Rosalind and Glenna as Celia!"
He mopped his brow. "What a relief. I have no idea
when we'll be ready to begin, but at least we have the
play."

We all toasted the decision happily—even I, "a
shepherdess" who would not appear until the fifth act!
None of us knew then that this was the play which
would change my life.

Shakespeare was to fill my life too, beginning with
that evening, as Mr. Markan decided that, to celebrate,
we would all attend Sunday's benefit performance of
Richard III, starring Edwin Booth.

"Perhaps," he added, "Nick might even deign to join
us."

Well, Mr. Van Dyne apparently had other plans, but
I did not think about him once as I sat in Daly's fine
theater and watched the greatest actor of his day perform *Richard III* before an audience more sophisticated
but just as moved as I. He limped horribly across the
stage, venom dripping almost visibly from his lips with
each line, a grotesque yet pitiable character. This was
the most moving moment of my life so far, and as the
long evening ended, I was on my feet with the rest of
the audience, cheering madly. Oh, what a glorious
life!—the life of an actor who held the world in the
palm of his hand. No matter that he was personally so
troubled and full of woe; on the stage he owned the
world. He was God.

One week later, *The Octoroon* was ready, and we went immediately into rehearsals for *As You Like It*. I was almost never needed, but was almost always there, seated in the back row of the darkened house, unable to tear myself away from the theater for more than a few hours at a time, and then only to go to the circulating library, where I read play after play, learning all the ingenue parts—to what end I wasn't even sure.

Although he mounted productions with a jolly attitude, laughing and sweating profusely, Lester Markan was, his looks notwithstanding, a theatrical giant. Glenna and William worked closely with him, since they would be the touring actor-managers as usual, but they, too, seemed in awe of his talent, and quietly left the initial staging in his hands.

And capable hands they were. During rehearsals for *The Octoroon*, I had sensed that something remarkable was happening to a play that was, in itself, of little consequence. But being on the stage so much of the time, I had not been able to watch in a detached manner as his genius took hold. Now I could see him shape and mold *As You Like It*, and I was enraptured. The parts played by Glenna and Clara Montrose were wonderful enough as Shakespeare had written them, but under Mr. Markan's direction, they came to life with a glowing beauty. Clara was almost thirty, I judged, and although not pretty by most standards, her flame-red hair and bright blue eyes lit up the stage, and she played the comedy with a flair. She also had a scandalous reputation, and she smoked cigarettes, which I had never before seen a lady do.

The play took shape magically as Mr. Markan directed his now greatly enlarged troupe. We were to have a call boy and prompter traveling with us this time, as well as a property manager. Cyril Montrose, Clara's ex-husband and one of the most famous scenic designers in New York, had created sets for *As You Like It* that added a dreamlike quality to the play.

Great excitement seemed to fill the air as the days

flew by, and all at once it was Christmas. We had
worked through Thanksgiving, not even taking the day
off for a turkey dinner. This saddened me somewhat as
I remembered the bounteous Thanksgiving dinners at
Magnolias, but we would celebrate Christmas by attending a grand ball. The Piersons had arranged an invitation for me and had given me a beautiful dress,
since I had no evening gown in my wardrobe and could
not yet, on my small salary, afford to purchase one myself.

I dressed for the evening with a feeling of mounting
excitement. My first ball, and at the Player's Club, with
many of the New York theater crowd attending! I must
look special—to see and be seen. The dress, of wine-
colored silk, was cut low, disclosing the roundness of
my breasts, which my tight corset pushed upward, and
accenting my small waist. A black lace overskirt gathered into a bustle in back. I wore long white gloves and
tucked two pale pink camelias in my hair. I used
makeup, but skillfully, just enough to look as if I wore
none. I whirled before the mirror. Yes, I was pleased,
really pleased with the effect. Daring, yet innocent.
Well, almost. I rarely thought of Drew these days, and
considered that part of my life a closed book.

The ball was everything I had hoped for, and more. I
danced every dance—waltz, polka, quadrille, even those
with which I wasn't familiar. I whirled into each one
easily, picking up the rhythm from my partners. The
Piersons seemed to know everyone, and I was as welcome as they; in fact, my notices had preceded me, as
had word that I was now a Markan player. News in the
theater world travels fast, I thought, but I didn't have
time to ponder the thought for long as I was swept onto
another arm, atop a wave of music, into a sea of floating dancers.

In the middle of a waltz—my favorite—I heard a familiar voice say, "Miss Lawrence, may I?" Then I was
in his arms. He held me very tight, tighter than any
other partner, his firm body molded against mine until I
seemed to feel his every muscle through the flimsy silk

of my dress. Without effort, he danced me from the ballroom to the hall and then into a small alcove.

"You have danced every dance. I expect you're tired."

"Dancing never tires me, Mr. Van Dyne, because I love it. But perhaps, as one gets older—"

He threw back his head and laughed. "Ah, Miss Lawrence, I see I still have to watch myself with you."

"I am sorry. I had no intention of being rude."

"No, I should apologize to you." He signaled a passing waiter and took two overflowing glasses of champagne from the tray. We settled on a small divan tucked into the corner of the alcove and surrounded by greenery.

"I was rude to you at the theater. I do apologize," he said.

"And I accept. Oh, I was so angry with you that day. I thought you were trying to block my career, and you were so superior and insufferable," I added boldly.

"You are not the only one who finds me that way, but you are one of the few who says as much—and the only one I would wish not to offend. Am I forgiven?"

I lowered my eyes from his level gaze. How handsome he was in his dark evening attire, his tawny hair gleaming about his face. And those eyes, which met mine at every opportunity—I could not name the color, for they seemed gray at moments and then green, framed with thick, dark lashes.

"Of—of course," I stammered.

"Then let's drink a toast. To friendship."

"To friendship."

Our glasses met with a symbolic clink of crystal, and then we drank.

He leaned back on the sofa, his eyes, interested and alive, still holding mine. "When does the tour leave?" he asked.

"The first of January. A terrible time, isn't it, for Pougkeepsie, Scranton, and Harrisburg?"

"You'll run into snow, without a doubt. In fact, I'm surprised we haven't had any in New York this season—just cold, damnable drizzle. Have you ever seen snow?"

"Once in South Carolina, but it melted quickly. No chance to make a snowman! Have you always lived in the North?"

"Born and reared in New York, with summers in the country and time away at school. Our lives have been very different, I suppose."

I nodded—how different, he couldn't know. I thought of the terrible, lean years of the war's aftermath.

His voice drew me back to the present. "But that doesn't preclude our being friends, does it?"

"I hope not," I answered.

After a long moment, he stood up, placed our empty glasses on a trestle stand beside the divan, and extended his hand. "Come, we should return to the dancing."

He helped me to my feet but continued to hold my hand. We stood very close together, close enough for me to hear his breathing, strong and rhythmic. A haze seemed to surround him as he moved back a step, slowly, for even as he moved, it was as if he were coming toward me, rather than going away. He placed his hands on my shoulders and gently ran them down my arms, sending a tremor along the surface of my skin. Then he encircled my waist, drawing me close.

"Katherine. What a lovely girl you are."

I raised my face to look at him, and his lips—warm and firm—found mine. My mouth relaxed, opening, feeling his tongue inside it. My arms pulled him closer, kissing and kissing until the haze that had surrounded him filled the whole room and my knees grew weak.

At last we broke apart.

"You feel it too, don't you, Kate? Don't you?"

"Yes, yes, I do." I lifted my lips again to his, and was lost in the world of his kiss. It was a world where I had never been, and I longed to stay there forever.

But I could not stay, and finally he spoke again. "We must go back now. The Piersons will miss you, and I dare not ruin your reputation."

"I don't care."

And I didn't. All I wanted was a continuation of this new excitement, this unknown experience. How different his kisses were from Drew's. One, the kisses of a boy; the other, the kisses of a man.

"I don't care," I repeated.

"I think you mean that, Kate, and it pleases me that you do. But it's almost midnight."

I knew he had come with someone, and I wondered who she was and if she clung to him as I had just done.

"Something has happened to us tonight, Kate, something that we will find again when I come back. I must leave tomorrow for Texas—"

"Texas!"

"You know Texas, it's down there in the South," he teased. "I have business there, railroad business. I shan't return until long after you're on tour, so it will be March before I see you again."

"Oh, Nick, no."

Must we be parted, I wanted to ask, when we've just found each other? Although I did not ask the question, my eyes must have.

"Don't be so bereaved, dear Kate. We'll be together when you return, I promise." He added, smiling, "When you return as the toast of the continent, or at least three states."

I did laugh at that. Of course I would see him, and March was not that far away. Meanwhile, I must not forget the tour and my future as an actress. Arm in arm, we walked back to the ballroom, and I found my way to William and Glenna. I cared nothing for further dancing. I cared nothing for toasts, nor for Christmas bells, but only for those bells that his name sounded in my heart—Nick, Nick!

My head spun crazily through the rest of the evening, until I climbed at last into bed. All my wildest dreams had given me no hint of the depths of feeling that lay within me, and now that I had sampled these feelings, I was frightened for the first time because I did not know what lay ahead. I only knew I was alive and open to him and ready for him. I fell asleep not with the usual images of Zoe or Mr. Markan's stage directions, but with thoughts of Nick—his mouth on mine, his body pressed against mine. And those thoughts became the dreams that filled my waking and sleeping hours.

Heavy snow began to fall as we pulled up at Grand Central Station to board the train on New Year's Day, 1876. I leaned back and turned my face to the night sky, licking the snowflakes with delight as they melted, cold and tingly, on my skin. Almost every day for the next two months, such flakes would fill the air, but I would not tire of them even when deep snow made traveling difficult, or simply crossing the street became a task requiring the dexterity of a tightrope walker. With part of my increased salary, I had purchased a heavy maroon wool cape with a detachable hood and high-button shoes. I was prepared.

Clara Montrose and I settled into the compartment which we would share. Ahead stretched a long line of drafty theaters from Poughkeepsie into Pennsylvania—Scranton, Harrisburg, Allentown, Philadelphia—and back through New Jersey for six nights a week, with travel on Sunday. Clara had decided that we were a perfect pair to travel together, since she was by no means small, and we made a good balance in the tiny compartment.

We began to share stories as soon as the train pulled out of the station. I took advantage of Clara's interest in the South, and before I knew it, Magnolias had turned into one of the grandest plantations in the Carolinas. But Clara didn't have to exaggerate at all when she talked about herself; the truth was fascinating enough.

"Married three times, and that's a lucky number, so I don't plan to enlarge on it."

"Then Cyril Montrose was your last husband?"

"No, he was the first. I married Cyril just as I was getting started on the stage, and I've been using his name ever since. It's a good thing too, considering the number of last names I've had. Wouldn't the public have been confused! Cyril doesn't mind. We're good friends now. As for the other two, well, I mustn't be disrespectful of the dead, but that second one was a mess. Drank himself into an early grave."

"Are you married now?" I asked, intrigued.

"Yes and no. LeClerq and I aren't divorced, but we don't live together. Since I never plan to marry again, why do I need a divorce?"

"But aren't you—lonely?" I was thinking of Nick; I missed him already.

"Now wait a minute, honey. I said I wasn't going to marry. I never said I wouldn't fall in love!"

The remark struck us both as hysterical, and in our laughter, a friendship was born.

My laughter froze like an icicle on a winter's night when, moments later, William knocked on our compartment door to tell us he had decided to open in Poughkeepsie with *The Octoroon*. I had assumed we would lead off with *Rip*, since it was such a popular play in New York State. Returning to my comfortable part of Lowena would be like rejoining an old friend. But *The Octoroon* rode heavily on Zoe, and the cast had not rehearsed together since November.

"There'll be a full dress rehearsal tomorrow afternoon, so don't worry," he said, patting my hand.

But I did worry, for the remainder of the trip and all the way through the rehearsal, although I was letter-perfect. I fell apart ten times before the curtain, and ten times Glenna and Clara put me back together.

All at once it was eight o'clock.

"You'll be all right as long as you don't step on *my* lines," Clara said with a throaty laugh. Then she gave me a little shove as my cue came, and suddenly I was in the middle of the stage.

I heard myself speak the first lines.

"Am I late? Ah, Mr. Scudder, good morning."

And he responded, and from then on I was flying, free and clear. At the final curtain call, I let the applause wrap around me like a blanket of love. I was home.

In spite of a snowstorm, late trains to Scranton, no water in the hotel in Harrisburg, and another storm in Allentown, I remained in good spirits town after town. Our second month began with two weeks at the Walnut Street Theater in Philadelphia. The Exhibition wouldn't open until May, but preparations were well under way, and everyone in Philadelphia was caught up in the Centennial mood.

I found the lovely Quaker town warm and friendly, almost like home, and I spent many an afternoon walking along the red brick sidewalks, exploring every block near the theater until I became a familiar face to the local shop owners. The house was packed each night, and my spirits were so high that I sparked the others into an almost flawless run, especially in *Rip*. Lowena seemed a part that belonged to me now, and I had the feeling that the audience sensed it too, and certainly the critics did. They were almost as kind to me as they had been in Trenton months before.

The night of our last performance, there were so many people backstage that I thought I would never get out of my makeup and costume. Since the cast had elaborate plans for dinner, I changed into my wine silk, wanting to look special before joining the crowd in the green room. The tradition of accepting friends and members of the audience in the large room adjoining the foyer after each performance was a ritual that I never missed. Some actors thought it was too much trouble and almost never bothered to attend, but I basked in the praise I found there, joining in the laughter and highjinks of the players and their admiring public.

I was talking with Freddie, the property manager, when a figure in the doorway caught my eye over the mass of bobbing heads. Nick was here! As he made his way toward me through the throng, his presence seemed to fill the room until I could see no one but him. The crowd parted to let him pass, and at last he was beside me, taking my hand and pressing it to his lips.

"Kate, my beautiful star. You were superb."

"Thank you, Nick."

Here he was, as close to me as I had dreamed he would be during all the nights of the tour, and I found myself trembling and almost speechless. "I thought you said Texas—" I began.

"So I did, but as soon as my business was completed, I decided to rush to your side. I've come all the way from Dallas to take you to dinner."

His light tone put me at ease, and I joined the banter. "Then you mustn't be disappointed. As a major stockholder, I'm sure you can be included in the party tonight. We're having a company dinner."

He groaned but did not object.

Just then, Clara entered the room, and I motioned to her. "Clara Montrose, this is Nicholas Van Dyne."

Their laughter reminded me that they were probably old friends. Hadn't I heard that Nick knew every actress in New York, at least all the stars?

"My dear Miss Montrose."

"Mr. Van Dyne, it's been a long time."

"Much too long. I enjoyed your performance tonight, but I am looking forward to seeing you play Rosalind. I hear Shakespeare wrote the role with you in mind."

"So the critics have said. I hope that doesn't mean I look two hundred years old!"

Clara howled at that, as did Nick and I. I had finally stopped trembling, but I could not tear my eyes from him. He was even more handsome than I had remembered, and I was completely under his spell.

William and Glenna joined us, and there were more handshakes and kisses all around.

Clara took the opportunity to lean toward me and whisper, "Nick Van Dyne. Well, well. I won't expect *you* home tonight."

"Clara! Shame!"

"Kate, honey, you must learn not to blush."

We moved as a group to the front of the theater, where hacks waited to take us to the party. Somehow, Nick and I were in the last carriage. The others pulled away, and we looked at each other.

"Where to, Kate?"

"You mean you didn't get the name of the restaurant?"

Nick laughed. "No, I thought you did. Well, I guess we'll have to dine alone. What a disappointment."

He had planned the whole thing! I looked at him skeptically.

"I'm a stranger to Philadelphia, but I hear the food at my hotel is quite good," he said, then caught my eye and laughed again. "Oh, Kate, I wanted you all to myself, can you blame me?"

Of course I couldn't, because I wanted just as desperately to be alone with him; as I had dreamed.

I was not prepared for the elegance of Nick's hotel. During the tour, we always stayed at the least expensive lodgings, cleanliness being our only requirement, and even that was sometimes overlooked. Obviously, Nick was used to the best. I caught my breath as we entered the huge dining room—a sea of white tablecloths, white-coated waiters, and glossy white walls and ceilings, from which hung dozens of crystal chandeliers. "A little overstated, I would say," Nick whispered as we were led to a corner table. "But just so the food is good . . ."

The few bites I managed to consume were good, but I'm afraid much of my meal was wasted. However, Nick did not appear to suffer from a similar loss of appetite.

"In my mad rush to be by your side, I haven't eaten all day," he explained, finishing up my dessert, a delicate caramel pudding.

Over coffee he told me about Texas, the cowboys, and the railroad. I tried to capture some of the excitement of the tour for him, but found myself babbling on, afraid of putting a wall of silence between us. Finally, he caught my hand and looked across at me, his gray eyes intent.

"Dear Kate, we have a long time." He saw my frown and went on, "We needn't cram everything into this moment, even into his evening."

He was silent then, and the silence was not so terrible after all. He lit a thin black cigar and smiled at me through the circling smoke.

"Yes, we have a lifetime," he said softly, almost to himself. Then, aloud, "Come, we'll have wine upstairs. I have a suite of rooms with a parlor."

"Would that be proper?"

"Probably not. Shall I take you home?"

"No!" I said automatically, and we both laughed.

"As your own Shakespeare said, 'We are the makers of manners, Kate.'"

We laughed again, and I took his arm.

"Old Willie comes in handy sometimes," he continued. "As which of his ladies do you plan your rise to stardom?"

"Oh, I haven't decided. Juliet, perhaps?"

"No, I think not. A comedy, I'll wager."

We continued to laugh as we crossed the great lobby and climbed the marble staircase, neither of us realizing how prophetic his words were, nor how soon they would come true.

Nick's suite was on the first landing, and the outside door opened directly from the foyer onto the parlor, a lovely room with deep wine velvet draperies and plush furniture.

"It's like a palace!" I exclaimed.

"Well, it's closer to one than my last lodgings—over a barroom with brawling all night long. A lot of Southerners have drifted West. Do you suppose that's why there's so much fighting?"

"You're still remembering my behavior at the audition."

"Yes. You were quite a scrapper; I liked that in you." He ran his hand absently through his thick hair and smiled down at me, the dimples etching deeply into his cheeks. "Would you like an after-dinner drink? Some cognac, perhaps?"

"Yes, thank you," I answered. I did not want a drink, but was anxious for him to move away so that I could catch my breath. But even as he stood at the sideboard, his back to me, I still could not rid myself of his image, his golden good looks. Suddenly I felt caged, unable to escape his powerful presence. I moved uncertainly about the room, finally settling into a soft velvet club chair. He brought a cane-backed chair from near the sideboard and placed it by mine. In his other hand he held two dram glasses. For a long moment he remained standing, the drinks in his hand. Finally he placed them on a side table.

"You don't want a drink, do you?"

"No."

"Neither do I." He sat down then, very close to me, close enough to touch, but he did not reach out. I ached for him to hold me, and yet was afraid that he would.

"I'm not going to seduce you, Kate," he said, as if he had read my mind. I looked at him in amazement. "I know that's what you're thinking, and it's true I want you. But not if you don't want me. And right now I'm not sure you do. I was sure at the ball; I was sure earlier this evening. But I'm not sure now. What is it, Kate, what's the matter?"

"I'm afraid, afraid you'll think me easy."

"Oh, Kate, I've known too many women who fit in that category ever to mistake you for one of them. Surely you know that. Besides, you came here because you wanted to. There's something else, isn't there?"

"Yes."

But I couldn't go on. He would think me a fool, a silly girl at best. A child. I didn't want him to laugh at me, and if I told him about Drew and my disappointment, he would laugh. He was a handsome, experienced man in his early thirties who probably couldn't even remember his first love affair. He would never understand. "You're so sure of yourself," I said, "and I'm so unsure. I want—"

"You want everything, don't you, Kate? Yes, I believe you do. You just don't know where to begin; there's so much, and you've had so little."

"I had a love affair once, at least one afternoon—"

He smiled, but it was a touching smile, and he did

not laugh. I told him about Drew, about my dreams of love and their bitter ending.

When I had finished, I was sure he was going to reach out to me, but he did not; instead, he picked up the glasses and handed me one. We both drank. The thick brown liquid stung my throat.

Nick emptied his drink before he spoke. "The boy was not right for you, Kate. That can make all the difference." His steady gaze reflected the meaning of his words.

A thousand thoughts flashed through my mind so quickly that I could not catch hold of them. I could not think; I could only feel, and my feelings drew me to this man. I sipped the cognac again, hoping to clear my head so that I could understand what was coming next.

"I want to be the one for you, Kate, but I'm not interested in a tawdry affair. I want the essence of Kate, the true quality of your loveliness and goodness, but I want it given freely."

At last he touched me, a strong touch, not a teasing one, as he took my hand firmly in his own and lifted me to my feet. We must have stood together for a full minute before he bent down and brushed my lips softly with his own. I gave my answer to him then, as I reached up and put my arms around his neck to return his kiss.

"Oh, Kate, I promise that this will be right for you. I promise." His voice was ragged in this throat. He gathered me in his arms and carried me to the soft rug that lay before the fireplace. There we made love with the fire roaring in our ears, the sparks shooting against the screen, echoing the flash of colors that at last exploded within me as every dream I had ever dreamed came true.

Sometime during the night, he carried me into his bedroom and lay beside me on the fresh white sheets. I awoke to hear him whispering my name over and over, as he buried his face in my hair and caressed my skin until I felt my whole body glow. We made love again, slowly, easily, but with no less passion than before, as I felt again that release of fire within me which I had imagined could come only once in a lifetime.

I heard myself say, "I love you." The words hung in the dark night, but when I drifted back to sleep, I wasn't sure I had spoken aloud. Maybe the words had just sounded in my mind. I'll tell him tomorrow, I thought. We'll talk of our love tomorrow.

But when morning came, I had to dress hurriedly and rush back to my hotel to pack and catch the eleven-fifteen train.

There wasn't time for tender words, only a quick goodbye at the door as I asked, "When will I see you again?" and wondered how many times I was to repeat that question.

"In New York when the tour ends," he answered. "We'll have time together then; don't worry."

Glenna made no comment about my appearance at the hotel in a cab, but she did speak later of Nick and of my career. We were to have a split week in Princeton and New Brunswick, and had played our first perfor-mance in the college town before a rather unenthusiastic audience. As a result of the cool reception, William had made some changes in stage business, which Glenna and I stayed on to rehearse. Twice during the brief reading I fluffed my lines, something I had never done before.

We finished, and as I closed my well-marked script, she said, "Kate, I know it's none of my business—"

"It won't happen again, Glenna, I'm just tired."

"I don't mean your reading."

I looked at her, surprised. She had never spoken per-sonally to me before, but now I knew she was talking about Nick.

"I love him, Glenna," I blurted out.

I avoided her gaze while waiting for her response, which did not come for some minutes. She moved downstage and turned out the gaslights, leaving us in blackness except for the one remaining light on the opposite prompt side. I followed her into the wings.

Everyone had left the theater except for Harry, the stagehand who usually closed up.

"Don't forget this lamp when you leave," she called out to him, her voice echoing through the empty theater.

Then she turned toward me, and I could see her raven hair gleaming in the faint light. She held herself beautifully—it was the one special quality that set her apart from so many other actresses, and one which I hoped to emulate. Her voice was firm.

"At your age, Kate, love often gets confused with other equally sensitive emotions."

Her words made me pause. True, I was confused because my first thoughts were no longer of acting but of Nick. But I was not confused about my love for him.

"I know it's impossible," she went on, "to ask you to regard your feelings for Nick as a part of growing up, but I feel an obligation to remind you of your goal, of your future as an actress. Don't forget that, dear."

"I won't," I answered as we went into our dressing rooms to change.

I was determined that I could have a career and Nick too. *You want everything*, he had said to me, and maybe I did. But why not?

Clara was more outspoken, once she got over her initial curiosity, which I satisfied by telling her everything.

"Personally, I don't give a hoot about your career," she said. "I'm thinking about your heart. First love—"

"First and only love," I corrected her.

"I'll remind you of those words some day," she said, chuckling. "Lord knows, I'm a poor one to lecture, with my record, but no woman has been able to corral Nick Van Dyne yet. I don't want you to end up just another name on a long list."

"I'm not going to. This is serious for both of us, Clara."

"Then you mean to marry him?"

I nodded.

"I'm happy for you," she said, giving me a great bear

hug. "Now sit down. We're going to have a long talk. A few actresses have been able to combine a career with a long-term relationship, even with marriage, but not many. Glenna and William, of course, but they are *both* theater people. Anyhow, there has never been a part written, that I know of, for a woman about to give birth."

Thus, very frankly, Clara told me about certain ways to ensure that I would not be confronted with an unwanted pregnancy.

At first I didn't like the thought of such precautions, which would make the act of love seem premeditated, but my practical side won out. Someday there would be time for children, after Nick and I were married. And we *would* be married.

Nick and I. The words rang in my head like the Christmas bells at the ball when we had met. I would never forget that night. I would never forget a moment of the time we shared.

My love for Nick began to flow over into my performances, and because of him, my Zoe improved. I knew that, from this time on, there would be a new depth to each role I played as my own life broadened, blossomed, and took on new dimension. Everything was ahead for me, and I was happy as I had never been.

When the tour was completed, on a cold, blustery day in early March, we left New Jersey, crowding onto the ferry for the ride to New York.

I had been so sure Nick would be there to meet me on the Manhattan side that, even when our luggage had been piled into a hack, my eyes still swept the empty waterfront for him.

A day passed, and I heard nothing. I began to doubt both him and myself. I was alternately gay and sad, displaying a moody disposition which was not at all my nature.

The morning of the second day, I awoke in the guest room at the Piersons' after crying half the night, and sat up abruptly in bed. This was ridiculous! We had to be at the theater at three o'clock for a meeting of the entire troupe with Mr. Markan, and I certainly wasn't about to turn up with a tear-stained face and puffy eyes.

I got out of bed, went to the breakfast nook, and poured myself a cup of hot tea, which I sipped as I walked down the hall to the bath. Large, fluffy towels were stacked high in the cupboards. I took one down, unwrapped a bar of lavender soap, and drew myself a bath, adding hot water from the kitchen stove. When it was just the right temperature, I sank into the tub, letting the water caress and soothe me.

Before my bath was over, I was my old self again. True, I loved Nick desperately, but I was eighteen years old and all my life was before me. I had no intention of turning into a recluse.

I stepped out of the tub and wrapped myself in the towel. For a moment I almost faltered as I thought of his touch on my bare skin, but I recovered quickly. I was young, and time was on my side.

Chapter 3

For an actor, work was always hard to come by, and
even the biggest stars suffered through long seasons of
inactivity. So when we gathered at the 14th Street Theater, it was with the hope that Lester Markan had plans
that would keep us all on the boards. Rumor as usual,
was widespread, but we were totally unprepared for Mr.
Markan's announcement.

"Ladies and gentlemen," he said from the front of
the house, as the last arrivals rushed to take their seats,
"I must congratulate you on your recent triumph. You
have just completed one of the most successful tours in
the history of the Markan Theatrical Company. Successful in financial as well as artistic terms. A producer
could not ask for more." He stopped to wipe his brow.

What an inconsequential man he seemed—except
when he was mounting a production. Then the lamb became a lion.

"As you may know," he continued, "the 14th Street
Theater is dark all this month, prior to opening the

spring season. I've decided to take advantage of the empty stage: you open on the thirteenth for three weeks."

Cheering and applause filled the theater. No one had imagined a New York engagement. My spirits soared, and I knew nothing would ever bring me down again—I was opening in New York in less than a week!

When the noise had died down, Lester went on, "We'll have an afternoon and evening rehearsal of each play for the next three days. They will be the toughest three days you've ever experienced. As good as you are, you're going to be better."

With that, he took a seat, looking somewhat embarrassed while everyone gathered around to thank him.

As the group dispersed, Mr. Markan called out, "Kate, stay behind for a moment, please."

I obediently took a seat in the front row. He finished instructing the call boy on the rehearsal schedule before turning to me.

"I've heard nothing but praise for you, Kate. It's time we put a permanent finish on all that talent with some acting lessons—diction and technique, I should think. I'm replacing you in *As You Like It*."

I started to speak, but he waved his hand impatiently.

"The part's of no consequence, and you'll need the extra time. You can begin as soon as rehearsals are over—two hours a day with Pauline Rossville."

He reached for his handkerchief, and I took advantage of the pause.

"That sounds wonderful, Mr. Markan, but I can't afford private lessons."

"Well, that's all been taken care of. I—we—the theater—will pay for it."

He was blushing! I could not help smiling—until I realized what had caused him to blush. Suddenly everything was very clear, and I was not amused at all. I stood up and put on my cape.

"What you are trying to say is that Mr. Van Dyne is paying for the lessons."

"You weren't supposed to know, Kate. He wanted to help with your career, and this seemed the best way. It was my suggestion."

"No, thank you, Lester." I had never called him by his first name, but we were not on the stage now, and I was riled—at him as well as at Nick. "Tell him I can pay my own way."

"No, you can't."

I had started up the aisle and Lester followed after me.

"Madame Pauline is very expensive, Kate. But she's good. The best."

I didn't answer, but I looked back at him over my shoulder, my eyes blazing.

"Kate, I admire your fire and fury. It comes across on the stage, and I don't want you to lose it. But try to be practical about this. With these lessons, you could become a great actress; without them, you'll remain a 'potential star.' "

I had started across the lobby toward the front door. Lester's words stopped me. He was right, of course; I would be a fool to let such an opportunity slip by me because of stubborn pride.

When I spoke, my voice reverberated around the empty room. "All right, Lester. I will go to Madame Pauline on Monday, and I'll study hard. I won't let you down."

With that, I turned and walked through the doorway into the cold night, my mind full of Nick.

Why? Why had he done this? I had not even seen him since Philadelphia. The thought of our night together there brought images of leaping flames to my mind—flames of passion and desire. Now the fire had died out, and what was left? Had he forgotten me so soon? Was this his way of dismissing me from his life? Was this my payment for services rendered, as if I were a common whore? Well, I'd take his fancy lessons, and I'd learn more than he expected. I had already learned not to trust my heart.

We opened *As You Like It* on Monday, and I watched from the wings, but I didn't care. I had spent the afternoon at Madame Pauline's. Lester was right: with her as my teacher, anything was possible.

In the three weeks that followed, she made me an actress. Madame Pauline Rossville was the best dramatic coach in New York, but she rarely left her house and saw only students and close theatrical friends. Her career had begun on the London stage, which she had deserted to come to New York to teach. As students emerged from her studio to success, a part of Madame Pauline went with them. This was the only success she ever wanted. She was almost six feet tall and stood as straight as an arrow. She was regal—a queen. Her presence dominated the narrow brownstone house that was dark—the shades were always drawn—and filled with memorabilia. She had strong features: glittering black eyes, a large hooked nose. She wore exotic caftans from North Africa, colorful Spanish shawls, and Mexican stoles. They would have been bizarre on anyone else, but on Madame they were somehow strangely fashionable.

I spent two hours each day with her, and my vowels grew round, my enunication clear, my timbre perfect. But I could not lose my accent entirely, despite Madame's persistent drilling. Nor do I think she regretted the touch of the South that remained, as it began to blend with the English lilt that I had acquired from her, giving my speech a quality that would one day set me apart.

For the first hour, she sat patiently at the piano as I sang the long phrases she had set to music. Over and over the notes rang out; over and over I repeated them until she was satisfied—or exhausted, I could never be absolutely sure which! Next, we practiced scenes. Because I was a quick study, I learned my lines after a few readings and was able to devote more time to understanding the character, guided by Madame's able interpretation. By the end of each session, I saw myself magically transformed into the role I was reading.

Madame was not always awed, but she did occasionally smile, which was her way of showing satisfaction. I was learning, and I knew she was pleased.

When the day's work was completed, we had tea and talked of the theater. She relived her days on the stage, but more often she talked about the success of her students. She did not mention her childhood; in fact, she spoke as if her life had begun with her first appearance on the London stage. Of course, I yearned to know everything, and the more relaxed our conversation became, the more relentlessly I pursued the subject until, at last, she threw up her hands in mock despair.

"Katherine, one must never tell all! Someday, you too will pull the curtain of mystery over your past. It will not seem romantic for the world to know that you were once little Kate Lawrence from Deaton, South Carolina. That is too small, too petty, too—bourgeois. And so it is with me. The world does not need to know that Madame Pauline Rossville was once Paula Rosenblatt from the slums of East London."

"Madame!"

"Enough. I have said enough. You will come tomorrow, and we will not mention the subject again. You are too persistent." But she was laughing, and I knew she was not angry.

As I was leaving the brownstone on a rainy day at the end of my first week with Madame, a carriage pulled up to the curb and the door swung open. The rain was falling so heavily that I could hardly see the man who emerged, but I knew immediately that she was Nick. I rushed headlong into his open arms. He pulled back my hood and kissed me longingly. Then he stood back to look at me as the rain soaked my face and hair.

"Kate, my dear Kate. You're more beautiful than ever. Damp, but beautiful."

"Shall we go somewhere and dry off?" I laughed.

He helped me into the carriage.

"That's just what I had in mind. Lunch at my flat."

"But it's three o'clock in the afternoon."

"Then we'll have an early dinner. I understand you

are performing tonight, so I must get you to the theater on time."

His arm was around me and he held me close. I forgot my anger, my tears. Nick was beside me. Still, I could not forget how long I had been alone, waiting for him; I could not ignore the question that must be asked.

"Nick, where have you been? I expected—"

"I know," he said. "I should have sent a note. It was business again; I had to go to Canada this time. But I'm here now."

"Yes."

I snuggled close to him, and we rode in silence to his flat. He leased the downstairs of a town house, with his kitchen and servants' rooms on the basement level. Nick's quarters consisted of a large parlor-sitting room and a bedroom. Instead of the heavy Victorian furniture I was used to seeing in New York homes, Nick's furniture had straight, clean lines—a Sheraton sofa, a walnut lowboy, Hepplewhite chairs—set off by soft Oriental carpets. Instead of clutter and darkness, we entered a room full of light and airiness. I was immediately drawn to four delicate prints, beautifully framed.

"There're Japanese," he explained. "Hokusai. I've tried to achieve an Eastern look here."

He indicated a blue and white porcelain bowl on the lowboy. It was the only piece in view, and seemed, for that reason, even more beautiful.

"I grew up in a home so cluttered with velvet cushions and bibelots and *objets d'art*, that I suppose I rebelled. This is the result. Is it too stark for your tastes?"

"No, it's beautiful."

Inside myself, I rejoiced that yet another aspect of this man showed itself to be everything I had hoped for. Could there be anyone like him in the world? I was sure there could not.

"Shall I ring for something to eat, Kate?"

"No, thank you, I'm not hungry. I never seem to be hungry when I'm with you. Oh, Nick," I said, the words tumbling out, "I was so afraid you would forget me."

"Forget you? Darling Kate, that will never happen. Here, let me hold you. Why, you're trembling."

He stepped back and looked at me. Then he smiled—that wonderful, wide smile I had seen a thousand times in my dreams.

"Dear Kate," he said softly, "the first thing we must do, I think, is warm you up and dry your hair."

He took my hand and led me into the bedroom. A tiny fireplace nestled in the wall. Without releasing my hand, he bent down and lit a match to the well-packed logs. Then he pulled the eiderdown quilt from the bed and spread it in front of the fire. We settled on the soft quilt as the flames began to build. Slowly, one by one, he removed the remaining pins from my hair until it all fell free, cascading around my shoulders.

"You're still trembling. What is it, Kate?"

"It's just—I want you to hold me. And kiss me. Please kiss me."

And he did: my lips, my face, my eyes.

"Sure you're not hungry?"

I shook my head as his mouth covered mine. The trembling stopped. He turned me in his arms until I lay on my back, his mouth still on mine. I slipped my hands under his jacket, feeling the strength of his muscles beneath the fine fabric of his shirt. He took off his jacket and flung it aside. Then he began to undress me slowly, his hands moving with great care as he unbuttoned my bodice and slipped it down. He kissed my bare shoulder, and then his lips moved to the cleavage between my breasts. Placing his hands on the small of my back, he arched me upward and slipped off my dress. My breath caught in my throat as he gently removed my chemise and cupped my breasts in his hands. I licked my parched lips and tried to speak his name, but no words came. He caught my pantaloons at the waist and pulled them down, his hands carressing the soft flesh of my stomach, my hips, my thighs. Then he removed my shoes and began to roll down my stockings, his fingers barely touching the sheer fabric. The pleasure that enveloped me was so great I felt I would scream.

At last I lay naked under his devouring gaze. He stood up slowly and began to unbutton his shirt, his eyes never leaving me, desire burning in them as fiercely as the flames that burned in the grate. For an astounding instant, the flames were reflected in the gray-green of his eyes as he stood over me. I found my voice in that instant and called out his name. He came to me then, wrapping me in his arms, bare flesh meeting bare flesh.

Together we soared beyond reality into another time, another place.

Much later, I felt Nick stir beside me and opened my eyes. He had reached for the poker and was trying to revive the dying fire. I watched the thick muscles rippling under his smooth skin, and wondered if a time would ever come when my breath would not catch in my throat whenever I looked at him. He turned back to me and smiled. I was snuggled into the quilt, my hair in tangles, my clothes scattered around us.

"We always seem to wind up on the floor in front of a dwindling fire," he said as he kissed me softly on the lips. "You are a beautiful mess, Kate. Get yourself dressed, and I'll ring down for supper."

He took me to the theater that evening and watched *Rip* from the wings. Glenna and William spoke to him cordially, and Clara greeted him with great enthusiasm before throwing a wicked glance my way.

Nick was in fine spirits after the show and invited Clara, Lester, and the Piersons to dine with us at Delmonico's. Since the rain was still falling, we took a brougham to the restaurant.

The evening was gay. The conversation was a mixture of politics, gossip, and of course, the theater. Nick ordered champagne for a belated toast to our successful tour and the end of our first week of repertory. Afterwards, we toasted every newspaper in town, one at a time, for they had all treated us kindly in their reviews. Some had been kinder than others, and those we toasted twice!

Nick was a perfect host, and I watched him proudly

from across the table, my body still glowing from his lovemaking only hours before.

As the evening ended, his eyes found mine and his lips formed the word, "Tomorrow." And so began two weeks that would live with me always.

We worked out a complicated schedule, spending every afternoon together and all the evenings that I wasn't performing. Glenna and William certainly knew of our liaison, but they did not admonish me; rather, they welcomed Nick when he came to call, and often joined us for a late dinner. I slept only a few hours each night; my energy was boundless. I was up with the sun to help Glenna with chores in the house, or to shop on Ladies' Mile for dresses and shoes and lingerie—squandering my hard-earned money at Lord and Taylor, A. T. Stewart, or McCreery's. But wherever I was, my mind raced ahead toward three o'clock, when I would leave Madame and step into his carriage.

Our afternoons were long and lazy and always began in each others' arms. After we made love, we would lie together and talk. I told him about the South. Actress that I was, Nick had no trouble getting me to do my imitations, and before long he had heard them all— Jamie, Laurel Ann, Sassy, the minister, and every shopkeeper in Deaton. As a special treat, I did my "throwing a fit" act, which, as a child, I had put on at the expense of every new teacher in school, fainting and falling out of my chair with such credibility that the untried teacher often ran screaming for help. As Nick almost choked with laughter, I glowed with pride, pleased that I could make him happy.

On rare occasions, Nick talked about his business affairs, and I listened intently, trying to grasp all the complicated facts and figures. I was particularly intrigued with his involvement in the new railroad. The idea of building a railroad from Brownsville, in the bottom corner of Texas, across the border south into Mexico seemed quite romantic to me, and I knew he had great hopes for the project.

"But won't that be difficult, crossing the border into another country?" I asked one afternoon when he seemed unusually receptive.

"It's been impossible, up until now. President Lerdo has kept the railroads and foreign capital out, but there are a group of us who know Lerdo won't be in power long."

"Why not?"

I snuggled up to him, running my hand across his chest. I wanted him to talk about his work, and I was anxious to know as much as possible, but at the same time I had difficulty concentrating when he lay so close to me, his lean body stretched the length of mine.

"His days are numbered. The *Porfiristas*—followers of Porfirio Diaz—are stronger each day. And when Diaz is president of Mexico, he will welcome the Southwest & Rio Grande with open arms. And then I shall be a very wealthy man."

I raised myself up and looked over at him. "I thought you were wealthy now."

"And you would forsake me if I were not? Shame, Kate." He was laughing at me with his eyes.

"No, of course not, but you seem so well off, so— rich." I said the word deliberately, savoring the single syllable. I had never been rich, had never even known anyone who was.

"My family is wealthy, but I don't depend on them. I live off my investments and a percentage from stock sales in the S.W. & R.G."

"Then who gets the rest of the railroad money?"

"Greedy, greedy little Kate." He pulled me to him, kissing my forehead. "Monte Powell, my partner, withholds some; the rest is used for construction and buying land rights in Mexico. When we get under way, hundreds of miles of track will need to be laid. But we have the money and power to do it. Building railroads has become this country's national pastime."

"Is there lots of money in railroading?"

"Lots," he said, kissing my nose.

"Thousands?"

"More than that." His lips slid to my throat.

"Millions?"

"Jay Gould planned to sell a hundred million dollars worth of stock in the Northern Pacific."

"A hundred million!"

"Does that overwhelm you?" His lips nibbled my chin.

"No, my dear Nick, it merely excites me."

"And I, my dear Kate, know just what to do about that."

He took me in his arms, and our day ended as it had begun.

Just before his lips found mine, I whispered, "I love you, Nick."

The kiss was his only answer, but I was sure that he loved me too. Someday he would tell me so. It was just a matter of time.

On my next free evening, we decided to attend the opera. I had bought a new dress at Lord and Taylor, and was thrilled with the prospect of showing it off. Nick loved the opera; he would be a perfect teacher for me, and I was anxious to share in everything that was special for him. Verdi's *La Traviata* was being sung—an apt choice, Nick said, for my initiation.

When he called for me at the Piersons', Glenna and William had already left for the theater, so I answered the door myself. He stood framed against the dark night sky, dressed in his formal evening clothes. I felt a warm glow spread over me as I looked up at him.

Before I could speak, he reached for my hand, pressed a narrow package into it, and said, "For the most beautiful girl in the world."

He followed me down the hall as I unwrapped the present and, with a gasp, lifted it from the silk-lined box to hold it over my hand. A diamond necklace!

"Here, let me put it on you."

The diamonds were almond-shaped and set in platinum. Never had I see anything so beautiful. He put the necklace around my neck and snapped the clasp; it was like ice against my skin.

"It's so cold," I said, laughing. "And heavy."

"The touch of diamonds," he answered. "It's time you got used to the feeling." He turned me toward the mirror. "Have a look, Kate."

I could hardly believe my own reflection. My hair, piled high with cascading curls, shone in the candlelight. My eyes seemed to be dancing. I turned once, and the emerald green dress swirled around me in rich, heavy folds. The bodice plunged to a deep V, filled with cream-colored lace ruffles and trimmed in velvet. The taffeta skirt was fitted tight at the waist and gathered back into a fashionable bustle. Around my neck sparkled the diamond necklace. I could see Nick's reflection as he stood behind me, and I knew he was proud.

The crowd at the Academy of Music was quite glamorous and well-dressed, but heads still turned as we walked by, and many pairs of opera glasses were focused on our box before the orchestra began tuning up. But once the first note was struck, I forgot everything except the music that enveloped me. I squeezed Nick's hand.

"Verdi suits you?" he asked.

"Perfectly," I whispered back.

At intermission, Nick ran into an old friend, and a little of the glow disappeared from my evening. We passed her on the mezzanine—a tall, elegantly dressed woman with raven black hair. Nick nodded to her. She stopped briefly, and whispered in his ear. They both laughed, and she passed on. The whole episode took just a few seconds; had I been walking in front of Nick, I might have missed it. But I was beside him. I saw her hand touch his arm, her lips brush his cheek. Nick walked on without looking over at me, but I knew he was waiting for my question.

"Who was she?" I asked finally, and he stopped.

"Just an old friend," was his reply. But his answer wasn't enough, and he knew it.

"She's from the past, Kate."

"And I'm from the present. Do you see the future here tonight?"

"Kate, don't be silly."

My eyes flashed. "There's nothing silly about this; in fact, it's very serious. A beautiful woman whispers something obviously very personal to you and you join her in what I can only call sensual laughter—"

"Sensual laughter!"

"—while I look on innocently."

"I'm still thinking about 'sensual laughter,' Kate. I've really never heard of such a thing."

"You have now."

I tossed my head and turned back toward the box. Nick caught my hand.

"You are without a doubt the most beautiful woman I have ever known, and damned if you aren't more beautiful when you're angry. Do you realize that I haven't seen those eyes blaze since the day we met?"

"Is she an actress?" I asked, ignoring his remarks.

"No, as a matter of fact—"

"Oh, then your list of conquests includes other professions. Dare I ask what hers is?"

Nick laughed. "Kate, you are extraordinary. She is a very rich, very married woman whose husband I once did business with. And before you make another sly remark, let me tell you something."

He had led me back to our box, and we stood in the narrow doorway. The mezzanine had cleared, and only a few people strolled by, paying no attention to us.

"I am thirty-two years old, and I have not led a celibate life. And yes, the list has been long, but at the moment you are the only one on it. You are the only one, Kate. My mind is too filled with you for me even to think of another woman, and quite frankly, I don't even remember what she said. In fact, at this moment, I can think of nothing but you. Not even *Traviata*."

He leaned back against the door jamb and looked down at me. The expression on his face had become serious.

"I want you, Kate. I want you now."

"Nick—"

"Let's go. To hell with Verdi."

I·stayed all night with Nick, and awoke at dawn in his arms. The ashes were cold in the fireplace, and there was a chill in the room. I snuggled next to him, breathing the sweet smell of his skin. My mind flashed back to our earlier passion. Never had he made love to me with such force, such fury. I could still feel the exquisite pain of his fingers as they dug into my flesh. I sighed deeply. He stirred and looked at me through half-opened eyes. Then he seemed to remember too, and he reached for my arm, kissing the bruises that clearly showed the marks of his fingers. "Darling Kate, I've hurt you."

"No, Nick, you could never hurt me. You've made me feel alive, more alive than I've ever felt."

"Even on the stage, with the applause sweeping over you?" He gave me a sly look. "Can you choose between us, Kate, the theater and me?"

"Must I?"

"No, and don't ever try. You will have it all, Kate. Don't settle for less than everything." He pulled me close, kissing me softly.

"But for now?"

"For now, it's good to wake up in the morning and find you beside me. Do you realize this is the first time since Philadelphia that we've been together all night?"

"Yes," I said, and then added guiltily, "and Glenna will remind me of it again, as soon as I get home." I sat on the edge of the bed and reached for my clothes.

"Then don't go home. Stay with me." He reached out and put his hand on my shoulder, but did not restrain me. "Kate, come live with me."

I did not melt into his arms with laughter and delight at those words, nor did I weep bitter tears that he was asking me not to marry him, but only to live with him. I simply collected my things from Seventeenth Street and moved to Nick's flat.

Perhaps it was a childish decision, perhaps it was a womanly one—but he had asked that we think only of the moment, at least for now, and that's what I intended to do. I made the decision without guilt or shame, and although my Southern conscience tried desperately to speak out, especially when I left Glenna and took the carriage back to Nick's, I simply smothered my conscience with my happiness, and thus kept it quiet.

I had not told Nick of my decision, but he guessed, and I was not surprised when Max, his butler, met me at the cab and collected my baggage before showing me into the parlor. Mr. Van Dyne, he told me, had been called out to a meeting but would be back in time to drive me to Madame Pauline's. I smiled my thanks, all the while wondering how many ladies Max had seen come and go. But even those thoughts took wing when I heard Nick's key in the lock. I stood in the middle of the room, and he paused at the door for a long look.

"You knew I would be here?" I asked.

"No, but I had hoped you would be." He flung his satchel onto a chair and crossed the room. "What did Glenna say?"

"Very little, but she obviously disapproves."

"Oh, I wouldn't be too sure. There's a little romance in the old girl yet."

"Nick!" I couldn't help laughing. "She's been very good to me. They both have, and I know they have my career in mind. And my reputation."

"Don't worry, darling. I shan't compromise you."

Nor did he. I felt proud to be with him, and we even entertained one evening with a late dinner for Clara Montrose and Johnny Byers, who was one of her close friends and a well-known actor with the Markan company.

The last week of repertory was an exciting one for me because my acting seemed inspired—because, Nick said, we were together.

. "Of course," he admitted, "I must share the responsibility with Pauline, but I take credit for a large part of your inspiration."

The company had planned elaborate parties for the last night of each play, and *The Octoroon* led off with a bang. Nick attended with me, and the jubilance over our success, the excitement of closing to a standing ovation, the superlatives that rang through the green room, went to everyone's head, including mine, as the party continued into the morning hours. Nick had recently bought a small brougham which he insisted on showing to the Piersons, Glenna, and Johnny, crowding them all in for the drive home. Clara was the last to leave, and she and Nick decided she should go to her door in style. Somewhere along the way, Clara had lost her coat, but that did not prevent her from cavorting with Nick in the rain, which had begun earlier and was now coming down in torrents.

The next night, when the curtain fell on *Rip,* Clara collapsed as she reached the wings. It did not seem serious since we were all just moving through our parts, exhausted, but when the doctor was summoned, he diagnosed the early stages of pneumonia and sent her right to bed with nursing care. There was no question of her appearing in *As You Like It* the following night. The party was canceled, to the relief of the cast, I expect, although no one would admit it. Lester and I took Clara home and remained to wait for the nurse. Clara was coughing constantly, a hacking cough that sent me scurrying around the house preparing homemade remedies that I hoped would bring temporary comfort until the nurse arrived.

"Kate," Clara said as I came into the room with hot tea, honey and lemon, "I'm not going to die—I just sound like it—so you stop fussing over me and go along home. You have a big day tomorrow."

"Don't talk; that just makes your cough worse," I answered. "Besides, Nick went to an investors' meeting and probably isn't even home yet. As for tomorrow, I don't have any plans at all."

Clara laughed, which just made her cough again. Between gasps, she said to Lester, "Could she possibly have forgotten?"

Lester chuckled and wiped his brow, which did little to enlighten me.

"Forgotten what?" I asked.

Clara started to answer, but I stopped her. "You just lie back and rest. Lester can tell me."

"Kate, you have no ego," Lester said. "None. I find it impossible to believe that you're an actress unless you're up on the stage, which you will be tomorrow. Must I remind you that you are Clara's understudy?"

I felt my face turn white.

"Tomorrow night you'll play Rosalind," Clara said, as I tried to calm myself and keep her from talking at the same time.

"No, I can't—I—" A deep breath stopped my trembling. I had understudied Clara from the beginning, had rehearsed with the company, knew the part perfectly, but I had never expected to play it!

"Will—will we have a run-through?"

"Yes," Lester said. "The call's for three o'clock. I advise you to skip lessons tomorrow and get some rest. Sleep late. And don't worry," he said, looking very worried himself, it seemed to me. "It's the last night. All the critics have seen the show, and so has half the town. Think of this as good experience, Kate, nothing more."

The lights were on when I reached Nick's flat. I rushed up the steps, through the open door, and into his arms, alternately laughing and crying, and somehow managed to blurt out the news. For an instant I thought his eyes seemed sad. Then he kissed my wet face.

"Dear Kate," he whispered, "a little sooner than I expected, your career is about to begin."

I realized, halfway through the rehearsal, that I was ready. A strange sort of calm came over me and lasted until the call-boy tapped on my door, saying, "Five minutes, Miss Lawrence."

Those four words sent me into a frenzy of nerves. I didn't think I could make it up the iron steps to the wings, much less onto the stage. I remembered that night in Poughkeepsie when we had first played *The*

Octoroon. I hadn't thought I could make it then, and without Clara, I might not have. I wished fervently for her tonight. I gripped the rail with clammy hands and slowly began the climb.

Backstage was crowded with stagehands and members of the large cast moving quietly among the flats and piled-up scenery. I joined them as though I were in a dream, a dream in which I found myself underwater, surrounded by faces that had become a sea of fish, eyes bulging, mouths opening and closing with words of encouragement as I tried to make my way to shore. The faces grew larger, and then smaller, and finally took human form again as I reached the wings. There, standing to the side, was Nick.

"Clara said you might need a little push." Without another word, he took me in his arms and kissed me with all the passion of a lover's first embrace. "She has her kind of push; I have mine."

Then I heard my cue.

I remember, at the end of the second act, hearing someone say that Nick's parents were in the audience; I remember chatting with Glenna during intermission; I remember walking into the green room to a burst of applause long after the curtain had fallen. Almost two weeks passed before I remembered the performance itself, and then it came back to me scene for scene, word for word. By then the course of my life had changed, and I was on my way to England.

Johnny Byers, who played Orlando, was the first to greet me as I made my way into the green room.

"Well, the newspapers weren't here tonight, Kate, but if this audience has its way, the whole town will know about you tomorrow."

"Oh, Johnny, was I all right?"

"All right! My dear, you were marvelous. I even caught a spark from your fire and turned in an adequate performance for a change."

"Johnny, you're always wonderful."

He bowed deeply and kissed my hand as Nick approached and also bowed low over my hand.

"My, I feel like a queen tonight!" I exclaimed.

"You are!" they said in unison, clicking their heels smartly.

"Nick, when will I meet your parents?"

"Later, Kate. Bathe in your glory for a while."

The cast was busy planning another party, and I joined in, between pauses to acknowledge the praise of fans who gathered around us.

But a new anxiousness had overcome me: I was anxious to meet Nick's parents, anxious for them to like me, and I was beginning to wonder why he didn't take me to them, when a voice called out, "Nicholas, Nicholas."

The voice belonged to a tall, stately man with white hair and mustaches. Beside him was a tiny woman, pale and fragile, with the saddest eyes I had ever seen.

"Father. Mother."

There was no particular warmth in Nick's voice as he greeted them. I stood beside him, but he made no effort to include me.

"We haven't seen you in a long time, son."

"Yes, and you're looking well, Father. You too, Mother." At that point he did lean forward to kiss his mother, who clung to him momentarily.

I waited awkwardly, somewhat apart. His mother noticed me first.

"Why, you're the young lady who played Rosalind."

Finally, Nick responded. "May I present Miss Katherine Lawrence? My parents, Mr. and Mrs. Van Dyne."

"How do you do?" I murmured.

They extolled my acting for a moment before turning back to Nick.

"We would like to see you more often, Nicholas, but I suppose you're too busy for us," Mr. Van Dyne said.

The statement was a challenge that Nick did not make any attempt to meet, answering only with a mumbled monosyllable.

"Still involved with that railroad scheme?"

Nick only nodded this time.

"Hmph," his father went on. "Thought you'd learn,

after '73. Too much expansion. Too many shady deals—"

Mrs. Van Dyne interrupted, but quietly. "This is not the time for business, Carlton. You'll bore Miss Lawrence. Have you known my son long, dear?"

I had started to answer when Nick broke in, "Miss Lawrence joined the company just last summer, Mother. This is her first New York run."

I felt my face burn. They knew nothing about us, and that was the way Nick wanted it. He introduced me not as the woman he loved, but as an actress in the company he backed. I felt cheated, wronged, betrayed.

Mrs. Van Dyne was about to respond to her son when I turned and walked away, my head high. I moved to the lobby without stopping to speak to those who called out. Someone said, "Kate, don't go yet. The party—" but the sentence dangled in midair as the speaker caught the cold look in my eye.

I gathered my wrap and stepped out into the night. I thought Nick might follow me, but when he did not, I hailed a cab and got in. The driver waited. Of course—I had not given my destination. Where to? Where to? Finally I leaned forward and gave Nick's address. I would pack my things and go back to the Pierson's. They had taken me in before; they would do so again. I would just have to depend on their understanding.

The season was over; one more week and my lessons with Madame would be finished. And tonight was the end of my liaison with Nick. I had made a terrible mistake when I went to live with Nick, who apparently thought no more of me than of any other actress who passed through his life. He probably had not presented the others to his parents, either. He looked down on me, used me, had no respect for me. Tonight was the proof. But I would not look back, for I was on my way in the theater. I knew Lester had more plans; he and William had asked me to lunch with them the next day, probably to discuss my future. Yes, I was on my way.

I paid the driver and stepped out of the carriage just as Nick's brougham drove up. "Get in," he said sternly.

"I certainly will not."

He moved across the seat, opened the door, and grabbed my arm. "I said get in, Kate. I'm going to explain something to you, and you are going to listen."

I climbed sullenly into the carriage next to him. "They don't know about us, do they, Nick?" I asked through clenched teeth.

Calmly, he lit a thin cigar and squinted at me through the rising smoke. "No."

"Why, Nick, why?" I almost screamed.

"You don't know them, Kate. You can have no idea what they're like."

I looked away from him, out the window into the dark, empty street. "Then suppose you tell me."

"I intend to tell you, but I can't promise you'll understand. They're from another world, a world you have never seen, a world you're not prepared to understand, not yet."

"If you had just given me a chance with them, I could have handled it. I have some pride, Nick."

"Darling, I know you do, but their world is one in which theater people have a place on the stage—"

"But one doesn't mix with them socially?" I asked with unconcealed bitterness.

Nick did not respond directly, but I knew that was what he had meant.

"I was not about to try and change their ideas in one night, your night, the most important night of your life."

I looked at him then, long and hard. "And are you ashamed of me? Do you look down on me as they do?"

"My darling Kate," Nick said huskily, "surely you know better." He reached out, and I let him take me in his arms. "I am nothing like them, and that's where the problem lies. They have always tried to control my life—who I was, and *what* I was. My father never asked me if I wanted to join him in the brokerage firm; he just assumed that I did, as Mother assumed I would marry into their set. I was meant to be just like them, pious and regimented, always knowing the right people, always doing the right thing. But I am not like them. I've tried to make my own way. I've made mistakes with my life, but all in all I'm satisfied. I like speculating and gambling and taking chances. Just as you do."

I looked up at that, and he smiled.

"Of course you do. Leaving Carolina, being on your own, coming to New York. You're an adventuress, and I like that in you, just as I like your independence and your drive. We see things the same way, Kate, and we want the same things: success and wealth. And pleasure, especially pleasure," he said, his hands reaching for me under my cape.

And what of love? I had wanted to ask, but my words were lost in a kiss, a deep, probing kiss that joined us once more.

And there, in his carriage on a dark New York street late at night, we made love, his hands searching, searing, kindling an instant passion within me.

But nothing remains static in life. Everything changes, and we somehow learn to live with the changes.

I met Lester and William for lunch the next day, and after the amenities were over, I saw that, indeed, something was brewing. Lester looked thoughtful, but William had a smile on his face. I waited until we were served before I finally asked.

"Something wonderful for you, Kate. A chance to act in England," William said with pride.

"England? You must be teasing."

"Not so. Tell her, Lester, my good man."

"We've put together a show—an 'international theatrical event,' I believe it's called. I'm sending over two American plays; they'll play in rotation with British and French companies. Now, Kate—" Lester took out his handkerchief, and I knew he was serious— "I'm thinking of you for the ingenue. You know both roles, and William and Glenna feel you can do it. I wasn't absolutely sure until last night. You've matured dramatically in the past weeks, and last night proved you are indeed an actress. Of course, we won't play Shakespeare, only

Rip and *The Octoroon,* which they love in England—
though God knows why. But the audiences are different, more demanding in many ways. I want to hear your
opinion."

"Can I do it? Of course I can. I can't imagine anything I'd love more."

All at once I thought of Nick. I would have to leave
Nick. My emotion must have been evident upon my
face, for I saw William shake his head. Of course, he
and Glenna wanted me to go, not just for the opportunity, but to get me away from Nick.

"How long will we be gone, Lester?"

"Leave in ten days; play through July."

Almost four months. Away from Nick for four
months. I could not bear that, yet a chance to act in
London—the London of Henry Irving, Ellen Terry,
Christina Sabine.

"Let me think, Lester. Who else is in the American
company?"

Lester sipped his drink. "Clara and Johnny Byers,
whom you know; the Whitcombs, whom you don't. It's
a good company."

"Yes," I responded thoughtfully.

"We're on a tight schedule," Lester went on, "and
I'm going to need your answer by tomorrow."

Although I had barely touched my lunch, I pushed
the plate aside. "I have my lessons now, and I'm late,
but I'll let you know tomorrow. And thank you, Lester."

My head whirled with thoughts of England. I would
have only the ingenue roles, but the experience could
never be duplicated. I felt torn between the two most
powerful forces in my life: my career and my lover. I
didn't mention my dilemma to Nick until we lay resting
in each others' arms after making long, satisfying love.
Then I told him quickly, not wanting to see his face.
What if he asked me not to leave?

But he didn't. "London! That's wonderful. You have
arrived, Miss Lawrence. Of course you must go."

"And you won't forget me in four months?"

He was thoughtful for a moment. "In six months, maybe, but certainly not in four." He laughed. "Of course, I won't forget you. This is a fine opportunity, one you can't afford to turn down. Maybe I'll come with you."

"Oh, Nick, could you?"

"Not right away, but possibly in June. In fact, things could work out well for me since Europe is a ripe market for railroad shares. I could combine work and pleasure. Would you like to see the continent? Paris? Rome?"

"Oh, yes, darling."

I leaned across his chest to kiss him. But I was surprised at the tears that blinded my eyes. Nick saw them too.

"And we'll travel as we are now, with me as your mistress?"

The words seemed to have formed themselves, apart from me, but my heart was beating loud enough to be heard across the room.

Although Nick said nothing, I could feel the change in his body. He took a deep breath. "That's all I can offer you now. Give me time, Kate. Give yourself time. You're so young, and you know so little of life. I'm not going to rob you of your future; you'd never forgive me if I did. Your dreams are too grand."

"And what of yourself?"

"I have dreams too, and a future that's still uncertain. The Southwest & Rio Grande is an emerging company with miles of track to lay over rugged, dangerous terrain, deep into Mexico." He rolled over and out of bed, drawing on a silk dressing gown. "Hell, Kate, I can't commit myself to anyone until it's completed. Be sensible, and go to Europe. I'll join you in June, and then we'll see. All right?"

I blinked back the tears and smiled.

"That's my girl. Now take a bath and get dressed. I'll have Max bring up some tea—no, wine. Chateau La Fite '68, eh? We'll celebrate."

Over the wine, we talked and planned. I was hurt. In

my fantasies, I had imagined that Nick would sweep me into his arms and say, "Marry me today. I'll follow you to London." Well, I was learning. Life is not all as we imagine, and none of the parts seem to balance out. If I had my career, I would be away from Nick; if I stayed with Nick, I would miss the chance of a lifetime. Oh, it all seemed so difficult. I sighed deeply.

Nick was sitting in an easy chair, holding his glass to the light. "Look at that color, Kate, the clearest of all reds. Here, come and sit on my lap and share it with me. And quit sighing."

"How can I, when I'm such a fool?"

"How so?"

"You say you only want me for a mistress, and what do I do? I accept it, when I should march out of here and tell you off for the cad you are."

"You've done that before, my little firebrand."

"Well, I don't care what people say. I love you enough to do as you ask—for now."

He laughed. "In the end, you'll have your way, my Kate." He planted a kiss on my forehead. "Your determination equals your talent." His mouth moved down to cover mine. "But I must say, it doesn't equal your beauty." Thus my immediate future was decided. I would sail for England on the ninth of April. Nick would follow in June. He would not marry me, not now, but I would wait. In the meantime, there was London, Europe—the theater, always the theater.

Chapter 4

Clara and I stood side by side at the rail of the Cunard liner *Scythia,* watching Manhattan fade in the distance. I still waved my handkerchief, hoping that Nick was there to see. He and Lester and the Piersons—in fact, most of the company—had come to see us off, and Nick had filled our stateroom with candy, flowers, and champagne. We had little time alone—only enough for a quick kiss as the champagne spilled into glasses and the well-wishers crowded against us, just a moment for a whispered word between spirited greetings and good wishes.

"Nick, I wish you were coming with us. I don't see how I can bear being alone, without you."

"Oh, you'll bear it, my Kate, because you won't be alone. All your dreams will be with you, and the time will pass quickly until I'm there."

"I'll count the hours of every day," I said, clinging to him, trying to memorize the way his body molded into mine, as reassurance against the lonely months ahead.

"It won't be long, darling." His lips brushed against mine as the whistle sounded.

Now spray and fog obscured our view of land, and we faced the open sea for the six-day crossing ahead. "Come, Kate," Clara said. "That wind is getting cold. Let's go change for dinner. I hear the food on these ships is just divine." She put her arm around me, leading me with her along the deck. "Oh, I know you could stand up here all day mooning over Nick, but I won't allow that. You'll see him soon enough."

"Will I? Clara, I have a terrible premonition that he's gone from my life. Oh, I know that's ridiculous," I went on before she could interrupt, "but I can't get the thought out of my head. He's filled my days and nights; he's become such a part of me that if I lost him I don't think I could go on."

"Oh, you'd go on, all right, but I wouldn't dwell on losing him if I were you. He's crazy about you, Kate."

I didn't doubt that, but still apprehension clung to me like a second skin, which I tried desperately to shed.

"I only know I love him completely and want to share my life with him, now as his mistress, maybe someday as his wife. Glenna says I'm foolish to pin my hopes on Nick's constancy. She thinks I'm foolish to—"

"Well, aren't we all? Look at me, with three husbands looming out of the past. Don't expect me to chide."

"That's just why I can talk to you, Clara. *You* don't tell me I'm a fool."

"Anyway, better to be a fool in love," she answered, "than to be afraid."

"Afraid?"

"That's right, afraid of life, afraid to break away. You could be rocking away on a decaying front porch in Carolina right now, the wife of a dull farmer and the mother of a whining baby. But here you are, on your way to England. Why, who knows? We may even see the Queen herself."

"Or at least Prince Edward."

"Now, I certainly do plan to get to know the Prince of Wales—intimately."

Clara's reading of that line made us both laugh. We had been poring over British newspapers and listening to all the gossip from abroad. We knew the Prince's reputation as a lover, especially of actresses. Clara gave her bright red hair a final pat and smiled seductively at her reflection. There was a sparkle in her eye that assured me her thoughts of England included conquering much more than the theater. I finished dressing quickly, and promptly at eight, we traversed the huge salon to enter the dining room.

Evan Whitcomb and his wife had left the week before to begin rehearsals, but Johnny Byers was sailing with us. He waved effusively from across the room, where he was already seated at our table. Johnny was older than he looked, but because of his slight stature and round, freckled face, he seemed unusually boyish, even with the addition of a bushy, sandy brown mustache. With Johnny was his friend Gideon Tennant, a self-styled poet who was making a pilgrimage to London to worship at the shrines of Shakespeare, Milton, and Keats, and perhaps to meet in person Tennyson and Hardy. Gideon was tall and thin, with flaxen hair that he wore unfashionably long. He wrapped himself in a flowing cloak to heighten his poetic image. I was impressed, as I was meant to be, by his intellectual fervor.

Johnny patted my hand in mock-condolence as Clara and I were seated. "Ah, Katie, I still see Nick's reflection in your eyes. Cheer up, darling, and think how exciting your reunion will be. Remember, distance lends enchantment to the view."

Johnny liked Nick and was intrigued with our affair, which he compared to the romances of the great stars like Bernhardt and Ellen Terry. Every actress he declared, should have an exciting, handsome lover to enhance her public image. Nick and I had laughed at that, but we were terribly fond of Johnny and constantly delighted by his quick wit. Yes, the trip was going to be amusing.

During the day, the four of us, wrapped warmly against the chill North Atlantic spray, took walks about the promenade deck. Our meals were filled with laughter and idle gossip, the latter supplied from Johnny's inexhaustible store.

I filled my spare time with letter-writing. I struggled over loving words to Nick and jotted down amusing anecdotes for my family. Finally resigned to my career, Jamie had even taken to bragging about his little sister, according to Laurel Ann. And as for Thelma, she was beside herself over the news of my trip. I decided to send her a picture postcard from London. How she would squeal over Buckingham Palace or the Tower! Laurel Ann had written that Thelma was keeping company now with David Goodwin. That made me smile, as I remembered how I had inveigled David into taking me to see Glenna and William that fateful night in Deaton. Well, he had helped to change my life, but Thelma was certainly welcome to him. I had Nick. Nick.

I closed my eyes and let the memory of him envelope me. I imagined his face growing larger as it moved closer and closer to me, until I saw the thick, tawny hair curled slightly over his forehead, the gray eyes filled with desire. I saw the curve of a smile begin to form at the corners of his finely etched mouth, saw the dimples widen and then fade as the smile disappeared and his lips hungrily sought mine.

Then a voice called from far away.

"Katie, Katie."

I opened my eyes, and was startled to see Johnny beside me.

"My dear, we can't have you going into a swoon on the promenade deck. Honestly, I'm embarrassed to think what must be going on in your head. Suppose someone could read your mind? Why, we'd all be returned to port!"

I laughed and roused myself for a walk with Johnny. The days were not going to be so difficult, but the nights—the nights! I longed for Nick beside me in my bed, touching me, holding me, loving me. I tried to remind myself that the time would pass quickly and that, once we were together, we would never be separated again.

Rehearsals with Johnny and Clara helped push Nick from my thoughts. For one so small, Johnny's voice was amazingly stentorian, and he was a capable actor. Since I was only five feet two inches tall, we made very believable lovers and played well together.

The rehearsals were rewarding and stimulating. For a while I would not have Nick, but at least I had my work. Johnny, and Gideon as well, treated me as a little sister, which was not surprising since they well knew my feelings for Nick, but I expected occasionally to be noticed as a woman. They did not seem to think of me in that way at all, and what was more surprising, they treated Clara similarly.

"Tell me," I said one afternoon to Clara as we made our way back to the cabin after rehearsal, "I know Johnny and Gideon like us, but why are their attentions so brotherly? After all, Clara, other men have showered compliments on our great beauty"—I laughed—"and if we plan to charm the Prince of Wales but can't even charm these two—"

"You mean you don't know?" Her voice was incredulous.

"Know what?"

"Honey, they're—that is, they prefer the company of men—" She broke off, waiting for me to respond.

"Do you mean—?" I thought for a moment. "I see. Like—like Hermaphrodite." The Greek word was all I could conjure up to explain the strange phenomenon.

"That's a more literary way of expressing it than I would have chosen, but yes, that's what I mean. I really thought you knew, but sometimes I forget how young and naive you are." She laughed. "Well, with the boys and me to educate you, you'll learn fast. To say nothing of Nick," she added with another laugh.

But my mind was still on Gideon and Johnny. The disclosure shocked me at first, I suppose, but then I became fascinated. There was so much of life that had escaped me, but as Clara said, I was learning. For a while I watched Gideon and Johnny very closely, but when I realized there was nothing to see, I forgot about Clara's disclosure entirely and enjoyed them as I had before, perhaps more so because I was safe with them. I could say or do what I wished and they would accept me. With no romantic possibilities, we could all be friends.

Johnny, who had traveled abroad before, took charge as we disembarked at Dover. I was anxious to see the White Cliffs, but Johnny said there wasn't time.

"Besides, darling, whoever said they were white must have seen them in a dream. I've been up there to have a look at the White Cliffs of Dover twice and haven't seen them yet. Too much rain or fog or clouds—or all three. No, save your sightseeing for London."

He organized our luggage and secured a compartment on the train, and when we arrived in the city, he had us transported by carriage to our hotel on Charles Street off Berkeley Square. The whole troupe was to lodge there, and although it was not one of the more fashionable hotels, like the St. James just down the street near Piccadilly Circus, the accommodations were adequate.

I had a private room on the third floor, next to Clara's. After removing my cape and hat, I stood in the middle of my room and looked around at the flowered wallpaper, the iron bedstead, the marble-topped washstand. It was not much different from a hotel in Richmond or Harrisburg or Poughkeepsie, but William often said that eventually all hotel rooms run together. He joked that, at times, he had to buy a newspaper to know where he was playing. Well, I knew where I was, and until Nick arrived, I would fill my time with the sights and sounds, the tastes and feelings of this exciting city.

But first, I came to perform. We met the next day at our theater, the Haymarket, with Sir Giles Overton, who had organized the International Festival. I learned that the *Theatre Paris* had been playing Molière and Racine since the beginning of April. The carefully planned itinerary allowed each company to play alone as well as in repertory with the other companies during the three-month tour.

I knew no names in the French cast from the playbills that were passed around—Johnny was distraught that Madame Bernhardt would not be with us—but I recognized a few members of the British cast, and one in particular: Christina Sabine, who was rivaled in London only by the great Ellen Terry. As a child I had been bewitched by her name—Christina Sabine. All the romance of the theater was in that name. I had collected pictures of her and followed her career as best I could from far-off Deaton. Soon she had taken the place of the formidable Mrs. Siddons in my heart, for she was alive and she was now. I had waited in vain for her memoirs, not knowing then that she considered herself much too young to begin looking back on her life. I would meet her in time and learn, most unpleasantly, how tenaciously she clung to the dream of youth.

Sir Giles, a large man, red of face with white whiskers, welcomed each of us personally and answered our many questions. He invited us to a reception at his town house where we would meet the other players a few nights hence. No, Sir Giles told us, Her Royal Highness Queen Victoria would not attend any performances, but certainly Prince Edward would appear. The Prince had recently returned from India and was eager to become involved again in the London scene. Clara gave me a broad wink which, fortunately, escaped Sir Giles's notice.

We spent the next days in rehearsal, accustoming ourselves to the deeper stage, the larger house, the acoustic peculiarities of the Haymarket, with its house divided into three wide tiers, each supported by fluted Corinthian columns. The distance from far upstage to the last row of balcony seats was half again as great as in the 14th Street Theater, and I spent hours alone after cast rehearsals were completed, projecting my voice into the dark as far as it would carry. A thrill went through me when at last I found that my voice was going to hold

up in this beautiful but cavernous theater. I longed for
William to share the moment with me.

Instead, Clara called out from the front row where
she waited to take me to dinner, "I think you've got it,
Kate. Besides, in another minute you're going to faint—
or I am."

"Do you think the projection is perfect? I want desperately to do the best I can in this theater; I can't
waste this opportunity." I went down the steps to join
her.

"Honey, this is an opportunity for all of us, but
sometime we have to eat! Yes, your voice is perfect.
You'll be a hit because your star is rising, so let's go
have dinner."

I pinned my hat in place and buttoned my cape
thoughtfully. Finally, I asked her a question that had
been on my mind for some time. "Were you glad for me
the night I took over in *As You Like It*?"

She too was thoughtful for a moment before answering. "Of course, I was glad for you, but at the same time
I was jealous. Oh, not of your success, but because you
were succeeding in a role that I had come to think of as
mine. I *am* an actress, Kate, and I'm entitled to a little
jealousy and egotism like everyone else in this profes-
sion. I have both, but fortunately for you—" she patted
my hand—"I am only half actress and the rest woman.
And that woman isn't the slightest bit jealous!" She
gave me another pat, and we walked up the aisle and
out into the chill London night.

The day had been cold once again. Unlike the poet
Robert Browning, I never did wake up in London and
find "some morning, unaware" that spring had arrived.
Rather, spring days followed winter days and alternated
in a kind of repertory of their own until, at last, the
warm weather seemed to make a final decision to stay
with us. The flowers began to bud and the birds took up
their songs while the sky shone blue, or the closest to
blue that London offered.

Before long, my feet began to ache from hours of
sightseeing, led by the indefatigable Johnny while Gideon

was off on a tour of the Shakespeare country. We saw
Westminster Abbey, St. Paul's Cathedral, the Tower of
London, the Houses of Parliament, and, one by one, the
museums. I was duly impressed, but I most enjoyed the
times when I could slip away and walk on my own,
along Berkeley Street to Piccadilly, meandering with the
crowds or strolling in the early morning when the streets
were empty except for the flower girls. I would cross
Green Park to stare in awe at Buckingham Palace, and
on my way back to the theater through St. James Park,
I would stop to watch children sailing their paper boats
at the edge of the ponds or rolling their hoops along the
footpaths.

One day, turning down a tiny alley to look in shop
windows, I found myself walking along the cobblestones, drawn by the sound of music in the distance. I
came out in a tiny park where a band concert was in
full swing. The sun caught the brass horns and brightened the colorful uniforms of the little band. How
delightful were these special moments I managed to capture on my own, and how I wished for Nick to share
them with me! I continued to count the days.

I was so entranced by this city of high stone houses
and sudden squares filled with fountains and statues
that at first I did not see the squalor that lay beneath.
Johnny, with his curiosity about all of life, had to point
this out to me: the white-faced child beggars, the thousands of prostitutes, the families who actually lived in the
streets, and those who lived off the trash they collected
there. It was no different, I suspected, from New York,
but here in London the contrast was more apparent.
Here the poor were surrounded by the glitter and shine
of the upper class—lords and ladies in London for "the
season," opening their town houses from April through
July, until they would return again to their great country estates. I closed my eyes to the poverty, or tried to. I
had seen enough in my own life, growing up in hand-
me-downs and patched dresses, living for long stretches
on turnips and potatoes. No more would I think of it. I
was Katherine Lawrence and, as Clara had said, my

star was rising. I was going to catch that star and hold fast.

The success of our plays gave us an entree into the private homes and clubs of London. The British adored *Rip* and *The Octoroon*. We played as they demanded—to the pits, with all the melodrama we could muster. And we were just the company to do it; Lester had chosen wisely. What a contrast, I thought, as I watched the French company in their calculated, classical presentation of Molière, and the British troupe in their stylized version of *The Way of the World*. Christina Sabine was just what I had imagined as a child: golden-haired and elegant, with a voice like a clear stream flowing over cut-crystal stones. She enraptured the audiences.

"She's a bitch, you know," was Johnny's comment when I gushed on about Miss Sabine.

"Johnny, how can you say that? Why, she's the finest actress in England, except for Ellen Terry."

"Ellen Terry is a fine lady. Christina is a bitch. When you meet her, you'll see for yourself, but remember to keep your distance."

Johnny's gaze usually cut through exterior charm to the real person beneath. That's why, he said, he liked Clara and me so much. But I knew he was wrong about Miss Sabine. I had seen her only from a distance at the reception and on the stage, but there she lived up to my childhood images absolutely. I chose to ignore Johnny.

The days passed into May, and the trees were in full leaf now; flower pots bloomed on window ledges as London turned lush and green. I didn't even mind the slate-colored skies; I was happy. Nick would arrive in late June, and in August he and I would travel. As I continued my exploration of London, all that I saw was filtered through Nick's eyes. I could imagine him, handsome and sophisticated, walking beside me through London, lending his own style to this very stylish city. After London, there would be Paris and Rome and Vienna, the most romantic cities in the world, and we would see them together, together as we had been in New York. Nick had lit a fire within me that even the distance separating us could not put out. Now the flame burned low, but when I saw him again, it would blaze brighter than ever before.

In anticipation of his arrival, I used my money extravagantly to buy new clothes on Oxford and Regent Streets. The styles had become more extreme, and I was determined to take advantage of them. I bought the clothes to show off for Nick, but I convinced myself they were necessary trappings, since I was constantly attending midnight suppers and receptions as a representative of the American theater.

My most glamorous purchase was a yellow silk dress that I planned to wear for the first time on the day Nick arrived. It was two-piece, the jacket tightly fitted below the waist, the neckline and sleeves banded with black velvet. White lace ruching filled the neck and flowed from the sleeves. The skirt fell in tiers of lace ruffles, which were gathered back into a modish bustle made more obvious by the horsehair pad underneath. I bought a matching length of velvet ribbon for my brooch. One of the few pieces of family jewelry that had survived the war was an ivory cameo which had belonged to my mother, and I planned to wear it pinned to the ribbon around my neck. Of course, I had to buy a new hat as well: black straw, tipped well forward over one eye, with a narrow band of black satin and a wreath of yellow flowers encircling the shallow crown. White and pale yellow egret feathers completed the decoration.

This was the most stylish outfit I had ever owned, and all the shopgirls gathered about to make a fuss over it as I had my last fitting, and to make a fuss over me as well. I was not surprised, as more and more Londoners had begun to recognize me. The press had given our plays favorable notices, and although the superlatives used to describe my performance were not as glowing as those lavished upon Christina Sabine's, they were very flattering. The London theater set, which had for weeks hounded the dressing room doors, passed their excitement on to the city at large, and I soon became one of the press photographers' favorite subjects: "Katherine Lawrence, exciting young American actress, views the changing of the guard," or "feeds the swans," or "buys a bunch of violets." Fame was a new experience for me, and I loved it. Besides, such publicity couldn't hurt the box office. Occasionally, one or two elegible young London swells joined the photographic sessions, but I had no interest. No man, however charming, however Etonian his accent, however well dressed, could supplant Nick in my thoughts.

Beginning in mid-May, the Haymarket featured our company—one week of *Rip Van Winkle,* followed by a week of *The Octoroon*—and I concentrated on my performance, relaxing during the days, which had grown foggy and overcast, and not good for exploring anyway. Then we had a few days' rest while the British played alone. During this time I began to haunt the other theaters. I was without Madame, without William, but I still felt the need to study and learn—and where better could I do this than in a seat in the audience, from where I could watch the work of the fine English actors. I went to the theater constantly, dragging Clara or Johnny or Gideon with me. They preferred the round of parties that had now become a way of life for us, but I wanted to watch actors on the stage, not on the dance floor. I attended a different theater every free night: the Gaiety, the New Queens, the Little Prince of Wales. Before the tour ended, I had seen Ellen Terry six times. When my friends refused to go again, I turned to other members of the cast—to Evan Whitcomb and his wife, and even to the call-boy, who happily escorted me to *The Merchant of Venice.* But my first view of Miss Terry had been with Johnny. After the performance, he took one look at the flush of excitement on my face, decided we needed a walk in the night air, and waved the cab away. Yellow gaslight flames danced along the street over the heads of the elegantly dressed after-theater crowd.

"How lovely she was, how special!" I raved.

"Just as I told you," Johnny said. "She's not only a great actress but a fine lady. When she left the stage door, did you notice her dress?"

"Yes, it was very simple. Not at all high fashion, and yet it suited her perfectly."

"You can get away with that too, my dear. Great beauties, like great kings, can set their own fashion. Remember that when we go to Sir Giles's ball."

"I shall."

In a few days' time, Sir Giles was opening his town house to all three companies for a fancy ball, and Clara and I planned to purchase new gowns for the event.

"I do wish Nick could be here to escort me," I said.

"My darling Katie, you may wish for him in your bed, but you do not need him by your side. Somehow I'm going to convince you that you are more than a mere extension of Nicholas Van Dyne, handsome and debonair as he is."

"He's more than that, Johnny," I countered. "He's my life."

"Nonsense. The theater is your life."

"I shall have both."

I did not voice my concern that Nick had not written yet, but Johnny knew, and it had been the reason for his remarks. He doubted that Nick would come; he was trying to prepare me to stand alone. But I did not doubt. I knew this was the railroad's busiest time; everything depended upon the successful issuance of stocks. I remembered when Nick had disappeared to Canada without telling me. The Southwest & Rio Grande had completely occupied his mind then, and so it did now. He would write soon to let me know an arrival date, or he might just appear, as he had done in Philadelphia.

One night as I was making up for *The Octoroon*, adding a false fringe and cascading ringlets to my hair, Clara entered the dressing room breathlessly.

"He's here."

"Who? Nick? Is Nick here?"

"Oh, Kate, you are daft. Look at you; you're white as a sheet. Pinch your cheeks and add more rouge. I'm not talking about Nick, silly; I'm talking about the Prince of Wales. Johnny just saw him go into the royal box."

I breathed a deep sigh of excitement tinged with disappointment, followed by momentary panic. "I've never performed before royalty!"

"Well, who has? We'll all be wonderful because we haven't had time to become blasé."

If we weren't wonderful, we were certainly inspired. The Prince stood up to applaud as we took our curtain calls (someone suggested he was just getting his coat, but no matter), and of course, the whole audience rose with him. After the performance, we all lined up backstage waiting for him to pay his respects. He arrived amid great hubbub, followed by an entourage of three men and two women, one an actress, rumored to be his current mistress. I raised my eyes from my curtsy to see a heavyset man of about thirty-five, with a red Van Dyke beard and mustache, bright blue eyes, and a pleasant smile—surely not the lady-killer I had been led to believe. He passed on down the line, speaking briefly with the men, and very obviously favoring the ladies, notably Clara. I couldn't hear her response to his words of praise, but it drew prolonged laughter from the Prince.

In the carriage going back to our hotel, the three of us—Clara, Johnny, and I—discussed the backstage appearance. "He is just too stout for me," I proclaimed. "I give him to you, Clara. Nick has a much better physique, and is certainly handsomer by far."

"Well, what about my third husband, Le Clerq? He is handsomer too, but he's not the Prince of Wales! I do think he was rather charmed by me, eh, Johnny?" she asked archly.

"Yes, but you'll have to stand in line. Have you heard the latest? About the scandal during his trip to India?"

Of course we had not, so Johnny told us, his face full of mischief.

"He made the trip earlier this year for *Mama,* accompanied by a certain Lord Aylesford, who is none other than the husband of Prince Edward's current paramour."

"I don't believe that!" I said, laughing. "How could Lord what's-his-name actually be on friendly terms with a man who seduced his wife?"

Johnny cut his eyes toward Clara. "What was Mark Twain's phrase? *Innocents Abroad*?"

"I'm not all that innocent," I retaliated, "but that hardly seems decent—"

"I daresay Continental morals differ somewhat from those of Delta, South Carolina, but perhaps not."

"In the first place, it's Deaton, not Delta, as you well know."

Johnny laughed. "Shall I finish the story?"

"There's more?"

"I haven't even gotten past the curtain-raiser. While Edward and Lord Aylesford were steaming toward India on the royal yacht, what was Lady Aylesford doing but precipitating another affair, this time with the son of the Duke of Marlborough, Lord Randolph Churchill's brother. I admit the plot is all rather involved, but if you can keep the participants straight, this is where it becomes fascinating, because Lord Randolph managed to get hold of letters from the Prince to Lady Aylesford. He used them to counter the scandal now brewing around his big brother. When he found out about the letters, the Prince acted in true princely fashion by challenging Lord Randolph to a duel. It put the Queen into a tizzy." Johnny paused to look out of the carriage window. "I do believe we're at the hotel."

"Never mind the dramatic pauses. Tell us what happened," Clara scolded.

"Well, no duel was fought, but Lord Randolph and his Brooklyn-born Jennie have been banished to Ireland. God, can you imagine? Ireland! See what can happen to a nice American girl if she gets involved with nobility."

"A good story, Johnny, but I still don't approve of all that flagrant adultery," I said as we climbed out of the carriage and waited for Johnny to pay the impatient driver. "It's shocking," I added as I thought of my own strict Protestant upbringing.

Johnny flashed his eyes toward Clara again.

"Oh, give her time, Johnny," she responded. "Kate is only on her first affair. Wait until the wealthy married men begin to dangle a few baubles—"

"Never, Clara. Nick is my first and last. You're just too cynical."

"Honey, just remember, happy endings occur on the stage, never in real life."

Together we climbed the stairs to our room. Clara's words had disturbed me, and the old nagging doubts and fears began to return. Surely I would hear from Nick soon. Surely he missed me as I missed him.

Sir Giles's ball was to take place at the end of the first week in June, and as the day approached, I began to realize that Nick would not be in London to attend with me. I became reconciled to having Johnny and Gideon as escorts, since Clara was being escorted by her latest admirer, the Honourable Julian Sandusky. I took Johnny's advice and purchased a gown with a modified bustle and clean, straight lines. The material was candlelight satin with a low neckline that shamelessly showed the cleavage between my breasts. The skirt draped once, simply, in an almost Grecian effect.

As I looked into the mirror to apply the finishing touches of kohl to my eyes and color to my cheeks, I spoke aloud: "Oh, Nick, you should be here. Damn it, why aren't you?"

The mirror gave no answer. I sighed and removed his necklace from its box. Although I had planned not to wear it until I was with him once again, I would wait no longer. It sparkled with a brilliance that actually made me smile at my reflection. Even without Nick, I would have a gay time. No one would know that beneath the glittering necklace, my heart yearned for my lover.

The anteroom of Sir Giles's Belgravia town house was far grander than the finest London hotel and almost as large. Paintings were hung high on the walls and along the winding marble staircase. I caught my breath as we moved around the room for a closer look at the art, much of which was the work of old masters. Gideon was particularly interested in one painting that showed a scene of a Roman feast. Peering out of the painting as the host of the bacchanal, I was amazed to see the face of our host, Sir Giles!

"It was painted by Sir Lawrence Alma-Tadema," Gideon said. "He wraps his rich patrons in Roman clothing and places them in a setting where they vicariously capture the romantic past."

"Some day," Johnny added, "we'll find you lounging thusly, your dainty hand dangling a bunch of grapes."

"Never," I vowed. "The whole idea is grotesque."

They both laughed as we entered the ballroom. Highly polished parquet floors stretched over an area the size of a South Carolina upcountry lake. The walls were white and gold, ornate and rococo. The ceiling was high enough to accommodate stairs leading to a balcony overlooking the ballroom floor. An orchestra played at one end, and dancers swirled out across the floor.

I grasped Gideon's hand. "I can't go out there!"

He laughed and swept me into his arms and onto the dance floor with an unexpected grace which put me immediately at ease.

When I complimented Gideon on his dancing, he smiled down shyly from his lanky height and nodded toward Johnny. "I'm just glad I dance, so at least you'll have a partner. Johnny won't go any closer to a dance floor than the champagne bowl, if he can help it. On the other hand," he added as an attractive young man approached and tapped his shoulder, "I doubt that you'll be a wallflower." He nodded politely to the young man and bowed gently to me as he handed me over to my new partner.

For the rest of the evening, I did not finish a single dance with the same man, and even when I stood sipping champagne with Johnny, we were joined by no fewer than three or four admirers.

At one point I looked helplessly at Johnny, and he

leaned over to whisper, "Men always gather around the most beautiful woman in the room."

The evening was almost over before I was able to break away long enough for Johnny to introduce me to Christina Sabine. We made our way along the edges of the ballroom to where she stood by French doors leading onto a wide balcony. Candlelight shone through the glass to illuminate her Titian hair from the back with a glowing halo. For her dress she had managed to find a soft, shimmering material the very color of her blue eyes; sapphires sparkled at her neck, and a matching clasp adorned her hair. She was truly the glamorous idol of my childhood. I looked excitedly toward Johnny, but he merely lifted his eyebrows and heaved a sigh as we approached.

"Christina, angel."

"Johnny! Johnny Byers. Darling."

They exchanged kisses on the cheek and purred a few words of endearment at each other. "Christina, may I present your most devoted fan, Miss Katherine Lawrence. Miss Lawrence is one of our bright new stars from across the water."

I almost curtsied, but managed to stop myself. "Oh, Miss Sabine, I've admired you for so long and thought you were just wonderful in *The Way of the World*. I've already seen it twice." I knew I was gushing, but I did idolize her.

She smiled graciously. "One is always gratified to hear praise from a colleague." Then she added, "I have been following your career in the press, Miss Lawrence. And tonight you have made another hit." There seemed to be an icy tone in that last remark, but I was sure I imagined it. "Darling—" she turned to a young man who had been talking with a group nearby— "Sasha, darling, come and meet this charming couple."

He turned toward us. What a handsome man, I thought. Dark hair worn long; piercing, dark eyes; an easy, catlike grace. Instead of the formal dinner clothes of white tie and tails, he wore a suit of velvet, with a white satin shirt and loose-flowing tie. He was exotic, different, sensual.

Christina reached out to him with her delicate, pale hand. "Sasha, pet, this is the young American actress Miss Katherine Lawrence, and my old friend Johnny Byers. Sasha Deschamps."

"Enchanté." Sasha bowed low over my hand.

Christina continued, "Sasha is also an actor. He has been coaching me. I plan to do Molière at the Comedie Français next season, and my accent is dreadful. Sasha is a great help with my French."

"It is my pleasure. I am fortunate to work with an actress of such talent." Now he kissed Christina's hand. His voice was low and charmingly accented.

Christina melted under his praise as she went on, "Sasha is also a playwright. We expect great things of him."

"I'm sure," Johnny muttered while I stared wide-eyed at the whole exchange. "This has been charming, dears, but little Kate longs to dance. *Au revoir.*"

Johnny and I moved slowly onto the floor. He danced stiffly, with absolutely no enthusiasm. "God, I do hope someone cuts in soon. Where in the world is Gideon?"

But I wanted time to talk about Christina and Sasha. I nodded in their direction. "What do you make of all that?"

"Surprised to find that she's flesh and blood? It's obvious, dear Katie; aging actress, young lover. He's giving her lessons all right, and I certainly would like to observe their practice! Maybe I'll enroll for a few lessons myself."

"Johnny!"

"Well, he *is* attractive, dear."

"Yes," I answered. "Yes, he is."

Just then, Johnny was cut in on, to his relief, and I ended the evening as I had begun, dancing from partner to partner. I did not think of Sasha again until the vagaries of the city of London threw us together.

On my sightseeing walks, I began to roam farther and farther from Piccadilly as each street, each square, showed me a new vista: a flower seller, her dress as drab as her flowers were bright and colorful; an old bookstore, its shelves crowded with volumes badly in need of dusting; a corner tea shop with fresh scones in the window; a vendor selling meat pies. I could still smell the pastry, the flowers, the musty odor of books long after I passed by. I loved the city. Even the squalor— the rats along the Thames, the beggars and prostitutes— were all a part of life, and London *was* alive.

One afternoon as I turned from the Thames riverbank where I had been strolling, I decided to go back along my favorite street, the Strand. The tall Gothic buildings rose all around me like delicate sand castles as I walked toward the Royal Courts of Justice, my mind empty of all but the sights around me. I was aware of a distant rumble, which I must have dismissed as thunder until the moment when it grew so loud that I could not ignore it. I turned to look back, and saw a crowd of people yelling and shouting. Some were throwing rocks and sticks at the bobbies who tried to control them. I watched for a moment as the blue helmets of the policemen wobbled among the crowd. Suddenly the helmets seemed to disappear into the mass of humanity that filled the street and came hurtling toward me from all sides. I panicked and, rather than moving into a side street, foolishly tried to outrun the mob. Faster and faster I ran, until, exhausted at last, I felt a hand on my arm. Someone pulled me into a doorway while the screaming mob surged past. The roar died down, and I relaxed. Now only a few stragglers remained in the streets. They seemed to be screaming up to the silent buildings above them, their faces filled with anger and frustration. I turned my eyes away, and only then did I notice the man beside me, my companion who had pulled me away just in time.

"Monsieur Deschamps—" I pushed my hair back from my face with a weary gesture— "I'm grateful. You arrived at an opportune moment."

"Yes, it was a close call, Miss Lawrence. But we're safe now. I expect you will need to sit and rest for a moment." Above the doorway in which we stood, the word "Romano's" was carved in bold script. "We appear to be in the entrance to a restaurant. Please join me for some refreshment." Monsieur Deschamp's English, though charmingly accented, was gramatically perfect and precisely phrased.

"That would be nice," I answered. "I do need to catch my breath."

Inside the dimly lit restaurant, white-clothed tables each held a single candle. Since it was early in the day, the room was deserted, and the owner himself showed us to a table.

As he handed us the menus, I asked impulsively, "The rioting—what was it? What happened?"

"It's the trade unions, ma'am. They're out on strike. Don't have the legal right to picket, but they picket anyway. Then the bobbies come in, and there's a bit of stone-throwing and pushing and shoving. Some bloke always gets hurt."

"Why do they strike?" Sasha asked.

"Poor conditions. Miserable pay. A man can't work from six in the morning until seven at night with nothing to show for it and be satisfied. Me, everything I work for, I get, not like those poor blokes who toil away so the factory owners can get rich. But come now—" all at once he was jovial again— "would you care for a nice hot meal?"

Sasha glanced at the menu. "Ah, I see your *specialité* is oysters. Miss Lawrence?"

"I love oysters. That would be fine."

"Excellent. Bring us a dozen—no, two dozen—and some bread, and a white wine. Pouilly Fumé, if you have it." Very soon the food was before us and, warmed by the wine, I began to relax. I had been more frightened than I realized by my brush with danger. We both ate heartily, savoring the delicacy of the oysters.

"Do you walk often?" Sasha asked.

"Yes, every day, but this was my first encounter with a riot."

Sasha laughed. "I too enjoy walking, observing the sights and sounds. Even that which is unpleasant can be interesting in a city such as London."

"Yes," I said. "I was just thinking the same thing myself, earlier. It's all a part of life."

"Exactly," Sasha said. "Now, Mademoiselle Katerina Lawrence, tell me about your own life."

"There is little to tell. I'm from a small town in the South—do you know the South?"

"Only the South of France," he laughed. "Were you an actress in your small Southern town?"

"Not really, but I dreamed only of acting, and I studied on my own before I joined the Markan Tours. After the tour was over, I went on with the company to New York, and then Mr. Markan gave me the chance to come to London."

"Ah, but you must have made a success in New York in order to be chosen?"

"I suppose I've come a long way very quickly. Perhaps too quickly," I added.

"I think not, for you are very popular in London. And besides," he said with a smile, "I have seen both of the American plays; you are a natural actress, I think."

I nodded my thanks.

"But what of Mademoiselle Lawrence's personal life? No beau, no lover? Ah, you blush. There must be."

"Yes, and he's coming to join me soon. We may go to France, in fact."

"*C'est bon.* Then I shall tell you what to do, where to visit."

We exchanged a smile, and I thought what a pleasant man he was, how comfortable to be with. No wonder Christina Sabine wanted him for a companion. Nor could I ignore the obvious—his fine, dark hair, his brilliant eyes, the smoothness of his skin. Yes, Sasha Deschamps was a charming man.

"And you, Monsieur Deschamps," I said finally. "Tell me about your plays."

"There is little to tell," he answered, mimicking me. "I write because I must. No one buys my work yet, but someday—"

"I understand. It's like acting with me. Only once have I played Shakespeare, just a single performance, but someday—"

We laughed together, and as twilight fell, Sasha—as he insisted I call him—escorted me to my hotel. On the way, he asked if I would attend the theater with him the following evening. I demurred, "I don't think so, Sasha. There is Christina, and then Nick will be here soon."

"*Mais oui*, there is Christina, and that is that, and will remain. But I am speaking of friends, *les amis*. We will see a play, have a little wine. No harm."

I looked up at him.

"No harm, because we shall tell no one."

I burst into laugher. "All right, Sasha. Once, perhaps. Christina performs tomorrow?"

He nodded. "Then shall we say seven-thirty?"

We did have a good time together, Sasha and I, at my first opening night in London. And what an opening it was!—Henry Irving, generally considered England's greatest living actor, playing *Othello*. Since my arrival in England I had been looking forward to the time when Mr. Irving would complete his tour in *Hamlet* and return to the Lyceum. The theater itself was even more ornate than the Haymarket, with sky blue ceilings, deep blue curtains, and gold trim; and the sets and costumes were splendid. And to see Henry Irving at last was a dream come true. Sasha's choice for the evening could not have been more perfect.

Afterwards, we walked back to the hotel discussing the play. Under his rather careless guise, Sasha had a quick mind and a real understanding of the theater.

"You are impressed with me, eh, Katerina? I am not the dilettante you thought at first?"

"I never thought you were a dilettante, Sasha. I simply did not realize that you cared so much for the theater."

"*Eh bien*, it is good to fool a woman now and then.

But what of Henry Irving's Othello? The first impression is that he does not have the physique for the role. So tall and skinny, with legs that are not flattered by tights."

"I know. But his voice—halting and compelling at the same time. I can't explain exactly why, but I found him quite pathetic as Othello. I was moved by his performance."

"Of course. Such a great actor should move you; that is his craft, and he is good, *ma petite*. I should like to see him as Iago."

"Yes, he would be perfect—or as Cassius. 'Yond Cassius has a lean and hungry look!' "

That the mystery and beauty of the theater had once more transported me out of myself was no surprise, but to see Sasha equally affected certainly was. As we walked along arm in arm, our conversation drifted from Irving to Booth and the possibility, which had often been discussed, that they would some day alternate in the roles of Othello and Iago. Too soon we were at the hotel, where he left me, discreetly glancing at the lobby clock, to insure, I knew, that he would be at the Haymarket in time to meet Christina.

I had hardly closed the door to my room when Johnny popped in for a chat. He perched on the bed as I combed out my hair. "Well, how was your evening with Monsieur Deschamps?"

"Really quite pleasant. I was surprised to find that he is not just a pretty face, Johnny. He knows the theater."

"Then shall we say you achieved a meeting of the minds?"

"We could say that. I certainly like him—as a friend."

"Well, friend or not, owing to her temperament, I suggest you keep the news from Christina. He's her property, you know."

"I can't imagine that she would object to our friendship. I think you misjudge her, Johnny, when you say she's not a charming woman."

Johnny leaned back against the pillow, his hands

clasped behind his head. His face wore an angelic expression, but his words were typically devilish. "Christina Sabine has the charm of Lady Macbeth."

"Johnny!" I had to laugh. "Well, she won't find out anything, because neither Sasha nor I are going to tell her. Unless you—"

"Never, darling. But I must warn you to watch your step. You've been apart from Nick a long time, and you're vulnerable. I've been noticing the way you're casting your eyes around, looking for a little—"

"Stop it, Johnny. You're disgustin'."

"Oops, I must have hit home. Your accent just returned."

"Oh, good night, Johnny." I pulled him up and headed him in the direction of the door. But once in bed I could not sleep. Johnny was right. I did ache for Nick, which probably made me vulnerable to the charms of Sasha Deschamps, but I did not intend to make a foolish mistake. Sasha belonged to Christina; in fact, his livelihood obviously depended on her. Besides, Nick would be here soon. I closed my eyes and tried to relax and think of Nick, but recently I had had difficulty capturing his image. Tonight I could neither remember how he looked nor how his kisses felt on my lips. I struggled to catch hold of him, my heart pounding wildly with the fear that I had forgotten, that his face had gone from my mind forever. I searched my memory for a specific moment when we had been together. I recalled the words he had spoken, where he had been sitting, what he had worn, until at last his face became clear. I had recaptured his essence and was able to relax and fall asleep.

ACT II

"There's not a minute of our lives should stretch
Without some pleasure now."

Antony and Cleopatra, Act 1, Scene 1

Chapter 1

The next week I received Nick's letter. I tore it open with trembling hands, certain that it contained news of his arrival. Then, in disbelief, I read his words—strong, slanted writing across the cream-colored paper—words that shattered my life.

My dearest Kate,

By now you have seen the news in the press. I am leaving New York but don't know where I'll go. It is best that you forget me. Just remember that I never meant to hurt you.

Nick.

I sank slowly onto the bed. The letter slipped from my hand and fell to the floor. I looked down at it. *Forget me . . . leaving New York . . .* What had happened? What did he mean? I clutched at my throat as I continued to stare at the terrible letter. Suddenly I heard a scream, and Clara was beside me. The screaming went on and on. It was my voice, but I had no control over it.

Clara grabbed my shoulders and shook me. "Stop it, stop it! Kate, for God's sake, what's the matter?"

Then she saw the letter and bent to pick it up. "News in the press? What is he talking about?" she asked, almost to herself.

I was still trembling violently, but no noise came from my throat. The screaming had stopped.

Clara put her arm around my shoulder, and her words were calm. "Get yourself in control now, honey. We'll find out what all this means."

Abruptly, I stood up and grabbed a shawl, and then, like a wild thing, I rushed for the door, calling out to Clara, "Get a wrap. Hurry."

I flew down the stairs and out into the street, with Clara not far behind. As I flagged a cab and grabbed at the door handle, she was beside me.

"Where are we going, honey?"

"The papers, I must find the papers."

"Of course," she said calmly. She climbed into the carriage, pulling me after her. "We'll go to the American embassy; they'll have the New York papers."

The carriage had barely come to a stop at the embassy when I opened the door and climbed out, leaving Clara to pay. The building was dark within, and the grilled front door was locked. I panicked and began banging on the glass.

A major domo in a frock coat appeared and opened the door a crack. "I'm sorry," he said stiffly. "We are closed now, madam."

Afraid he would turn me away, I began to shout. "Please, let me in, let me in! I must see the American papers, please!"

Clara was beside me, talking, explaining. He relented at last, ushered us down the hall into a reading room, and lit a gas lamp. The room filled with light. Hundreds of newspapers lined the walls on wooden racks.

I stood helpless, staring at them. "Clara," I called numbly.

I watched her move from rack to rack until she found a recent copy of the *New York Times*, which she brought to me, guardedly displaying a headline at the bottom of the front page. I reached for it, and my eyes focused on the words—the unbelievable words—that suddenly blurred as my head began to spin and my knees grew weak.

"Are you all right?" Clara asked.

"Just dizzy for a moment. Don't worry," I said, seeing the look of concern on her face. "I'm not the fainting kind." But I did need to sit down. Once on the sofa, with the bewildered embassy employee still hovering about, I looked at Clara. "Read it to me, please."

Nicholas Van Dyne Sought in Fraud

New York, June 10. Nicholas Van Dyne, scion of the illustrious New York family, is sought in a scandal involving the Southwest & Rio Grande Railroad. According to Monte Powell, Mr. Van Dyne's partner, five hundred thousand shares of stock were published and subsequently sold 'on the railroad scheduled to connect Brownsville, Texas and Mexico City. Sources indicate that no track has been laid and no land rights have been secured. Mr. Powell states that Mr. Van Dyne was head of financing for the railroad and absconded with all funds. The city attorney has issued a warrant for Mr. Van Dyne's arrest. . . .

"It's not true," I whispered. "It's not true."

"Honey, it's here in the paper."

"I don't care; it's still not true. This Powell is lying. Nick is not a thief, and I'll prove it. I must prove it."

"The only thing you *must* do now is get back to your room. Let me help you up. Can you walk?"

I nodded wordlessly. Clara, aided by the major domo, who was anxious to hasten our departure, helped me to the street and secured a carriage.

Back in my room; I pulled out my trunk and began to pack.

"What are you doing? Are you mad?" Clara said.

"I'm going to New York to find Monte Powell and make him admit that he lied."

"Kate, be reasonable. He's told his story to the police, to the city attorney, to the papers. Do you suppose he's going to change it for you?"

"Then I'll find Nick. I'll—"

"Honey, Nick is not there. He's left New York, and no one knows where he is."

She was right. Nick had gone. He had left me, and I would never find him. He wanted me to forget him. Aimlessly, I sank to the bed. I was tired, so terribly tired. "Clara, please leave me. I need to rest, and to think."

"Can't I stay with you, honey? I'll sit right here beside the bed—"

"No. I'll be all right. Truly, I'll be fine."

I knew Clara was not convinced, but after covering me with a blanket, she left quietly. I lay back, watching the deep afternoon shadows move across the room. *Forget me . . . forget me . . .* The words rang in my ears. How could Nick write those unbearable words? Did he think a letter could shut him out of my life? Did he think I could dismiss him from my heart and mind so easily?

In my exhaustion, I fell asleep and dreamed terrible dreams. I saw myself alone and lost in a raging storm. All at once a house appeared, with soft lights beckoning to me through the windows. Inside the house, Nick waited, warm and loving; he held me tight to keep me safe from the blackness outside. But I could not stay. For some reason, he shut me out of his house, and I was once more stumbling alone in the storm. Cold. Afraid.

I awoke to find the room grown chill and the sun gone from the sky. Something in me was gone too—dead, ended. The flame that had burned so brightly within me was extinguished. Nick had not had faith in me or my love. When he should have turned to me and let me believe in him, he had abandoned me. I was alone and he was alone. But I would not forget him. I would never forget him.

Still exhausted, I dragged myself from the bed and began methodically to prepare for the evening performance. Clara and Johnny rode with me to the theater, and I could tell they were deeply concerned. But the pain was too great for me to talk about Nick. And I would not cry; I was too dead inside to cry.

I played *The Octoroon* that night. I spoke my lines; I adhered to my blocking; I took my curtain calls. Clara gave me a hug afterwards, Johnny kissed my cheek, and they both breathed a sigh of relief and told me how well I was holding up. The next night it was the same, and the next. They congratulated me on my excellent recovery. But they did not know that, every waking moment, those words ran through my head—*forget me, forget me*—over and over, until I thought I would go mad.

I had tried to convince them that I was fine, and I had succeeded because I could not bear their pity, nor could I bear to hear criticism of Nick. Although they both liked Nick, their sympathies were with me, so we did not speak of him at all. I divided myself in half; the line was as clearly defined as if drawn along the edge of a ruler—the public Katherine and the private Katherine. The one performed, both for her friends and her audience; the other alternately wept and screamed inside.

Shortly after I received Nick's letter, I heard from Glenna, who had additional news to share. The gossip was dying down at last, she said. Nick's family had shut their New York home and gone to Newport for the summer. Mrs. Van Dyne, she heard, had suffered a slight stroke. Nick had left his flat hurriedly, and the

furniture was being sold at auction. Nick had claimed to
Lester Markan that he had turned over the entire issue
from the stock sales to his partner, yet Monte Powell
swore that, although he had originally received small
amounts from Texas sales, Nick had remitted nothing
since. The securities investigators had, at Powell's insis-
tence, gone through his financial records, bank accounts,
and safe deposit boxes, but were unable to find any evidence of the burial of unusual amounts of money. Nick
had sworn to Lester that he was innocent, and Lester
had believed him. (Glenna did not say, however, that
she and William shared that belief.) Nick had given
Lester no hint as to where he was going, but had vowed
that he would never stand trial. And trial was inevitable
if he did not run—trial and prison—so stacked was the
evidence against him. Glenna ended her letter with
words of comfort for me, saying that I always had a
place with her and William, that their thoughts were
with me.

For a long time I believed, however naively, that
Nick would get word to me somehow. But each day that
passed brought me closer to reality. He was not going to
write. He had forgotten me as he had asked that I forget
him. But there was more—another thought that tried to
work its way into my mind: he had never really loved
me, never believed in a future for us. I had been no
more than another name on his long list of conquests. I
would not, could not, let that thought into my mind for
fear that it would push me over the fragile edge that
separated the two Katherines, and finally let loose the
agony that dwelt inside me.

If spring had been late, it seemed that summer would
never arrive—at least, not what I called summer. July
brought damp fog, rain, and depression. To avoid that
depression, I forced myself to continue my walks, re-
gardless of the weather. Once or twice, Sasha joined
me. He had a sensitivity about him that I had not at
first recognized, and somehow I felt more at ease with

him than with my other friends. They knew about Nick;
and worse, although they never spoke of him, I was
afraid they believed him guilty.

One Sunday afternoon—a bright, clear day following
a week of mist—Sasha urged me to accompany him to
the Crystal Palace, the huge exhibition hall in South
London. I refused, as I did not possess the strength,
must less the enthusiasm, to be cooped up inside looking at exotic birds and plants all day.

"Then come with me to St. James Park," he suggested. "I know it's your favorite. You can feed the
ducks, and I'll make a paper boat for you to sail."

I laughed, half tempted.

"Please come. Christina is having tea with a maiden
aunt until six, and I am *persona non grata* in that
household. You will do me a favor."

I did go, and once we were out in the fresh air, I
began to enjoy our day together. Although I did not
feed the ducks or sail a paper boat, I took pleasure, as
always, in watching the children at these pastimes. We
sat on a bench, taking advantage of the London sunshine, pale though it was.

Sasha looked over at me, and said, "I love the sun."

I smiled but did not respond.

"I have been thinking recently of France," Sasha
went on. "Of the warm sun and rich soil of the Loire
Valley. We have this in common, Katerina, we are both
of the sun and the soil, and it beckons, does it not?"

I nodded, and he stopped to look at me.

"What is it, Katerina? You have changed."

"How, Sasha?" I was surprised that he had seen
through the screen that covered my deep inner feelings,
when no one else had.

"On the outside you seem the same—as lovely as always, more so perhaps—but there is such a sadness
about you. Has your lover brought this sadness to your
face?"

I could not answer. All at once, tears welled in my
eyes and cascaded down my cheeks.

"Here, *ma petite*, take this handkerchief. Is it so bad you cannot tell? I thought we were friends."

"We are, Sasha, but I feel so sorry for myself, so alone."

"You are not alone, Katerina; you have your friends."

Then he put into words what I could not: "The sadness surrounds your heart because your lover is not coming, because he has left you."

I knew at once that he would understand, and I was able to tell the whole story of my love for Nick, his troubles, my feeling of pain when he turned away from me rather than toward me. Sasha sat quietly as I spoke, occasionally touching my hand or arm, the way one would touch a frightened animal. The tears flowed more easily now, as if a great dam had broken within me, releasing the waters of my despair that had been held back for so long.

"Oh, Sasha, look at me, crying here in public."

"And why not? In Italy or France we might draw a crowd, but not here in London. The British are too well-bred to stare." He smiled. "Wipe your eyes and blow your nose. There, that's better." He inspected my face and pushed back a lock of hair. "So, you feel great love for this man?"

"Yes."

"But you think he does not love you?"

"No, he doesn't. He couldn't, or he would not have cut me out of his life so easily."

"Perhaps he did this to protect you, Katerina. Perhaps he wanted to spare you the pain of his humiliation and defeat. A man's pride is a powerful force. Have you thought of that?"

I had not, for I was too involved in my own pain to think of Nick's. I considered what Sasha said, and then I spoke my thoughts aloud: "He always wanted me to have a career, to do well. Maybe he felt that if I followed him, my career would be ruined." I paused a moment, and then added, almost to myself, "He knows how I love the theater. He just doesn't know that I love him more." Sasha had forced me to search for ways to understand Nick, and if I was not entirely satisfied with the explanation he offered, at least the pain was not as bad as I had expected.

"Thank you, Sasha. Talking to you has helped."

"I am glad, Katerina. I see that you still love this man, and I would never wish to take his place. Instead, let us remain as you once promised—*les amis*. Do you remember?"

I did remember. "Yes, the day you rescued me from 'the madding crowd.' "

We laughed together and walked, hand in hand, back across the park. He had restored a little hope to me. I did not feel utterly abandoned, for it was possible that Nick had thought of me. It was possible that he thought of me still.

At last the end of July was in sight, and with it, the end of the tour. In August, all of London would shut down as the social season slowed to a halt. I breathed a sigh of relief; it was time for a rest. I wanted to get away from London, but now, after my first frantic hopes of finding Nick were dashed, I knew I wasn't ready to face New York, the city that was linked so strongly with him in my mind. Clara presented what she declared was the perfect solution. Sir Giles had invited the American and British troupes to his country house in Surrey for a long weekend, the French having returned home the week before. Johnny and Clara were going, and she insisted that I join them. At first I declined.

"Kate, don't be an idiot," Clara said. "How often do you get a chance for such a grand holiday? We're planning a weekend of fun and rest, both of which have been in short supply recently."

"What if Nick tries to get in touch and can't find me?" At times I knew Nick would find me, just as at other times I knew I would never see him again.

"Now think, Kate. He's had weeks to contact you

and we'll only be gone four days. If you insist, we'll leave a forwarding address here at the hotel, and at the theater as well."

I sank into a chair by the window and looked out on another dreary London day. "I feel like a puppet. Someone pulls the strings—you or Johnny—and I execute my little dance."

"Honey, whatever do you mean?"

"First, you convince me that I mustn't return to search for Nick, then Johnny literally holds me up during my performances. Now you're goading me into a trip to the country. I begin to wonder whether I have a mind of my own."

"I can't believe what I'm hearing. Aren't you the girl who ran away from a nice Southern home into the unknown wilds of the theater world?"

"The only decision of my life."

"And the most important one. Honey, you've had a bad shock, and you need some direction, that's all, until you are over this terrible time."

I started to speak, but she would not be interrupted.

"Don't think I've been fooled, Kate, by that calm mask you wear. I know the turmoil you're going through. Remember, honey, you aren't the first to be hurt in love. I've had a few romances in my life, and they didn't all end in marriage. I don't mean to manipulate you. You're too intelligent to be manipulated. I just mean to show you both sides so that you can make your own decision."

"Clara, I don't even know how I feel about Nick, and that's the only decision I'm trying to make now."

"Perhaps you shouldn't try."

"But I must. I've been avoiding every thought of him this past month, avoiding even the mention of his name, as you know. I'm being torn apart by my own fear . . ." My words drifted off, leaving my head spinning.

To have placed my faith in love and be afraid that faith had been misplaced—*that* was my fear. I wanted to damn him for the hell I was in, but I could not.

Clara remained silent until at last I spoke again, spoke my fear aloud to her: "He may have been lying to me all along, lying about his love for me."

"I don't think so, Kate."

I went on, ignoring her weak response, "And if he were capable of deception, might he not also be capable of criminal acts?"

This time she did not respond.

"Perhaps, as Sasha suggested, he's trying to protect me, but might he not be protecting me from the reality of his guilt? At least I can ask myself that question now. I'm just frightened that I may never, never know the answer."

"And do you plan to mope about until you find the answer, assuming you ever do? No, Kate, it's not your nature to be so despondent. You either love Nick or you don't."

"Of course, I do."

"Then, if you love him, you must believe that someday you'll see him again. You must stop worrying about him and have a little fun. You can't sit here in this hotel forever. In the first place, Lester's no longer paying the bill, and you can't afford it!"

I laughed. "I was thinking of going home, to Magnolias, that is, for a while."

"That shows a real spirit of adventure! I don't believe I'm talking to the Katherine Lawrence who laughed at two feet of snow and a broken-down train in New Jersey, or who dared to taste tripe on our first night out in London. No, that Katherine Lawrence would be downtown on Regent Street right now, buying a dress to wear to the country."

"And a new bonnet as well?"

At that, Clara's eyes lit up.

"Of course I'm going," I said. "There was never any doubt."

"What? And you let me spend an hour convincing you, when we could have been out shopping! Come on," she said, bustling about, "let's don't waste any more time."

Thus, on a hot, sticky Thursday morning in early August, Clara and I, along with Johnny and Gideon, boarded the train at Charing Cross Station for the trip south to Thornfield Keep. As we left the city behind and chugged into the Surrey countryside, the sky brightened and my spirits grew lighter. Green-hedged fields rolled lazily off toward distant woods, which parted to disclose tiny villages. Ancient bridges spanned slow-moving streams that meandered by strawberry-colored brick houses. Small flocks of sheep spilled out of brick-and-timber barns onto green pastures. Behind each curve, over each crest, was another picturesque scene that could have been torn from the pages of a travel book.

Carriages waited at the tiny Bitterford station to transport us to the manor house. My first look at Thornfield Keep made me gasp aloud.

"Don't get so carried away, Katie. It's just another forty-room castle," Johnny quipped. But Clara and I, and even Gideon, were speechless. We motioned for the driver to stop at the top of a hill so we could look across the valley to the keep.

"I take it all back," said Johnny. "It looks like a set Clara's husband constructed for *Hamlet*." Then he added with a smile, "I'm just carrying on like this to keep from fainting."

We all laughed and climbed back into the carriage.

As we crossed the valley, I realized that Johnny's words did have a ring of truth: Thornfield Keep resembled nothing so much as an elaborate set. Constructed of gray stone weathered over centuries, the four wings of the house surrounded an open courtyard, and a mass of twisted chimneys and turrets rose above the corner towers.

As we drove through the wide entranceway, Johnny sat back, feigning disappointment. "And I was so hoping for a moat and drawbridge."

"Shush," I remonstrated. "Here is Sir Giles."

Apparently, Sir Giles greeted each carriage personally, followed by a bevy of servants who gathered up
luggage effortlessly and disappeared into dark hallways.
His ruddy face beaming with pleasure, Sir Giles ushered
us through the main door into the flagstone entrance
hall. We climbed massive, carved oak stairs to a long
gallery that ran the length of the castle's south side. Its
walls were crowded with ancestral portraits. The gallery
windows looked out over a sloping lawn where pea-
cocks wandered freely near a lake and regal swans
glided in their intricate water ballet.

"Do you see the canopy down near the first terrace?" Sir Giles asked.

We gathered at the windows as he pointed it out.

"We serve high tea there, about five-ish. Some of the
ladies dress, but others wear their tennis togs. We have
a rather nice grass court on the east lawn, the only one
in Surrey, so you must all have a go."

Sir Giles soon departed, and Clara and I were left
alone in our adjoining rooms.

"Do you think we're dreaming?" she called out.

"Don't wake me if we are," I answered, crossing to
examine an ancient tapestry that hung on the wall
above my bed. "Clara," I exclaimed, "come quickly!"

She crossed the room to stand beside me, her eyes as
wide as mine. The tapestry depicted what seemed, at
first glance, an innocent pastoral scene, but on further
examination revealed half a doen full-bodied nymphs
romping, unencumbered by clothing of any sort, across
a lush glen. They were hotly pursued by minotaurs and
satyrs of every description.

"Look here," I said, pointing to a corner of the tapestry where two of the figures were coupling in obvious
ecstasy. "I do hope this room was chosen for me by
chance." We broke into giggles, the first of many to
overcome us that day.

My eyes swept the room, but I found no more such
treasures. Pale green draperies hung heavily beside tall,

narrow, leaded windows. The carpet was Oriental, worn by the use of many years. The massive oak furniture was impressive, but did not look particularly comfortable. It was not a charming room, nor a cozy room, but rather, like the house itself, overpowering.

I perched carefully on the edge of a huge chair. "I'm afraid to touch anything. And how do you suppose I'll ever get into that bed? It must be four feet high."

Clara laughed and pulled a footstool from under the bed. Gingerly, she stepped onto it and collapsed under the spreading canopy.

"Do you suppose there are secret passages and haunted rooms?" I asked.

"I certainly hope so—all bedecked with pastoral tapestries!" Clara stretched languidly and puffed up the downy pillows. "Mmm. These covers smell like a spring garden. I wonder if there's time for a little nap."

I reminded her of our "five-ish" invitation.

"I suppose we should shake the wrinkles from our new tea dresses," she replied as she climbed almost relunctantly from the bed. "I wonder if I dare smoke a cigarette at high tea?"

I looked aghast, and we giggled again.

Finally we were ready. My dress was a rose-colored faille silk, trimmed in braid, with a deeper rose chiffon panel in front. Clara wore turquoise, the front plunging deeply to reveal her ample bosom, and carried a matching parasol. "To protect my creamy complexion," she cautioned, but I did without, anxious to feel the strong sun on my face again. We retraced our steps along the gallery, down the stairs, and into the entrance hall. The black and white flagstones were set in intricate diamond patterns, and our heels clicked as we crossed them. There was something strangely affluent in the sound, as if it were an echo passed down through generations of wealth.

"I wish I knew the history of this place," I said.

"Don't worry. If Johnny doesn't know, he'll make up something." More giggles. "Actually, Gideon is quite a serious historian; I suspect he'll know all about Thornfield Keep. It's bound to be in the history books."

We strolled across a carpet of thick green grass toward the tent where liveried servants stood in attendance at lavishly spread tables. Fragrant, spicy teas were offered, along with platters of sandwiches, pastries, cold meats, jellied consumés—an endless list including the usual English tea cakes, crumpets, and red currant and mint jellies. We piled our plates high and joined Evan Whitcomb and his wife. The Whitcombs would be traveling to Dover the following day for the New York crossing. Lester was already busy making plans for the fall season.

"He expects both of you soon," Evan said, "so don't be lingering too long in Europe."

Neither of us answered. Clara was much too busy buttering a crumbly seed cake; I had no answer to offer; I was unable to plan beyond the weekend. The Whitcombs soon excused themselves and returned to the house. Clara and I were at last satiated, and none too soon, for there was Sasha approaching us. My eyes swept the lawn for Christina, whom I glimpsed in the distance, conversing easily with Sir Giles and looking coolly elegant in white linen.

"*Mademoiselles,* how lovely you are." Sasha bent low and offered an arm to each of us. "I've been watching you from across the lawn."

"I hoped you were gallant enough to ignore our incredible appetites," Clara laughed.

"I saw nothing!" he quipped. "But how good to know you are enjoying yourselves. Christina has not tasted a bite. She is afraid, I suspect, of an unwanted inch or pound." Sasha was dressed in white flannels with a soft silk shirt and a pale blue scarf which was knotted loosely around his neck. My eyes lingered on his solid, manly physique.

"I wish to propose further enjoyment for you," he was saying. "I have walked around the lake and found a dock

with punts, canoes, and rowboats. When will you ladies
go boating with me?"

"Never!" said Clara emphatically. "I wouldn't dare
get in one of those devices. You'll have to take Kate.
She's the adventurous one."

Sasha smiled at me. "Then we will make a perfect
team, as I am adventurous also." He was full of charm
today, and not a little flirtatious.

I eyed him mischievously. "Doesn't Christina like
boating?"

"*Mais oui,* but not in summertime. She fears the freckles."

"Freckles! Mustn't I avoid them also, Sasha?" We
were caught up in the spirit of gaiety which had begun,
for me at least, with my earlier giggling in front of the
tapestry.

"Yes, but with your dark hair and eyes, your beautiful coloring, freckles will not be so noticeable. But if
you insist, I shall supply a straw hat. Please, *cherie.*" He
boldly took my hand and gave it a squeeze.

"Well, we'll see," I teased. "Come, let's join Gideon
and Johnny at their table."

Clara had been correct. Gideon knew all about the
keep, and happily shared his knowledge. The original
foundation dated from the twelfth century, as did the
kitchen, which boasted a fireplace lintel of an ancient
material called hamstone. The main part of the house
had been rebuilt in the fourteenth century, with east and
west wings added a hundred years later. Much of the
furniture was original, but all of the tapestries were recent, if one could consider a hundred and fifty years
recent. (I avoided Clara's eyes as best I could at that bit
of information.) In the 1700s, Sir Giles's family had
purchased the keep from the descendants of the original
owners. The history of the family, Gideon said, was
filled with romance as well as scandal, which he promised to research more completely for Johnny's sake. Apparently, they had been Yorkist sympathizers during the
War of the Roses, for the stone entranceway was carved

with the York emblem of intermingled suns and roses. And there were secret stairs, Gideon assured us, built into the thick walls; moreover, he said to Johnny, there had once been a moat and drawbridge!

"Lord, it's a medieval fortress," Johnny drawled. "We should be putting on *The Murders of Udolpho*."

"Maybe Lester would consider extending our tour," Clara retorted. Once more we were overcome by laughter, which Clara and I determined to stifle by dinner time. She finally left to take her longed-for nap, and the boys drifted toward the tennis courts to arrange a match.

I glanced over at Sasha, to find him watching me thoughtfully.

"Some of the light has returned to your eyes, Katerina, but I wish to bring it all back, to see you as you once were. Will you go boating with me in the morning?"

"Of course."

We sat quietly with our own thoughts. The friendship between us had grown slowly over long weeks until, today, it seemed we had known each other always. Sasha spoke finally, in a spirit of more than mere friendship: "Katerina, I must tell you of what will soon pass between Christina and me." His eyes, serious now, met mine across the cluttered table. "We have been long enough together. The lessons are over, and now Christina begins to make demands of me, demands I cannot meet. Soon, very soon, we shall part."

I could offer no encouragement; I could only hope that he would not expect more from me than friendship, for I could not give more.

The tennis players returned, the tables were cleared, the canopy was lowered, and the straggling guests moved slowly toward the house to dress for dinner, where another spectacle awaited us. I was fast becoming accustomed to opulence, but because the scale seemed grander at each turn, I could not feign indifference; my wide eyes betrayed me. The banquet hall was domi-

nated by a long Chippendale table, decorated with her-
aldic flags and lit by a double-tiered chandelier. As in
medieval times, musicians played while we made our
way through the sumptuous meal of soup, suckling pig,
roast beef piled high with vegetables, and finally—those
most English of desserts—stewed apples, rice pudding,
plum pudding, and cheese, vanilla, and chocolate souf-
fles. Wine flowed generously, along with stout, and by
bedtime, Clara and I were quite tipsy. We had spent the
evening at the whist table, playing with the abandon of
inexperience and ending as happy losers, our IOUs dis-
tributed willingly and at random.

"What if they try to collect, Clara?" I asked as I gave
my hair a thorough brushing.

"I hope Julian Sandusky does try!"

"You are shameless."

Lord Sandusky had long been Clara's most ardent
suitor, and I suspected that he had already tried to "collect," and possibly even succeeded. Weaving precariously, I shut the door after Clara and slipped into my
batiste night dress. When I climbed into bed and turned
out the lamp, I could see, through the myriad panes of
leaded glass, the moon—just the sliver of a crescent,
faint in the sky. I snuggled into my covers and thought
once more of Nick. Where was he, I wondered. Was he
safe? Did that same moon shine down on him?

After breakfast, I joined several others from the
American company in the Elizabethan drawing room.
Sir Giles had agreed to give us a tour of the drawing
rooms and show us some of the treasures they held.
Gideon accompanied me, spellbound. As we passed
through the yellow drawing room and returned to the
main hall, Sasha joined us. Sir Giles urged us to feel
free to roam the grounds, especially along the yew walk
that led to a brick Palladian bridge only recently completed, of which he was obviously proud. Sasha whispered that that was just the walk he had in mind for us,
since it led to the boat dock. I agreed to meet him in the
garden later. The kitchen would prepare picnics for any

guests who preferred taking lunch out of doors rather than in the dining room, Sir Giles told us. I took a second cup of tea to my room and dressed in a leisurely fashion, choosing a light muslin of pale yellow to set off the rosy glow that had crept into my cheeks after a day of sunshine.

I found Sasha stretched out on a lawn chair, the picnic basket beside him.

I must inadvertently have glanced around, for he hastened to assure me, "Christina will sleep until well past noon. Come, we'll drift away below Sir Giles's famous Palladian bridge to the middle of the lake with the swans, and watch your freckles grow." Then he laughed and presented me with his own straw hat, which I placed at a jaunty angle. "Ah, Katerina, you look just like a little girl."

He took my hand, and together we ran across the sloping yard to the dock. Sasha chose a sleek canoe, loaded the basket, and gave me a hand in. He paddled across the lake with strong, even strokes, the muscles rippling under the light material of his shirt. He wore no tie or scarf today. The neck of his shirt was open almost to the waist, exposing a tangled mass of dark hair. The loosely woven linen of his trousers hugged his legs and flared out over the tops of shiny boots. Squinting against the sun, I allowed my eyes to linger on him momentarily, then I leaned back and dangled my hand in the cool, clear water, which was marred only by occasional thick patches of water lilies. My thoughts drifted as freely as the boat, dwelling neither on the past nor on the future. It was a moment of complete peace, the most perfect such moment I had known in a long time. At length, Sasha picked up the paddle again and headed for the far side of the lake, steering us under the shade of an overhanging willow.

"*Voilà*, the perfect place for our picnic, out of the sun but still adrift." He leaned back lazily. "Do you enjoy the water, Katerina?"

"Oh, yes. As a child in Carolina, I used to go fishing.

Except our streams were brown and muddy, not clear blue like this, and we didn't have a canoe, just an old rowboat. Look, Sasha, at the school of minnow below. Let me have some bread, I want to feed them."

He laughed and handed me a thick slice of bread. "They're probably stuffed with English pastry."

"Hmm, it tastes good." I took a bite before I tossed the crumbs on the water and watched each one disappear as the fish surfaced to feed. "What else have they packed?" I asked, amazingly hungry again.

He opened the lunch basket and rattled off the contents with an auctioneer's voice. "Cold meat pie—looks like beef. And what is this? Pastry? Oh, no, crumpets again. Fruit—apples and bananas, slightly green. But look here, a roasted bird of some sort."

"It looks like a partridge or a quail. What a strange selection of picnic foods," I mused.

Sasha broke off a chunk of meat from the bird and passed it to me. The taste was gamy and succulent. "What would you take on a picnic in Carolina, Katerina?" His words were light, and yet something unspoken hung heavily in the air, something I could feel but could not name. I answered the spoken words, ignoring the unspoken ones.

"Let's see. Ham, of course. My brother's sugar-cured ham is his pride. If I packed the basket, there would be plenty of wild raspberries and red, juicy tomatoes. Chess pie too." He looked puzzled, and I smiled. "Pie made with brown sugar; I can't imagine where the name came from. And a big pitcher of ice-cold lemonade," I added. "And if we were picnicking in France?"

"Very simple. Wine, bread, and cheese. The bread, always the same—thickly crusted outside, soft within. But the cheeses, so many to offer: Brie, Camembert, Roquefort. And an infinite variety of wines from which to choose, each one as delightful as the one before." Then he seemed to draw from those words which hung in the air. "But you must come with me to France, and I will let you see, let you taste."

I treated the offer lightly, in the manner in which it had, I suspected, been made. "I had hoped to go once, but now I think not; I don't feel up to traveling."

"But of course you can still come! I once offered to show you my country, remember?"

"Yes, but that was when Nick and I . . ." My voice trailed off, and I stared out across the lake.

"You think of him yet, do you?"

"Yes."

"Do you plan to wait for him forever?"

"Yes, if I must."

We sat quietly, the two of us in our separate worlds, filled with our own thoughts, until at last Sasha said, "I cannot bear to think of your waiting, Katerina, when he may never come back to you."

I knew that was true, and my eyes showed that I knew.

"Oh, Katerina, how I wish I could make you understand that life is to be lived, not wished away. Such unhappiness as surrounds you will not bring your lover back, and ignoring me is useless, for I shall not let you ignore me. As you see, I have you now in the boat alone. There is nowhere for you to go, so you must listen."

"I will listen if you talk of something else. Of yourself. Where will you go next?"

He laughed. "I will speak of myself, but you will find that, in doing so, I speak of Katerina. I must begin my work once more; I must return very soon to France; I must ask that you come with me!" He bit loudly into an apple and eyed me playfully, but I did not respond. "Ah, yes, about myself," he said with feigned meekness. "I return to France to write, for I cannot work here at my best. I need the fragrance and feeling of my own country, not the stale air of England."

"Christina knows you are leaving?"

"She knows that in time I must."

He told me about his play, which he had long carried within him and which he had begun at last to put down

on paper. He was well into the first draft, and, with his
return to France, would find the direction, the motiva-
tion, the inspiration to complete it. We talked once
more of the theater, of our hopes for the future. We
both longed for more new works of importance.

We did not speak personally again until after the boat
ride. As Sasha ran the canoe alongside the dock to tie
up, he touched my hand lightly. "Perhaps," he said,
"when I look at you I am misunderstanding what I
seem to see in your eyes."

"You see a look of friendship, Sasha. That's all I
have to offer."

"Have I asked for more?"

When we reached the house, his eyes turned merry
again. "You will save a dance for me tonight? For that,
no special look is required!"

I laughed and nodded. I had forgotten that Sir Giles
planned another of his fancy balls for tonight, but I decided then and there to have a long afternoon nap in
preparation for the event. As I drifted to sleep, Sasha's
words continued to dwell just outside the periphery of
my consciousness.

I had not seen Clara all day, nor were she and Lord
Sandusky present at dinner. I smiled to myself, almost
enviously, thinking of how easily Clara drifted into a
liaison which was so very lightly painted with the
brushstrokes of love. For some, such affairs are freely
entered into and just as freely ended; for others, love
comes only once. Perhaps I longed to be like Clara, but
I was not. Oh, well, I thought with a sigh, I would
dance tonight, and the dancing would be, as it always
had been, my release.

The furniture was cleared from the Great Hall and
the orchestra positioned above in the minstrel gallery.
Since the dance at Sir Giles's townhouse, Gideon and I
had practiced often, working on the intricate steps of
the European dances that had not reached New York
and certainly not South Carolina, where even the names
were unfamiliar. Tonight we flew across the floor on
winged feet, and in the midst of a mazurka, I heard the

rhythmic clapping of a few pairs of hands, soon taken up by many, and looked around to see that we were the only dancers on the floor. The others were now by-standers, keeping time with their hands and tapping feet. My momentary embarrassment fled with Gideon's reassuring smile, and I caught the look of pleasure on Sasha's face as we whirled by. Sasha and I danced but once that night, and then only briefly, just long enough for him to whisper, "I have told Christina that I am leaving. She knows I cannot work here in England, and she understands. I did not need to tell her the rest."

"That you no longer care for her?" I asked.

"I speak of my feelings for you, Katerina, not for her. I believe you know this." I was swept into another's arms before I had a chance to form an answer.

As I returned to my room later, exhilarated but with a clear head, having sipped only one glass of wine during the evening, a voice from the next room told me that Clara had returned. She came through the adjoin-ing door, her face happily flushed. "My, you danced the night away, Kate."

I smiled and lay back on the pillows of my bed, still fully clothed. "I didn't even see you on the floor. Where have you been all day?" I asked lazily.

"Oh, I was dancing, but we moved into the anteroom to avoid changing partners." She smiled slyly. "Oh, yes, Julian has definitely stolen my heart."

"Will you marry him?" I asked in all innocence.

"Marry? Don't forget, honey, that I'm already mar-ried, and Julian has a wife and several children. I'm an actress, Kate. Marriage with an Englishman who sits in the House of Lords would be unthinkable, not to men-tion ridiculous. Can you see me entertaining the Lon-don social set? No, I'll be a happy mistress. Julian makes the crossing to New York quite often."

"I just don't see how you can be happy under those circumstances."

"Well, take my word for it, I can. With Nick, you had greater expectations, Kate. That's why it's difficult for you to understand."

"Do you suppose that's how Nick saw me, as an actress who was willing to go on being his mistress?" I did not even mention Sasha and his offer to take me to France.

"Don't be silly, Kate. American society is quite different, even in Nick's set. You certainly know that. You've said yourself that Nick will be back some day. Also, I need hardly mention that he has no wife and you have no husband."

"Sometimes I think I hate him, Clara."

"You don't hate him; you just hate yourself for loving him so. Now let's think about tomorrow—and the hunt. Will you ride?"

"Oh, I doubt it, Clara. I love horses, but I have never been interested in chasing down an innocent, lonely fox. Perhaps I'll take a quiet ride alone. The estate seems to be crisscrossed with bridle paths."

"So Julian and I have noticed. We might just ignore the fox ourselves!"

Clara seemed happy, and I was glad. She had her Julian, and I had—what? My memories.

Sunday, a day normally spent in church in South Carolina, or resting in bed in New York, was spent riding to the hounds at Thornfield Keep. The riders gathered quite early, just as the sun rose, blood red, over the far treetops, and I went out into the courtyard to watch them mount up. Stable boys paraded sleek hunters for the guests to choose from, and the air was filled with the clopping of well-shod hooves on the paved courtyard, neighs rising in the early dawn, the slap of saddles being cinched, the rattle of shiny bits and decorated martingales, the clinking of spurs. Soon the long horn sounded, the fox was let loose, and the hunt was on. Sir Giles was present to see the riders off, but did not join in the hunt himself, complaining of an unusual case of gout after two days of overly rich food and heady wine.

He noticed that I was in my habit but had not yet mounted. "Ah, Miss Lawrence. I suspect you do not fancy the chase?"

"I must admit not, Sir Giles, but I would enjoy taking a bridle trail, if I may."

"Certainly. I'll have one of my own mares saddled for you. She's become disinterested in taking jumps in recent years, but is still an excellent saddle horse."

I was soon trotting along a gravel path and into the woods on soft, well-cleared trails. They led through deep pines where the sun seeped through only occasionally when the thickness of the forest opened for a moment and then closed again, plunging me into a fairytale world of pine needles, mushrooms, and wild berry patches. I sighed deeply. It would be a perfect morning, my last in the country, for tomorrow we would return to London and thence, I supposed, to America. I thought of Nick, who would not be there, and of Lester, who would. Perhaps when the fall theatrical activities were firmed up, assuming I would be included in the Markan program, I would have time to go home, however briefly, to Magnolias and my family, before Lester put me to work again. Work. My family. If only I were ready to face them. But I wasn't ready! Oh, God, I prayed, prepare me for what lies ahead in a future without Nick.

I crossed a shallow stream and came out on the edge of a large clearing. I tapped the mare lightly with the crop, but she balked, tossing her head in gentle defiance. "Come on, girl, there's nothing here to frighten you."

Then I saw. On the far side of the clearing, a blanket was stretched over the short-cropped grass, and atop the blanket were two figures. I strained to see better, although I knew I should turn back and not intrude. But what I saw froze me like a statue. The man's trousers were lowered well below his hips, exposing pink, generous buttocks that moved convulsively up and down. Beneath him was a woman whose dress was pulled up, all but covering her face. Her arms were locked around his neck, her legs entwined with his, her hips rising to meet him and then falling as he plunged within her. I watched mesmerized until, with a violent spasm, the man collapsed heavily, emitting a moan that carried across the meadow and caused the little horse once more to toss her head. I flattened the reins against her neck, and she turned quickly to the stream, eager to be away, and waded a few yards to where another path crossed the water. We doubled back in the direction from which we had come.

I did not have to see the faces to know that the couple were Clara and Julian. I felt fiushed with embarrassment. Or was it excitement? There had been something ridiculous and, at the same time, strangely beautiful in the scene I had witnessed. I felt a terrible longing in that quivering, private, empty place where my thighs spread over the hard leather of the saddle. I cursed Nick, cursed him for awakening those hidden desires, for lighting that glorious fuse of fulfillment, and then for leaving me with nothing but a terrible, aching emptiness. Fighting against the spasm that threatened to envelop me, I spurred the horse to a gallop, and through the woods we ran. Low-hanging branches stung my face with welcome pain, pain I hoped would make me forget. We emerged, horse and rider as one now, onto a wide path, clear and straight for hundreds of yards ahead. I bent low, burying my face against her neck, breathing the sweet, heady smell of sweat, giving myself over to the race, the race against my own feelings. On and on we flew, tearing against the wind until my head cleared and my body relaxed. I pulled the mare up at last, and dismounted in one movement to fall beside her in the grass. Oh, Nick, Nick! How much longer could I fight against this growing desire?

I lay stretched out on the grassy knoll for a moment—or an hour, I could not know which—the mare grazing nearby. When we were both breathing more easily, I led her down to where the stream converged once more with the bridle path. I knelt down beside the clear water, scooped up handsful, and splashed my burning face until at last I felt cool and refreshed. The horse, white with foam, heaved and blew as she drank. When at last she lifted her head, I took up the reins and walked along the path beside her. A long time had passed, I was sure, since the little mare had been run so hard, and I did not want to return her to the stables in a lather. We had not gone very far when I had my second encounter of the day—this time a more welcome one— for ahead in the road was Sasha. I called out to him, "Did the fox elude you?"

He looked up, surprised. "A double catastrophe. I became separated from the field, and the roan threw a shoe. I fear I must walk him back. You seem to have a similar problem, eh?"

"No, but we had such a hard run that I thought my horse deserved a rest."

"Then let's walk back together. Let the others run down the poor fox."

We walked along in companionable silence, the reins loose in our hands, the horses nuzzling us occasionally from behind, as if to urge us on toward the stable where oats and barley awaited them.

"So you are really returning to France?" I asked.

"Yes, tomorrow, I think."

"Tomorrow?" The news both surprised and disturbed me. Then I would not see him when we all returned to London. This would be our last day together.

"I can get a train from Bitterford to Southampton, and take the ferry across to Cherbourg. Oh, I've left a few belongings behind in London, but nothing I can't do without. Have you considered my offer, Kate, to come with me?"

"Sasha, you are impossible. You have barely freed yourself from your entanglement with Christina, and you know how I feel about Nick—"

"Before you say more, please think. I am leaving Christina; this is for good. Nick has left you; perhaps this is not for good, but it is for now. Could it be that fate has thrown us together for some reason?"

I could not answer.

"I understand who you are, Kate, and how you feel. I would not wish you to change. I am not asking that you love me, only that you trust me. I could teach you so much of life; I could show you how to laugh and be happy again. Katerina, I can take care of you; I can heal you. And then one day you will be free to return to your lover, or to a new life. It does not matter which, so much awaits you."

"And we would remain as we are, *les amis*?"

"If that is your wish. But if that is not your wish, and I think it is not—"

"No, Sasha, I—" Fear possessed me, for I knew from my reaction to what I had seen in the clearing how close to the surface my feelings dwelt, how at any moment they could explode and betray me.

He put his fingers against my lips. "Don't answer yet, *ma cherie*, just think about it. Until tomorrow."

Rather solemnly, we approached the long walk to the main gate. The guests were already returning from the hunt, their faces flushed with victory. Apparently the fox had been cornered and, if I guessed correctly, torn apart by the dogs. Still walking our mounts, Sasha and I were among the last to enter the courtyard. Among the last, but not the last. The muted tones of grooms soothing horses were silenced by the onrush of Christina as she galloped into the court. Her horse tossed his head and half-reared in confusion when she laid her crop alongside his flank, coming through the gates. She suddenly pulled him to a stop before Sasha and me.

Not waiting for help to dismount, she jumped off, a figure of fury who hurled herself at us. "Liar, liar!" she screamed at Sasha. "It's this bitch you're after, this whore! And to think I believed your cunning tale of going home to write! To write, indeed!"

Then she was on me like a lioness, her gloved hands yanking at my hair, tearing at my dress. Her shrill voice filled the air with vile curses and obscenities. I threw my hands up to protect my face as Sasha reached for Christina and tried to hold her flailing arms. She drew back her crop and slashed at his face, leaving a ragged mark across his cheek. I tried to pull her away from him, but her rage was uncontrollable, more animal than human. All at once, Sir Giles was between us, holding the now sobbing Christina, leading her toward the house while Johnny ran to Sasha, a towel in his hand to wipe away the blood that now poured from Sasha's face. Gideon guided me away from the gathering crowd. I was too shocked to cry, too amazed to speak. I only felt anger that Christina had so completely misunder-stood.

"Well," Gideon was saying, his arm supporting me as we climbed the stairs, "Johnny said she was jealous, but my Lord, I believe she was sired by a cougar."

I didn't answer, but leaned heavily against him until we reached my room. Without shame, I allowed Gideon to help me out of my tattered dress and find a robe for me to slip into.

"You lie down now, Katie, there's a good girl. I'll just go find Clara and send her up to you."

I did not have to wait long.

"Honey, what happened?" she asked before she was even in the room. "Gideon said Christina flew at you like a wild woman. Are you hurt?"

"No, but she certainly left her mark on Sasha. Oh, Clara, her anger was so unjustified. We simply met on the trail and walked back together."

"That was all?" Clara seemed amazed, even a little doubtful.

"Yes—no. Oh, Clara, I might as well tell you; he wants me to go away with him to France. He knows about Nick, that I still love him, but Sasha understands, and it doesn't matter to him. Sasha wants only to make me happy again." I thought of all that Sasha had said to me, and I believed him. He would never hurt me. "Would you think I was crazy if I left with him? I've never even kissed him, and I certainly don't love him. I love Nick."

"But Nick is gone."

"Yes." We were both silent. "What should I do, Clara?"

She laughed. "For once, I don't have the answer. I don't even have any advice."

There was a faint knocking at the door, and Clara moved across the room to open it.

There stood Sasha, a heavy valise in each hand. "Please. I must see Katerina."

I nodded and he came in, setting the bags beside the door. The ugly red welt protruded from his tanned face.

"I am returning to France today," he said, "within the hour. I asked that you give me your answer tomorrow, but now tomorrow is too late. Must I say farewell, Katerina, or will you come with me?"

A thousand images flashed through my mind, the thousand Kates of my past merging into one: a strong Kate, a daring Kate, a Kate who wanted to taste life. I did not know what Sasha offered me, but unless I took this chance, I would never know. "Yes," I said, "I will come, Sasha. Just give me a little time to pack." I would go as a friend, but if, in time, he asked for more than friendship, I knew I would give him what he desired.

"Kate, are you sure?" Clara asked.

"*Ma chere* Clara, do not worry." Sasha took her hand and raised it to his lips. "I will take good care of her. I promise. I want only what is best for Katerina." Then he turned to me. "There will be a carriage at the east gate in twenty minutes. And don't worry, I will explain everything to Sir Giles."

With a smile, he was gone. I began to throw my clothes pell-mell into my trunk. Clara joined in, and between us, everything was soon packed and ready.

"Honey, I think you're a little crazy, but if this can make you happy, then I'm all for it. Just remember, there's no future for you with Sasha, certainly nothing permanent."

"That's why I'm going with him. I don't love him, and I don't believe he loves me. But we're good companions, and we shall have fun together." I stopped long enough to give her a hug. "I need this now, Clara, do you understand?"

She nodded and held me tightly for a moment before undertaking the practical aspects of my departure: a formal note to Sir Giles, a footman summoned for the luggage, extra money in my reticule.

As Sasha and I rolled away in the carriage, I could see Clara standing outside the courtyard gate, still waving.

"No backward looks, Katerina. Let us only think of now."

Chapter 2

I had never known the word *hedonist* until I met Sasha. He was a man who lived for the pleasure of the moment, that same pleasure I had so often reached for, even grasped and held onto—but briefly, only briefly. Such happiness was a part of Sasha, and if he sensed that it was escaping him, he took whatever action was necessary to reclaim it. This was why he left Christina and took me away to France; I never had any delusions about his motives. I also knew he took me away not just for himself but for me, because he knew that, to save myself, I must go with him. He was never cruel in his pleasure-seeking, and never looked for happiness at the expense of others. As I learned to know him and his world, I found that Sasha was that most remarkable of men—a man content with himself. He appeared not to care about the past or worry about the future. His world was today. He was to bring sunshine into my life, and I would soon bask in its warm rays.

All these thoughts and more passed through my mind

as our train pulled into the tiny station at Naval, in the
Loire Valley of France. My exhaustion was com-
pounded by the lingering mental agony of my terrible
scene with Christina and my impulsive decision to run
away with Sasha. It had been a difficult trip: a slow
local train from Bitterford to Southampton, the boat-
train to France, the short but uncomfortable trip from
the port town of Cherbourg to connect with our train at
Caen, and now the final leg of our journey. I was tired
and dusty, wrinkled and rumpled, feeling far from he-
donistic. Yet I was somehow content, as throughout the
journey I slept sporadically against Sasha as a child
would sleep against a protective parent. How strange, I
thought, that Sasha and I had never even kissed, yet I
entrusted myself to him, knowing nothing of what tomorrow might bring, knowing only that I needed time,
and he would give me time. And yes, I was apprehensive over the mystery that surrounded Sasha—or at
least this French Sasha, whom, on the soil of his own
country, I did not know at all. But at the same time I
was intrigued, even excited, by the mystery itself, by
what lay ahead and would soon be revealed to me.

As we prepared to leave the train, I wondered momentarily what his father would be like. He had not
mentioned his mother, and I assumed that she was not
living. How would Sasha explain my presence to his father, and must I look forward to the kind of treatment
from him that I had received from Nick's parents? No, I
told myself, this was France, not New York, and my
conduct would not be judged so quickly here. Besides, I
would be safe with Sasha; I could trust him. So I put the
thought easily from my mind as, together, we stepped
out onto the platform at Naval. The town was as tiny as
Deaton, unhurried, even sleepy, gentle, and unpreten-
tious—very like the whole of the Loire Valley, I would
soon find.

Sasha roused the dozing driver of an open wagon and
arranged transportation to the chateau. The afternoon
sun beat down heavily, and there was a shimmering

haze on the white stone of the houses with their rust-colored tile roofs.

"Look, there, Katerina." Sasha pointed out the wide Loire River, placid and slow-moving, just visible through the poplar trees that bordered its banks.

Even the air was quiet, interrupted at intervals by the squeak of our wagon wheels. There was no other traffic on the road. In less than half an hour, we turned onto a crushed-stone lane, thickly fringed with lime trees, their scent heady in the air. The wagon completed a half-circle, coming to a halt before a low white wall. Iron gates, supported by two massive pillars, were open invitingly, exposing a small formal garden. Within, where I had expected to see the round towers and triangular roofs that had ever been associated in my mind with a typical chateau, I saw instead a large country house, from which wide steps led down to a veranda and thence to the garden

I stood for a moment as Sasha dealt with the driver, who had begun to unload our baggage. Five tall windows stretched across the main front of the house, which was framed between two pavilions. The ground level was constructed of local stone set in random patterns, and the windows were topped with rounded arches. The two levels above were of stucco, their five windows lined up symmetrically with those below, but framed by narrow pediments so that the architectural simplicity remained, but was beautifully tempered. I watched two servants, a man and a woman, hurry down the long row of steps, circle the round centerpiece of the garden, and approach us with obvious joy. They did not hide their feelings for Sasha, hugging him repeatedly with almost childlike adoration, all the while chattering madly in French much too rapid for me to understand.

"Here, Katerina," Sasha said with an arm around each. "Meet Louis and Solange. *Voici, Mademoiselle Lawrence.*" And then to the woman, *"J'ai faime, Solange, est'il possible de manger maintenant?"*

I too was hungry and was delighted to follow Sasha into the cool house. The entrance was set slightly to one side of the main facade and opened into a grand salon, beautifully but simply furnished in the style of Louis XVI. There we sipped a refreshing glass of wine before going up to our rooms, where Sasha had asked that we be served. We had adjoining apartments in the east wing. Mine was charming, with white hangings against blue walls, again decorated in Louis XVI, and the comfortable armchairs in the sitting room, like the bed hangings, were covered in blue and white stripes. The bath was dominated by a mahogany-and-marble sunken tub, with a dressing room set off by Oriental screens. And everywhere, windows offered a view of the Loire, which wandered among thickets and meadows. In the distant hills, grape arbors lay slumbering in the sun.

Sasha joined me after changing into light cotton trousers and an open shirt. I suddenly wished I had taken the time to change, but he told me not to worry, as I would be asleep very soon after our late lunch and one more glass of wine. He was right. Solange and Louis brought trays and served us cold sausages, fruit, and wine on the breakfast table in my sitting room. Sasha's father, the marquis, was not in residence. He spent July in the Tyrol and probably would not be returning for a few days, but the house apparently ran in his absence quite as well as if he were there. Solange had even placed a vase of freshly cut flowers on the table. She and Sasha kept up a running conversation—some I could follow, and some I could not—as she remained to pour our wine and slice the obligatory bread and cheese with which she supplied us from a huge tray on the buffet, wielding her knives lovingly and not allowing us to refuse a taste of each variety of cheese. Sasha must have seen my eyes begin to droop before I even realized that the exhaustion he predicted had overcome me, for he motioned to Solange and the table was cleared.

"Come, Katerina, let me close the curtains so you can sleep. We shall talk later." With a light touch on my arm, he left the room.

I drew off my soiled dress and undergarments, throwing them in a heap. With the heat, I would need no

nightgown or cover, and as I lay down on the cool
sheets, sleep came immediately. When I awoke, the sun
was low in the sky and Sasha was at the windows, pulling back the curtains. The last feeble rays of the day
filtered across me as I lay naked under Sasha's gaze. I
could tell that he had not slept, for he still wore the
same crisp trousers and shirt, and his face still showed
the strain of travel, although his eyes were bright as he
looked down at me. I reached for the sheet, but Sasha
was quickly beside me, taking my hand in his.

"You have a beautiful body, my Katerina. Do not
cover yourself."

The look in his eyes was the look of desire that, when
I left England, I had no doubt I would see in time. And
with that look, I entered another phase of my journey,
the journey beginning with the letter from Nick that had
led me into a dark tunnel. With the appearance of
Sasha, I had begun to feel a force drawing me toward
the end of the tunnel. Now, at this moment, I emerged
into the light. The tunnel was behind me still, and I
would, I knew, pass through it again on my return trip.
But until then, until then . . .

I tried to speak, but could not. We remained frozen
as in a tableau: I lying back on cool sheets that smelled
of sage and thyme, and Sasha poised above me. The sun
produced a faint aureole behind him as he leaned
closer, still closer, watching me with his soft, dark eyes.
His hand reached out to touch my face as time froze
once more, creating another tableau: his face close to
mine, just inches away, his hand resting tenderly on my
cheek. The moment was endless. I remembered other
eyes, other hands—I could not put down the memory.
The touch was so different, the look was not at all the
same, but the desire within me was as great. And then, as
his lips finally brushed mine, the other memory flew, and
the desire was all that remained. His lips were warm
and sweet, surrounding mine greedily as if inhaling, ab-
sorbing, drawing into himself my very heart and soul.
He lifted me into his arms, and I felt the soft cotton of
his shirt against my skin—skin so sensitive that even the

cotton seemed to bruise it. His lips left my mouth and moved across my face, my neck, my shoulder and my breasts, encircling the taut nipples. I heard my own breath—my first, it seemed, since he had touched me—turn to a moan as his lips moved now across my abdomen and down my thighs. I felt as if every nerve in my body rested just below the surface of my skin. I was on fire. But still he was not content, as he explored my legs slowly to my toes and then back, touching the skin of my ankles with his tongue, tasting my calves and my thighs, at last probing the soft moistness between my legs. Now he could no longer ignore the trembling that ravaged my body, and he quickly stripped off his trousers to lie beside me. I held him close, touching him, kissing his face, running my hands softly over the jagged red mark still visible on his cheek.

He took my hand and placed it between his legs, letting me feel the strength and hardness there. "See how I want you, Katerina. Do you want me?"

At last I spoke. "Yes."

And he was inside me, moving with me, rousing me to the fevered edge of my desire, for which there was only one release, a release we found together.

Trembling, I lay in his arms, close to the warmth of his body. He held me to him, murmuring my name. "Katerina, Katerina. Are you awakening, *ma petite*? Are you coming back to life?"

I nodded wordlessly and suddenly began to cry—not tears of sorrow, but healing tears for the comfort that I had found with Sasha.

He held me until the tears stopped, and then smiled as if he knew my thoughts. "Those will be your last tears for a long while, Katerina. We shall love and laugh and sleep and eat; and we shall do so whenever, however, wherever we please! That is the rule here."

"But when your father comes—"

He broke into laughter at that. "Have I not told you that my father is the greatest hedonist of them all? You will see. Lie beside me now while I sleep for a time before dinner."

I slept again too, and we both awoke refreshed, dressed leisurely, and went down together for dinner. The hour was well past nine. Very late to dine, I thought, but once more, all was in readiness for us, as if Solange had anticipated our arrival.

Sasha began that evening to tell me the story of his life, a story that made him all the more appealing to me and seemed to increase, rather than diminish, the exotic aura that enveloped him. I was now deeply under the spell of his beauty, his sensuality, his appetite for life. I learned why Sasha, surrounded by all the wealth and abundance of Chateau Merliac, found it necessary to live as a teacher and actor while hoping to find success as a playwright. He was not the Merliac heir. Although the Marquis of Merliac, a man now in his sixties, was Sasha's natural father, Sasha had been born of an affair and had spent his first years far from his father's world. The father had felt responsible for the child, however, and had seen that he was well-educated. After the death of the Marchioness, Sasha had come to live part of every year with his father, who could finally open his home to the illegitimate child. But there was also a legitimate child, Sasha's half-sister Maria, who had married a count and lived in the South of France. Her sons would inherit Chateau Merliac, according to French law and custom. Sasha accepted this with no regrets, and enjoyed the hospitality and comradeship that his father offered him. He received a small allowance from the marquis, which he supplemented with acting jobs or by "tutoring" wealthy women. As he spoke, the mystery that surrounded him seemed to fade. Yet something of it still lingered, and I wasn't sure why until I asked, "And what of your mother, Sasha? Did you know her?"

"*Mais oui*. She was a *gitane*."

"*Gitane?*" The word was strange to me.

"A gypsy."

A gypsy! So that was why Sasha seemed exotic, foreign, different. The blood of the Rom ran through his veins. I listened in awe to the rest of the fascinating story Sasha had to tell. Reared by his mother, he had traveled with the gypsies during his formative years, as the caravans roamed France. He was one of them, wild and untamed. His mother had made her way by telling fortunes, dancing in cafés, reading palms. When Sasha grew older, his father intervened just enough to see that the boy received an education, sending him during the winter months to a private school where he studied history, literature, and the classics. In the summer, he returned again to the Rom and his roots. Later, when the marhcioness died, Sasha began to spend the brief school holidays at the chateau with his father. And from the age of twelve, he was writing—stories at first, and then his plays. There was never any bitterness between his parents; neither wanted to marry the other, although this could have been possible after the death of the marquis's wife, but both preferred to retain their own lives, with the boy sharing in each. Thus he had the best of two worlds.

But writing was the real world, the deep love that could not be ignored.

"I have completed many plays, Katerina, but this new one, the one I am working on now, is the best. It is a play about my mother, about the Rom."

"And you've come back here to France to finish it?"

"So I hope." He held his wine to the light, smiling through the glass to me. "Rosé d'Anjou," he said lovingly. "It is best drunk young and fresh, and it is for such a taste that I have returned. To taste the wine, to taste the sweet air of this Happy Valley. So it is called, did you know?" I shook my head. "Yes, the Happy Valley—that is my inspiration. Still, I need my muse." He looked at me with teasing eyes.

I took up the challenge, why I will never know. I had not read the play and couldn't have realized, then, the depth of emotion he would draw on and the freshness of concept that would emerge. At a time when I had not read one word that he had written, I couldn't have known; yet I knew. "Sasha," I blurted out, "I will be your muse."

He laughed and took my hand. "I shall need time to

work," he said seriously. "Even a *bon vivant* such as I must work."

"I'll give you that time every day, and at night we can talk over what you have written. That will be good for me too, Sasha. I need to keep the theater with me. I can't lose it completely." I did need the theater. Perhaps not the actual experience of appearing on stage—I had not missed that yet, although in time I would—but at least being a part of Sasha's work. More, I needed to give to this man, to share his life. I knew my trip had not ended, and that this time with Sasha was just an interruption to allow me to live again. One day I must take up my search for Nick and the answer to our love, for even though I could be alive without him, I could never be complete without him. But that was for the future, and now—today—I wanted to give. I had never been able to share Nick's life, had known almost nothing of it, so that when tragedy struck him, he had not turned to me. Now I wanted to share, and now I could. Each and every day.

We slept to the song of the nightingale and awoke in each others' arms the next day, and for many days to come. He worked with me beside him, in my bed, over breakfast, in the shade of the oak trees near the river. We did not need to speak, and I knew his concentration was complete, even with me so near. In fact, he often reached out to touch me, hardly aware of the gesture and its tenderness. But I was not always there. Often I wandered far downstream so that I could recite aloud, not from his play, not even from my volume of Shakespeare that I carried with me and from which I continued to memorize. The words I spoke aloud were French conjugations—not terribly interesting, but more important to me at this time than any other words, for I had laboriously begun to perfect my French so that I could read and fully understand the lines Sasha created. Oh, I knew the plot and the characters. When he completed each scene, he read aloud to me, translating into English as he went along, but I wanted to read his words myself, in his own language. Somehow that seemed important to me.

Those were our mornings, filled with intense concentration but blanketed by the peace we seemed to instill in each other; long mornings which stretched into midday when, at last, the work was put aside. We took our late lunch out of doors, usually beside the river at Sasha's favorite boyhood haunts: the wooded spot where a rope hung from a thick limb of the sturdiest poplar, the rope knotted low to accommodate bare feet of long ago; the bluff where the bank was highest, its paths so narrow that I could barely traverse them without gripping the flimsy branches of shrubbery that protruded from the narrow crevices; the wide stretch of beach where sand bars jutted far out into the river and the waters were perfect for swimming. All of this, Sasha was able to see through a child's eyes but looking back from the maturity of an adult, and my memories flooded together with his as he awakened my senses to all that surrounded me and memories of all that was pleasant from my own childhood.

He loved the river, loved to swim in its cool waters, fish for hours from its banks, explore its hidden places.

"La Loire," he explained, "is a woman, without doubt."

We were lying on our backs in the sand after a long swim. I looked over at him, puzzled, as he continued.

"Lazy and soft-hearted here in this valley, but farther north, in the mountains where the river passes through deep gorges, dangerous and unpredictable. Yes, assuredly a woman."

My eyes narrowed as I searched his face to see if he was teasing, and he laughed to show that he was. He touched me softly, his hand caressing my bare skin.

"But everywhere it is beautiful, everywhere desirable, everywhere—" His voice trailed off as his mouth covered mine in a long, exploring kiss that I returned with equal fervor. Along with awakening my senses, Sasha had also rekindled the physical passion that had long lain dormant within me. Each day, my need for him had grown stronger as we explored the very limits of our sensuality. Sometimes the depth of my response to him was almost frightening, yet, like one addicted to a powerful drug, I could not break away. Today, free of clothing to encumber us, free of walls to surround us, with no eyes but those of nature herself to watch over us, we possessed each other with a passion of pure pleasure, that pleasure which was everything for Sasha, and which he had passed on so easily to me.

Earlier, we had stripped off our garments and swum together in the waters of the Loire. I believe it was this abandon, the naturalness with which I was able to shed my clothes before him, more than the freedom with which I gave myself to him, that surprised me most. I had never suspected in my own nature a willingness to display my body so easily, but Sasha seemed never to tire of looking at me and touching me, and whether we were together in a moment of love or just sharing a swim, he wanted to be able to reach out freely to me. He told me that each day my body became more beautiful, and the mirror echoed his words whenever I glanced into it. I could see there the rosy color that brightened my skin, the firmness of my breasts, and a new suppleness in my limbs.

Sasha found delight in my body. But more, he taught me to find delight there as well, as he explored with his hands and lips, sensitive to those places that tantalized me most, relishing my whispers and moans of rapture. He taught me to touch myself in those secret places— my breasts, between my legs, in all the pockets and folds of desire, and to bring to myself gratification of my own deepest urgings. Often he would watch me touching myself, touching himself, too, as he watched, until at last, driven to a frenzy of need, we turned to each other to find satiation of our exquisite longings.

And he taught me to explore his body as he explored mine. I would kiss his eyes, his lips, his chest, pausing to dampen his own sensitive nipples with my tongue, then moving down, my mouth searching his flat abdomen and then, at last, encircling that most manly part of

his body as he turned me around to find the corre-
sponding part of my body where the hidden bud of desire flowered at the touch of his tongue and we joined in
another different but equally satisfying pinnacle of full-
fillment, our mouths alone bringing to each other the
thrill of love.

Sasha's attitude toward love was the same as his approach to life. To him, lovemaking was as natural as
breathing. He made no moral judgments and accepted
every act that gave pleasure as wholesome, and very
easily I was able to put reticence aside and follow him
down the paths of sensuality. Ours was an idyll that was
too perfect to last. Nor was it meant to last, for it
brought with it no ties, no bonds, and I wanted none.
But I did wonder about Sasha and his own thoughts of
the future, and whether he did not sometimes yearn for
permanence in his life.

Those thoughts were revealed to me by chance that
same late afternoon on the beach. I had finally slipped
on my dress and he his trousers, as we thought of returning to the house but changed our minds and lay
back again on the sand bar to drain the last of the bottle
of rosé we had brought in our now empty picnic hamper. I was very relaxed, even slightly tipsy. As I lay on
my back, watching the soft white clouds above, I felt
like a cloud myself, floating high over the earth, swimming in the cerulean blue sky.

"And if you are that cloud, what am I?" Sasha asked.

"The sun," I answered without thinking. "The har-
binger of light and warmth and goodness."

"You think too highly of me, Katerina."

"How could I think too highly of the one who has
brought me back to life? No, Sasha, darling, you mean
very much to me—" I let my serious tone drift into
playfulness— "as you have to so many women."

But he remained serious. "Are you disturbed by
that—the other women?"

"No, because you and I are very special together, and
I'll be sorry when our time comes to an end."

"I too, my love."

"Sasha, will you ever settle down and marry?"

"Marry, marry. That is all you Americans think of." He had loaded the hamper, and we began reluctantly to gather up the rest of our scattered clothes and head back to the house.

"Perhaps because it seems so natural—to marry the one you love."

We crossed the sand bar slowly, hand in hand, and made our way through the brambles along the bank onto a cleared path.

"To answer your question," Sasha said, "I probably will marry someday, when I am ready."

"An actress? A dancer? A gypsy?"

He laughed. "*Non*. I will, I suspect, marry an older woman, perhaps a widow with a nice home which she manages efficently, a woman who will take care of me."

"That sounds like a mother!"

He smiled but did not answer, apparently unperturbed by my remark.

"Won't you love her?" I asked.

"I shall care for her, certainly, but love—if you mean *la grande passion*—no, for this does not blend with marriage, as all Frenchmen know. We marry for one reason; we have affairs for another. Ah, Katerina, you are shocked?"

"No, I'm just surprised by your honesty. I also wonder if it would work out to marry someone you like or respect but do not truly love—"

"For the Frenchman, yes, but probably not for Katerina. Katerina will marry a man she loves and adores, and he will love and adore her, eh?" He dropped my hand and put his arm around my waist. This was done casually, to show he was not thinking of Nick. But he was, and so was I.

For a moment I felt a terrible despair sweep over me. I reached up and kissed Sasha, feeling the warmth and sweetness of his lips on mine—those lips that could, for now, blot out all memories. He dropped the hamper and held me for a long moment in his arms, as if to apologize for bringing even a hint of sadness into my day.

Along with learning French, I was also learning the art of French country cooking, with Solange as my guide. We began with simple dishes like steamed artichokes and mushrooms in heavy cream. These I mastered quickly. I was a good cook and had been helping Laurel Ann in the kitchen since childhood, but I had to put away many of my Southern habits—no more gravies, overcooked vegetables, or fried fish and poultry. Here I found delicate sauces, lightly sautéed meats, crisp vegetables. After I mastered *jambons de volaille*— a delicious boned chicken dish which was one of Sasha's favorites—Solange taught me to make a rich pastry dough, cutting the butter into the floor with a knife and then working quickly with my hands to blend the ingredients before the butter softened. She watched carefully as I beat eggs thoroughly with cream, grated cheese, and ground nutmeg to achieve my *pièce de résistance*: a delicious cheese tart. Sasha was thoroughly impressed, and after that I could hardly stay out of the kitchen. Often in the evening, Sasha and I would shoo a chuckling Solange away, and I would prepare our entire meal. Solange would eye us merrily as she wiped her hands and hung her apron on a peg, as if to say she knew there was more to my preoccupation with cooking than love of food! Dressed in soft muslin, barefooted, and with my hair hanging loose, I would putter about the cool stone kitchen while Sasha sat in a chair, tilted back against the wall. He would give advice as I prepared one of his favorites, *Brochet de la Loire*—fish with butter sauce, using pike which Louis had pulled from the river only an hour before—or roast lamb with white beans. I refused to learn to cook eels, a supposed delicacy, or *grenouilles sautees*, which I insisted on calling by its most literal American translation—fried frogs! But I enjoyed preparing the other dishes, especially the locally cured ham and pork sausages that Sasha liked so well. At these times I was completely happy. Sasha and I would laugh together as we sat at the long oak kitchen table and talked about the theater, about London and New York, as if they were as far away from our world as another planet. We would laugh at the image of Sir Giles or Evan Whitcomb coming upon us suddenly in this setting, with me barefoot and up to my elbows in flour. We joked about how the London papers might handle the story: "Miss Katherine Lawrence, the actress, enjoying life as a French peasant-woman." Well, I was enjoying life, a life in which I was a part of everything around me.

As we lay with our books and papers scattered about in a chestnut forest several miles from the chateau, I tried to explain this unity that I felt with nature to Sasha one day, a day that turned out to be our last alone at Chateau Merliac. We had ridden out on horseback just after dawn, and Sasha had been working quietly for several hours in this, another of his favorite spots, where the sun could barely reach us through the thick ceiling of leaves and branches. I had read all that he had written now, in the original French, and had thought of translating the play myself. My French had improved dramatically with my studies and the long hours of conversation with Solange—even Sasha and I spoke French much of the time now—but I found that the improvement was not great enough for such a difficult job, and finally I gave up. Now I sat beside him, my head resting against the dark gray trunk of a giant old chestnut tree, surrounded by a carpet of rich green ferns. Through the silence came the sound of the bells of a faraway, ancient abbey. The moment was too perfect, and I breathed a sigh. Sasha put down his work and looked over at me with questioning eyes.

"I'm just thinking of how close to nature I feel at this moment, how much a part of the earth and sky."

He smiled and reached for me. "One has only to know my name to know how well I understand your feelings. As I have told you, Katerina, we are both nature's children. Literally, Deschamps means that I come from the fields, the soil, but for me it means that I am a part of all that surrounds me, just as I am part of you,

and you are part of me." He had pushed my dimity
dress to my waist and loosened his clothes so that our
bodies could find each other, so that in our total embrace we could once more prove his words.

Later on in the afternoon, we returned to the house
and entered as usual through the kitchen to be met with
a torrent of French from Solange: Sasha's father, the
marquis, had returned. Once again I felt the same
shiver of nerves as on the day we had arrived in France,
brought on by the fear that Sasha's father might not approve of my presence in his home. "Do you think he
will like me?" I asked Sasha.

"He will think at first that you are a beautiful girl,
and he will find in time that you are much more." He
kissed the top of my head. "Don't be concerned; I'll
wager Father has not come home alone either, but we
shall know soon enough. Dress beautifully for tonight,
cherie. I will go see him now. *À demain*."

Despite his words, I remained tremulous over the
prospect of meeting the man who was not only Sasha's
father, but also a French marquis, and meeting him under such compromising circumstances. From the little
Sasha had told me about his father, I had deduced only
that he was an attractive and intelligent man. Well, I
would endeavor to look my best, and happily, I would
be able to converse in French, however awkwardly. I
rummaged through the dresses in my closet. My eyes
fell on the yellow silk that I had bought in London so
long ago, and that I had not planned to wear until—My
head swam for a moment, and then I reached for the
dress. After all, it was too beautiful to hang uselessly in
the closet, and I would look better in it, now that my
color was so heightened, than I had that day in the fitting room when I had tried it on for a final time to the
delight of all the salesgirls. I would simply not think of
whom I had bought it for; I would wear it tonight for
Sasha's father. I pulled the dress over my head and
fluffed out the lace ruffles until they fell deliciously
into place. "You look good enough to eat," Sasha said
as he appeared to dress for dinner. He helped me with

the tiny covered buttons on the jacket and gave me a long, lingering kiss of approval.

"But will the marquis approve? And is he alone? And what will—"

"One question at a time," Sasha said as he crossed the room to draw his bath.

I followed and stood by the door while he stripped off his clothes and stepped into the marble tub.

"*Oui,* he will approve; *non,* he is not alone. There is a companion, a Mademoiselle Veronique, a girl of— well, you shall see for yourself." He bathed quickly and dressed in the formal dinner clothes Louis had laid out, while I stood at the mirror reviewing my appearance.

"I wonder if I should wear Mother's brooch?" I fastened it to the matching piece of velvet ribbon and held it around my neck for Sasha to see.

"Wear it, by all means, as it is very lovely, but your beauty needs no embellishments, Katerina," he said, as he helped me secure the ribbon. "Come now, dinner is formal tonight, and we must be down by eight." I took his arm, and we walked down the staircase and through the salon. Louis opened heavy double doors as we approached. The dining room was large and sparsely furnished, but the brilliantly painted ceiling and decorated wainscoting around the walls saved it from austerity. The room seemed alight and alive, with fine silver, china, and crystal gleaming in the candlelight of the long table.

Standing at the sideboard was a slim man with wavy gray hair and the thin line of a mustache, and by his side stood an exquisite young woman, or rather a girl of not more than seventeen, with the face of an angel. Her hair was corn-colored and pulled up in a cascade of curls. Her eyes were clear and blue, her complexion flawless. We were introduced, and the marquis gallantly kissed my hand. Neither he nor Veronique spoke English, so we conversed in French—his flowery and elegant, hers monosyllabic and barely audible. Over dinner—seven courses, each a perfect example of Solange's culinary art—we talked about the theater, and the mar-

quis seemed genuinely impressed with my success so far
and interested as well to hear that Sasha was finishing a
new play, although I noticed that the son did not reveal
to his father what his play was about. Veronique did not
speak unless spoken to, and then only if the marquis
were addressing her; otherwise, she simply nodded her
head. I assumed she was extremely shy; I would not
learn until later that she possessed no more than the
most rudimentary conversation, even though French
was her native, and only, language. The marquis
treated her as an ornament, touching her hair or her
arm as if she were a rare but—I shuddered as I realized—inanimate object. He seemed almost surprised
when she actually moved.

Dinner was followed by brandy and coffee, which we
took in the library, a huge room complete with an inlaid
billiard table. Sasha and his father moved to it almost
automatically, as if this were a usual after-dinner challenge, began chalking their cues enthusiastically, and
made outrageously high wagers. Ladies did not play,
of course, but Veronique and I stood by to watch for a
while. She soon moved away disinterestedly, and I followed, hoping for a conversation at last now that we
were, for all practical purposes, alone. But in facing
her, I found myself facing an almost invulnerable wall
of silence. I learned that she was from Paris, which intrigued me since I had always wanted to visit there, but
I could learn nothing of Parisian life from her. I did
wonder, though, about this child, how she came to be
with a man more than three times her age. But this I
would assuredly not learn from her.

Soon Veronique drifted wordlessly from the room,
unobserved by the men who were still bent over the
billiard table. I took a chair nearby, and while Sasha
pondered over his shots, the marquis stood beside me,
chatting amicably. No mention was made of Veronique's
disappearance, and I felt strangely as if she had never
been there at all.

At last, the game having ended and the brandy having been consumed, we climbed the stairs to our rooms. The marquis admitted that the day had been long and the trip tiring. Usually, he added, he could stay up until the morning hours. *"Mais je vieille,"* he said—I grow old. Sasha laughed at that, but his father, I noticed, did not.

Sasha undressed and came into my room to stretch out lazily under the canopy on the cool sheets. I joined him, and we talked in the quiet moonlight, the words drifting away gradually as he took me in his arms and made love to me gently, sweetly, as in a dream. I moved from that dream into a deep sleep and back into the dream again. Or was I dreaming? A hand caressed my bare leg.

I twitched slightly and mumbled, "No, Sasha, I'm too sleepy."

Again sleep came, but still the light touch remained on my leg. Reluctantly, I opened my eyes to see Sasha asleep beside me. Then whose hand—? I sat up abruptly, tugging at the sheet. There before me stood Veronique, her fingers still resting lightly against my leg, a faint smile on her lips. I must still be dreaming, I told myself. I closed my eyes and then opened them again slowly. The apparition remained.

"Tu es jolie," she said hesitantly, *"et Sasha aussi."*

By now Sasha was awake, and we both looked in amazement at the figure by the foot of the bed. She was completely nude. Her long blonde hair hung below her shoulders; her breasts were pink-tipped and firm; her skin was fair, almost translucent. Rounded hips and shapely thighs joined in a golden triangle of silky down upon which her other hand rested provocatively. I grasped Sasha firmly to convince myself that I was not dreaming, and dug my nails into his arm.

"What does she want? Is she sleepwalking?"

"No, she is very much awake and wants, I believe, to get into bed with us. The marquis must not be the man I thought. Are you interested?"

"Of course not, you fool," I laughed. "Please, Sasha,

get her out of here. And get some clothes on her," I
added, as he swung out of bed and reached for his shirt
to put around the girl. Talking softly, he led her from
the room with an amused glance over his shoulder at
me. In a short time, he was back. I was wide awake and
ready to talk. "What in the world! I have never been so
surprised. She must have wanted you."

"Or you, *cherie*, or both of us! Who is to know? At
least now she understands that we want our beds to ourselves."

"Who is she, Sasha?"

"I do not know anything about her, but I would
guess that she became a prostitute very early—at thirteen, perhaps twelve. She has no education at all. You
noticed, did you not, that she could barely speak a complete sentence? But she is beautiful—for the moment.
Certainly she does not love my father; he pays her, and
well, I am sure. He will be good to her, but in time she
will become bored. I would say that she is already
bored." He laughed. "She will leave him and go from
man to man, and by twenty-five she will be an old
woman."

"How very sad."

"*C'est vrai*. But all in this world is fate. You were
lucky to have a family who cared, an education, a career. You can always take care of yourself. But many
women, even those more intelligent than this poor
child—well, life can be terrible for them."

I shivered. "Maybe I should get in touch with Lester—"

Sasha fell back onto the bed, laughing. "Lester hasn't
forgotten you, and you aren't on the streets yet!" At
last he stopped laughing long enough to add, "Besides, I
have some plans for us."

"Oh? Tell me. What?"

"My father brought word that the Rom are not many
miles away and will be camping tomorrow on his land.
Would you like to spend some time with my people?"

"The gypsies? Yes. Oh, yes!" I lay back against him,
relaxed now.

We would go away from the marquis and Veronique and the decadence that seemed to be impinging upon us, away to stay among his people, outdoors where we had always been happiest. I needed more time, just a little more time.

Chapter 3

The next morning, Louis helped Sasha bring down a huge trunk from a storage room. They left it unopened in the middle of my room while Sasha disappeared to dress. He returned quickly and flung open the trunk to reveal a conglomeration of clothes splashed with every hue of the rainbow. Bending over the trunk, he pulled out costumes for me to choose from, for our trip to the Rom. Conspicously absent were any of the stiff fashions of the day, with overdone bustles and tight waists. Instead, there were soft, low-necked blouses, flowing skirts, and leather sandals. The skirts were multicolored and many-layered, and fell to just below my ankles. I spent the morning choosing the colors that suited me best, and Sasha added several gold chains for my neck. Then, wading through the mass of clothes strewn about the floor, he made his way to the trunk and pulled out a pair of riding boots for himself.

"Most of the men do not wear boots, but I have been away too long, and I will be tender-footed at first."

He chose several pairs of dark trousers and brightly embroidered shirts, a few kerchiefs and a floppy old hat. "This is my favorite," he said. "I am never without it when I go to the Rom. Now close your eyes. I have something for you," he demanded.

I did as I was told, then felt his hands at my waist and neck, loosening my clothes.

"Sasha—"

"Quiet, my Katerina. I have often seen you without clothes!"

He drew off my blouse, and I felt the skirt fall around my ankles. My eyes remained tightly shut as he put something soft and silky around my shoulders, sending shivers through me.

"Open your eyes, *cherie*."

I saw myself reflected in the beveled glass mirror, my dark hair hanging free, my bare arms and legs tanned from the sun. Around me was draped a shawl of a thousand iridescent colors, shimmering, changing colors in the light.

"Oh, Sasha, it is gorgeous. Look at me!" I whirled around, the shawl billowing about me until, dizzy, I dropped into a chair. A shaft of sunlight fell across me.

"Look at you in the sun, how beautiful you are."

I smiled at him, my darling Sasha, my friend.

"You are as lovely as a Manet painting. If he could see you now, he would immortalize you as *La fille dans le chale*."

"Manet?"

"Edouard Manet. He is an artist in Paris. Someday, I have no doubt, you will meet him—when you are an international star."

I laughed. Such a day seemed unattainable, even undesirable, as we made our plans to visit the gypsies. "I'm not sure that I want that day ever to come," I said.

"But it must, because you are Katherine Lawrence, and the choice has been taken from you. The public will not let such an actress disappear even if she wants to. Which you do not, my Katerina, no matter what you think at the moment."

"Maybe I could hide forever with the gypsies!"

He laughed and pulled me to my feet, turning me slowly under his outstretched hand. Then he stepped back and spoke seriously. "You are Nadja." He saw that I understood the meaning of those words. Nadja was his mother, the young gypsy woman in his play. "I wrote it about my mother as a girl, but you must also know that I wrote it for you to play."

I started to object that I was not a gypsy woman; I could never pretend to be one. There were other doubts as well, but he anticipated each of them as he answered, "You are thinking that a gypsy must play a gypsy? My Katerina, you know better. A great actress must play the part, an actress who can *become* a gypsy." He did not pause to let me object. "As for the dancing, do you not remember how my eyes never left you when you danced the mazurka with Gideon, danced in such a way that everyone left the floor to watch. With that same ease, you can learn the gypsy steps."

I stopped him then, long enough to ask about the language, but again he was not concerned.

"Your accent will be delightful, French spoken with a touch that is somewhat foreign—exactly what would be expected. As for the Romany words, your ear will become accustomed to them very quickly."

"Then you are taking me to your people so I can learn to be one of them?"

"I am taking you to them because I am going, and I want you with me. There I will finish my play, and there—if you choose—you can study the gypsy ways. Soon I will take the play to Paris and find a producer. It is my greatest wish that you will be Nadja, but the choice is yours, my Katerina. This you know."

I moved back to the chair and sat down thoughtfully.

"Do not bother yourself about it now, for now we go to the Rom to relax and play like children in the sunshine." He came and knelt beside me. "Like children we play, but like a man and woman we love." He slipped his hands under the shawl and caressed my breasts until my nipples were taut beneath his exploring hands. "How I want you, Katerina." He lifted the shawl away and brought his mouth to my throat, to the cleft below, and at last to my breasts, kissing them until I moaned and drew him near, running my fingers up his back and neck into his thick, dark hair.

"Sasha, darling, now. Make love to me now."

He looked at me with his brown eyes, which were so dark that, as the sun moved behind a cloud and threw a shadow across his face, they seemed black. From the shadow those eyes searched mine as if to find the depth of my desire. "You ask for my lovemaking, Katerina. That is good. I am pleased that you want me as I want you. But wait—" Once again his lips touched my skin as he pushed the shawl aside, and his hands moved to the intersection between my legs until his fingers, damp now with the evidence of my desire, withdrew to spread my thighs apart, leaving their wet touch imprinted on my skin.

"Now, Sasha!" I cried. I leaned back in the chair, and he raised my hips, kneeling above to enter me, so deep I felt I would scream, pulling my hips upward, upward toward him until I could stand it no longer and let myself come to him as he to me in a long moment of thrilling release. When my breathing was soft and easy once more, he turned me around and pulled me onto his lap as he leaned back in the chair. And there, curled together in a space hardly large enough for one, our arms and legs entwined, we slept.

I awoke, cramped and uncomfortable, and started to giggle as I squirmed to free myself from Sasha's limbs. He woke then too, and laughed with me.

"Next time, remind me that chairs are not for sleeping." He lifted me up onto the floor. "But they are for making love," he added, "as is any place where we two are together." He gave my cheek a pat. "Dress now in your favorite gypsy outfit, and I will have Solange pack a lunch. We leave in an hour."

We rode to the camp in a two-wheeled cart pulled by a dappled gray the Marquis had long ago put to pasture. But she loved an occasional trek to the Rom, so Sasha always asked for her to be caught and hitched to the cart, even though the pace at which she traveled was leisurely to say the least. We were in no hurry. The Rom themselves, I learned, traveled no more hastily than the gray, since their destination was often unknown, even to them.

"They simply move on when they feel it is time," Sasha told me. "Throughout France, there are those, like my father, who accept the gypsies and allow them to camp freely. But often it is necessary to stay near the border, in case a nighttime escape becomes necessary."

In some regions, the gypsies were blamed for any catastrophe from fire and theft to child-stealing, and even witchcraft. I was shocked at this, but Sasha's smile assured me that the accusations were far from true, within his tribe at least, a tribe where honest work was pursued. The men did horse-trading and metalwork, as well as the manufacturing of simple vessels and tools. The women danced and sang for money, made their own primitive jewelry, and, of course, told fortunes.

I watched Sasha as he spoke, observing his dark head, his strong arms, his brown hands holding the reins loosely with the easy skill of a born horseman. At that moment, when everything seemed so perfect, I somehow knew the end was very near. I closed my eyes against the thought, and behind my lids loomed the train, dark and foreboding, that would carry me again through the tunnel of despair into the dim light of reality. The world in which we were suspended now was an unreal world, outside of time and place, bounded by pleasure and desire. Sasha, too, knew it was all a dream; when the time came for me to leave, he would know as well as I. Yet he did not realize, as I did, how soon it would happen.

We traveled on slowly, letting the mare set the pace, for the days were long and we followed no schedule. I found it difficult to believe that, after hours of travel, we were still on the marquis's land, but apparently his holdings stretched mile after mile along the valley near the river. We lunched in the wagon, stopping only once in the afternoon to let the mare drink from a stream and graze briefly in a meadow before Sasha flicked the reins and put her back on the rough path.

After we had driven a few more miles, I felt a sudden sense of activity in the air and looked ahead to see the camp: perhaps a dozen wagons were pulled into a wide circle, brightly painted wagons set on four high wheels, with wide boards lowered to serve as back porches, and three narrow windows on each side open to catch the breeze, their vivid curtains fluttering. The air was alive with happy voices, which, though they spoke another language, carried the enthusiasm that surrounds a circus just before the big top rises to the sky. And the colors! And the sounds! The children at play created blurred rainbows as they ran; the men and women moved in the clearing, gathering wood, lighting fires, talking among themselves; young girls' voices joined in a spontaneous song; and everywhere, laughter filled the air.

All at once, the cacophony of sound grew still, as someone spied us. And then a shout rang out. "Sasha!"

He stopped our cart, swung down, and was immediately surrounded by men dressed almost exactly as he except that, as he had said, most were barefooted. The women stayed a little back, but were equally as enthusiastic as the men, clapping and laughing with joy at the sight of Sasha.

Eventually he lifted me down beside him. "Katerina, meet my friends, the Rom."

The women did not come forward, but the chattering stopped as the men formally bowed their heads to me and muttered indecipherable words of greeting.

"Romany," Sasha explained. "You will not understand. But most of them speak French—an unusual dialect which I will translate until you become accustomed to it."

I groaned inwardly as I realized that I would have to begin new lessons if I were to communicate with these people. And for a moment I was not at all sure I wanted to communicate. The women had drawn still farther away, and the men stared openly, the word *gajo* flowing like quicksilver among them.

"Anyone who is not a gypsy is called *gajo*," Sasha explained. "Do not be offended; they are shy of strangers."

But the look in the eyes of the men did not seem at all shy to me, and I indicated as much to Sasha.

He laughed. "The Rom men are faithful to their wives, and those who are unmarried must be encouraged before they will impose themselves. We Rom are very proud," he laughed.

We were shown to a wagon that had been cleared out for us, and we placed our few belongings inside. I hung my clothes on a row of wooden pegs, set out of my comb and brush (I had brought no makeup with me), and was unpacked. I laughed to myself. Never had I settled in so quickly and easily. I looked around. The wagon was clean and shiny, the bed a soft pallet covered with flowered material, the walls of varnished oak. In a corner stood a white table and chairs. "It looks as if they expected us."

"And so they did. The wagon belongs to one of the old men of the tribe. He will drive our cart and sleep out of doors, which is customary anyway, during the warm weather."

"But how did he know that we were coming?"

Sasha explained the complicated gypsy method of communication. Messages were left at friendly houses, shops, or more often, taverns across the country, messages which were picked up at intervals by younger members of the tribe who rode out alone. Letters were posted and received in this same way, but more often, as in our case, word of mouth was all that was needed.

Hours before our arrival, perhaps soon after Sasha had
made his decision to join them, they knew. The men
were gathered at the porch end of the wagon now, waiting patiently for Sasha to join them.

He looked at me, and I nodded. "Go ahead. I know
you want to gossip with your friends. I'll just wander
around and explore." I watched as he joined the others,
and they all gathered under the trees, laughing and talking as a leather wine bag was passed among them.

I stepped out onto the porch and looked around.
Close among them, the carnival atmosphere disappeared. Even though they moved about intent on their
tasks or at their play, there was an air of casualness in
the camp. No one hurried; everything moved easily. I
stepped off the porch and walked into the clearing,
moving among a group of children and stopping to retrieve a ball gone astray. The children laughed and
grouped near me as I passed, but the women continued
to keep their distance. Although they were not friendly,
neither were they hostile. They simply observed me with
dark-eyed curiosity, much as I observed them, and one
or two of them returned my smile before looking
quickly away. The gypsy women, like their men, were
dark-skinned, much darker than Sasha, but whether
their skin was colored naturally or from constant expo-
sure to the sun, I could not tell. Bracelets jangled at
their wrists, and golden rings hung from pierced ears.
Otherwise, their dress was similar to my own: colorful,
full skirts and low-cut blouses. I was glad I had let my
hair hang down freely; true, it was not glossy black, but
I hoped I was not so different that I would not in time
be accepted. But it would not happen right away, of
that I was certain. Not wishing to intrude, I wandered a
little away from the wagons near the woods, where a
broad stream flowed toward the Loire.

As darkness fell, Sasha found me and took my hand
to walk me back toward the caravan. "Josef has returned," he said, "and you must meet him. He is the
vataf, the chief, and we have long been friends."

We approached a figure leaning against a gaily decorated wagon, a man not as tall and slim as Sasha, but with a powerful physique, strong features, dark brows, piercing black eyes, and a hawk's nose. His was not a handsome face, but rather a memorable one. The man smiled, revealing even, white teeth, and bowed low. He spoke softly in Romany, and Sasha made a laughing reply.

In French, Josef said to me, "Welcome, Katerina, to our camp. May you find happiness here." His dialect was unfamiliar, but I was able to understand more easily than I had expected. I responded in careful French. Then Sasha pointed to my feet and said something else to his friend in Romany. Josef nodded his head, and suddenly Sasha swung me onto the porch, leaned over to untie my sandal, and held my foot up in his hand.

"What in the world are you doing?" I exclaimed, this time in English.

Sasha laughed. "Josef is a bootmaker. I have asked him to tailor a pair for you—red kid boots."

Josef bent down in front of me, and before I knew it, he had taken my bare foot in his hands. The touch was so unexpected, so personal, that I felt as if a bolt of lightning had struck my foot, sending jagged shocks through my whole being. Our eyes met, but I looked away quickly, blushing at this sudden incredible attraction. His grip tightened around my ankle. With one hand he turned my foot tenderly, almost as with a caress. But he seemed completely calm when he measured the length with his hand. Then he took my sandal from Sasha and replaced it, resting my foot solidly against his groin as he slowly tied the straps. With a few more words to Sasha, he was gone, and we returned to our wagon. I could not speak about what had happened, but Sasha did.

"You are upset."

"Why do you say that?"

"I know you. You are upset because you feel attracted to Josef, but you say to yourself, no, this is wrong. Why is it wrong, Katerina?"

"Because I don't know him. Because of you. Because he is a stranger. Because—oh, Sasha, there are a thousand reasons."

He turned to me at the steps leading into our wagon. "It is not wrong that you feel attraction for two men at once. What is wrong is to suppress this feeling. You do not even realize yet how beautiful and desirable you are, but in time you will. There is a flame within you, Katerina, that has been twice kindled. That flame burns in your eyes for others to see. You must not let it go out. Promise."

"I can't promise that. I'm afraid, Sasha, afraid of my own feelings." I blinked back the tears that threatened to spill over down my cheeks—tears not of sadness, but of bewilderment. I did not understand those feelings, and I tried to explain my confusion to Sasha. "I have been so intimate with you, shared such passion with you. I have given myself in lovemaking—but not in love. Now suddenly, today—"

"You feel pleasure from another's touch? Silly little Katerina, you are learning that within your body are pleasures of many kinds, and you must not ignore them. You were born to taste all of life, to find delight in your career, in your body—" he smiled— "even as in the taste of a good meal or the sight of a blazing sunset. So do not be afraid." He drew me to him. "Go to Josef if you must, but I shall not fear that he will take you from me—neither he nor another like him. There are two things only that will take you away. One is your work, the theater. You cannot deny that part of you which calls. And Katerina—" he gazed deep into my eyes— "we both know what the other is."

I looked down and away from him.

"Do not be sad, my Katerina, but just promise that you will not let the memory of that great love deny you other pleasures, for you are meant to live. With me you have done so, and we will stay together until we part;

such is the way of things. But I must ask again for your promise—the promise that when you leave, you will not become sad and melancholy, but that you will keep the flame burning and live." He looked at me intently until at last I nodded my head. "Good," he said. "Now let us prepare for the *patshiv*."

"*Patshiv?*"

"A celebration of my return." He laughed. "Any reason for a party; in that way, the Rom are very like our friend Sir Giles." He smiled and kissed me gently. "And how glad I am for his grand party which brought us together. Now brush your hair and let us go."

The *patshiv* was like nothing I had ever seen. Four huge campfires blazed in the night, and over each, a different delicacy simmered in a heavy iron pot: roast pig, a leg of lamb, a side of beef, sausages seasoned with rosemary and peppers. On tables which had been scrubbed until they were spotless, enameled bowls were piled high with apples and currants, cabbage leaves stuffed with beef and rice, fried potatoes, and fresh vegetables. Beer and wine splashed from heavy pitchers. The food was served from the tables, but the gypsies ate lying down, resting on one elbow, and they ate with their fingers. I struggled for some minutes until I was finally settled in an agreeable posture. Then I began to wonder why all people didn't see the advantage of dining so comfortably in this ancient position of the Greeks and Romans. The meal was consumed slowly and with savor, and a warm glow pervaded the camp. Even the children were quiet as they ate their fill with the rest of us before falling asleep in front of the fires, under the wagons, or in their parents' arms; wherever they happened to lower their lids for a final time, there they were left undisturbed.

As we stretched out beside the fire, Sasha told me the names of his friends and something about each one, and I noticed, as the evening wore on and they came up to pay their respects, some of the shyness at my presence began to disappear. And by the time the music started,

they seemed to forget that I was among them as, one by
one, the women and then their men rose and began to
dance, moving gracefully and sensuously to the haunt-
ing strains of a lone violin.

How I wanted to dance, especially when, across the
flames, a young girl beckoned and Sasha rose to join
her—a girl of barely sixteen, whose gleaming hair fell
well below her waist. They danced beautifully, and I
watched with fascination blended with envy. Somehow,
I would learn the gypsy dances. My eyes swept the
clearing, and I saw Josef. His gaze locked on mine in a
way that told me he knew I had been searching for him.
I looked away. Finally, Sasha returned to sit beside me,
his body wet with perspiration. He pulled off his shirt
and wiped his face and chest while the music continued
plaintively in the background. He was slightly drunk
from the wine and the dance, and he pulled me to him.
"How like a gypsy you are tonight, Katerina, with your
dark hair and eyes. A beautiful gypsy who stirs my
blood." He kissed my neck and hair as I clung to him.
Over his shoulder other eyes blazed, and once more I
looked away.

By midnight, I could no longer hold my eyes open.
With Sasha's approval, I tiptoed quietly toward our
wagon while he remained by the fire, listening to the
stories that were being told and telling some of his own.
Once inside, I undressed and lay down on the flowery
eiderdown quilt that covered a wide pallet on the
floor—our bed. The windows were open and I could
hear soft voices drifting through the night, smell the
sweet scent of spices and roasted meat that lingered still
in the air, see the flickering of light from the one remaining fire. How few people, I wondered, in a world
where life was regulated by clocks and schedules, knew
that such peace could exist. I slept.

Near dawn I heard Sasha enter, and when I awoke
late in the morning, he was still asleep. A woman from
a neighboring wagon brought our breakfast, which she
silently left just inside the door: pancakes piled high, a

plate of fruit, and a pot of steaming coffee. The sweet, heady smell filled my nostrils, and I was happy to see that Sasha had begun to stir. It was very late, near noon, I guessed, and I was hungry. He raised himself on his elbow and smiled at me. I took the tray and placed it on the floor near our makeshift bed, where, together, we lay down and ate our breakfast. The pancakes were light and fluffy, and stuffed with chunks of tender meat. Sasha told me that they were called *bokoli*, and that I must eat my fill, since our next meal would be at sundown.

"What about lunch?" I asked.

"There is no such word in *Romany*. But the meals in the morning and evening are hearty ones, and you will find that they satisfy." We ate in silence, with our fingers, washing down the *bokoli* with strong black coffee in heavy, enameled cups. Between bites of pancake and sips of coffee, we sampled slices of fruit—apples, oranges, and melon, fresh and juicy.

As we sat on the steps of the wagon, sipping a second cup of coffee while the camp awoke, I asked Sasha about the girl with whom he had danced.

"She is called Zara. A lovely girl, is she not?"

"Very. She seemed to like you." I could not avoid the tinge of jealousy that crept into my voice.

"That may be, but I must remind you that the gypsies are protective of their young girls. To go to her husband a virgin is very important, not like—"

"Not like the *gaje*," I said, finishing his sentence and remembering that I too had once thought that I would go in innocence and chastity to my husband.

"Don't look so glum, Katerina. Zara is a girl who will live in the tribe all her life, so she must obey the rules of this closed society. But she is a beautiful child. Would you like to meet her?"

"Do you think she will talk with me? The women are all so shy; I feel such an outsider among them."

"Of course you do, because they consider you so, but in time they will all come to accept you. The younger ones, such as Zara, are not so timid, however. You have noticed the children, how they love strangers? Well, Zara is the same."

"Sasha, do you think she would teach me to dance?"

"Of course. Come and meet her, and you can begin right away."

Sasha was right; Zara enthusiastically agreed to give me lessons, and that day and every day for the next week, I spent long hours with her, learning the intricate steps, accustoming myself to the rhythm and flow of the gypsy music, trying to imitate the grace of her movements. We would go into the forest and find a clearing with space to turn and twirl and jump. I was pleased with my progress, for I meant to dance soon for Sasha, not as Katerina, but as a real *gitana*.

Although Zara's French was rudimentary, I had begun to learn a little Romany, and as our friendship grew, we came up with a language all our own. I told her something of my life and the stage. She endeavored to teach me palmistry, but I had difficulty remembering what the whorls and lines of the hand meant. Zara laughed and gave up her attempt, and we returned to the dancing lessons where, at least, I had a little natural skill.

During that week the caravan moved twice, once closer to the chateau, and then north toward Orleans. We traveled no more than ten or twelve miles at a stretch. Sometimes I would drive the wagon, and at others walk beside it. The old man who owned the wagon rode farther back in the caravan in our cart, so that we had the illusion that we were gypsies and this was, in truth, our home. As we traveled, Sasha told me stories about his own life among the gypsies, a life that he could not remove from his blood, that would continue to draw him back for as long as he lived.

"Even as I grew to be a young man and lived at the chateau in the summers when I was not in school, I still ran off sometimes, once for the whole summer, to be with my people." He laughed. "When I returned, my

skin was almost black, and my clothes were tattered—I
never took extra clothing with me. I washed my one
pair of trousers in the river now and then—not often, I
must admit. My father would always feign horror at the
sight of me when I reappeared after being so long with
the gypsies, but I think, in truth, he was pleased. There
is an education to be had from all of life, not just at the
university."

I, too, had much to learn, and an early lesson came
when I stopped to pick some freshly bloomed flowers
beside the road. Just as I reached for them, Sasha's
hand caught mine, encircling my wrist fiercely so that I
released my hold on the flowers and they sprang up,
still rooted, in place.

"Always leave the flowers growing where nature intended, Katerina, for to pick them means death to the
gypsy."

I drew back, frightened by the intensity with which
he spoke, but I was learning the customs of a people
unlike myself, learning respect. Rather than being upset
by Sasha's harsh words, I smiled and leaned against him
in thanks.

"You are quite a girl, my Katerina," he said, and I
knew then that the bond between us would be lasting,
for it was one of friendship and understanding that
would never die.

I felt that I could walk forever, traveling with this
band of people, sharing their lives and Sasha's. My skin
became darker and my figure firm from exercise—
dancing, walking, working with the women over the
cook fires at night. As we traveled, the older women
spread out, going from house to house, telling fortunes,
selling trinkets, and often, I am afraid, picking up items
that were not theirs—eggs and fruit and sausages—
tucked quickly into large pockets in their skirts. But this
was a friendly province to the gypsies, and the French
people in the Loire Valley obviously did not object to a
little pilfering. I wondered that the Rom did not stay
here, where they were so well liked, but as Sasha re-

minded me, it was their nature to move on, ever on,
roaming toward destinations even they did not know,
often through areas where they were not smiled upon.

While we were camping near the chateau, Sasha's father appeared and was the honored guest. For a
hundred years or more, the Merliac family had opened
their grounds to the Rom. Sasha told me that when the
marquis's affair with Nadja, Sasha's mother, had been
revealed, the marquis might well have been killed but
for the loyalty the Rom felt toward his family. He had
given a large dowry, and Nadja had found a willing
gypsy husband in time. Today the Marquis de Merliac
was held in great esteem; he knew, however, how close
he had come to having his throat cut in the night for
behavior so abhorrent to the gypsies. But the marquis,
as I already knew, was a man easily tempted; however,
I did notice that he had not brought the girl Veronique
with him.

Again, there was feasting and dancing. Earlier in the
day, a pair of beautiful red kid boots had been placed
on the steps of the wagon. The fit was perfect, and I
wore them to the *patshiv*.

"Will you dance tonight?" Sasha asked.

"No, Sasha, I am not ready—but soon."

"When you find him, thank Josef for the boots."

I nodded my head. I had been avoiding Josef because
of the emotions he aroused in me, and because I knew
he was somehow a threat to me.

But it was impossible to ignore him when, at last, he
came to speak to the marquis, at whose side I sat. As he
turned to leave, I said softly, *"Merci, vataf, pour les
botes."*

"De rien, Mademoiselle."

That was all, but my heart pounded violently as a
terrible image surged within me: I felt his lips on mine,
his strong body next to me. I imagined him as my lover
with a clarity that I could not shake off. My hands
clutched at the coffee cup I was holding until the heat
surged through to my palms, and I dropped it to the
ground. Sasha glanced my way, then silently picked up

the cup and poured more coffee for me. The marquis, I was releaved to find, had noticed nothing. But the sensation would not pass. My head swam until I began to feel that there was nothing left of me—no face, no limbs, not even a soul—only that throbbing place of desire, that bud ready to open into a flower of passion. I grasped Sasha's hand and held it tightly in my own. His eyes narrowed for an instant, and then he stood up, his hand still in mine, and led me around the fire—its heat heightening my own flaming desire—across the clearing and into our wagon, where he stripped off my clothes in one motion and was inside of me while my hands touched him in all the places that excited him and my mouth aroused him to a fever pitch.

When, much later, we lay together, languid and spent, he said to me, "What aroused this passion that turned my Katerina into a tiger tonight?"

I dared not admit my attraction for another man, my fear of that other man, indeed of myself. Rather I said, "It is because I have such feeling for you. You have given me so much, Sasha, that I don't want to hurt you."

"Pain is a part of life, *cherie*. I know you care for me, but I know that I do not possess you, nor you me. So do not worry, *ma petite amie*."

I curled up against him to sleep. He knew. He knew of my feelings for Josef, yet he would not interfere. He would want me to do as I must. Because of his trust, I vowed not to give in to the feelings that had, that evening, possessed me.

Among the Rom, there were two seasons only: summer and winter. Summer was spent in the fields and on the roads; in winter they huddled together in the caravan, waiting for the thaw. Now the summer days drifted by, melting into one another, and once more I was at peace. I kept my vow and made another. Before the green leaves of September faded into October's red and gold, I would return to America, to New York, to the stage.

I continued to practice each day with Zara, for now I

had a secret dream which I would not divulge even to Sasha, and there was not much time left.

All traces of shyness had passed, and Zara was now my friend. We exchanged clothes and arranged each other's hair and walked together in the woods like sisters, speaking a language that was all our own. Gypsy women were modest and had certain stringent taboos regarding men. Zara seemed to accept that I was from the outside and therefore different; she understood that I was Sasha's woman. I knew she cared for him, but I also knew, as did she, that to care was foolish, for Sasha would not tie his life completely to the Rom, and Zara would be a misfit in the world of the *gaje*. As we sat on a hillock beside a stream where we had washed out hair, she took my hand and said she would tell my fortune. I jokingly promised her a piece of silver when we returned to camp, but I saw that Zara was not joking as she bent studiously over my palm. I was skeptical. The gypsies did not tell fortunes among themselves, and for that reason I had always suspected that the art of seeing the future in the palm of one's hand was a ruse. Slowly, in careful French, she began, and as she spoke, I became increasingly less sure that this was a game.

"I see a journey for you. Many journeys over water." That was easy, I thought. She knew I would return to America. "There will be children, but not for a while. A long while." Again a good guess, I mused. "And wealth. There will be wealth very soon." Who would not want to hear that? Clever girl. "Your love line shows many men, Katerina, many." Those were the words that began to ruffle my composure; she knew of no man in my life but Sasha. "There was once a man," she went on, "who brought much pain. I see him leaving. I do not know why. I see other men who love you, but you do not love them. I see—death, a man dying. I see—" Suddenly she thrust my hand away. "No more, Katerina. No more." She stood up as if to leave, but I stood too, and held her back.

"Now that you have begun, Zara, you must tell me the rest. What man? What man will die?"

"I cannot say. In truth, I cannot."

"Because you don't know, or because you won't tell."

"Because I do not know."

I thrust my hand toward her. "Then look again."

She shook her head and turned away from the stream, back toward the camp. I followed.

"Zara, don't be silly. Fortune telling is just a game, anyway; we both know that. You made it up, didn't you?"

"No, Katerina, I did not. It just came to me; it was there. I cannot explain."

"Then why won't you look again?"

"To look now would be of no use. I would see nothing more."

Suddenly there was a chill in the air as a dark cloud covered the sun. We moved quickly through the woods and into the clearing. Zara was silent. Why, if she knew fortune telling to be a trick, had she looked into my hand with such fear?

That night I threw myself feverishly into the activities of the tribe. I helped prepare dinner, serving the plates and later washing up, scrubbing heavy iron kettles with crusts of bread. After dinner, as we sat around the flames, a young gypsy boy began playing his violin. The strains were different, more poignant, than any I had ever heard. Sasha told me that this was the first time the boy had played before the fire for his *companeros*. Something in the music, in the boy's fine touch, beckoned to me, and I knew I must dance. I moved from the shadows and raised my hands slowly upward toward the stars, and then I danced as I never had, as I never would again.

As my dance ended, the *vataf* stepped from the trees to take my hand and lift me to my feet. Then, silently, he disappeared. I did not think about him again until the morning when I stepped from my solitary bath in the clear stream's pool, until I searched for my towel and saw him standing before me, his hand outstretched, the towel dangling loosely from it just out of my reach.

I spoke to him in French: "My towel, please, Josef."

He opened it wide, as if to wrap me in it. "Come, Katerina, come."

"No." But even as I said the word, I moved toward him.

Reaching over my head, he placed the towel around my shoulders and began to dry my back as I stood motionless before him, my eyes closed. Then he leaned over and rubbed the towel down my legs, drying each one with great care. When I opened my eyes at last to look at him, he raised his face to me, and I saw the deep scar across his cheek, the gold ring in his ear, the swarthy skin, the heavy cast of stubble on his cheeks, the dark mass of hair that protruded from the neck of his shirt. My own skin was alive and tingling from his touch. He pulled me to him, began to kiss me hungrily, and I responded to him, pressing myself against that solid, firm body. Suddenly I was no longer in a forest in France; I was no longer with this fierce, demanding gypsy. I was somewhere else, with someone else. With—Nick.

"Nick!"

The name was torn from my lips in a scream of desire and then horror—he was not Nick; he was not! I did not need to struggle, for Josef released me instantly and stepped away. The towel dropped to the ground. I reached to pick it up and cover my nakedness. Neither of us spoke, but as I turned to retrieve my clothes, he vanished into the trees.

Everything was as it had been. In the low bushes, a bright bird sang a melodic song. I moved close and watched as its deep orange throat opened wide, emitting a powerful sound for so tiny a feathered creature. Probably that same bird had sung while I was in Josef's arms, but I had not heard it until now. I began slowly pulling on my clothes. I was as much at fault as Josef for what had happened, I thought with a shiver. A ghost haunted me, the ghost of Nick. No matter how I might give myself to Sasha, no matter how I might be attracted to Josef or others like him, my need for Nick would never die. My love for him was the constant flame which burned within.

I turned and walked back into the woods along the path that led to camp. The bird's singing had stopped.

I knew that my time here was over. I knew that I must go home, back to America, before I became the kind of woman who would give herself to any man. I must return to my work and my life. If I could not find Nick, at least I might hear of him. The tunnel loomed ahead, and I must enter it once more.

INTERMEZZO

Four o'clock in the afternoon in Santarem, Brazil, and the air hung hot and heavy. Nowhere in the world was the heat so tired, so lazy, that it came to rest with such great weight on anything that dared to stand in its path. Even now, with the rainy season at least a month away, the steam that rose from the earth was as heavy as rain.

Nick Van Dyne stared out into the jungle, its tangled branches and vines a green mass that crept to within a few feet of where he stood on the porch of the Brasilia Hotel. He sighed, pushed open the swinging doors, and returned to the bar. The bartender had fallen asleep, his heavy head resting on his heavy arm as he leaned forward from his stool onto the handcarved mahogany bar. Nick, in his linen suit that had been crisp and fresh only an hour before, could feel the perspiration running down his back, causing his shirt to adhere to his skin.

He shook his head in disgust; the German was late. How long must he wait? He could wake the bartender and order another beer, but drinking only made him feel the heat more intensely. He stayed with beer now, after his experiences in the jungle with *chachaca*, the fiery Brazilian rum, coarse and gut-rotting, which had been all he could afford for a long time, and was often all that was available in the dank hole where he lived with the other human and subhuman creatures, far below the light of day. The drink had seen him through—dulled the pain, blurred his senses, and probably allowed him to survive. Nick gave a silent *salut* to *chachaca*; he would never drink it again.

He moved to one of the small tables, took a black cigar from his breast pocket, clipped off the end, and lit it, drawing slowly to inhale the fragrant smoke. Thank God, he could get good cigars here; that was one pleasurable vice he would not have to do without. Damn it, where was the German? Nick took off his jacket and tossed it over the back of a chair, where it crumpled in limp defiance of his attempt to maintain sartorial style. He loosened his tie and smiled philosophically. At least he was alive, and Santarem was paradise compared to Porto Manos, that stinking hellhole up the Lapajos River.

He thought back to the last days in New York, when the bottom of his world had dropped out. The accusations of fraud, which had begun with subtle hints in the press and ended with a warrant for his arrest, had moved with explosive speed—too fast, in fact, for Nick to track down the man at the top, the man into whose trap Nick had fallen, the man to whose rook Nick had played pawn. For there was such a man, someone much bigger than Monte Powell, someone who had conceived the whole intricate scheme, and Nick could have found him if there had only been time. He'd had to run, but he ran with the name pounding like an anvil in his head. The pounding continued through long jungle nights, with an intensity that threatened to drive him mad. At the same time, it was all that kept him sane. He'd seen the name only once, on a handwritten note on Monte's desk—a well-known name in the world of finance, the blue-ink signature scrawled across the page with the flourish of success.

Nick stubbed out his cigar thoughtfully. He had long ago fit together all the pieces of the puzzle, and the picture they formed was imprinted on his brain, awaiting the moment of his return to New York—the picture of a scheme of intricate simplicity: fake certificates are printed, Monte is set up as a front to pass the funds on, obviously skimming some off the top—that would have been part of the deal—and Nick is brought in to sell the stock, aided, of course, by the reputable Van Dyne name. Then, quickly and noiselessly, the operation folds. Nothing can be traced to Monte because the phony stock, the certificates, the letterhead were all provided for him. And the instigator of the million-dollar swindle, his profits tucked away in a foreign bank, is confident that he can never be touched. Except by Nick; he knew the name, and somehow, by God, he'd get back and find the man who belonged to that name. But first he needed money—a great deal of money, much more than he had now.

Nick's eyes swept the room. Time stood still, as still as the never-changing heat. The bartender slept on; there was no sign of the German. Today and yesterday were one, and all the days before, all the way back to the day he had left New York, furtively in the night, on a freighter bound for Belem at the mouth of the Amazon River. Belem—a whore of a city; on the outside beautiful and perfumed, underneath corrupt and evil. The city rose high above the docks at the water's edge, crowded into a clearing cut from the ever-encroaching jungle. Its perfumed outside was lined with cobblestone drives leading to magnificent houses behind marble walls. The rich came out at night to travel those drives on their way to the theater in sleek carriages. Lamps burning turtle oil lit the way; Indian and African slaves, dressed in costumes from the pages of *The Arabian Nights*, drove the carriages of the rich—the coffee-rich, rubber-rich, gold- and diamond-rich of Belem—while underneath, the city showed its rank, stinking sores. Shanties and huts with mud floors housed the natives whose land this was: natives conquered by the Portuguese, saved by the missionaries, and now manipulated by the powerful from every country but their own. Garbage rotted in ditches, waste drained into stagnant water, and above it all, the vultures circled, waiting. Their time would come.

Nick had no trouble losing himself in Belem. He had grown a beard on the voyage, and after the ship docked, he changed his dress to the cotton pants, loose shirt, and straw hat of the thousands of other fortune-hunters— Greek, German, Italian, English, Oriental—who swarmed over Brazil from the four corners of the earth in a search for gold that rivaled the California rush of almost thirty years before. There was another way, even faster, Nick had heard, to get rich—panning for diamonds far to the north in the Serras do Frio, the Cold Mountains, where nothing grew on the land, but where the crystal-clear streams carried Brazil's finest diamonds. Preparation for the mountains would be more costly and time-consuming, and the trip itself would be twice as long as upriver to the Minas Gerais, the Brazilian gold fields. Nick was in a hurry. He chose gold. Outfitted with supplies, he made his way up the Amazon by steamship toward Santarem.

Even in the heat of midday, on that first trip Nick could not resist standing out on the uncovered companionway, staring across the river, the overwhelming, huge, unbelievable Amazon, so wide that there were times when neither bank was visible and Nick felt as if he were not on a river at all, but a thick, brown ocean. Along the banks, where they were visible, the trees were a mass of green in this land of no seasons, but from the green emerged splotches of color—parakeets and cockatoos and flocks of bright birds that Nick could not identify. Clinging to the trees and hanging from the banks were the colorful jungle flowers—orchid, bougainvillea, passion flower, lily—in every shade from pure white to deep purple, even black. Nick slapped at the insects and continued to stare in wonder. How beautiful the jungle and the river were from topside of a sturdy ship, its dependable boilers stoked with coal, its engines oiled and reliable. He wondered what it would be like when he went into that jungle by canoe along the Rio Tapajos. Too soon, he found out.

With an Indian half-breed as his guide, he made his way slowly upriver to Porto Manos—two weeks of paddling, fighting white-water rapids, and portaging where the river was not navigable. To capsize meant sure death in this river that was the home of the anaconda—the biggest snake in the world, five times longer than Nick—and the piranha, that deceptive little fish that swam in schools of thousands and could completely devour a man's flesh in a matter of minutes. Porto Manos was one of those towns torn from the jungle that appeared one day and, as the miners moved out, disappeared the next, covered again in a blanket of green as if it had never existed. The town itself was no more than a camp of several hundred shacks, some consisting of only four poles in the ground, supporting a roof of palm fronds. The center of town was a store that sold supplies and liquor at exorbitant prices. There was no sanitation, and the one street was a mass of holes and ruts. It was worse here than in the poorest section of Belem, but no one cared. They only cared for gold.

Nick paid off the guide and slung his rifle over his shoulder. As he looked around at the riffraff of four continents in Porto Manos, he grasped the wooden stock tightly, glad now that he had spent the extra money in Belem for a gun. He might well need it. Nick wondered, as he scanned the terrible faces of the men in this camp, if any of them knew what drove them to pursue the gold nuggets at the risk of death. Perhaps he alone of all of them was driven by an emotion other than pure greed. Nick was driven by hate, and that emotion was so overwhelming that he would do anything to gain his revenge. Anything but lose. He had

planned carefully, and this camp was but the first step
in his plan. He shouldered the gun with as much confidence as he could muster. He would survive.

The routine at Porto Manos was simple. The men
rose at dawn from hammocks stretched in their huts.
Until dark they sieved in the river, hunched over, their
bleary eyes scanning the water. At night they ate whatever they could. Some drank, some fought. Nick went to
his hut, his gold nuggets tied inside his clothes. He
avoided contact with the other men, but he sensed almost at once that this was a mistake. A man alone was
fair game.

Then he met Stephen Chapman, and his life became
easier. Chapman was also an American, as reticent as
Nick to talk about his past. They met one late afternoon
as Nick was returning from the river. Half a dozen butterflies darted across his path, their vivid blue wings
catching the last rays of sun that filtered through the
trees. Nick stopped for a moment to watch them. A
voice spoke from behind him, down the path.

"Amazing, isn't it?"

Nick whirled around, his forefinger nursing the trig-
ger of his rifle.

"I was just going to say that it's amazing how such
beauty can exist down here in hell."

Nick was face-to-face with a man about his own size,
with a month's growth of light brown beard on his pale
face, a tiny monkey perched defensively on his shoulder.

"I'm Stephen Chapman, obviously a countryman of
yours." He held out his hand. "I thought we both might
benefit if we banded together."

Nick hesitated, then took the outstretched hand, still
cautious. Down here in hell—as Chapman called it—
one could not be too careful.

"I arrived a couple of days before you, and I have a
larger hut. Recently I've had the distinct feeling that a
man alone doesn't stand much of a chance. They have
their eyes on us."

Nick realized that Chapman spoke the truth. He had

seen the other American once or twice and had noticed that Chapman, like himself, stayed away from the others as much as possible. Either way, Nick would be taking a chance, but his instincts told him to join with Chapman. He nodded and the partnership was formed.

Nick's instincts proved to be right. He and Chapman shared a hut, sieved together in the river, pooled their food and supplies, and felt safe against the cutthroats all around them. The monkey helped. If anyone approached their hut, his chattering sent the prowler scurrying and alerted Chapman and Nick of possible danger.

Danger and death were all around. Once, during a fight that broke out near the cantina, two men were killed; the bodies lay unburied for day. Human life had no value. Only gold had value. The days were full of unrelieved misery, as they hunched over the streams, keeping a watch for snakes or—just as deadly—other men; pulling off the leeches that clung, bloodthirsty, to their bodies; fighting the insects, especially the mosquitoes that sometimes swarmed in masses thick enough to blot out the sun. If they could only last and not give in to disease or alcohol. If they could only fight the loneliness and the terrible despair that could easily turn to insanity. . . .

With several thousand dollars worth of nuggets accumulated, little by little, over six long months, Nick began to see light at the end of his road. He rarely saw a calendar, never knew the day of the week, and often not even the month. Christmas came and went without his even knowing it. And then Chapman became ill. For several days he struggled on, but soon it was impossible for him to work, or even to get up. Nick couldn't help. He watched in horror as chills alternated with fever and Chapman became weaker by the hour. He built a fire to warm him, and then put wet cloths on his head to fight the fever. There was no quinine, no doctor, no hope. The storekeeper, a sullen Portuguese named Silves, diagnosed malaria and departed, shaking his head.

In his delirium, Chapman talked incoherently, only

occasionally speaking words Nick could understand.
"Gold," he said once, clearly. "Take it before the cutthroats—" And then, just before he died, he whispered
clearly through parched lips, "Let the monkey go. He
never liked you much, anyway." He smiled weakly and
was dead.

Nick went to the store to report the death. Silves only
shrugged and suggested that the body be thrown into
the jungle, to be scavenged by animals. Burying bodies
here was no use, since the animals managed to dig them
up eventually.

It was midday. Most of the men were working at the
streams. Nick knew he must leave before news of the
death got around and he found himself alone again. Nor
would he leave Chapman's body in the jungle. He hired
a canoe and a paddler and took the body with him.

Two days down river, he came upon a more permanent settlement that boasted a small church built of logs
from the jungle. There, for a few gold nuggets, he per-
suaded Father Gomez to bury Chapman. Whether the
gold went into the parish coffers or into Gomez's
pocket, Nick did not stop to wonder. He helped dig the
grave and construct a rough marker.

Then he made another decision: he gave the padre a
wallet, a gold signet ring, an address. He said they were
the possessions of the dead man, but in truth the objects
were his own. At that moment he became Stephen
Chapman. The padre agreed to get a message to the
family of Nicholas Van Dyne, a message that their son
lay buried in Brazil.

Nick returned to Santarem, unloaded his gear at the
docks, and dismissed his guide. He stood and watched
the boy paddle back into the mainstream at the mouth
of the Tapajos, where the river's blue water joined the
chocolate of the Amazon, the two rivers flowing alongside each other until they finally merged, blue into
brown, and became one. Then he picked up his belongings and headed toward the hotel.

Santarem was a growing town which, at the outset,
held little appeal for Nick except that it had a large

English-speaking population. Southern Americans had
settled in Santarem, fleeing Reconstruction and defeat
in the Civil War, searching for a new life. They had not
fared well, for they were men who had depended for
generations on slaves to work their great plantations,
and the Negro slaves in the vicinity of Santarem had
long before been enlisted, by others stronger and more
persuasive than the Southerners, to work on rubber and
coffee plantations. The Indians were not so easy to harness. But the Southerners stayed on, eking out what living they could from this wild land, and holding fiercely
to their pride. At least Nick would not have to depend
entirely on the few words of Portuguese he had picked
up.

He traded in the gold that he and his dead friend had
accumulated during their more than six months in Porto
Manos ad opened a bank account in the name of Stephen Chapman. He bought new clothes and checked
into the Hotel Brasilia. The most elegant building in
town, it too was beginning to lose its fight to the jungle
and the weather. Mold formed in corners and spread up
cracked walls from which vines fought to escape into
the light. Boards warped, paint peeled, insects wrought
havoc with the fabrics and tapestries, but compared to
Porto Manos, this was heaven.

Nick relaxed in his first real bath since leaving Belem. He trimmed his beard, dressed in light flannels,
and ordered dinner. He did not leave the room again
for the better part of his first day in Santarem.

He had already made inquiries and learned what he
needed to know. Kurt von Stagner, a German, was the
chief *aviador* of Santarem. Von Stagner controlled the
money-lending, the latex exporting, and financial trans-
actions both legal and illegal. He was the man to see.

Nick knew von Stagner the moment he stepped
through the doorway into the bar. A tall man, he was
ramrod-straight and held himself with military demeanor. His fair hair was brushed back from a high
forehead; his eyes were pale gray under slightly arched
eyebrows. He, like Nick, wore a light-colored linen suit,

but von Stagner also carried a gold-headed walking
stick and a broad-brimmed straw hat. Nick rose as Von
Stagner approached.

"Chapman," the German said in a friendly voice,
"good to meet you. I'm always happy to get together
with potential investors." He called to the bar for a
brandy. The bartender awoke with a start and rushed to
fill the order.

"I hope you can help me, Herr von Stagner." Nick
plunged right in, stating that he had a large amount of
money to invest, and wanted to make a quick profit.
Von Stagner seemed impressed by the sums mentioned.
How Chapman came upon so much money could not
have interested him less, just as long as it was available.

"Well, Mr. Chapman, there is latex—raw rubber, as
you know."

The bartender brought the brandy, and Nick ordered
a beer before nodding for von Stagner to continue.

"Let me explain the system. I am the *aviador*. I buy
the latex that is delivered to my warehouses by the *patrons*. I have a certain number of these men under me;
they are scattered throughout Amazonia in small settle-
ments; they run the general stores and buy up latex
from the *seringeiro*, the tapper who gathers the raw rubber. You might be interested in buying out one of my
patrons."

Nick was silent. He had heard of the system. No matter how many rubber trees were tapped, no matter how
much latex was gathered, the tapper was never out of
debt; rent, food, and supplies always ran more than
payments. The system was little better than slavery. In
fact, Nick had heard rumors in Belem that, in some
camps, Negroes were kept penned up, and only released
to tap the rubber trees. These were the same black men
who had been captured and brought to this continent as
slaves, just as their brothers had been brought to North
America. And while slavery had been abolished in the
United States, it still existed in Brazil. Even the Indians,
who had always lived wild and free on this land to
which they had belonged since the dawn of time, were

now being lured into the system. Nick smiled wryly to himself. He might object to working in such a system on moral grounds, but there was another catch: the *patron* fared only slightly better than the tapper, since he acted only as a middleman, selling latex to the *aviador*, who, in turn, provided transportation and resold on the international market in Belem at a profit—an enormous profit, in fact. And there was but one *aviador*: Herr von Stagner.

The German had downed his brandy and was watching Nick out of the corner of his eye, well aware that his offer would be refused, curious only to know what the excuse would be.

Nick did not have to make excuses. "No, Herr von Stagner," he said at last, "I have just come from upriver on the Tapajos. I do not plan to go into the jungle again."

Von Stagner laughed and nodded his head. "I understand, Mr. Chapman. I have another possibility—a risk, perhaps, but not a large one."

This was the proposition he had intended to make all along. He had sized Nick up immediately as a determined man, after more than the small profits afforded the *patrons*, who were weak-willed and satisfied with a pittance. He had needed to make sure Nick was not such a man. He was sure now. Anyone who went into the gold fields had to be tough to survive—tough and perhaps somewhat desperate.

Von Stagner continued, "I have now only two riverboats that ply from Manaus to Santarem to Belem. I would like to buy four more—small but swift steamboats built for this river. The down payment would be large, but I think we could get our investment back in less than a year. After that, the profits should be enormous."

Nick was interested. "Do you have figures?"

"*Ja.* Here I have the overhead, the expenses—" He took a paper from his breast pocket. "See, these figures here and here." The two men pored over the paper.

"The idea seems sound," Nick said, "but we'll need to discuss it further, and I'll want to see the boats."

"They are presently docked in Belém, but I have a copy of the master plan at my house. All four boats were built from the same plan, designed by an Englishman who was more interested in speed and mobility than in beauty. Do you know much about seagoing vessels, Mr. Chapman?"

"A little. I sailed frequently as a child, and my father keeps a yacht which I took on fishing trips during my summers away from college."

"Excellent. Then you will certainly be able to envision the steamboats from the master plan. I also have a model that should interest you. Come to dinner tonight, and we'll talk more. My sister, the Baroness Hoffman-Manz, is here visiting. She, like myself, enjoys a dinner companion."

The German was pleased, as he had hoped to be able to extend a dinner invitation, but naturally had to look Chapman over first. One could not be too careful; the man must be the right sort. And so he was—worldly and sophisticated. Lise would be charmed.

Von Stagner rose and reached for his hat and stick. "Tonight at eight, Mr. Chapman, at the Villa Alegre. Any carriage driver knows my house. Until then, *guten tag.*"

With an almost military click of his heels, he was gone, leaving Nick to mull over the proposition. Profits from transporting raw latex to Europe and North America were known to be considerable. There were risks—shipwreck, sabotage, theft—but with rubber in such demand, and so few vessels presently exporting . . . He wasn't sure. He needed to talk further with von Stagner.

Nick was surprised that evening, when he strolled from the hotel to a waiting carriage, that the air was so cool. The driver told him such weather was not unusual in Santarem, which was often stirred by breezes from the ocean, hundreds of miles downriver. Here also, the driver assured him, there were fewer mosquitoes. Well,

Nick had his doubts about that, but the driver was obviously happy to be in Santarem rather than working in the jungle like so many of the Negroes. Nick would wait and see; one cool evening does not make an agreeable climate.

Villa Alegre was on the fringe of town, as it was impossible to build too far out without being overtaken by the jungle. Even here, Nick noticed, as a servant swung open the iron gates to let his carriage through, the jungle was uncomfortably near, and the ravages of climate were obvious. All of von Stagner's wealth could not stop the flaking paint, rusting balustrades, rotting wood. Another servant showed Nick into a tiled hall, and beyond, to a grand salon.

The room was ablaze with lamps burning turtle oil. Nick was surprised to see that the furniture was all Brazilian, handcrafted from the native piacaba tree. The cushions and pillows were covered with bright woven fabrics made even more vivid by the contrast with rough, whitewashed walls. The room was large, but the furniture rather sparse, with sofas and chairs placed for conversation. The atmosphere was friendly, the effect cool and airy. After von Stagner greeted him and mixed two large whiskeys, Nick commented on the room.

"Any compliments go to Lise, my sister. She is dressing and will be down soon, or so she says; I expect we'll have ample time to discuss business. But first, tell me what you think of Brazil. Quite a place, eh?"

"That is an understatement. I feel as if I am in not just another country but another world. Brazil must be quite a contrast for you, as well." Nick wanted to know more about this man before he entered into business with him, if, indeed, he decided to take von Stagner's offer.

Von Stagner leaned back against the yellow and green sofa pillows. "Yes, quite a contrast. Of course, I still keep my *schloss* in Germany, at Nurnberg, a lovely town in Bavaria. Do you know Nurnberg?"

Nick nodded, and the German smiled. Chapman was well-traveled, too, a welcome surprise.

Von Stagner went on, "It is peaceful there, perhaps
too peaceful. I am the adventurous type, and I always
want to see what is over the next hill. Or beyond the
next river, in this case. Brazil is a new world, much like
your America of a hundred and fifty years ago."

"But the conditions here—"

"Yes, yes, I know." Von Stagner stood up and paced
about the room to emphasize his words. "With the jungle on three sides and the river on the one remaining, it
is rather like a disease-infested jail, filled with Indians
and wild animals. Yet it is an exciting place, and I must
admit that I have done well here financially. You will
be surprised, too, that Santarem's climate is actually
rather pleasant. The cool weather this evening is not at
all unusual."

"So my driver assured me," Nick laughed. "I'll withhold judgment. It's certainly an improvement over the
jungle. Have you ever been into the 'Green Hell,' as it is
called?"

"Only briefly. Tell me what it was like, Mr. Chapman."

"Please call me Steve," Nick said with a smile. He
was becoming accustomed to the name. "It is just as described: hell. I don't know which was worse, the heat or
the lack of proper food or the sickness. I'm sure, too,
that if I had not carried a rifle at all times, I would not
be alive today. Men in search of gold are not men one
would choose for dinner companions."

The German laughed. Steve Chapman was certainly
an exception.

"Sleep was the only escape, and for the first few
weeks I was barely able to sleep because of the noise."

Von Stagner frowned.

"Yes, I know," Nick went on, "the jungle is supposed
to be quiet, but for one used to the lulling nighttime
sounds of a city, the jungle is the noisiest place on
earth. Bullfrogs fighting with cicadas and night birds to
be heard. And the monkeys—you can't imagine how
much noise those little creatures can make. But at least
they are comparatively harmless, not as frightening as

listening to the roar of the jaguar." Nick paused a moment and thought back. "But I don't suppose anything could compare with the insects. My God, I couldn't believe the kinds and numbers—mosquitoes, flies, gnats, tarantulas. There is one species of fly that drinks liquid from the eye, and another that lays eggs under the skin. There's one called the matuca fly, which somehow grabs onto the skin with lancets and draws blood, leaving a string of bright red gashes behind. I expect I will carry those scars to my grave." Nick took a long drink. "Not terribly appetizing, I'm afraid."

"No, it is not, but I get a good idea about the man who survives it."

"I have an instinct for survival, Herr von Stagner, and I don't want to get into a situation where my survival might be in jeopardy."

Von Stagner poured two more large drinks from the crystal decanter. "Your point is well made, Steve. I would be wary of a man who undertook a venture such as the one I propose without careful consideration. I won't say there is no danger involved. Every time a boat casts away from the dock and moves into the waters of the Amazon there is danger—of running aground on a floating island, of flooding rains, of collision, or even of malfunction, although I would not foresee the latter. The boats we would be purchasing are particularly sound. As for dealing with the authorities in Belem and traveling abroad, you are admirably well-suited. The actual purchase of the boats would involve investing the greater part of your funds, which I, of course, would match with an equal amount. This would be finalized through the banks and would be completely honest and legitimate. Now, you may not approve of the *patron* system that supplies our latex; it is not difficult for a European to understand, but perhaps more so for an American—"

"Slavery was abolished in the United States in 1863. I would find it difficult to adjust to what I consider a cruel and archaic system."

"And that is the difference, or one of them, between

the New World and the Old. We Europeans see that, just as in feudal times, the strong must protect the less fortunate." The German detected a look of skepticism on Steve's face, and quickly went on, "But this philosophizing is beside the point. The system exists, and it is legal. In any case, you would not be involved. I deal with the *patrons* myself, but I need a partner who can travel for me both here and, occasionally, abroad. I handle most of the European business, but because of my other interests in Santarem, I cannot be away constantly. I need someone I can trust." Von Stagner did not completely trust Steve, any more than Steve trusted him. Could any man trust another? But these two were on the brink of a tremendous money-making opportunity, and they would both have to take their chances. "Shall we have a look at the boat?"

Nick nodded and followed von Stagner to a table in the corner, where the boat's plans were laid out for his perusal. He did not have to study them at length; he could see immediately that this was just the vessel for their purposes—built for speed, sleek, with a shallow draft to avoid the thick debris in the Amazon, but large enough to carry big loads. Von Stagner handed him a scale model of the boat, which Nick turned carefully in his hands. Yes, it was perfect.

"And you say we can make a great deal of money quickly?"

"We can more than quadruple the amount of rubber I am now transporting to Belem."

Nick carefully returned the boat to its stand and raised his glass to von Stagner. "Here's to our success."

"Gentlemen, is the business completed, or shall I come back later?"

They turned at the sound of the woman's voice.

"Lise, dear. Come in. Yes, we are finished. Here, Stephen Chapman, my sister, the Baroness Lise Hoffman-Manz."

Nick looked across the room at one of the most stunning women he had ever seen. She was quite tall, only a few inches shorter than his six feet two. Her hair, a tawny shade of blonde, was piled high on her head. Her face was broad, more Slavic than Germanic, with high cheekbones and a wide, sensual mouth. Her large eyes were gray-green, and slanted like a great cat's. She moved toward them, the gold silk of her gown showing off every voluptuous curve of her figure.

"Baroness, I am honored."

"And we are delighted to have you, Mr. Chapman. Kurt tells me that you may join him in a business enterprise."

"Yes, that is true. In fact, we've agreed."

"*Wunderbar.* Now we shall have cause for a real party. Shall I tell Vincente to bring out champagne?" she asked her brother.

"Of course. As you say, let us celebrate."

The dining room furniture was made of the same carved, highly polished native wood, but the china and silver were Bavarian. At Nick's question, Lise answered that she had had a complete set of dinnerware shipped from Europe.

"Each time I come to visit Kurt, I am glad to have this one touch of home. Otherwise, we do try to live in the style of the country, taking advantage of the native crafts and using them where we can. And of course, Kurt has no trouble indulging himself with Brazilian port and cigars, as you will see after dinner. And did you notice the sculptures in the entranceway? They are carved from the jacaranda tree, and are quite exquisite, I think. Only the food here pales in comparison, and I do occasionally long for my own chef."

"But the meal tonight is excellent," Nick responded.

"Thank you, Mr. Chapman. Alfonso is a good chef, if one likes Portugese cuisine. I enjoy it occasionally, but day to day, I prefer French cooking."

Nick was indeed delighted by the meal, which consisted of cold soup; fish croquettes, flaky and delicate; rice garnished with shellfish, nuts, and pineapple; crayfish with hot sauce; and roast kid. He thought of what he had forced himself to consume on the Tapajos— boiled river fish, rattlesnake, turtle, even lizard. And endless bananas. He could not complain about the lack of a French chef.

After dinner, they moved into the salon once more for coffee and port—products, as Lise had said, of the country, and fine ones. The conversation was light and centered on amusing stories of travels the brother and sister had made abroad and in North America, to which Nick was able to add his own reminiscences. He did not speak further about his trip to the gold fields. He had told von Stagner as much as he would ever tell anyone, and he hoped to put the experience out of his own mind in time. He would never be able to do so completely. Nick did notice that he was not asked for details of his own past, and for that he was grateful. Von Stagner, by his own admission, was an adventurer, but Nick was curious about the baroness—Lise, as she insisted he call her. Why would a beautiful, fascinating woman hide herself away here? To escape? Or to find adventure? He could not prevent his eyes from straying again and again to the beautiful face and form of Lise Hoffman-Manz, the most desirable woman he had seen since he had left New York. He drew himself up sharply. He had but one goal now: money. Money to enable him to track down the man who had betrayed him. Money bought power, and power could buy anonymity. He did not need to become involved with the baroness. That wasn't part of his plan.

As he watched her, she also watched him. She had not delved into his background with questions. Nor did she intend to. There was something exciting about the mystery that surrounded him, something that appealed to the spirit of the woman, a spirit equally as adventurous as her brother's. She looked over at Kurt. He obviously liked the American too, and that was good. Kurt's approval was important, for he was the standard after which she had always patterned her men. Kurt's eyes caught hers and held. From across the room, Nick saw something in the look that sent a shiver up his spine; he could not say why. Quickly, the moment passed.

Nick stood at the rail as the boat pulled out of the slip and made its way up the Tocantins River to the wide mouth of the Amazon. As many times as he had made this trip, Nick still could not get over the vastness of the huge river as it spilled into an ocean that seemed no more overpowering than the river itself. He walked slowly along the companionway toward the bow, and climbed up into the wheelhouse to get a better view. God, it was overpowering. As long as he lived, Nick would never look out on a scene that would move him more. He stood silently beside the pilot and lit a cigar.

A fortnight had passed since he had left Santarem; he would be glad to get back. Spending time in Belem was unpleasant, but the work he had accomplished there had been profitable for him. His load of latex had brought a good price, and he had purchased two new boats, bringing their total to eight. The figures von Stagner had shown him that first day—the day they had met in the bar of the Brasilia, over two months before—had been low; the profits had far exceeded their expectations. And he had the best crew on the river. Money talked, there was no doubt about that. Their company was able to pay the highest wages, so they got the best men. Everyone was satisfied, and so far the problems had been few.

Each time he traveled the river from Belem to Marnaus, he found himself looking forward, as now, to reaching Santarem, if only for a few days. What drew him to the town? Perhaps its people; they liked Americans and welcomed them. Nick had met a few of the Southern families who remained in the town, and had visited their *faziendas*, the plantations they struggled, with a hopeless tenacity, to hold onto. Hopeless, because they continued to depend on slavery, and Nick could see the future as well as any man. Slavery in Brazil was nearing its end. And good riddance. Nick detested the system in a way even his staunch Republican family would not understand. The Van Dynes had fought in the Civil War, not so much to abolish slavery as to unite the country under one central government. If the truth be known, Nick doubted that his relatives actually objected to slavery itself. But Nick did, and against Kurt's wishes, he had even returned once to the jungle he hated, just to assure himself that the tappers were being paid decent wages and that the stories he had heard were not true of the fields von Stagner bought from. Nick raised the wages of the tappers and the *patrons* over Kurt's objections, too, but he had been right. The workers in the fields, like the crews on the river, took incentive from better treatment and higher pay.

Nick leaned back and watched as the boat threaded its way through the narrows, those twisting channels separating the hundreds of islands that made this river so unique. Some of the islands were larger than his own island of Manhattan; others were smaller than the native rafts that skimmed among them as skillfully as his own pilot negotiated their waters now, with Nick watching in admiration. Yes, his crew was the best, a crew that worked hard and stayed on.

His thoughts drifted again to the Southerners in Santarem. Even though he objected to their views, he could not help but admire them as they struggled on against such overwhelming odds. Perhaps he felt sorry for them, worshiping a past long dead. But there was obviously a bond between him and these people; they welcomed him into their homes, and he returned more than once, even though many evenings ended in argument. Why? Because they were Americans; because they were well-educated and interesting; because of their manner, their speech, the soft beauty of their women.

Yet there was more—he did not try to deny it. They reminded him of Katherine. He had even met a family who knew the Lawrences, at least by name. When he had first left New York, he had tried not to think of her at all, and for a time he had been successful. But recently she had been more and more on his mind. He would see a girl in the street, perhaps a Portuguese with dark eyes and hair, and he would think of Kate. He would hear a Southern voice and turn, looking for Kate when he knew she was not there, could not be there.

He wondered where she was now. She would have returned to New York, and probably, returned to work with Lester. She was a fine actress, and he hoped she was still as determined as ever to pursue her career. She was a beautiful woman as well, and someday she would meet the right man and forget what they had shared. Yes, Kate was young, with an inner strength to carry her on. She would be all right. Now he needed only to think of himself.

He put his mind to work, carefully going over, step by step, the business he had to finish when he reached port in Santarem. A lot of paperwork loomed before him, and he sorted mentally through the pages. He knew every figure, every item that needed his attention. He forgot nothing, and his mind worked more quickly than ever before in his life—the quick mind of a desperate man who was nearing his goal. In a year's time, possibly only eight or nine months, he calculated, he would be ready to go home, ready to find the man who had brought him down and whose name even now rang in his ears. The past year had left many scars on his body, but, except for losing Kate, had not harmed him. He was only thirty-three, and he had survived what few men before him had survived, and he had come out ahead.

Something in him had changed, and although he carried a terrible hate for one man, he knew there was more. He had begun to value life; he was not so pleasure-seeking; he no longer wanted everything. No, he would be satisfied, his own battle completed, to settle down to a peaceful life.

He laughed aloud. The pilot turned to look at him, startled.

"It's nothing, Pat," Nick assured the man. He had just been thinking that he had spent most of his life avoiding a permanence that today he actually yearned for, that in time he hoped to find. But not yet, not until the cold hate that burned within him burned no more.

He sighed deeply and spoke to the pilot: "Let me take the wheel now, Pat."

"Sure thing, Mister Chapman," the salty old Irishman responded. "I'll just go below and rest up a bit. Had a mighty full coupla days, I did, in Belem." He laughed and handed over the wheel to Nick. The narrows having been negotiated, Nick had clear sailing ahead, and he enjoyed the last hours of daylight as, serene and peaceful, he watched the clouds roll through the skies—pink, then mauve, then purple—toward another mangificent river sunset. He watched the waters of the river change from yellow to olive to brown, as the last lingering shadows of twilight played across its surface. Along the shore, the Amazonian jungle lay intriguing and seductive like a ripe, overblown woman, lying in wait. He knew from experience how dangerous an excursion into her depths could be.

On arriving in Santarem, Nick found a handwritten note from the Baroness Hoffman-Manz at his hotel. Kurt had gone by steamer to Manaus; would Stephen be able to join her for dinner at the villa? Unless she heard to the contrary, she would expect him about eight. The time was now barely four. Nick stuffed the letter into his pocket and climbed the stairs to his room. He had seen little of Lise in the past month, having been to the house only twice, and then only for business meetings after dinner in town. He had caught a fleeting glimpse of her on one of those evenings, just enough to whet his appetite. He wondered now, as he stripped off his grimy clothes and relaxed in his bath, whether, with that glimpse, she had meant to tantalize him. If so, she had succeeded.

After a much-needed soaking, Nick stepped from the tub refreshed, splashed on a cooling cologne, and stretched out naked on the bed, his thoughts still on the beautiful German woman. Just to be in the company of someone soft and feminine was a luxury Nick had long been denied, and he looked forward to the evening. He could not ignore the urges that swept over him as he lay thinking about her. He had not had a woman in far too long. There had been little opportunity, but more than that, his mind was on another goal; he did not want anything to interfere, certainly not an entanglement. Somehow, though, he felt that whatever came of this dinner with Lise, she would not expect anything lasting or permanent. After all, there must be a Baron Hoffman-Manz somewhere. And, too, there was Kurt.

Later, in the carriage on his way to the villa, another thought occured to Nick: the evening might not be for him alone. Quite possibly, Lise had planned a dinner party at which he was simply another guest. He smiled to himself and stroked his beard philosophically. All of his dreams during his siesta earlier might turn out to be just that—dreams. The carriage pulled up at Villa Alegre promptly at eight, and Nick emerged dressed in white linen trousers and a soft cotton shirt. He was glad he had thought to add a coat, collar, and tie, just in case there were other guests. He was ushered through the cool, tiled foyer into the salon, where Lise was seated on the sofa. She rose and moved toward him. They were alone.

"Stephen, how kind of you to come. One becomes lonely with only servants about." She extended her hand toward him.

Nick took it, turned the palm up, and kissed her just below the wrist. There was a personal implication to the kiss, and Lise knew it too. She did not withdraw her hand until a servant appeared in the door. Lise gave instructions for drinks before turning back to Nick.

"I thought you might enjoy something different, so I have concocted a fruit punch."

Nick raised his eyes heavenward, jokingly.

"Do not despair," Lise laughed. "There is a wine base—French wine, in fact, which Kurt brought back from Belem. I also added a little rum," she confided.

Indeed she had, Nick realized with his first taste. The punch was potent as well as refreshing.

As before, Lise was a sophisticated and elegant hostess. Dinner was served in the European manner, flawlessly, ending with a chocolate soufflè, which, she admitted, had taken her cook some time to master. "I insist on an occasional French dish, even though I find that teaching Alfonso anything new can be more trouble than it's worth."

After dinner, they sat with cups of rich, dark Brazilian coffee. Now candles were lit, and the air cooled quickly. Outside, night birds serenaded them noisily.

Nick leaned back, a smile of contentment on his face. "Only here in this villa do I feel close to civilization again, Lise."

"But I understand that you have spent several evenings among our American immigrants."

Nick smiled. She had obviously kept up with him from a distance. "Yes," he admitted. "I do enjoy their company. But here the touch is more European. And more personal," he added.

Apparently satisfied, Lise changed the subject. "Tell me about your time in the jungle, in the gold camp."

"I've tried to put that out of my mind. I can't think of anything I experienced there that would appeal to a beautiful woman."

She took a sip of her coffee and once more turned the gaze of her incredible eyes on Nick, asking boldly, "Were there women in Porto Manos?"

"Sometimes. Now and then an enterprising soul would bring in a boatload of prostitutes and rent them out. I believe the custom is called *cegamonen*."

"And were they young and attractive, these women?"

"Young, yes. Attractive, no. Most were sick and ill-used, and more than likely diseased. To become involved with one would not have been sensible."

"Oh, and you always do that which is sensible, Stephen?" There was another meaning, he knew, behind her teasing words.

"No, I often behave very foolishly, Lise, but where women are concerned, I am quite particular."

A secret smile curved her lips as she placed the demitasse cup on the low table beside her. "My dear Stephen, I have been so remiss. You have never seen the rest of the house. Please let me show you around now. I have the feeling you will like it very much."

She was right. Although they did not share the same tastes, he appreciated her decorating skills. Missing was any sign of clutter or overcrowding. The house, although not very large, had high ceilings and gave an impression of spaciousness.

As they moved from room to room, Lise walked in front, just close enough for Nick to follow with his eyes the movement of her curvacious body. She reminded him of a seductive Rubens painting—full-bodied and golden-skinned. But she assuredly lacked the comfortable, satisfied look of Rubens' women. This was a woman whose eyes reflected an inner fire, a restlessness. As he admired the house, his gaze kept slipping toward her, a gaze she must have felt but did not acknowledge. Soon they emerged again into the foyer.

"Would you care to see the second floor?" she asked.

He nodded and followed her up the stairs. The air was filled with words unspoken, looks unanswered. Nick's head swam as much with desire as with the effects of too much rum. Beads of perspiration broke out on his forehead, although the evening was now quite cool. He could hardly keep himself from reaching out for her. She pushed open the door of a small, pleasant room. A native quilt covered a large bed, its mosquito netting thrown back over the canopy. He knew immediately that the room was hers. A single lamp flickered on the bedside table, spreading a soft, intimate light across the room, across her comb and brush on the vanity, across her flimsy gown, thrown casually over the back of a chair.

"Do you like my room?" she asked.

He knew that when he answered, he would answer more than that question. Her eyes met his gaze at last.

"I like you, Lise." He reached for her, and she came quickly into his arms.

Her lips found his almost at once, and he heard himself moan under the onslaught of her mouth and tongue.

His arms tightened around her as he pulled her lush body close. She filled his arms with a warmth and passion that he had almost forgotten. Nor was she passive; her hands moved beneath his coat, pressing him closer and closer.

"My dear," she whispered, "has it been a long time since you have held a woman?"

"A day can be a long time, Lise, but yes, it has been—a very long time. And I want you desperately."

"That is good, Stephen, for I want you too."

Hurriedly they undressed and lay on the bed, tented by the folds of mosquito netting. Nick meant to be gentle with her, but he could not be. All at once he was within her, as if driven by a demon. He knew he must be hurting her, but he could not stop. "Lise—Lise—I don't want to hurt you," he moaned.

Her only answer was to wrap her strong legs about his back and dig her nails into the flesh of his shoulders. "Hurt me, Stephen. Hurt me. Hurt me!" Her cries turned into a scream of pleasure as, with one final thrust, he emptied into her ripe and waiting body the nectar of his passion.

He awoke, disoriented, in the night. The moonlight cut a brilliant swath through the room and over the bed. In its path he saw Lise. And he remembered. She was still asleep, lying on her back, her hair falling across the pillow. He raised himself on one elbow to look at her. What an extraordinary woman she was, and what extraordinary fortune to find her here in Santarem, this beautiful Teutonic goddess.

As he watched her sleep, he wondered why the Baron Hoffman-Manz had let this prize stray from him. Theirs could only be a marriage of convenience, he supposed. The baron must be old or infirm; otherwise, he would not have let her roam. Whatever the circumstances, she was here now, beside him—a beautiful, exotic, foreign creature, as mysterious as the jungle that surrounded them.

Who was she, this woman so charming and sophisticated over dinner, so wild and passionate in bed? He took a lock of her hair in his hand, bent to inhale its aroma and bury his face in its silky fragrance. His lips brushed her throat, and once again he could feel, rising in his loins, the desire to possess the body that lay beneath his gaze. He could not bother now to wonder what had brought her to him; he could only be glad that she was here, that he was here.

His mouth found the soft lobe of her ear, and enclosed it as he would soon enclose the beautiful wide mouth, for she had opened her cat-green eyes and, smiling, drawn him down upon her, kissing him, slowly and fully. Now, with his first terrible need for her satisfied, he could embrace the wonderful body more completely. He kissed her lips again and again, using his tongue to taste the honey-sweetness of her mouth. He clasped her full and magnificent breasts in his hands. So soft, yet so firm beneath his touch, which grew stronger now as he grasped her breasts. His fingers tormented the dark, tender nipples until he drew a gasp from her lips. He pulled her compliant body over on top of him and lost himself in the thrill of her, his mouth hungry to taste every wonderful part of her. They filled each other's arms, turning over and over again, holding, tasting, biting, until their heads swam with the ecstasy of each others' embrace, until at last he had to be inside of her, until she eagerly accepted him. But this time there was no rough taking of her. Instead, together, they moved, slowly now and deliberately, in perfect union, each determined to prolong the unbearable pleasure, until they came to the inevitable moment of release.

Lying side by side, their limbs interlocked, they fell asleep again in time, and Nick did not awaken until the sun was high in the sky. When he did open his eyes, Lise was standing by the bed, wrapped in a cotton robe, holding a cup of coffee out to him.

"I had Luisa bring our breakfast up here. Coffee?"

He swung his legs over the side of the bed and took the cup from her hands. The coffee tasted strong and sweet. She tossed him a towel.

"Here, darling, we don't have to be too formal this morning. The servants are discreet."

He wrapped the towel around his hips and tucked it in at the waist with a laugh.

Strewn unceremoniously over the floor were their clothes from the night before, rumpled and wrinkled.

"And am I to wear the towel back to my hotel?"

"Oh, no, one of the servants will press your clothes out. But not now. Now, we'll have breakfast."

He joined her at the table that had been set up for their meal.

"Lise, you are as beautiful in the daylight as by candlelight. Or moonlight," he added, as he reached across the table and placed his hand behind her neck, drawing her to him for a long kiss. "How hungry I am," he said.

She understood the double meaning in his words and laughed. He watched as she took two steaming pastries from the linen napkins in which they had been carefully wrapped, and began buttering them. Her hair hung loosely in a golden mane to her waist. She placed one of the pastries on his plate and smiled.

"I must tell you that I have only the best of everything—food and houses and clothes and wines. And lovers." She looked at him seductively from under lowered lids.

"Do I take that as an indication that my performance met your high standards?

She took his hand and raised it to her lips. "More than adequate."

He held tightly to her hand. "When can I see you again?"

"Must you leave? Kurt will not return for three days."

"Yes, Lise, I must. There is work to be done." He drained his coffee cup, and she poured him another. "But I can return tonight. Tell me, would Kurt disapprove?"

"Of you? Oh, no. I shall tell him you are my lover, but we must be circumspect when he is in the villa. He does disapprove of mixing business and pleasure. Now, darling, try your pastry. I have buttered it for you."

Nick bit into the flaky croissant, which melted in his mouth, hot and sweet. They finished the meal in silence, each watching the other as they ate, until Nick leaned back with pleasure, relaxed by her lovemaking, satiated by her food, warmed by her presence. It was the closest to peace he had come in a long, long time.

He filled the day with activity, but his body cried out for Lise. In Kurt's office by the wharf, as he worked steadily over applications for the new crew, he thought of her; as he listened to the skipper of the *R. G. Tatum*, who was having trouble with one of his deckhands, he thought of her. A dock worker had been strickened by the fever. Nick went down himself to get the bundles of latex loaded on the *Moulton Fipher*, already two hours late casting off for Belem, and Lise was still on his mind. Nick handled these and many other details skillfully, but all the while he watched the shadows through the window of his office, waiting for them to lengthen, waiting until he could go to her.

At last his work was done, and although the time was not yet five o'clock, he closed up and took a carriage straight to the villa, without stopping by his hotel to bathe and change clothes.

When he arrived, he was shown to her room by a silent, barefooted servant. She was seated at a desk by the window, writing letters. The door stood open, but he knocked before he entered, and in a moment she was in his arms. He untied the loose robe she wore to expose her naked body. The robe fell to the floor, and he ran his hands over her smooth shoulders, down her back to her hips, drawing her close, feeling her tremble with desire under his hands. She unbuttoned his damp shirt and lay her face against his bare chest as he pulled off his shirt and unbuttoned his trousers. She laughed with surprise to see that he too was naked beneath his light cotton trousers. They moved to the bed and lay together in the late afternoon light, oblivious to the heat as they buried themselves in each other.

He learned that afternoon that Lise was as bold as she was passionate and yielding, that there was no variation of lovemaking that did not thrill and delight her, that the more unusual the position, the more excited she became. The exotic nature of her requests aroused him and enabled him to sustain his own desire so that when they lay back at last, laughing and wet with perspiration, he was amazed that the sky was dark. Evening had long ago fallen.

Lise slipped from the bed and, lithe as a panther, moved to the dressing table to brush her hair. He watched as she admired her own reflection. She was beautiful, a beautiful animal who stalked her prey and, having trapped it, finished it off heartlessly or, her appetite glutted, tossed it aside. He wondered what became of the men she tired of. Even though he knew he could handle her, he was glad they would both move on to their unfinished lives. Part of the thrill was that they must taste quickly and fully before their passion was spent.

"Come, Stephen," Lise was saying, "I'll have a bath drawn for you. I'm starving, and dinner will be served soon."

Later, sitting across the table from Lise, Nick was amazed at her elegance and aloofness as she dealt with the servants and conversed with him. He had difficulty connecting the regal baroness with the wanton creature who had raked his back with her nails and whispered obscenities in his ears just a short time before. Mystery did not appeal to him, and he wanted to know more about this woman.

"Tell me, Lise," he said, "about the baron. Why does he allow you to slip away like this?"

"And after I tell you, may I then ply you with questions, and will you answer?"

"No," he said firmly.

She laughed. "I will tell anyway. I do not mind that you will know everything, and I will know nothing. I like for my lover to be shrouded in mystery." She sipped at her wine thoughtfully. "You think that the baron is old or sick, eh? Or crippled?"

Nick did not answer, but that was just what he thought.

"Everyone thinks so," she continued, "but this is not true. He is young, my baron. He is handsome and tall. Like you, his body is hard and firm. He is intelligent also."

"Then why—"

She finished the question for him, "Why do I spend so much time away? Well, like myself, my husband has his diversions. Mine is—well, you know mine. His is to hunt. The deer in the Black Forest, the boar in the Italian mountains, the wolf in Transylvania. Now he is in Nubia, after the lion. The hunt I enjoy is of another kind, so I travel. Kurt and I are close, so I spend time each year with him."

"Does your husband mind?"

"That I stay with my brother?"

"No, I mean— Well, yes, that too. Lise, do you and Kurt—" Nick, as sophisticated as he was in the ways of love, found that he could not finish the question.

"Would you be repelled if I told you that I have made love with my own brother? Or," she said before Nick could answer, "would you be excited by my confession?"

Nick laughed. "Probably something in between the two feelings."

"Well then, I shan't tell you. I shall have my mystery too, and you will always have to wonder." Much later her long hair cascading over her shoulders and partially covering her breasts, she did tell him more, not of her husband, not her brother. "You see, my darling Stephen, I do not love my husband. I respect him and admire him; therefore, because he feels the same for me, we never experience the petty jealousies of love, nor its pain. I am beside him at receptions and balls; I shall return before he does, to open our house for the season. So you see, I am the perfect wife for my baron and, for me, he is the

perfect husband. And you—" As she leaned across him,
her mouth found his in a kiss that said everything.

In April, after a prolonged stay in Belem and a difficult
trip upriver to Santarem in violent rains, Nick received
a piece of news that particularly pleased him: the baron
would be traveling next month to Russia, and the baroness would stay longer at the villa, until the end of the
summer. He was obsessed with her beauty, her sexual-
ity, and her undisguised desire for him, for his body,
and the things he could do to her. Now, except for a
trip he must take with the new skipper to Manaus, Nick
would be able to spend uninterrupted evenings with her.

When Kurt was at the villa, Nick slept at his hotel in
deference to him. But the nights that were difficult
without her were made even more unbearable by the
knowledge that she was so near. He avoided dining at
the villa with Kurt, because he had tired of the pretense
that needed to be maintained in such circumstances. He
and Lise had long ago dispensed with formalities.

While Kurt was in residence, all business was conducted at the office or over dinner in a restaurant, and
there was no talk of Lise except in passing. The partnership between Kurt and Nick was firmly cemented;
they were well on their way to making a fortune, and
what passed between each of them with Lise would not
be allowed to disrupt their plans. Nick could not have
known that Kurt was secretly pleased; Lise's happiness
was his own.

When Kurt was away—and he traveled often during
the late spring and summer—Nick spent every night at
the villa. He continued to be obsessed with Lise, sometimes even startled by her, always unable to get enough
of her. Once she had stolen the key to a chest in von
Stagner's room and brought out stacks of ancient ero-
tica that her brother had collected. Sitting nude on the
bed, she and Nick poured over the pages, alternately
amused and perplexed by the positioning of the bodies.
Lise, her hair pulled back and tied at the nape of her
neck, scrutinized a particularly intricate position, and

Nick laughed as she exclaimed, "There are three bodies here! Shall we call one of the servants?"

"No!" he said, when he realized that she was quite serious. "I have no interest in the servants. You fill my arms quite adequately."

She smiled with her green eyes and flipped through the pages until she found another picture to intrigue her. As Nick watched, he could almost see the desire rising within her. Her pupils dilated and her breathing became ragged.

"This one, Stephen, darling."

He leaned over her shoulder to see.

"Here, I will sit like this, and you must sit so . . . "

Smiling at her intentness, Nick placed his out-stretched legs over hers as she indicated, loosened the ribbon that held back her hair, tossed the book aside, and with increasing passion, took her as she desired.

Aided by the pictures and her own vivid imagination and inventiveness, Lise daily found new experiences in the art of lovemaking, with Nick as a willing, even enthusiastic, partner—up to a point. He steadfastly refused to involve a third person, and on another point he was equally adamant.

"But why not, Stephen, darling?"

"Lise, I am not going to beat you."

"Not beat me. Just hit me here—" she indicated the soft curve of her hip— "with this leather. Oh, please, I think that would excite me so. Please, darling." She pressed her soft, yielding flesh against him as she sought his mouth with her moist lips and tongue.

"I'll excite you, Lise, but not with this ridiculous strap." He took the leather from her and pulled her close. "I'll excite you with my body, my lips, my hands, like this and this and this—"

"Oh, Stephen," she moaned, "how can I ever find another lover like you?"

He held her tightly and laughed. "My dear Baroness, I'm sure you will find another easily. But until then—"

She forgot about the leather, forgot about the pictures that had so intrigued her, forgot everything but him, as he brought her time and again just to the pinnacle of her desire, but time and again held her back, until that final moment when they reached the summit of passion together.

Lise sailed for Europe in August. She had promised to be home to open the house in Bavaria before the baron returned from Russia. Nick saw her off almost gratefully. Their time together had ended just when it should have. Just, as Lise had said, before they had tasted the last delicious morsel. He held her in his arms for a brief moment before she stepped aboard the liner at Belem, and then he watched until the great ship was out of sight. Lise had given him the comfort and warmth he had needed, and now he could put her out of his mind. Kurt, however, was very depressed over her departure, and Nick found himself in the unenviable position of having to cheer von Stagner up. Together they visited the one reputable bordello in town, but Kurt left early, before the festivities began. Nick shrugged and let him go. He had no intention of playing nursemaid.

So he was especially pleased when, a few months later, his partner's depression unrelieved, Nick was able to travel abroad himself, representing Kurt in Hamburg, Rotterdam, and Liverpool, arranging the direct sale of the company's latex. He received a fine commission, and, in December, arrived in Monte Carlo. He had dismissed the idea of visiting the baroness at Christmas; he was not eager to face another of her lovers—this time her husband—and risk another confusing entanglement. So he traveled to the Riviera for some sun and warmth, and to try his luck at the casino.

There was a smart crowd at the Palais-Royale Hotel: Americans living abroad, a few Italians, numerous Frenchmen. He fell in with a group that gambled and drank through the night, and often into the morning. Nick had known these carefree types before, on earlier trips abroad. They were rich and idle. He spent time with them, but he was not one of them. Years ago, he could have been, but not now. He tasted their wine and even one or two of their women, but he dismissed them easily. Nick was here for another, more important reason. This was the first time he had been away from the seclusion of Amazonia in close to two years. He wanted to see if he would be recognized by those Americans and Europeans who would have read about him, who might even have known his family. He was not. He had shaved off his beard and wore only a mustache, which, against his sunburned skin, gave him the look of a pirate. His hair was worn longer, in the European style, and his face bore the scars of Porto Manos. Nor were his eyes the same. They were icy cold now, and reflected the determination of a man obsessed by a single mission. He looked older than his barely thirty-four years, and he realized that only those who had known him well would recognize the sophisticated Nicholas Van Dyne beneath the hardened Stephen Chapman.

On New Year's Day, 1878, he attended a ball at the Internationale, and overheard a name that made him pause. "Where is she?" he asked the Italian who had mentioned the name.

"Over there, Chapman. The pale, rather thin girl. See, near the palms. She's pretty enough, I suppose."

"I see her now. Introduce me. She's a lady I must meet."

ACT III

"All the world's a stage,
And all the men and women merely players."

As You Like It, Act 2, Scene 7

Chapter 1

I returned from France with two treasures: Sasha's play, and the shimmering, multicolored shawl that had belonged to his mother and was now entrusted to me. Our parting had been inevitable, but our knowing that the time must come did not make its coming any easier, nor did our knowing make the memory of the stolen moments from our lives any less bittersweet. There were only memories now—the memory of Sasha kissing me goodbye, the memory of my tears and of his sad smile, the memory of his words.

"This is only *au revoir,* Katerina, not goodbye," he had said.

"I'm sorry, Sasha, that I—"

"No, *cherie,* do not speak of regrets. There must be no place in our lives for regrets. We have laughed and loved and played. Now we must part and return to our separate lives. But our paths will cross again someday, that I promise."

"Oh, Sasha, I hope so. I hope so." He enclosed me in

his arms and held me tight, repeating his promise until at last I believed. We parted with warm hugs and kisses, to meet again, yes, but not for many years. . . .

At the other end of the trip, there were more hugs and kisses, for Clara was there to meet me. She threw her arms around me in genuine pleasure, then stepped back to take a long look.

"Good Lord, don't you look like a regular gypsy yourself. But otherwise, beautiful, just beautiful. And healthy."

"I spent most of the time outside in France. I'm sure Glenna will say I've ruined my complexion. Where are they, Glenna and William?"

"On tour, where else? Connecticut and Boston. That's why I'm a greeting party of one. Come on, let's get your luggage and go to my house. Or would you rather stay at the Piersons'?"

"Oh, with you tonight. We have so much catching up to do. I may go to Glenna's later. Are the servants there?"

"Of course, and the house has been offered to you, but I'm glad you want to be with me. Johnny will be over for dinner; I couldn't keep him away. He's dying to see you and hear all about the divine Sasha. Your letters were appropriately vague." She gave me a sly look which I ignored with a laugh. "Here, customs is this way."

With her arm under mine, Clara guided me to my trunks in the customs shed. After I was cleared through, and the porters had piled all of my luggage in a hack, we headed downtown. I looked forward to the cozy warmth I remembered at Clara's.

She lived in a two-story brick house on Grove Court, a charming area at the foot of Grove Street near Hudson. Her house was not very far from the theater, and on fair days she could walk, or so I always reminded her, but she had yet to heed my suggestion! The house had been built in the 1830s, and Clara had purchased it from the estate of the originial owner. Although her mortgage payments were steep, she was a shrewd enough businesswoman to recognize the value of her investment, which had more than doubled as the neighborhood grew around her, in size as well as popularity. I knew I would enjoy my stay there with her, for the house was, simply, like Clara herself. As the carriage made its way through the West Side, I gazed with excitement out of the window. There was already a crisp bite of autumn in the air, and the trees lining Eighth Avenue were just beginning to show edges of red and gold. I was surprised at the sense of excitement that overcame me, pushing away the last vestiges of sadness that had held tenaciously onto me. I was happy to be home, happy to be back in America, and eager to work again, so eager that I asked Clara if we could go a little out of our way and stop by the theater.

"You mean to see Lester?" she asked me, with a look that was, at the very least, perplexed.

"Of course."

"Honey, you've only just gotten off the ship. You must be tired. An ocean crossing . . ." As she went on making excuses, her voice began to drop.

"He's angry, isn't he?"

"Well, if you must know, yes. He had tours going out at the beginning of September, and he needed you, especially after your wonderful London notices and all the publicity in the press. You may not recall, Kate, but you were the darling of the season, the rising American star, and Lester very much wanted his little star to come home to shine."

"I'll more than make up for the trouble I've caused, Clara, because I have a wonderful surprise for him, for all of you. Sasha finished his play, and it's marvelous. We had planned to take it to a producer in Paris, but— well, I decided the time had come for me to leave. We talked about the play and agreed that Lester should have the first chance."

"The first chance! Honey, you do keep amazing me. Lester is not even going to want to hear the name Sasha Deschamps! He'll certainly not be thrilled that, besides being your abductor, he is also a budding playwright!"

Just as I started to answer, the carriage rocked to a halt at Clara's house and the driver, after helping us out, began to unload the luggage. Under Clara's supervision, he placed my trunks in the guest room, where I fell onto the bed exhausted, but somehow unable to close my eyes. Clara insisted that I take a nap, but I was much too excited, and finally she filled the teapot and we settled in the parlor, that comfortable, crowded room where anyone would feel at home. I leaned back and listened to Clara's description of life backstage with the cast of *The Way of the World*, the play she and Johnny were currently rehearsing. Clara had the leading role, the same part Christina had played so successfully in London, and which we had seen several times.

Clara admitted having picked up a few nuances from Christina. "But," she added, "I thought her performance was a little subdued. I've decided to play Mrs. Wishfort as a fiery woman. Lord knows whether it's going to work, but Lester agreed—finally." She laughed huskily. "And speaking of Lester—"

"Can we talk about him later, Clara? I've been wanting to ask you—" No, I thought to myself, that's not the best way to begin. "All the way home on the ship I could think of nothing but— Oh, Clara, have you heard anything?"

She looked puzzled at first, and then realized that I was talking about Nick. She shook her head.

"Nothing?" I cried.

"No, honey, nothing."

I started talking unheeding, unable to make myself believe her. "I was sure that there had been some word, that he'd been in touch with you, even that he'd be at the ship to meet me—" I broke off, confronted by the irrefutable fact that I had come back, not to New York and Nick, but to New York and the ghost of Nick.

Clara's comforting arms were around me. "Oh, honey, I hoped you had forgotten him. I hoped this time with Sasha—"

I pulled away. "Forgotten? Forgotten Nick? Clara, I love him; he means everything to me. He—"

"He ran off," she finished, "without so much as a fare-thee-well. If Nick had wanted to get in touch with you, he could have. A letter could have been sent to me, or to the Piersons, or to Lester."

Her words stung me, as they were meant to. I rose and walked to the window, where I pulled back the heavy curtains to look out on New York. The first careless taste of excitement that I had felt at being back suddenly faded. Oh, God, I thought, will I never forget, will I never give up hope? I felt the tears behind my eyelids, but I would not cry. I had done with crying.

Clara watched me quietly for a moment before continuing. She did not change her tack. Obviously she was going to do everything in her power to make me see things her way—the way, as it turned out, of nearly everyone else in New York. Except Lester. And, I would soon discover, except Johnny.

"You are going to have to face the facts someday, Kate, and I think now is as good a time as any. You steadfastly refused to doubt him when we were in England, and I went along with you because we knew so little, and we were so far away. There seemed to be some hope then, but now— Do you want to hear what they're saying and what everyone believes—even, I'm told, his family?"

"No. Yes. Oh, I don't know, Clara."

"Well, I'm going to tell you. Nick planned the swindle, and he was in it alone. He had the stocks printed and sold them, with Monte Powell as a dupe. A thorough investigation has turned up no evidence to the contrary, and Nick did not stay and defend himself. He ran, Kate, and unless I'm very mistaken, he's running still."

"Stop it, stop it! I won't hear any more!" Even though my words were sharp, I was not angry at Clara; I was angry at what she wanted me to believe and what I would never, never let myself believe.

"Kate, you know I love you and don't mean to hurt you," she said, "but you must try to be realistic. I think, in time, you will find that the hurt will be less if you just let go of the hope."

"No. I never will. Oh, Clara, I never will. So let's just not talk about him anymore."

She nodded, and the tension began to pass, as it always does between true friends.

"But Clara," I added seriously, "if his name does come up, please remember that I will never hear a word against him."

"All right, love, I recognize that stubborn look, and I promise. Come now, let's get dressed for dinner. Johnny will be here soon."

Johnny's presence was just the tonic we needed. He was in effervescent good spirits and full of his usual lightly fabricated tales, further adorned by his wide store of theatrical knowledge.

"They say Bernhardt may come over this season," he said as we sat down to dinner.

"Oh, Johnny, you've been believing that rumor for years," Clara laughed. "You'll be dead before she ever gets here. Or I will."

"Or she will," Johnny put in. "Just imagine, Kate was in France and made no effort to see the glorious Sarah Bernhardt."

"We weren't in Paris, Johnny, I told you."

"There's someplace else in France besides Paris?" he quipped back. "Well, never mind, I did see Fanny Davenport. An unrestrained Camille, to say the least."

We laughed at his ability to capture a performance in one or two succinct words and pressed him for more, which he willingly supplied through dinner, over dessert, and after we had moved into the parlor for coffee.

He settled comfortably in an overstuffed chair and accepted a brandy from Clara, never pausing. "Speaking of actresses, if that's the word to describe her, Edwina just got married, Kate. I thought you'd love to hear that another of Nick's old flames is out of the way."

Clara flashed her eyes at him in warning, but I didn't mind. Somehow, I was cheered to hear Johnny speak of Nick.

"Yes, she married into millions; not old money, I'm afraid, very *nouveau riche*. No one who counts will have anything to do with her, but she acts as though she doesn't care. Poor thing."

I laughed easily, and Clara relaxed with a sigh. A little later, when she had left the room for a moment, I was able to ask Johnny what he thought of the scandal.

He answered without hesitation, "Nick's arrogant and hot-headed and impulsive, but he is not a thief." Johnny gave my hand a squeeze, and I smiled with relief. Nick had another ally.

When Clara returned, Johnny switched the conversation to Lester. "So, sweetie, when are you going to face the lion in his den?"

"Tomorrow, I think. The sooner the better."

Johnny raised his eyes toward heaven and asked what I planned to tell him.

"Maybe I'll just tell him the truth."

"No, you have to do better than that! Lester is not going to be gratified to hear that a sexy pair of dark eyes and white teeth caused his leading ingenue to forget the fall season."

"Yes, he will, because I have something to pacify him." Quickly, I ran up to my room and returned with Sasha's script. "Here, look at this." I proudly dumped the pages onto Johnny's lap.

"My God, Kate, what *is* this mess?"

"It's Sasha's play."

"Just what Lester needs. Katie, Katie, have you taken leave of your senses? What do you suppose Lester wants with an unproduced—my God, it's in French!— an unproduced and untranslated play by the very man who swept you away and ruined the fall season?"

I was undaunted. "Don't judge too harshly until you've read it." I settled on the floor and looked up at Clara and Johnny. "It's about Sasha's father and mother, although, of course, he's changed much of the

real story for dramatic effect. A nobleman—Sasha's father—falls in love with a gypsy woman—Sasha's
mother. She was a gypsy, you know."

"I didn't know," Johnny answered with an undisguised lack of interest.

"Naturally, her father opposes the affair."

"Naturally," Johnny echoed.

"To further complicate matters, she is betrothed to
another, who is the gypsy chief," I went on. "A number
of minor characters are woven into intricate subplots,
and throughout, there is music and dance. The girl does
a beautiful dance on the night that she and the count
become lovers. In time, of course, the two rivals must
face each other and fight for the woman they both love.
The nobleman is fatally wounded and dies in his sweet-
heart's arms."

Clara looked speculatively at Johnny, who had
stopped smirking. "You do have to admit, Johnny, that
is the kind of play Lester loves."

"It certainly doesn't lack for pathos. Just who do you
imagine will star in this drama, Katie, my pet?"

I blushed as I realized how well they knew me.
"Sasha *did* name the girl Katerina," I laughed. "And
I've learned the gypsy ways, the gypsy dances, even
some of their language. What do you think? Will Lester
consider the play?"

"Kate, Lester is as unpredictable as you. Who knows
what he'll consider." Johnny was thoughtful for a moment. "You are a valuable commodity, and he won't
want to lose you to another company. That's at least
two high cards for your hand." Suddenly, a twinkle
came into his eyes. "I feel an inspiration coming on. Is
any of this mess translated?"

I shook my head.

"Too bad. But never you mind, I have an alternate
idea. Do you feel like taking a chance?"

"Johnny, dearest, my life has been ruled by chance.
I'd stop at nothing to win Lester over."

Johnny told us his plan, amid fits of giggles mixed

with dramatic pauses, as, together, the three of us conspired to give the showman a show.

The next morning, Clara went with me to the 14th Street Theater. Johnny was already there with one of the stagehands who, given brief instruction, set the scene for us. Clara took a seat in the front row, and Johnny, after giving my hand a pat, went off to find Lester. I stood alone in the middle of the stage. How good it felt to be back! I closed my eyes and inhaled the sweet, musty scent of the theater I loved so much and felt the indefinable anticipation that always seemed to be present, each time I stepped onto a stage.

Then I heard the echo of a voice from the rear of the theater, a voice that was unmistakably Lester's, raised in irritation, if not anger. "What the hell is this, dragging me away from my desk? You know the schedules I have to meet. This is ridiculous, just ridiculous, just—"

I took a deep breath, trying to calm my pounding heart as Lester went on and on. His voice, which was nearer now, was finally interrupted by Johnny's saying, "A surprise, Lester, I told you. If you'll sit here and try to calm down." Johnny was using the fatherly approach at which he had never been very convincing, and as Lester sputtered on, I was momentarily afraid the plan would fizzle. Then, quickly, Johnny said, "All right, Harry, the light, please."

I was bathed in diffuse light, soft, but bright enough for Johnny's purpose—from where Lester sat, there could be no mistaking who I was. I paused just long enough to feel him catch his breath, but before he could start to fume, I began, my voice quivering slightly at first, until I gained assurance and the character emerged.

"The quality of mercy is not strain'd,
It droppeth as the gentle rain from heaven
Upon the place beneath. It is twice bless'd . . ."

I heard a faint stirring, and then all was quiet as I continued, Portia's words now my own, her feelings mine. My voice ached as I spoke the final lines.

". . . We do pray for mercy,
And that same prayer doth teach us all to render
The deeds of mercy."

I sank to my knees and, like a ballerina, extended my
arms upward in supplication toward Lester. There was
a long silence—the silence I had heard so often just before the curtain fell and the applause began. But now
there was no applause. I dared not raise my head, for
fear I would see him walking away.

But I heard him coming down the aisle, and then I
heard his voice: "Damn, Kate, you've bamboozled me
again. Stay there, I'm coming up to give you a kiss, you
baggage."

He bounded up the steps, and in a moment we were
hugging. He took a step back, folded his arms, and
looked at me, clucking in distress.

"You'll have to stay indoors for a while and get rid of
all that color. Otherwise, you do look good, Miss Lawrence."

"While you, Mr. Markan, look exactly the same—
simply wonderful!" Indeed, he had not changed—he
was still chubby, perspiring, and altogether marvelous.

"I am glad to see you, Kate, and after such a performance, I'll admit there were tears in my eyes. Now,
whose idea was it to dredge up that scene from *The
Merchant of Venice?* As if I didn't know."

On cue, Johnny and Clara appeared from the wings.

"Well, these two won't be around much longer;
they're leaving soon for three months, so I'll be able to
relax."

"Don't try to fool us, Lester. You'll miss us every
moment, but now you have Kate back." That was
Clara, holding onto Lester's arm, looking into his eyes
for a definite answer.

"All right, all of you, you win. Yes, she looks beautiful; yes, it's great to have her back with the company;
no, you do not have my permission to go out and celebrate."

"Who said anything—"

"Oh, I know you two; you'd celebrate the prop boy's birthday with a costume ball. No telling what you have in mind for this occasion."

"Actually," Johnny said, "we were planning to go home and learn our lines, but since you mention it . . ." He offered his arm to Clara. Without another word, they swept down the steps and up the center aisle.

Laughing, I picked up the parcel Clara had left for me, and followed Lester through the theater to his office—a room crowded with posters tacked on the walls, letters, telegrams, and newspapers stacked in every corner, and scripts spilling over the top of his desk.

Lester cleared a chair for me and sat down behind the desk, mopping his brow. He looked at me sternly. "I should be angry, Kate. You behaved unprofessionally, running off like that when I had planned for you to go out again in September with Glenna and William. The girl we replaced you with is barely more than adequate. I simply didn't have the time to hunt down an available ingenue, and frankly, this girl irritates me more than I can say. Maybe *she'll* run off," he added as an afterthought. "Actresses! If it's not one thing, it's another. I'm in the wrong business. I've known that for years, but what can I do?" He wiped his face a final time and replaced his handkerchief. "There's nothing for you in *Way of the World,* you know, so we'll have to wait until December. Damn, Kate, I wanted to capitalize on the British publicity."

I looked down without answering.

"I hear you were good," he went on. "Really good."

"I was, and I can be again. I don't know how to explain why I went to France with Sasha, except to say I needed to, Lester. I couldn't bear to think of coming to New York and no Nick— Oh, Lester, have you heard anything?"

"No, Kate."

I knew this was not what he had meant to talk to me about, but I had to make him understand. And I had to know how he felt. "Do you believe he's guilty?"

Lester leaned back in his swivel chair and looked at

me. "I've known Nick for ten years, Kate. He's not guilty."

I felt the tears building in my eyes and reached for my handkerchief.

"Now, honey, please don't cry." Lester squirmed uncomfortably. Actresses all seem to wear their hearts on their sleeves, but years of dealing with us had not made Lester any less uneasy, and I determined not to embarrass him further.

"I won't cry, Lester, but thank you for your words, for your faith in him. That means so much to me."

Lester avoided my glance for a moment as he looked away, blinking, and I thought that his eyes, too, seemed glazed over with tears.

He cleared his throat and immediately assumed a more businesslike manner. "Whatever you go out in, I want you to have the lead. We'll let the papers know you're back, and maybe build up a little anticipation so we don't lose all that British press stuff. What the hell, I may even try you in something here at the 14th Street."

"A lead?" I asked in disbelief.

"Maybe. Remember, I said maybe. I would have to find just the right part, and I'm not at all sure I can, but I'll admit one thing, Kate: that performance on the stage just now was moving. Very moving," he repeated. "You've changed."

"I've grown up, Lester, and although you don't approve of my sojourn to France, I feel stronger and more sure of myself because of that time with Sasha. Lester, I'll never be that scared little girl again, the girl Glenna and William brought to you. I know this sounds dramatic, but I've loved and I've lost." Dramatic or not, the words I spoke were true. Lester had seen the change I had undergone. "Now all I want to do is work as hard as I can."

"I believe you, and that's why I'd like for you to go back to Pauline for a week or two. Lessons are important, even for the most seasoned actresses."

"I know, Lester, and I would like to go back. I need the discipline after this time away from the stage. But afterwards, when I've finished my lessons, I would like to go to South Carolina and see my family."

"No problem. Just be sure you're back by the first of November to start rehearsals, *if* I find something suitable."

Now was the moment to show him Sasha's play. I hesitated, and then, before he could stop me, plunged right in with a scene-by-scene description, more detailed than I had offered Clara and Johnny, except that today I talked faster. The play was on his desk, and he fingered the pages distractedly as I talked. I thought he was interested, but the only response I received was an occasional grunt—more, I thought, of approval than of disgust. But I couldn't be sure. Finally, after a few questions, he said, "Well, maybe I'll have a look at it."

I grinned broadly and started to thank him, when he looked down for the first time at the script.

"My God, this is in French!"

Trying to be casual, I said, "Of course. Sasha is French. But there are any number of *emigrés* here who can translate; that's not really a problem. But Lester, do try to find someone who is also a writer, so we don't lose the poetry of Sasha's words." I reached for my cape and began to move toward the door as Lester stood up, his mouth open. "Of course, if you aren't interested, maybe I should take it to someone else." I was as the door now, my hand resting on the knob.

"I—I'll take the translation fee out of your salary, do you hear?"

I opened the door. "Yes, Lester."

"And if I say no, that's it."

I flung on my cape and turned toward him. "Yes, Lester."

"And you'll be back here in November."

I moved into the hall. "Yes, Lester."

"And Kate—welcome home."

To awaken in my own bed was still a strange sensation, even after a fortnight in South Carolina. All was familiar, yet, at the same time, foreign. There was the spool bed, the cherry nightstand, the braided rug, the gingham curtains, the prints from *Godey's Ladies' Book*. These were very real belongings, memories I could touch. A part of me still belonged, for here was my first home, and here I could always return. And how I was being pampered! Thinking what fun I had playing the celebrity, I smiled and rolled over lazily. Courtney had kept a scrapbook about me, and had dug up everything from my high school days that could be considered theatrical. She had added several pages of clippings from the two American tours, and had carefully annotated each item in her neat script. On the cover, one of the boys had burned my name into the polished wood. I returned with newspaper features from London as well as a stack of publicity photographs of the Markan troop, which Courtney carefully pasted into the now bulging book. My dear friend Thelma, more affable than ever, had asked hundreds of questions about my travels and my career, although she could not prevent her starry gaze from returning to David Goodwin's diamond engagement ring, which flashed on her hand.

Finally I threw back the covers, but lay snuggled into the pillow, thinking over the events of the past days. The first time I had been asked about my future plans, I was well into an explanation of the new play I hoped to do, before realizing that, to the women of Deaton, "future plans" meant marriage. Now I met such questions with evasive replies about finding someone who would be understanding of my love of the theater and my need to keep working, while inwardly I smiled, wondering at the gasps that would greet the real truth about the men in my life, in this small corner of the world, where there was but one man for each woman. Laurel Ann had found that man in Jamie, and considered herself especially blessed; Thelma was preparing to settle down into a lifelong marriage with David, and even the mention of that prospect set her into nervous giggles of excitement. I suspected, however, that both women, and little Courtney as well, must have some idea that my travels through Europe had not been made alone.

When, at the end of the day, as everyone in the house settled down, Laurel Ann inquired tentatively whether there was any special gentleman friend, I managed to put her off by giving the illusion that I had been pursued by dozens of admirers, but had given my heart to none. There was no need to speak of Sasha, for Laurel Ann would not be able to understand. Nor could I bear the pain of telling her about Nick. These were the men who had been and would ever be a part of me, and I would keep the memory of them like flowers pressed in a book for me alone. These were not memories to share.

I closed my eyes for a moment, fully aware of the face that would appear. I tried to think of Sasha, of the laughter and love we had shared, but then, as in all my dreams, whether by day or night, *he* interfered. Nick. Every man became Nick. I felt his arms about me, his lips on mine, his hands at my breast. He filled my mind as he filled my heart, and for a precious moment I let it happen, let him enter and envelop my being. But such a dream was futile, for I could not hold onto it, and when at last I opened my eyes, I was left with more unhappiness than comfort.

I stood up finally, and flung off my gown. Damn it, would I never be able to forget him? I needed something else to occupy my mind. Perhaps I would hear from Lester soon, about the play. With an opening night to look forward to, with a new run before me, I could almost be complete.

As I began dressing, I saw the absurdity of my mental theatrics, and managed to laugh at myself. Here I was, just another country girl, preparing for a day of gossip and housework. Nothing, looked at from the point of view of Deaton, South Carolina, could be as dramatic as I envisioned; my problems were of no greater consequence than anyone else's, just because I was an actress—they were simply colored with a more dramatic flair. And as I caught a glimpse of myself in the walnut-framed mirror, I thought with amusement that I wasn't even going to be an actress much longer, unless I stopped gorging myself on Laurel Ann's cooking. I was absolutely fat! The chubby girl I saw before me, cheeks round and arms plump as a milkmaid's, bore little resemblance to Katerina, the passionate gypsy dancer. Drastic steps would have to be taken.

When I confronted Laurel Ann with my decision to pass up cornbread and rolls, she just laughed and took a plate off the stove, where it had been warming since breakfast. I looked down in horror at the thick slices of country ham and biscuits swimming in honey.

"Katherine," she said, oblivious to my plight, "do you want the rest of these grits?"

"Lord, no, Laurel Ann. Please. I'm absolutely rotund."

"Pshaw, you're thin as a rail. Why, everyone says so."

"An actress needs to stay thin. Unless she wants to play Henry the Eighth or Falstaff."

Even Laurel Ann had to laugh at that, as she sat down opposite me to have her second cup of coffee. The morning sun cut across the kitchen, and she moved aside to avoid the glare. Laurel Ann possessed all the poise that Glenna and Pauline had tried to instill in me, yet she was not even aware of this. Just looking at her always filled me with warmth and love, but today I noticed, for the first time, gray in her fine gold hair and tiny lines around her eyes. Laurel Ann, I realized with disbelief, was almost forty, but with her superb bone structure and golden coloring, she was still beautiful, and I knew that Jamie loved her very much. In his way. He was not a demonstrative man, except in anger. And he was still angry with me. Yet each day was becoming easier, and I was confident that, with Laurel Ann's help, Jamie and I would find an easy peace soon. We would never be as before, because I had grown up; I was no longer his baby sister.

"Where's Jamie?" I asked.

"Down at the creek with some of the tenants, trying to patch up the dam. That last rain almost did it in." She paused for a moment, knowing what had passed between Jamie and me. "Honey," she said at last, "no matter how he acts, Jamie is mighty proud of you. He's just going to take a while admitting it."

"I know, Laurel Ann. The fact is, he may never admit it, but I understand. Yesterday, when you and the kids were turning the ice cream, we sat down in the parlor. We didn't even talk, except for a few words, but I had the feeling that he was pleased to be with me. I felt good about that, because I know how hurt he must have been when I ran off with the Piersons; I know he wanted to kill me, and I can't blame him."

"Oh, he was fit to be tied. He went into one of those towering rages that sends the dogs running to hide under the house, the way they do in a real storm. Your daddy always said those rages come from the Sloanes— your mama's side—but I doubt that's any comfort to the dogs! Anyway, when we found out you were all right, Jamie calmed down, and if you could have seen him at church with that clipping from the New Jersey newspaper— My goodness, he almost popped his buttons." We both laughed at what must have been Jamie's dilemma—anger at my improper behavior, mixed with pride at my success.

"I'm just glad I have achieved some success. Suppose I'd had to crawl home with my tail between my legs?"

"Famous or not, Katherine Sloane Lawrence, this is your home. I'm just sad because, when I look at you now, after only a year has passed, I somehow know you've gone from us for good."

I started to correct her, but she went right on.

"Oh, I don't mean you won't be coming home for a visit. But I'd still love to see you settled down here in Deaton, with some nice boy. I know Jamie'd like that too, but it's not to be."

She was right, of course, but I was sorry to see her hurt by what I knew she could only think of as my desertion, and I answered jokingly, "All the nice boys in Deaton are already married."

"I suppose, especially now that Thelma has given up

Marshall Hammond for David Goodwin. Why, David was crazy about you. If you hadn't run off—"

I laughed and reached for her hand. "Laurel Ann, you know you wouldn't want to see me married to someone I didn't love."

"Of course not, honey. I just want you to be as happy as Jamie and I have been. But I know there are different kinds of happiness." She gave my hand a squeeze. "I guess a mother can't help but want what's best for her children, and ever since your mama died, I've always thought of you as one of mine."

"I know, Laurel Ann."

She looked at me with her lovely, dark-lashed blue eyes and said, "Oh, Katherine, sometimes I think that since you came home, you're more grown-up than I am. I just hope that when you have a family, you'll be able to make the right decisions. It's so hard to know what's best . . ." She broke off and began to clear the table.

"What's the matter, Laurel Ann? Are the boys—"

"No, not the boys. Courtney. Here I am talking to you about settling down, and at the same time, I'm petrified that Courtney will do just that."

"Why, Courtney's only a child, and she's still in school."

"She's seventeen—only two years younger than you—and she's already finished all her course work at school. Miss Wylie just tutors her in French and Latin, and Courtney helps with the younger ones. We wanted her to go down to Charleston this fall. She's so bright, and a year at a ladies' school down there would be just what she needs. I don't mind admitting I'd be pleased if she met some nice young man at the Citadel or the medical college. Now that we can afford to do something for her, she comes up stubborn—like all the Lawrences. And that, my dear, comes from your father's side."

"I assume the boy she's interested in is not a 'nice young man.' "

"Nice enough, but his family—" With a look of dismay, Laurel Ann sat back down. "Honey, they're just tenants, just poor whites. He's Buford Pickett, old Tom's son."

I thought back to the Picketts' four-room cabin down by the bluff. "I just remember a passel of towheaded kids."

"Well, Bufe is the oldest. He's Courtney's age, and I must say, to his credit, he did finish his schooling, but he has no background, no future, no money. Oh, I do sound stuck-up and hardhearted, but I can't bear to think of her living in some shack by the river, with a new baby coming every year."

"Surely things haven't gone that far."

"How do I know? Courtney is as secretive as you were open. You were always into trouble, but at least it was trouble I knew about, like riding bareback and scaring the cows, or stealing the Fergusons' apples, or using my best sheets for stage curtains, but Courtney lives within herself. She is a romantic girl, the sort of girl who might throw over everything for love." There was a kind of quiet desperation in Laurel Ann's voice when she asked me, "Kate, would you talk to her?"

"I'm not sure I would know what to say."

"You could tell her how you feel. You can't possibly believe that marrying Bufe at her age is a sensible choice, so just tell her. If you could convince her to try Charleston for a year, I know she'd see things differently. And Kate, find out if she and Bufe have—well, if they've been intimate." Before I could protest, she went on, "I don't expect you to tell me, but warn her, honey. She thinks of you as very glamorous and sophisticated. She'll listen to you. Please try."

How could I refuse? I agreed to talk to Courtney at the first opportunity. Laurel Ann's was certainly the sensible solution, and I saw no reason why I couldn't convince Courtney. A year was not such a long time.

The chance did not come that day. Sassy arrived to help with the heavy housework, washing the windows and polishing the wood and brass, but Laurel Ann and I kept busy, canning the last of the fall vegetables. A far cry, I thought, from my days at Thornfield Keep, where

scores of servants stood in readiness, or even at the chateau, where Solange and Louis were always at hand. I
was learning more and more about my capacity to adjust to change and still remain myself. Nothing was farther from Deaton than the gypsy caravans winding
through the meadows of the Loire Valley, yet I felt
equally at home in South Carolina and France. Oh, I
impressed the folks here with my sophistication and
worldliness, and they marveled at the notoriety surrounding my homecoming and its aftermath. My own
family, however, no longer stood in that gaping group;
after the initial awe wore off, they discovered quickly
that beneath the celebrated actress was only Aunt Kate.
The boys had been excited by their many presents from
New York and London—popular new games and puz-
zles and sets of lead toys—and Courtney was thrilled
with the bolts of Liberty print silks I had brought to her
and Laurel Ann, but by suppertime of my first day
home, everything was back to normal and the teasing
had begun.

Over a typical meal of pork chops, collard greens,
and cornpone, I mentioned the banquets at Sir Giles's
houses, adding that I had not immediately taken to the
Continental cuisine. I might as well have said "heavenly
manna" as "Continental cuisine," from the ribbing the
boys gave me. I retorted with a lengthy description of
the dishes, delivered in rapid French so that only Courtney could follow me, and she just barely. That quieted
Phillip and John for a while, until we got on the subject
of what Phillip called "the boring old castles filled with
pictures and statues of dead people." I had always
thought of the past as history rather than "dead people," but I had to admit that his description was apt!

"But I *would* like to travel someday," Phillip added
appeasingly, "just as long as I can always come back to
live in Deaton."

John agreed that he would like to see some of the
world, like his roving aunt. But Courtney demurred.

"I'm never going to leave," she said adamantly.
"Never."

Laurel Ann shot a look first at Jamie and then at me, her eyebrows raised slightly. "You might appreciate Deaton more if you took some time to see other places first."

I saw the message that Laurel Ann wanted to get across. So did Courtney.

"I know what I want, Mother," she said with quiet firmness.

"So do I," John spoke up, dispersing the gathering clouds. "More peach cobbler!" My family. How I loved them, I thought, yet what meanderings I had taken from the broad, slow-moving river of their lives, to the rapid swirls of my own.

My opportunity to talk with Courtney came the next day, as we dressed for the engagement party the Goodwins were giving Thelma and David at their plantation, Montjoy. Courtney and I had decided to take our time preparing for the evening, and closeted away from the boys in my room, we gave each other buttermilk facials and splashed the rosewater I had brought from France over our arms and shoulders. I laid out my hoard of makeup before a delighted Courtney, cautioning her to avoid a heavy hand. She sat down before the dressing table and began dabbing into shades of kohl. Before long she let out a squeal, and turned to me in desperation. I laughed as I saw the smears beneath her brows, and picked up a damp sponge to remove the damage. Carefully, I applied just a touch of blue to bring out the color of her eyes. Then I took the hairbrush and pulled it through her heavy chestnut hair, thinking how pretty she was. All the children had different coloring. Jamie and I were both dark, like our father, but Jamie's marriage to Laurel Ann had produced Courtney's brown hair and blue eyes, Phillip's blond good looks—made more startling by his deep brown eyes—and John's red hair, with his sister's cornflower eyes. The only similarities I could find among us were the set of the eyes and a certain stubbornness of the chin.

"Ouch, Kate, that hurts."

"Sorry, pet, my mind was wandering. Suppose I pull

you hair up like this and let just a few curls fall over your shoulders?"

"Umm, that's fine; of course, I really don't care, since—" She broke off, looking at me in the mirror under lowered lashes.

I sighed audibly as I realized that the moment had come for me to plunge ahead. "Since what?"

She got up and took my hand. "Come and sit with me, Kate, on the bed." The robe she wore fell open, and I noticed the creamy white skin and heavy breasts pushing against her flimsy chemise. Courtney was three or four inches taller than I, and even at seventeen, her figure was mature. I saw now why Laurel Ann was concerned. We sat side by side, still holding hands.

"Can you keep a secret?" she asked with childlike seriousness. I nodded.

"Kate, I'm in love."

She laid the first stone with those words, which I knew were difficult for her to speak, not only because she was shy, but because, after a year away, I must have seemed more like a stranger than a surrogate sister to her. But upon the difficult first stone, she began to construct her dream for me, a dream which, I soon realized, she was determined not to have destroyed.

The words poured out. "He's wonderful, just wonderful, and we're very happy together. Of course, Mama and Papa are so—so haughty. If they would just get to know him! But they won't even try. You'd like him, Kate, I'm sure you would."

There was pride in her voice as she continued, anxious to tell me everything at once, "Do you remember the Picketts? He's their oldest boy. Oh, I know they're sharecroppers and poor and uneducated, but they are decent, hard-working people. And Bufe wants his life, our life, to be better. We have so many dreams. All we need is a chance to make them come true. But no one wants to let us have that chance—not my parents, not even his parents." She looked down, watching abstractedly as her fingers traced an aimless pattern along the quilted bedspread. I tried to choose my words carefully.

"He sounds like a fine young man, and I can tell that your feelings for him are sincere. But you must think about your parents and their dreams—"

She looked up with a frown.

"The dreams they have for you, Courtney. If you could just wait a year—"

"You've been talking to Mama!"

She pulled away angrily, and I was afraid I had lost her trust. But something must have told her that I could believe in dreams too, for she spoke with assurance: "There's no reason to wait a year. I want him now. In a year I will just want him more. Kate, think of all those moments that would be wasted—a year of precious moments."

"Would you defy your parents and marry him?"

"Yes, if I thought we would have a chance." Her next words showed a surprising maturity. "If we ran away, that would just make things worse. Papa would be furious, and so would Bufe's father. Who knows what they might do? We have so much against us, Kate, that we can't afford to start out wrong. I'm not a child; I know how serious our problems are. If they just give us a chance, we can make it."

"Could you possibly compromise, Courtney? I'm sure your mother doesn't want you to be miserable, but if you would just try Charleston, maybe for this spring term—"

"Even a few months is too long, Kate, when an hour's too long. We can't wait; I mean it."

"Are you lovers, Courtney?" She looked startled by the bluntness of my question, and I quickly added, "I wouldn't condemn you, darling."

She seemed to believe me as she answered, "We're not lovers, not yet. But not because I don't want it. Bufe says no." She wrapped her arms around her breasts and leaned forward. "Oh, Kate, sometimes I think I'll die if I can't have him." Her words laid open all her naked longings and all her pain. "He's so handsome and strong, yet he's so sweet and tender. Until I fell in love with Bufe, I never dreamed a man could be like that. Do you know what I mean?"

"Yes, I know." I reached out to touch her shoulder, and she grabbed my hand and held on in desperation.

"Once we slipped into his house when his family was down by the campground at a revival meeting. We undressed and got in bed." She paused for a moment to assure herself that she could tell me all that was in her heart. "At first I felt embarrassed, and I made Bufe turn out the light when we took off our clothes. But later, I wasn't shy at all. He held me next to him and said I had a beautiful body. When he touched me— when he touched my breasts—I thought I would explode inside. And I touched him too; you know, there. And then I wasn't embarrassed anymore, and I let him turn on the light so we could see each other. He was beautiful. Oh, I know that sounds funny, but it's true. I knew right well how he would look. After all, I've got two brothers." She almost giggled, but then she was serious again. "And I had put my hand there before, but never right on him, only over his clothes. I just didn't know how much I would want to touch him; I didn't know how I would ache for him to be inside me. I begged him to make love to me, but he wouldn't. He said I might get pregnant, and he didn't want to shame me." She began to cry, her body shaking. "I can't bear it much longer, Kate. I want to be with him and sleep with him and have his babies. What can I do?"

"I don't know, darling. I don't know." I held her against me until her sobs lessened.

"Kate, I've never told anyone this, but I knew you wouldn't be shocked. You're so beautiful, so glamorous; I'm sure you know what it's like to be in love."

"Yes, I know."

A radiant smile shone through Courtney's tears. "Then you can help me. You can tell me what to do."

"But I can't. No one can tell you. I can only tell you that there is a bright side of love, but there is also a darker side. I just hope you can avoid the darker side of love—the pain, the hurt, the separation."

"I hope I can too. But even if I can't, he's worth the risk."

I stood up and walked to the wardrobe where my dress was hanging. This conversation had not turned out as I had intended, and certainly not as Laurel Ann would have liked. I had done nothing to dissuade Courtney. Rather, she had reawakened in me all those emotions I had felt with Nick. I knew I should play the role that Laurel Ann expected of me, but I was beyond play-acting now. I could only say what was in my heart. I turned back to look at Courtney, still seated on the bed, her eyes pleading.

"Life is very short," I heard myself say. "Sometimes I imagine it's no longer than this room, and happiness flies through the door and toward the open window so quickly that it's almost impossible to catch. But if you are lucky enough to catch it, then hold on with both your hands."

Courtney's face lit up as if I had given her a present.

"Wait a minute," I said, "I'm not finished. Life *is* short, but the world we live in is wonderful and wide and very full. Why not see a little of it first, before you settle down?"

"I'm not like you, Kate. I don't want to gobble up the whole world. I only want Bufe; he's my life."

I smiled and took her hands once more. It was then that she saw the sadness in my eyes. I would not have to tell her about Nick. She knew.

"Are you terribly unhappy?" she asked.

"No, Courtney, I made a choice, just as you will do. Perhaps both of our choices will turn out to be the right ones. We can only hope so. But whatever happens, you are still my dear Courtney, and I love you."

"Kate, Kate. I love you too." She hugged me tight. "And I thank you. I know Mama wanted you to change my mind, so let's keep this our secret. And Kate," she said, cheerful now, "some of David's snooty relatives from Savannah are going to be at the party, so look your most devastating. I want my famous aunt to knock them off their feet."

"Shall I cause a sensation?" I asked.

"Oh, do, do!" Courtney giggled.

Well, why not? I thought to myself. When Courtney had finished dressing, I shooed her out and completed my toilette alone, putting on my wrap before going down, so that when I joined the others, only the green edge of my dress was visible as it swept the floor. I had come home to rest and visit with my family, but as we approached Montjoy, where stringed instruments were already sending soft music from open windows, and other carriages were lined up to discharge passengers, I had to admit that I was excited by the evening's allure. Whether in New York or London or Deaton, I loved to dance.

Montjoy, which was larger than Magnolias, could in fact be called a plantation house, with its double portico and Palladian doors, and its roomy interior, the hallway of which was dominated by a suspended spiral staircase—one of the few in the state, and still considered an architectural wonder. A few guests had gathered at the foot of the stairs. Beyond, the adjoining parlor doors had been thrown open and the rooms cleared for dancing. I could just see into the dining room, where the brightly candlelit table was laden with cakes and punch, an appetizing display upon yards of cream-colored heirloom lace. The Goodwins apparently intended to make this an evening to remember, since parties during Reconstruction had been few and far between. The guests had risen to the occasion. The ladies wore brightly colored dresses, and their hair was carefully coiffed. The men were in dinner suits and starched collars, looking a bit uncomfortable, but making the most of the situation. After a few cups of punch, even the pinching shoes would be forgotten!

The butler came to take our wraps. I slipped off my cloak and heard Laurel Ann's quick intake of breath, followed by Jamie's soft, "Great God in heaven."

Even Mrs. Goodwin, always the gracious hostess, looked decidedly flustered as she approached. I wore the emerald green dress I had first worn the night Nick took me to see *La Traviata*. But for my debut in Deaton, I had, rather naughtily, removed the lace ruching in the neckline, which now plunged very low, partially exposing my breasts. At my neck, Nick's diamonds sparkled, perhaps inappropriately for a country cotillion, but when I caught Courtney's eye, she flashed a dazzling smile of approval. I had grown used to being the center of attention, onstage and off. Even more, I had grown used to—yes, needed—the attention of the men in any crowd, and tonight I was assured of that attention. After the first moments of stunned silence had passed, Mrs. Goodwin composed herself.

"How elegant you look, Katherine. My, those European styles are—are—"

"This is a New York design, Mrs. Goodwin, but I like it, and I'm so glad that you do."

"Yes." She faltered briefly, then went on, "Your jewelry is lovely too, my dear." She was dying to know more about the diamonds, obviously, and no doubt Laurel Ann and Jamie would have questions themselves, later. I would find an answer to satisfy them, but Mrs. Goodwin would have to continue to wonder! She led me from group to group, showing me off like the prize heifer at a county fair, at last coming to stop before an attractive older couple standing near the fireplace, which remained unlit in the warm October evening.

"Irene and Carlyle, at last we're here," Mrs. Goodwin said breathlessly. "Honestly, everyone has wanted to talk to this lovely child. I thought I'd never get her through the crowd." She fanned herself uselessly with her hand, and then, satisfied that she had stirred up the semblance of a breeze, reached for a lace handkerchief with which to dab her face and further smear the powder and rouge. She was undaunted. "Katherine, dear, these are my cousins, Irene and Carlyle Wharton."

I greeted each in turn, aware that they were the "snooty relatives" Courtney so wanted me to scandalize.

Well, I would do my best. They were not, as I had at first thought, husband and wife, but brother and sister. The resemblance was striking. Both exuded a rare sophistication and ease of manner. Miss Wharton, dark and thin, was in a black gown I guessed to be designed by Worth; Mr. Wharton was coolly elegant in perfectly tailored evening clothes.

Mrs. Goodwin's voice interrupted my musing. "Carlyle's firm is based in New York," she said, waiting for me to take up the cue, which I did easily.

"And how often does your business take you to New York, Mr. Wharton?"

"Carlyle, please. 'Mr. Wharton' makes me feel like someone's doting old uncle."

I did not know his age, but guessed him to be in his late forties. He was extremely tall and quite slender, like his sister. His dark hair was thick and abundant, especially around the temples, which were just beginning to gray. His face was narrow and his mouth rather small, even slightly pinched, but his cool gray eyes were large and brightened a tanned face.

"To answer your question, Katherine—as an investment banker, I must travel to New York several times during the year, and I keep quarters at the Brevoort."

"And the rest of the time?" I asked with interest.

"Irene makes a home for me at the family place in Savannah. I also have a summer house in the mountains. Ah, here's the punch."

He signaled to the butler, who served us instantly, and since Mrs. Goodwin and Irene were deep in conversation, we moved to a sofa nearby. Carlyle told me he had just returned from the mountains, where he had been since a number of cases of fellow fever had been diagnosed in Savannah.

I knew that the heat had been particularly unyielding during the time I was in France, and while the fever had not spread, hundreds of people had closed their homes and fled to the country. He told me about his mountain retreat, describing the rolling vistas that could be seen in every direction from his house.

I listened attentively, flattered by his attention, for my worldliness, such as it was, was newly acquired, while his was the result of upbringing and long experience, and was worn with the ease of many years. Nor did his interest in me seemed feigned. I learned that he knew the details of my career and that he did not expect this brief encounter to be our last.

"I was recently in London. Unfortunately, it was after the close of the International Festival, where I understand you achieved great popularity."

My efforts at denial were dismissed, and he inquired about future Markan productions. I found myself telling him of my hope that Lester would present the play I had brought back from France, and he immediately vowed not to miss me again, even suggesting that we dine together soon in New York.

We chatted on, despite frequent interruptions from Mrs. Goodwin's ever-increasing hoards of friends and relatives who were, she insisted, "dying to meet our celebrity."

Then the music began, and I was swept onto the floor. Carlyle watched from a distance, not willing, apparently, to line up with the young men who were anxious to give me a whirl. Whenever I looked in his direction, he seemed to be watching, but his manner was such that I could not be sure.

The last dance of the evening was a Virginia Reel. Mrs. Goodwin asked me to lead the first set. I suggested that that honor should go to Thelma and David, only to be answered with, "Pshaw, you are the one everyone's looking at."

"But I have no partner."

"Katherine Lawrence, you are the one! Almost every man here has danced with you, and those who haven't are still standing in line. Carlyle," she called out lustily, although he was standing quite nearby, "will you lead the reel with Kate? The poor girl has no partner."

Carlyle agreed, and with the stipulation that he would tolerate no interference from the 'competition,' he bowed gallantly as we led the other couples onto the floor.

I whispered that I had not led a reel since my school days.

He admitted the same, adding with a smile, "Just think how long ago that was!"

Then, dropping hands, we formed two lines with the men and women facing each other. The violins sang out. Carlyle and I stepped forward with a right-hand swing, turning through the line until we reached the foot and then sidestepping back the length of the room. Our memories didn't fail us, and although he did not possess the flair of Gideon or the sensuality of Sasha, Carlyle partnered me with a special grace as we whirled through each dance. Finally, exhausted, we finished with a lively promenade, and Thelma and David took our places for the next set.

At last the evening came to an end. Hugs and kisses were exchanged with the engaged couple and their parents. I joined Courtney on the porch, and together we collapsed into the carriage, where Jamie and Laurel Ann were waiting. I slipped off my shoes with a groan. "Oh, I don't know when I've danced so much."

"You were beautiful, Kate," Courtney chimed out, and Laurel Ann agreed.

"All three of you were beautiful," Jamie said, almost glowing. "But Kate's the only one who acquired a new suitor. Carlyle Wharton seemed mighty taken."

"I only talked with him for a few minutes, Jamie."

"*And* led the reel," Laurel Ann added.

"Besides," Jamie said, "when he wasn't talking to you, he was talking to me *about* you."

I heard Courtney breathe a deep sigh, and I knew what she was thinking: Carlyle Wharton was an old man.

Laurel Ann, however, could not resist a further nudge. "A girl would have to look far and wide to do better than Mr. Wharton."

"Mother!" Courtney gasped, her voice filled with

disgust. "He's twenty-five years older than Kate—at least. And he probably has an old wife somewhere."

"He's a widower," Laurel Ann said, "with a grown daughter."

"And I bet his daughter is older than Kate."

"About the same age, I believe," Laurel Ann responded.

"Ugh," said Courtney.

I laughed. "Carlyle is very attractive, and I enjoyed his attention. But Courtney's right; he's much too old for me."

"Age is not so important," Laurel Ann went on. "Besides, it's just as easy to love a rich man as a poor one, whatever his age."

I knew that remark was meant as much for Courtney as for me. Not wanting to be involved in a family argument after such a pleasant evening, I tried to end the discussion. "Well, the Whartons will be returning to Savannah soon, so that takes care of anyone's romantic fantasies."

"We could have them over for dinner before the leave."

Laurel Ann never gives up, I thought.

"Let's talk about that tomorrow," I sighed. "I'm too tired tonight."

But the next day a telegram arrived from Lester, which ended all discussion of further plans for Carlyle Wharton.

The Gypsy and the Soldier-Count goes into rehearsal November 1. Report to the 14th Street Theater.

Chapter 2

Life had come full circle. Once again, on a cold, rainy November day, I was alone on the stage of the Markan Theater. My mind raced backward in time, and I did not have to close my eyes to see him there in the rear of the theater, engagingly out of place in his elegant clothes, his tawny hair gleaming, his gray eyes alight. But now I was not auditioning for the part of the ingenue in a touring company, and there was no Nicholas Van Dyne to act as my nemesis. Now I was a star, or so the newspapers said. And Nick was gone.

The Gypsy and the Soldier-Count, long before the final scripts were prepared, had become the focus of theater gossip around New York. Sasha was being described as a mysterious Frenchman whose great passion for me had inspired him to write this play. Except for an occasional unsuppressed giggle I allowed to slip out, I did nothing to squelch the rumors, for I was as aware as Lester of what would be good for business. The house would be filled for weeks with the curious, and if the play was a hit as well, we would all benefit. So I kept quiet and read the newspaper and magazine pieces with delight. One I liked particularly told of my sojourn in Paris with Count Deschamps. The fact that I had never been to Paris, and that Sasha was hardly a count, did not deter these yellow journalists.

I was the first to arrive at the theater, except for Charlie, the stage manager. I took a seat in one of the straight chairs arranged in a semicircle on the stage, and waited. I was pleased that Charlie, who was Lester's mainstay, would be working with us, and I felt that his presence was a good omen for our successs. We chatted quietly as he moved about, clearing the cue board, prop lists, and lighting charts for a new play. This was a world that encompassed many, all equally important to the life of a play, all equally dedicated to its success, and all, star and call-boy alike, equally nervous at the start of a new production.

I missed Glenna and William though, and Johnny and Clara, all of whom were on tour. My supports were gone, leaving me, for the first time, on my own. No longer a puppet pulled by invisible strings, I would have to depend on myself and make my own decisions. To meet this challenge, I had decided that some trappings were necessary and had purchased, on credit, a splendid floor-length green velvet cape lined with silver fox fur, which made a shimmering halo around my face when I pulled up the hood. I did so now, in spite of the heated theater, to bolster my somewhat shaky image as a star. Then I remembered, with a blush, my antics of the night before when I was undressing for bed in my room at Clara's . . .

The cape still lay unopened in the box. Like a small child saving the best for last, I had refrained from even taking a peek since I had left the store. I parted the tissue almost gleefully and lifted it from the box. With the gesture of a matador, I whirled the cape around, flung it over my shoulders, and then wrapped myself in the thick, cool fur lining that seemed to nestle against my bare skin, filling me with a sensation of such rare pleasure that I had to stop for a moment and catch my breath. Awakened to heights of physical awareness in the past year, I had begun to believe that I was indeed, as Sasha had once said, a woman made for loving. But just as surely, I was now a woman without a man . . .

My reverie broken, I arranged the cape in becoming folds around me when the first sounds of activity drifted out from the wings and grew in intensity as old-timers and new players greeted each other happily, in a way that only theater people about to begin a new venture can. They were glad to be back, glad to be inhaling the most compelling perfume on earth—the scent of an empty theater at the start of a new production, an essence at once musty and clean, new and old, proud and evasive.

Lester arrived, sweating profusely, with Evan Whitcomb, who would play my lover's father, and an older actor, Boris Golding, who was cast as my father. Lester's secret plan—a secret to none of us—was to lure Madame Pauline back to the stage in the small role of the gypsy fortune teller, but Madame had not yet given an answer. Always the consummate actress, she believed in letting the suspense build until the final moment. Also missing, as the laughter died down and the actors made their way onto the stage, was my co-star . . .

I had been, if not appalled, at least apprehensive about Lester's choice for the Soldier-Count, and had actually dickered with him over the decision; I was still dickering, whenever I could catch his attention. But my opinion was of little value. I was the leading actress, not the producer. The day I had dropped Sasha's play onto Lester's overcrowded desk, I had released any authority over its production, and the day Lester had decided to accept it for the fall season, his word had become law. Besides, he tried to assure me, Terry O'Neill was blazing like a comet across New York stages. He was the perfect choice to play my lover. Based on the reviews I had read, I had to agree. O'Neill had appeared in Dion Boucicault's plays—*Daddy O'Dowd, The Sidewalks of New York*, and *Colleen Bawd*—with great success, and he had played Shakespeare just recently to receptive critics and audiences alike. He was obviously a gifted actor with a magnificent stage presence and a voice, I had read once, like fine marble. To the ladies, his was the voice of a man who had spent the evening making love; to the men it conjured up long nights of drinking with his cronies in a pub. His appearance too, I understood to be impressive. But I had not seen him. Nor, it seemed, would I see him today. Lester was obviously not concerned. He had faith in this man, who was known to everyone as a womanizer, drinker, and brawler, but who was also known to be a great actor.

I, fearing that our success would be threatened by Terry O'Neill, had been prepared to plead with Lester at length for a capable understudy. I found this unnecessary. For this task, he had decided on an actor who was everyone's choice, a young man who had worked for Markan Tours previously, and who had just completed a year of strenuous repertory in California.

Coming down the aisle toward me was that actor—Drew Dowd. We rushed into each other's arms, replacing with laughter and tears the apprehension we had both felt over this meeting. Our friendship had outlasted our memories of those summer days in Virginia when we had groped with immaturity and found bitter disappointment. Drew took a seat beside me as a hush fell over the stage. We were ready to begin, although Mr. O'Neill was not present. Lester rose, mopped his brow, and plunged into his usual first-rehearsal speech, introducing the cast members and reminding us all of the tough six weeks ahead. This time he added a few words about the beauty and excitement of the new play, words that brought a glow to my cheeks.

I had written to Sasha in care of the chateau, enclosing, with delight, the first of a series of bank drafts from Lester. I had no assurance that Sasha was still in France, but I knew the letter would reach him eventually, and he would realize that our dream was being fulfilled: I would star in the play that he had created for me. Someday, somehow, Sasha would see his work brought to life. Lester passed the scripts around, and at once the reading began. Drew read his own part—that of the Soldier-Count's friend—and the lead as well. No one mentioned Terry O'Neill's very conspicuous absence. Even in this rough run-through, I felt the inherent power of the play. Katerina is a beautiful gypsy girl betrothed to Andreas, *vataf* of the tribe. One day, deep in the forest, a nobleman is thrown from his horse and brought, unconscious, to the camp. He is Maurice Le Marc, the Soldier-Count. Katerina nurses him back to health, and in doing so, she falls in love with him. Maurice shares her feelings, but realizes that theirs is a love that cannot be.

In the second act, the Soldier-Count returns to the ancestral home of his father, but he is unable to erase the image of Katerina from his mind, even though he is also betrothed—to the Lady Clarisse. All of his former pleasures, including hunting with his companion, Claude, seem foolish and inane to him. Katerina, deserted by her lover, has her fortune told by Anya, the old gypsy, who sees death written in her palm.

In Madame's absence, Lester read the fortune-teller's part. While the other actors delivered their lines seated—stumbling with the unfamiliar dialogue, unsure of the plot—such was not the case with Lester: he stood, he strutted, he glared into his imaginary glass ball with blazing eyes. Those who had not seen his amazing talents before were spellbound by the transformation as Lester became, before our eyes, the fortune-teller. We dared not applaud the performance, but went right ahead with the reading, knowing that any show of approval would be an embarrassment to him.

In the third act, Katerina prepares to marry Andreas, even though she is carrying Maurice's child. The wedding feast has just begun when Maurice returns, determined to win Katerina back. A knife fight ensues between the two rivals for her love, and Maurice is killed. In the final scene, Katerina cradles her dead lover in her arms and delivers a soliloquy to the unborn child who will bear his name. The part was a tour-de-force for an actress, and I was determined that no one, not even the inimitable Terry O'Neill, would spoil my chance for success.

O'Neill did not show up, and Lester dismissed us early, with instructions to learn act one for a nine o'clock call the next morning. I walked out to the street with Drew Dowd, who hailed a cab, insisting I have tea with him at the Fifth Avenue Hotel before returning to Clara's house. I agreed. I was terribly curious about how he had fared during the past year, but no more curious, I knew, than he was about me. As we climbed into the carriage, I turned to have a long look at Drew, and he struck a serious pose for me, delighted when I told him that his boyish look had fled. He was still just as handsome, with fair hair and blue eyes, but the hollows in his cheeks seemed more pronounced, and this gaunt look added maturity to his young face.

That he had become more of a man of the world was shown by the easy manner in which he dealt with the maitre d', securing a quiet table for us in the hotel tearoom.

"And now," Drew said, after the waiter had taken our order, "tell me all about New York's newest star."

"I intend to, but you first."

"Well, California was like a training ground for me. I've learned so much, Kate, but when Lester called me back, I must admit I was ready to return."

"Oh, Drew, I've often wondered whether or not my behavior in Virginia had anything to do with your going West. I was such a child."

"Don't fret, Kate. I was very young myself. A year has made a difference for us both, and the California experience was just what I needed. I've played an amazing range of parts—a microcosm of the theater— Romeo, Marc Antony, Sebastian. American plays, too. We even dragged out ol' *Rip* again, plus *Uncle Tom* and *The Sidewalks of New York*."

"All within a year?"

"Our company was repertory, and San Francisco is a growing town. We had to meet the audience's demands,

and they demanded variety. But now you, 'my sweet
Kate, my fair Kate.' " He laughed. "I haven't played
Petrucchio yet, but I never read *The Taming of the
Shrew* without thinking of you."

Dear Drew! I remembered how we had talked often
about the theater that meant so much to both of us.
Suddenly, I felt that we were the same boy and girl we
had been a year ago, that no time had passed, and that
we were just two hopeful actors with wonderful dreams.
But of course I was wrong; more than time had changed
us. I smiled, a little modestly.

"Where shall I begin? Let's see, I finished the Markan tour last fall. I don't believe my Rowena took on
any great new depths." Drew laughed. "Then Lester
sent me on another tour after Christmas, playing in *Rip*
and *The Octoroon*. Those reviews were good, so good
that he brought us back here to play for a month at
Fourteenth Street. He added *As You Like It*, and one
night when Clara was ill, I went on as Rosalind."

"And you were a great success."

"How did you know?" I asked.

"Well, your fame didn't spread across the continent
because of one performance," Drew answered with a
smile, "but one of the Markan players told me about
that exciting night. What did you do next? Was that the
England trip?"

"Yes. I gather you didn't hear about that in California, either!" We laughed together.

"No, I didn't, but I have since heard a few rumors.
Tell me the rest, Kate."

I knew, of course, just what he was referring to.

"Now, Kate, don't be coy. Tell me about Sasha Deschamps."

"He's a friend—a special friend whom I care for
deeply."

"That seems a rather mild way to describe the man
who, in fiery passion, wrote a play with you as his
muse. Isn't this the great love that I predicted for you?"

"No," I admitted. "There *was* such a love, or at least
I thought so, but it's over now. I haven't seen Nick in—"

"Nick? You don't mean Nicholas Van Dyne?"
I looked up, startled.

"Remember, I started out with Markan Tours. Nick and I go way back." His expression became serious. "I'm sorry about what happened, Kate—about the railroad scandal. I gather you haven't seen him since he left New York."

"No. I've tried to forget him, to make a fresh start, but sometimes he is very much with me."

"Then Deschamps was a distraction?"

"I suppose so, although I am very fond of Sasha."

"Well, now you have another distraction, one I hope you will also become very fond of." Drew's smile was wide, his handclasp firm, accenting the warmth of his words. We began to talk about the play and our roles. I also wanted Drew's evaulation of my co-star, Terry O'Neill.

"He's brilliant," was the immediate response. "I saw him two years ago in *Daddy O'Dowd*, and I was jealous, green with envy at the man's talent, but I understand he is unpredictable." He saw my look of obvious agreement and added, "To say the least. But if anyone can handle him, Lester can, so let's not borrow trouble. Come, we'll have more tea. Waiter!"

Drew's optimism cheered me as his friendship had warmed me, and I returned home to work diligently on my lines. On the way, I stopped at a newsstand on the corner of Clara's street to pick up a copy of the *Globe*. There was to be an article about me in the paper that evening. Lester had demanded that I be selective with personal interviews, allowing only one reporter to have an exclusive story. At Clara's suggestion, I had chosen Barney Helm of the *New York Globe*, unaware then that this would be only the first of many stories Barney would write about me for the *Globe*.

Whether by affectation, choice, or disregard, Barney was the least well-groomed man I had ever known. His garish plaid suit was rumpled and stained, his brown bowler hat, which he was never without, was shapeless, even crushed; he spoke from behind a cigarette that always dangled from his lip, spilling ashes down his vest front. His eyes were small and bright and the color of ginger, as were his bristling mustache and side whiskers. Each onrush of sentences was punctuated with a guffaw, immediately followed by a raspy cough. But there was an inordinate amount of intelligence hidden behind the rumples and stains, and I found, when I reached Clara's and read hurriedly through the article, that his style dominated the interview, which was clever, amusing, and factually correct. Not without a little pride, I clipped the story out to mail to Deaton for Courtney's scrapbook.

The next day, I dressed carefully again, determined not to be intimidated by Terry O'Neill. Under my new cloak, I wore a bronze crepe dress with brown velvet trim, dismissing the matching bonnet in favor of my fur-lined hood. Again, I was on time for rehearsal; again, there was no Terry O'Neill.

I considered approaching Lester with my complaint about his choice of a leading man, but he avoided conflict, quickly involving us in another reading of the first act before we began blocking. He also announced that Madame Pauline would be joining us the following week when we began rehearsing act two.

We had stopped to discuss a piece of stage business when, all at once, a whirlwind swept onto the stage—a swirling cape of royal blue, a cap tossed on a chair, curly red hair, bright eyes, flushed cheeks, the voice I had read about, which no amount of description could capture.

"Holy Jesus, Lester, what do you mean, scheduling a rehearsal for nine in the morning? That's a time for farm hands, not actors."

Before Lester could speak, Terry O'Neill was moving among the company, introducing himself to some, dispensing hugs and kisses to others. Finally, he stood before me.

"Ah, here she is, Miss Katherine Lawrence, as fair a flower as ever bloomed. What a pleasure it's going to be working with you, Miss Lawrence."

"I certainly hope so, Mr. O'Neill," I answered, fully intending to add that his failure to show up the previous day represented unprofessional behavior, but something about the man—not just his charm and determination to win my favor, but something else—told me that this was not a man who took easily to criticism. So I remained silent. This time.

With O'Neill present at last, we began our third reading of act one. Despite the quality of his voice, O'Neill's reading was stumbling and uninspired, and I assumed that he had not looked at the script, until I noticed that it was well-marked.

Drew whispered to me later that O'Neill was known as a notoriously slow study, the kind of actor who felt his way through a part. I shrugged off Drew's explanation. So far, I was not impressed by Terry O'Neill. Again, Lester made himself unavailable for my complaints.

In the next days, as we blocked the first act without scripts, everything moved smoothly, aided by Lester's always brilliant direction—everything, that is, except Mr. O'Neill's performance. While the other actors were quickly letter-perfect in their parts, O'Neill continued to fumble. When O'Neill played against other cast members, he still stumbled over his lines and confused the blocking, but during his scenes with me, he was quite impossible.

"Miss Lawrence," he would say in the roundest tones, "aren't you reacting with excess emotion?" Or, contrarily, "Wouldn't a bit more excitement be desirable?" And always, "Obviously, I can't play off that kind of reading."

When his complaints became too heated, Lester would simply stop the rehearsal. Then followed endless arguments, often over one line, while the rest of the actors scattered themselves throughout the house, their feet draped over seat backs, as they attempted to achieve a semblance of comfort during the long periods of inactivity.

As the week dragged on, I grew increasingly angry with Terrence O'Neill. How dare he? I was tired of his fumbling, irritated by his upstaging, and resentful of his criticism. The man was impossible.

Late on a Saturday afternoon, the final blow came. O'Neill and I were alone on the stage, rehearsing our love scene for the first act curtain. Again and again, he muffed his lines. When at last we reached the final action, a passionate kiss between the gypsy and her noble lover, I was seething inwardly. I had long ago learned to fake a stage kiss by pressing my lips together and rotating my face a half-turn upstage, away from the audience. But Terry O'Neill had other ideas; his kiss was not a stage kiss at all, but a passionate, openmouthed one, his tongue probing mine. That outrage was more than I could stand. I yanked myself from his embrace furiously, hot with anger as I tried my best to ignore the memory of his body against mine, his mouth on mine—an outrage made doubly humiliating because I had felt the beginning of desire and had almost responded to it.

"Mr. O'Neill," I said, my voice as taut as my body, "I have suffered your incompetence and your insolence, but I do not have to put up with your kisses. Don't ever do that again."

He was on his feet now, towering over me, his presence as large as his rage. "I was acting, Miss Katherine Lawrence, when you were a babe in arms. I know how to act, and I know how to make love, and God damn it, the audience will never believe that lily-lipped peck you call a kiss."

Now my anger was as high as his. "If you know anything about acting, you have yet to reveal it, but you certainly know a great deal about being a boor. This play was written for me. For *me*, Mr. O'Neill, and I know Katerina, what she feels, what she thinks. I'm warning you, leave my lines alone. And leave me alone!"

"This isn't the first time professionals have had to suffer because some poor writer with a modicum of talent fell in love with a pretty face," he retorted. "And just because you've slept in the author's bed doesn't mean you understand his bloody play."

For an instant, I was blinded with a rage as red as if a huge paintbrush had been splashed, dripping and bloody, before my eyes. For the first time in my life, I drew back my hand and slapped a man. The sound of my open palm on the flesh of his face stunned me, and as my vision cleared, I stepped back in horror, too frightened by my own violent act to acknowledge his muttered obscenity.

Lester was on the stage, and Drew, and most of the company. I looked about at them wildly, and then, with a muffled cry, turned and ran. I grabbed my cloak and raced into the street, where I was almost run down by the cab I hailed.

On the way to Clara's, the tears began. Thank God, I thought, O'Neill wasn't here to see me cry, that bastard. I would not let him ruin this play. So help me God, I wouldn't. I'd see Lester tomorrow—no, Monday—and changes would be made. The play would be performed as Sasha had intended or—or— Would Lester agree to replace Terry? Well, he would have to, if he wanted me. Sasha wrote Katerina for me, and no arrogant, ill-bred Irishman would ruin my chance for stardom. Not now. Not ever.

Curled up on the overstuffed sofa in Clara's comfortable, crowded parlor, I looked around at all of the knicknacks, bibelots, souvenirs, and memorabilia of the theater, in a room that was at once full and empty— empty because Clara was not here, and I desperately needed to talk over the debacle of the afternoon. As if in answer to that need, Drew arrived shortly after twilight to tell me what had happened following my precipitious departure from the theater. Lester and O'Neill had closeted themselves in the front office, and nothing could be heard until the door was flung open and O'Neill stormed out, followed by the perspiring Lester, who sent the rest of the cast home until Monday morning. Drew had gone with some of the men to a nearby tavern, where bets were taken on who would emerge the winner—the Gypsy or the Soldier-Count. No matter who was victorious, Lester stood to lose unless he could bring his two stars together, and if he lost, so did the entire cast. I understood this and was sympathetic, but I was not going to give in to the kind of treatment I had received all week at Terry O'Neill's hands, nor could I understand why Lester, usually the tyrant of the stage, could not make use of his own authority.

"He can't lay down a separate law for each of you, Kate, and he knows it. Lester's playing a waiting game now, and that's all he can do—wait and hope his two stars can come to terms."

Drew followed me into the kitchen, where, together, we scraped up a light supper of cold meats and cheese, Clara's servants having left for the day.

"I'm perfectly willing," I said in answer to Drew's remarks, "to come to terms with Mr. O'Neill, but not if he continues to harass me at every turn. Drew, the man is a marvelous actor, or so I'm told. Why must he behave like such a fool?"

"You forget how childlike most theater people are. Kate, you have so little ego—you just want to act and do a good job. O'Neill has already achieved stardom, and now everything he does will be measured against his past work. He can't afford to be less than perfect, less than the center of all attention. You stand to walk off with the laurels in this one, and he knows that."

"Then I must convince him that doing Sasha's play as it is written is best for both of us—for all of us. And I must convince myself, too. You're wrong when you say I have no ego, Drew, because as recently as this afternoon, when I ran from the theater, my only thought was that Terry O'Neill, in his misplaced passion, was going to ruin my chance for stardom. I wasn't thinking of the play, or of anyone else in the cast, or even of Lester."

"Well, you're not a saint, and you deserve an occasional lapse into pride; after all, the play was written for you, Kate. It *should* bring you fame."

We sat together at the dining room table, our meal

completed, drinking coffee. I was silent, thinking about the other plays I had done, where the only problems were snowstorms and drafty theaters and misplaced props. "Working with Glenna and William, even Johnny and Clara, was so easy because we pulled together to help each other."

"Those are all very good performers, Kate, and very nice people. But they're not of O'Neill's caliber. They don't have his talent, or his needs, or his drive to destroy himself."

"Destroy himself?"

"Drinking, fighting, missing rehearsals. Does a man who wants to succeed behave like that?"

I had no answer.

After Drew had left, I cleared the dishes and then went upstairs, where I climbed into bed to study my script, all the while thinking about what he had said. The play would benefit from O'Neill's presence; his name alone was a drawing card, but damn it, we could not continue at such odds. I decided to try again, to subdue my anger and ignore, if I could, his jibes. I made this silent vow with some apprehension, for there was something about the man that I could not understand. He was, Drew thought, plagued by demons that drove him toward failure, and while he was afraid to fail, he seemed to take delight in the terrible prospect that it could happen to him.

Such conflicting emotions were difficult for me to understand. And I too was afraid when I considered the prospect of a long run opposite this man. Even if we did solve our problems, what other of his demons might I be faced with? I must have drifted off to sleep, for about midnight, I was awakened by a terrible pounding at the door. Wearing only my red satin dressing gown, I made my way down the narrow stairs to the front hall. The pounding continued.

"Who is it?" I asked through the locked door.

I heard the muffled response of a man's voice.

"Who is there?"

Again, an incoherent mumble, which I recognized as the voice of Terry O'Neill.

I could not be confronted with him. I must have more time to think about my decisions, made earlier and under the pressure of Drew's clear-headed optimism. No, I would not open the door to him now.

"Go away," I called back. "You're disturbing the neighbors. Leave."

The shouting and pounding continued. I turned and leaned with my back against the door, trying to control the anger which I had promised myself would not get out of hand again, at the same time trying to consider my options.

If he didn't stop, everyone in the court would hear the fool, the police would be called, and a scene would ensue, adding fuel to the gossip New Yorkers loved to spread about theater people. Our reputation was precarious already, and Lester had problems enough, without two of his actors appearing on the front pages of tomorrow's scandal sheets.

The alternative was as unpredictable as the man himself, but I would have to take my chances. I opened the door a crack. There he was, drunk, even reeling, shouting my name over and over.

I changed my mind. Better for the neighbors to be faced with this raving maniac than for me to let him in the house. But I changed my mind too late. When I tried to push the door shut, his shoulder was against it and his foot wedged in it. With effortless strength, he pushed the door back and was in the hall. I strained against the force that he brought in with him. I was afraid—afraid of his passion as much as of his power. I turned and ran toward the parlor, but his hand shot out and grasped my arm tenaciously. In one unsteady motion, he pulled me against him, his lips finding mine.

"I will kiss you now, my Kitty, as you would not let me kiss you before. By damn, I will."

His lips were demanding, insistent, unrelenting. I tried to fight him, but his strength was too much for me.

I could feel him overpowering me, making me yield to him, making me want him in spite of my fear of him.

With one last effort, I managed to pull away and get into the parlor. There, I thought, I could reason with him, if it was not too late. I moved across the room, my arms outstretched in a futile gesture, to keep him away.

"Terry, please," I whispered hoarsely, "stop and think. You don't want to do this, not now, just when I was so determined that we could work things out on the stage—"

"This is not the stage, and you won't tell me what I want."

In two strides he was across the room, and then I began to scream.

"You drunken Irish bastard. I find you disgusting, boorish, repulsive—" Every terrible word I could imagine spilled from my lips as he moved toward me. But even as I saw him coming, I continued to scream. Then, without warning, he hit me. I fell back against the fireplace and, through glazed eyes, saw him stagger forward and crumple in a heap onto the sofa. We both lay still. I heard his heavy breathing and my own. I stood up unsteadily and looked at him in disbelief. His shoulders had begun to shake; he was crying. I thought of sending someone for the police. Then I remembered that the servants had left, and I couldn't go out for help until I dressed; besides, looking at him now, as he sobbed helplessly on the sofa, I was no longer afraid. He seemed so harmless, so strangely pathetic. I took a step toward him and touched his shoulder, causing him to jump as if attacked.

"Whiskey," he slurred. "Get me a drink."

"Let me make you some coffee," I responded.

He stared at me without answering, his eyes hard.

"All right," I added quickly, "but I don't know where—" My voice trailed off as I moved into the dining room. I lit a lamp on the sideboard and began searching through the cabinets until I found a half-full bottle of whiskey. I straightened up, the bottle clutched in my hand, and saw my reflection in the mirror's faint light. I looked disheveled, but that was all. There was no mark on my face where he had hit me. I must have been caught off-balance; I was more startled than hurt.

I found a glass and returned to the parlor. He was sitting up now. There were tears on his cheeks. He indicated that I should sit beside him. I didn't know what else to do, so I obeyed.

"My wife," he mumbled, "is a cold woman."

I hadn't known that he was married, and I strained to hear his next words.

"Very little emotion," he went on, "except, of course, when she fights. Those Irishwomen fight like hounds in the chickenhouse. I love her, though, in my way; and she loves me, in her way." He laughed. "God knows what that means. She'd as soon tear my hair out as look at me, that's *her* way. What's mine, Kitty, what's mine?"

He stood up, the drink sloshing over the rim of the glass onto the floor. I reached to take the glass from him, but he pushed me away as, with one gulp, he drained the whiskey.

"Don't ever try to take a drink from a drinking man." He picked up the bottle and poured another. "She takes my money, though."

For a moment I didn't know what he meant.

"Yes, I support her and the darlin' child, and that damned cause." He collapsed back on the sofa, and I thought that he had passed out. His eyes were closed, but he continued to speak, far less clearly now. "The cause," he repeated. "The bloody Irish cause. Single-handedly, that woman plans to drive the British out of Ireland. Well, she drove me out, so I wish her luck with the British."

His head drooped back against the pillows. If he would just sleep, I could dress and go for help. I sat beside him, barely daring to breathe, for what seemed like hours. Finally, his hand relaxed its hold on the empty glass, which fell noiselessly onto the rug. I picked it up, along with the now almost empty bottle, and set them on the table. Quickly, I climbed the stairs to my room and pulled a dress from the closet. In his stupor, he seemed harmless enough, but I could not anticipate what would happen when he awakened. I must go for help.

I was untying the ribbons of my dressing gown when something made me turn. Terry was in the hall. He walked with amazing steadiness into the room, removed his jacket in one motion, and crossed to me. I bent over to retrieve my gown.

"No," he demanded. "I want to see you."

I dared not move, as, before my disbelieving eyes, he stripped off his shirt and trousers. We were surrounded by a heaviness which, like a fog, had crept into the room and enveloped us in its thick haze. I wanted to run, but the air was heavy—so heavy it seemed to clutch at my limbs and weigh them down. I could not move.

But he moved—through the fog—closer, still closer. Broad chest, slim hips, muscular arms and legs, were only impressions until my eyes dropped to his groin. There, nestled in a thicket of curling gold hair, I saw his manhood, lengthening, strong and powerful.

He swept me into his arms and carried me to the bed. The fog lifted. I struggled to free myself, but his hold was binding. I looked up into his eyes, clear now, and bright. He was cold sober. Something within told me that this mustn't be. The passion that swirled within us, if released, could bring us both down. This must not be!

I twisted and turned, but still he held me, his body rising over mine, his red hair crowning his face like a jagged halo, his skin flushed, his cheeks pitted with tiny scars. Closer now, I saw the pale growth of beard on his chin. I closed my eyes and turned my head to avoid the hungry mouth. No! my brain screamed, no! I pushed against him, trying to free myself.

"I'm going to fuck you, my Kitty, as you've never been fucked before, and when I finish, you'll beg for me."

Suddenly, I knew the words he spoke were true. I *would* end by begging for him and, God help me, I

begged for him now, even as I fought, biting and kick-
ing with a fury that only aroused his passion—and my
own.

"Look at me!" he cried. "Look at the man who is
making love to you."

I opened my eyes as his manhood pushed within me,
pushed and pushed until I forgot everything but him,
until he bore me through the wind into the vortex of a
cyclone, whirled around and around until at last I was
lost, blown and scattered into a thousand pieces.

When I awoke, I thought I heard singing. I turned in
the bed, cramped and uncomfortable. Sparks of memory tried to light my mind, but I pushed them away, not
wanting to know, when all the while I knew. I sat up
and looked around the dark room. I was alone.
Snatches of singing filled the air again, and suddenly
the door burst open.

There stood Terry, carrying a lamp in one hand and
balancing a huge tray in his arms; on the tray were a
pot of tea, two china cups, a plate of bread, butter, jam,
and fruit. He was still singing.

I fell back against the headboard, alternately laughing and crying. Who was this giant Irishman in whom
the fury of a storm gave way to the calm of a summer
day?

"Terry, I don't understand—"

"Don't bother worrying about things you don't understand, dearie, or you'll cause wrinkles in that beautiful forehead." He placed the tray on the foot of the bed
and pulled up a chair, with a gesture for me to sit beside
him. "Best hurry if you don't want to miss out." He had
put on his trousers but not his shirt, and he was barefooted. "No time for snacking like the middle of the
night." He buttered a piece of bread and pushed it toward me.

"I just don't believe this," I said as I took a bite of
the bread, cut, I realized, from a loaf I had left in the
breadbox, and very stale. "I don't believe you and me,
together this way."

"Can't imagine why. I knew from the first."

"From the first? But I hated you!"

"Love and hate are both strong emotions. They're kin to each other. My little girl, hate is not the opposite of love. Don't you know that? Indifference is the opposite of love. And we, my dear, are not indifferent."

"No, we aren't," I agreed.

We finished the tea and fruit in silence. Although I could not begin to understand the complexity of what had happened to us, there was something I felt must be asked.

"Terry, about the play. We need to—"

"Tomorrow, Kitty. Tomorrow. Come, let's sleep." He pulled off his trousers and stretched out on the bed. "We'll talk tomorrow. Lie close to me and sleep, love."

And so I did, curled up beside him, through the rest of the night.

I was out of bed first, downstairs in the kitchen, embarrassed by the man in my bed upstairs, sleeping as if this were his house. I started the coffee boiling and the bacon frying.

"Lord love us, she cooks too. Good mornin', my precious." There he was, his shirt hanging outside his trousers, acting as if this were an everyday occurrence. "Sleep well, Kitty?"

"Yes, I did, and you?"

Amazingly, I found that I was as casual as he, although I could not explain why. A surprising uncontrollable wind had swept over us both. How could anyone explain the wind?

"My sleep was wonderful, to be sure," he said. "But I'm hungry now, really hungry."

And indeed he was. He polished off toast, eggs, bacon, fried potatoes, and quantities of coffee, commenting somewhere toward the end of his breakfast, "You look amazed, Kitty, at my appetite."

When I nodded, he continued, "Once I thought I'd never have enough to eat, and now I enjoy food when I can. I learned early that life is short; a man must gobble it up in huge chunks and taste a bit of everything.

That's what I've done. But I've yet to taste it all. Lord knows if there'll be time."

I wasn't sure what he meant by that last remark, and when he began to look rather pensive, even dejected, I changed the subject and asked about his child.

"You know about Maeve, do you?" He did not remember his words from last night, kind words about the child and less kind ones about his wife. Nor, I guessed, did he remember the tears. Something told me not to mention either. "She's getting to be a big girl—eleven now, almost twelve. She lives in Dublin with her ma, but she's the light of her old da's life." A devilish grin lit his face. "Ah, that's a chunk of life not to be missed, having a wee one. You'll find out one day."

I dismissed the thought with great effort, a little pensive myself. How varying were the moods we showed to each other, and in such a short span of time. Once more, I changed the subject. As I poured him yet another cup of coffee, I asked what had brought him from Ireland to the New York theater.

He leaned back and smiled what I would always remember as his raconteur smile, and began to tell me a story I was to hear again many times in various forms, all a bit different and some, I was sure, a bit exaggerated.

"We-ell-ll," he said, stretching the word into three syllables, "my lucky star decreed that I be born in 'forty-five, the first year of the potato famine. My ma and da were actors with a touring company—a poor one at that—the Galway Players. Once the famine started, there was no money to go to the theater. No money for food. No food. Aye, those were terrible times. You know what the poor Irish did, Kitty? Ate grass. Ate grass like cattle, and died with their mouths green. I remember those days well, and I just a babe."

I suppose I must have looked a little skeptical, for he quickly insisted, "You'd be surprised what a little feller can remember of the terrible times. They say memory doesn't go back to infancy, but I'm telling you it does."

"How did your family survive?" I asked.

"My da did what a million other Paddies did; he emigrated in 'forty-eight, but we never heard from him. I guess the fever got him like it did me. See these scars on my face? Smallpox. But I survived. Ma and I went to live with Gran-da on his farm, which was more what you might call a rocky hill. A real bitch of a place to work, but I helped Gran-da and went to school and studied acting with my ma, who was a good teacher, God rest her soul. When I was eighteen, I went to Dublin and acted here and there. Then I moved on to London, and finally here, to Boston and New York. I met Boucicault; we got on, and couldn't I play those Irish lads of his to a fare-thee-well!"

"I hear you are a very fine actor," I said sincerely.

"And I believe you hear the truth." Again, he gave me that wonderful, devilish grin, which wrinkled his large, freckled, oft-broken nose.

"Then why are you so difficult in rehearsal? You have been rude and have upstaged me—"

"Now the latter is a hazard of the trade, my kitten. Perhaps I have been rude, but I've been a little galled by your noble, self-righteous, holier-than-thou act." Apparently he had not run out of adjectives, for he threw in a few more before adding, "And I don't like to be bossed about, especially by a woman."

My immediate response was anger, but that was replaced at once by curiosity. "Do I act bossy?"

"Like this play was your private property. And other actors can have ideas, you'll learn. For example— Do you have a script?"

"Of course."

"Then get it." We moved to the parlor and spent the rest of the morning going over our roles—discussing, arguing, fighting, agreeing.

"Terry, this is so good between us now," I said when we had broken off at last. "Why must everything be so difficult on the stage?"

"Because, my love, here I'll admit you're right, but never before the cast. I'm too proud, Kitty. I've come a long way from that shack in Galway. I've been put down and thrown out and spat on. Well, no more. So don't try to make me appear small in front of my peers, do you hear me?"

Chilled by his voice, I nodded.

"Good, darlin' girl. Now, I have an appetite again."

"Terry, we just ate!"

He laughed infectiously and gathered me into his arms. "Obviously, you haven't yet played Cleopatra." In his most Shakespearean tones, he quoted, " 'Other women cloy/The appetites they feed, but she makes hungry/Where most she satisfies.' That is the hunger I speak of, the hunger a man has for a beautiful, exciting woman. My appetite, Kitty, is for you."

He lifted me gently and carried me upstairs, where we made love again, but this time it was different. Terry had been more violent in his first taking of me than any man I had known, yet now he was gentle, kind, almost childlike, in the way he touched and kissed me. What a confusing man he was! In one moment he could strike out at me in fury, and in another, be reduced to tears by an unknown turmoil; a man at once weak and strong, passionate and vulnerable.

We lay close to each other, flesh touching flesh.

"You are quite a woman, Kitty Lawrence."

"And you, Terrence O'Neill, are quite a man."

"Are you still surprised that we are here together?" he asked.

I nodded my head against his chest.

"Well, I'm not. You're a woman made for loving." Sasha's words. And now Terry's.

I must have slept, for when I opened my eyes again, I was alone. I bathed and dressed leisurely, expecting to find him downstairs, but when I went down he wasn't there. My mind raced wildly around after every possible explanation: he had gone out to a bar, he would return drunk and abusive. Or worse, he would not return at all.

I heard him long before he reached the front door; no doubt everyone else in the court heard him too.

"Singing hushabye loo-la-loo, singing hushabye—" he warbled at the top of his lungs.

I rushed for the door to hurry him inside. There he stood, bathed and dressed and spruced up, his unruly hair temporarily slicked down. And in his arms, roses and violets and tulips and pansies—more flowers than I had ever seen—overflowing and falling onto the steps. He bowed ceremoniously.

"To the Gypsy from the Soldier-Count," he said in a grand tone.

And so we began a partnership that spilled across the stage and flooded our lives. I had the feeling he would come to me whenever he wanted me; I knew I would not turn him away.

Chapter 3

For a time, by chance if not by design, our affair was kept away from gossip-mongers and out of the newspapers. We arrived at the theater separately, on stage we behaved like professionals, and we left separately.

That first Monday morning when Lester decided the time had come to lay down the law, he found, to his surprise, that both of us were amenable to compromise. He pocketed his handkerchief with delight, spared the task of playing the tyrant. Terry would never be able to control his outbursts totally—even the most hopeful among us knew that—but for the duration of rehearsals, we experienced no more conflict as long as we discussed our differences alone.

Terry continued to stumble over his lines, but almost before our eyes a miracle began to take place, the miracle we had all been waiting for. Maurice, the Soldier-Count, emerged with dimension. His duty to his family and love for the gypsy girl created a poignant conflict which tore at the character in a way that perhaps even

Sasha had not anticipated. When the character emerged, the lines began to come as if Terry had had to know the man before he could speak the words.

I was forced by his brilliance to draw on resources within myself, resources that I did not know I possessed. And Terry helped. He would not be upstaged or surpassed, but he too saw how we sparked together on the stage, and knew that these were sparks that could ignite an audience.

Madame Pauline was at the theater frequently now, and I drew also on her expertise. Alternately charmed and exasperated by Terry, she was not oblivious to his talent. Secretly, when he was not in earshot, she coached me in the nuances of playing opposite such a strong actor and vibrant personality.

"Once," she said, "in the provinces of England when I was very young, I toured with an Irishman of such combined temperament and talent. Never have I done so well, for I knew that to be less than brilliant was to be trampled artistically by that brute of an Irishman. You must be the same." I intended to be, for, whatever our feelings toward each other, once we were on the stage, we were not Kitty and Terry but actor and actress—working together, yes, but each aware of the other's strength and determined not be be overpowered.

Offstage, our physical needs ebbed and flowed with the tide of our days at the theater; sometimes gentle, sometimes violent, our lovemaking had many moods. We vied with each other on the stage, took our differences to Lester to mediate, and then went home to argue once more until agreement was reached or until, failing that, we took our battles to bed where we used our bodies to gain power, one over the other. Many a morning, Terry awoke with the marks of my teeth on his shoulders and the tracks of my nails across his back.

The tension and its accompanying passion filled our days and our nights, and sometimes I felt that I could not live at his pace. He asked too much of me, he asked for more than I could give—he asked for *all*. Just when

I thought I would break under the force of him, he would settle down to a sort of peace.

We went through such a time as the rehearsals took shape and the play began to look like a hit. Terry settled into a merry period, with happiness as his only stimulant, but even the merrymaking had something of a fury about it, as he tried to live up to the myth that he and his public had created. I saw something desperate in these times too, but no one else saw, least of all Terry. Night after night he would literally scoop us up into his arms—Drew, me, even Lester—and pile us into a hack bound for dinner at the most expensive restaurant he could find, and afterwards he would take us to a nearby pub. There he would take out his old pipe, light up, and begin to tell his stories. All around us silence prevailed, and the entire pub became his audience.

Like most Irishmen, he was in love with words and could spin a magic web with them. His tales were wildly funny, with every word a gem of delight. During these times, he wove tales of purest gold with no misery in them, no despair; this he saved for his blacker moods, which were always just around the corner, for the peace was never a lasting peace. He was, he had told me once, like the wind that hurls itself across the Irish Sea.

"You can't hold the wind in your hand," he had said. "All you can do is move with it or be left behind." And so I tried to move with the wind that was Terry O'Neill.

I would have to say that I was happy during the weeks of rehearsal, although moments of true serenity· were few. One such moment was when I danced. Then the stage belonged to me alone. Lester had hired a guitarist who was Spanish, not *gitano*, but who played beautifully and seemed to sense the meaning of the gypsy dance movements. Together Manolo and I attempted to evoke the essence of the Rom. During my dance, the other gypsies and Maurice gathered around imitation fires on the periphery of the stage to watch, as I danced alone under imaginary stars. I wore Nadja's wonderful scarf, its soft touch as indescribable as the flutter of a breeze, its fresh scent as cool as the shade of the Loire Valley, reminding me always of Sasha. I put all the sensuality and all the innocence of Katerina into this dance, for with this—and the final scene—I hoped to capture the audience.

But I had misgivings; we all did, for I shared responsibility for our success not just with Sasha and Lester, but with Terry and Evan Whitcomb, who were stars, and Madame Pauline, who was a legend; with Drew and Boris and Aurora Spence, who played Lady Clarisse. We would soar or fall together.

The day before opening, I began to taste the tension. I arrived early at the theater for dress rehearsal. The backstage area was a clutter of costumes pinned up with last-minute tucks. Frantic notations on scene changes and final instructions were called out by Charlie from his overflowing clipboard of notes.

Finally, everything was ready. We assembled on the stage behind the lowered curtain, Lester took his usual place before us, and we waited. Terry had not arrived. A voiceless murmur seemed to sweep over the stage. Then all was quiet. Lester parted the curtain and disappeared. When at last he returned, he motioned Drew out with him. Moments later he reappeared alone, and asked to speak privately with me. In silence, we descended the iron stairs to the dressing rooms. The expression on Lester's face was not charitable.

"Kate, have you seen Terry since we broke last night?"

"No, he left the theater alone. Lester, do you think he's ill?"

Lester was not sympathetic in his answer. "I don't believe 'ill' is the word you want. Besides, we just checked his flat, and he's not there. Hell's bells, opening night is hardly more than twenty-four hours away."

He paced the tiny hallway. I knew the despair that Lester felt, but there was no way I could help. Terry's gaiety had flown to be replaced with that devouring, black mood that sent him off in a frantic search for himself, a search that would lead to the comradeship of a barroom and the warmth of a whiskey bottle. My heart cried out to him, yet I was angry—angry at his ego, which dismissed the waiting cast, dismissed me, dismissed everyone but himself.

"Damn you, Terry O'Neill," I thought with a passion that imitated Terry himself, "I'll see you roast in hell if you ruin my chances tomorrow."

Lester continued to pace. He was helpless, as were we all. He could wait no longer.

The final run-through began with Drew playing Terry's role, and barely adequately, so haunted was he by the specter of a disastrous opening night. I hardly remember the rehearsal, for I was haunted, too, by the thought of that proud Irishman who refused to live by any rules but his own.

"You bastard," I kept repeating inwardly, "I won't let you ruin this play; I won't let you ruin my chance."

After rehearsal, I waited for Drew at the stage door. We had promised Lester to find his star actor and get him to the theater for opening night. We had promised to catch the wind. The iron door swung open and Drew appeared. He sank onto the cold cement steps.

"Are you all right?" I asked.

"Yes, considering the alternative. I could be dead, I suppose. Hell, Kate, like any actor, I want the chance to go on for the star. But opening night? They've all bought tickets to see Terry O'Neill, not Drew Dowd."

I knew he was right, but I couldn't have him falling apart too. "You can do it, Drew, if you have to, but let's hope you won't have to." I sat down beside him. "Oh, Drew, where is he? Do you think we can find him?"

"We can try, but there are hundreds of saloons in New York. He could be in any of them."

"No, I don't think so. He once told me about an Irish-American society called Clan-na-Gael. He spoke of the group with admiration, yet he belittled their goals, so I've never known just how he felt about them. But they're Irishmen, and he would want to be with Irishmen now. Do you know the Clan-na-Gael?"

"Only from hearsay. I have no idea where they

gather, but I would expect in the Irish section around lower Manhattan."

"I have a crazy idea!" I said suddenly. "Barney Helm!"

"The newspaperman?"

I nodded. "He knows New York and the theater, but more than that, he knows the saloons."

"Kate, be sensible. You might just as well offer Terry to the lions. Helm would spread the story across the front page of tomorrow's *Globe*."

"Somehow I don't think so. But what if he did? This story pales beside what the papers will write about him if he misses opening night."

"You're right. Come on."

At the curb in two steps, we hailed a cab and headed downtown to Park Row. Drew went in search of Barney, while I waited in the hansom. He returned alone. Barney was not in his office, but a copyboy had told Drew he could probably be found at Solly's, a saloon just two blocks away.

From the outside, Solly's was less than cheerful; inside, it was worse. Still, I scrambled through the frosted door after Drew, against his wishes. Women were not welcome in men's saloons, but propriety hardly mattered to me now.

I felt fifty pairs of eyes on me, and I grasped Drew's arm tightly as we peered into the smoky, dimly lit gloom. "Look, Drew," I cried, "there he is!"

Barney sat at the far end of the long bar. He was in shirtsleeves, his derby tilted back on his head, sipping a beer. Quickly, I made my way toward him, with Drew close behind.

"Mr. Helm, I need to talk with you."

He sputtered as he recognized me. "Migod," he wheezed, "Miss Lawrence. Here?" Then he threw back his head and laughed that hoarse, infectious laugh. "Will wonders never cease? But do sit down while I order you a beer." Passing a large platter of food down the bar toward me he added, "And have something to munch on."

"No, thank you, I'm not here to indulge my appetite. I'm here to see you and ask a favor."

"I've not refused a lovely lass yet. Now what is your problem?"

As I told him, his face became alive with interest. "I gather you wish to keep this search out of the press?"

I nodded.

"But if I help find him, as a newspaper man, I would expect a generous reward."

"As a newspaperman, you might be interested in an exclusive interview with Mr. O'Neill and me. You are aware of the rumors that have been circulating. Well, you can ask any questions, and we'll answer honestly. Yours will be the only interview we give together." I lifted my chin somewhat defiantly, as if daring him to doubt me.

"A deal, Miss Lawrence. Now, let's find our wandering Irish laddy. Do you have a cab?"

"Just outside," answered Drew, who had been silently waiting.

"Then let's go."

Barney drained his beer, pulled on his coat, and led us into the cold December night. Our breaths formed silvery clouds of vapor as we huddled together in the cab, heading for lower Manhattan. We rolled along through unfamiliar parts of town where narrow, shabby houses lined deserted streets, dimly lit by flickering lamps.

"You won't find many folks here on the streets at night," Barney told us. "The women and children are crowded into the houses and the men are crowded into the saloons. But they'll all meet in church on Sunday." He chuckled. "I might warn you that these fellers aren't going to take kindly to strangers like us, so be prepared for a little bribery." When we looked surprised, he added, "Nothing makes a Paddy talkative like a couple of beers."

I smiled nervously and looked back toward the streets. We were in a part of New York that I had never seen, had never known existed. This was another world.

Finally, the cab bumped to a halt. We had arrived on
the Bowery. Barney paid the driver, and the three of us
continued on foot.

After our first few forays into the dark, dreary gathering places, my fright gave way to curiosity as, saloon
after saloon, Barney bought beers and talked on about
his dear friend Terry O'Neill, while Drew and I stood
beside him or joined him at the bar or at one of the
plank tables grouped around a pot-bellied stove. Evil-
looking bartenders eyed me suspiciously, tightlipped patrons wore fixed sneers, and buxom barmaids leaned
provocatively over to serve Barney, revealing bad teeth
behind wide grins.

The more Barney talked, the more they all warmed
up, and soon evil looks gave way to laughter and story-
telling. But soon, too, I began to tire of all the talk. We
had not found Terry, and in each saloon the answers
were much the same: "Sure now, I know Terry, but we
haven't seen him in weeks." Or, "Terry O'Neill, a fine
Galway lad he is. No, he hasn't been in tonight." Or,
"Terry? Saw him just last week. That boy can drink,
can he not?"

The hour grew later as we moved from the bitter cold
of the night air into the sultry warmth of a saloon, and
back out again. Unsuccessful once more, we trudged on.

"Let us put you in a cab, Kate. You should be home
resting," Drew begged.

"No, I want to stay with you until we find him. If I
went home, I'd go mad alone, wondering and waiting."

At last, just when I had almost given up hope, we
found him in a tavern called Costello's, much the finest of
the establishments we had seen that night, with a wide
mahogany bar illuminated by multicolored lights painted
to look like stained glass. Terry was seated at the bar, so
drunk he did not even recognize us at first. He wasn't
alone. A woman stood beside him, holding onto him as
tightly as he held onto the whiskey-filled glass before
him.

I walked up to Terry, and with a cool, "Pardon me,"

directed to the woman, I put my hand over the rim of his whiskey glass.

"Terry, it's time to go home."

He turned and looked at me, his clothes wrinkled and stained, his appearance disheveled and unshaven, and a terrible, haunted look behind his red-rimmed eyes.

"Holy Mother of God, Kitty!" The shock of seeing me in the saloon roused him from his stupor.

"Yes. And Drew and Barney. We've come for you."

For a moment I thought he would follow us out docilely, but only for a moment. Then his face changed as, with a great roar, he pushed my hand away. "So you've come for me, have you? Then you've bloody well come for naught, because I'm not leaving this barroom. Or this barstool. Or," he continued with delight, "this bar." He leaned forward to pound mightily on the bar, and his stool tottered dangerously, almost spilling its occupant onto the sawdust-covered floor. I reached out to steady him, but again he pushed my hand away.

Drew and Barney both wanted to speak, but I motioned them to silence. "Terry," I began again, "the play opens tomorrow."

"Without Terry O'Neill, you might add. Because I'm not performing. What's more, I'm not even attending."

"Of course you are," I said gently. "Now come, we'll get a carriage."

He seemed not to hear me as he droned on, his voice rising to a stentorian level, his words slurred, but as always, carefully chosen: "Maurice, the darling Soldier-Count, is of no importance, and if he never graced the stage at all, nary a soul would be the wiser."

I tried to interrupt, to no avail.

"However, we have here," he said, indicating Drew, "a fine young actor who can bloody well climb into the bloody costume and walk through the fuckin' part, because Terry O'Neill has deserted the army. The soldier is now a civilian. Another whiskey!" he shouted.

As his voice rose, so did my anger. Damn the man, weaving clever phrases through a drunken haze while the fate of our play hung in the balance.

Just then, the prostitute still standing beside Terry made the mistake of entering the conversation. "Leave him alone, honey. If anyone can take care of him, Lollie can. In fact, me and Terry is old friends." She smiled condescendingly at me with brightly painted lips.

"Not tonight, Lollie," I snapped back. "First, I doubt if Mr. O'Neill, in his present condition, could satisfy your needs; second, he has a previous commitment."

Obviously, I was not going to be able to talk Terry into a cab, and if he wouldn't leave on his own, he'd simply have to be carried.

"Drew, Barney, help me."

They both understood my meaning. Unfortunately, so did Terry, and as they grabbed for him, he swung. I was able to get Lollie out of the way, or Terry's broad reach would have caught her instead of Drew, for whom he had aimed, but who had also swerved aside. Barney grabbed Terry from behind, trying to hold down his arms, but he was flung backwards, and they both crashed to the floor.

After that, confusion reigned. Arms and legs were tangled as another man threw himself into the melee. Sawdust filled the air. And through it all, the patrons laughed and clapped. This was, a man standing near me declared, "a regular delightful donnybrook."

At last Terry was subdued. Drew flung some bills onto the bar, and he and Barney, with the barely conscious Irishman between them, headed for the street. Drew pulled me after him with his one free hand. A hack stopped, and we piled in.

"He's not hurt, just drunk as a lord," Drew assured me. Terry leaned heavily against him, his eyes half-closed, his breathing laborious.

"We have twelve hours," I said confidently. "He'll go on."

Barney sat beside me, shaking his head in amazement. "You are a surprise, Miss Kate. All that beauty and softness, with steel underneath. You're determined, aren't you?"

"Pigheaded, my relatives call me, but I usually get what I want, and I want a hit show."

"I think you'll have it now," Barney mused. When we arrived at Clara's, he helped us carry the now inert Terry into the parlor, where he was deposited unceremoniously on the sofa—the same sofa he had collapsed on once before.

"My deepest thanks, Barney," I said. "I knew we could count on you."

"Good luck, Kate." He turned at the front door with a twinkle in his eyes. "By the way, when do I get my reward?"

"After we open. You'll be interviewing either a star or a failure."

"The first, without a doubt. Good night, Kate."

With Barney gone, Drew and I were left with the task of sobering up a very drunken Irish actor. The black coffee we forced down him helped. At least it helped to send him rushing into the bathroom, where he coughed and sputtered and vomited up two days of hard drinking, while I leaned against the door, alternately cursing him and feeling sorry for him. His stomach empty, he stumbled back to the sofa and slept. After Drew had sponged him off and loosened his clothes, he too went home, convinced that there was nothing more for him to do. I could watch and wait through what remained of the night.

As the sun came up, I went to bed myself, awakening near noon when I heard the clatter of dishes in the kitchen. Wrapped in a robe, I went downstairs on bare feet, to stand in the kitchen doorway and watch as Terry, tousled but steady on his feet, stood gulping down a glass of water at the sink. He spoke first.

"A man has a powerful thirst after a bender like that. But not for liquor, that I vow."

"Oh, Terry." Against all my best intentions, I was across the room, hugging him, feeling his arms around me.

"Kitty, oh, my sweet Kitty. I'm sorry, Jesus, I am. I

don't know what comes over me—the old fears, the old panic. I almost ruined it this time, didn't I?"

"Almost, darling."

"Except for you, Kitty. Thanks for caring, darlin'."

All at once we were kissing and laughing and crying with a crazy kind of wild euphoria, at the opposite end of our world from the dark sadness that had almost dragged Terry down.

"I won't let you down again, my Kitty. I promise."

I had helped Terry, made him strong for opening night, but who would help me? We were to enter from opposite sides of the stage; Terry's first scene came just before mine. I stood in the wings and looked across at him as he awaited his cue. He seemed larger than life in his magnificent hunting costume. I saw him take a deep breath just before he stepped onto the stage. Then he was bathed in light; his golden skin glistened like a Greek god's. The audience roared its approval, and suddenly I was scared to death. From behind me, a voice whispered, "Ah, my little Katherine, this is truly the night we have waited for. Your tour, even London, was only a prelude to this."

"But Madame, I'm so afraid."

"Of course. The good ones always are. But you are ready, Katherine. Now don't let that burly Irishman step on your lines!"

Did I dream the rest? Terry's brilliance, his magnetism, the magic that seemed to happen when we played together, the thunderous applause that greeted my dance, and the endless moment of silence just as the curtain went down, before the cheers rang out? The first sensation I can remember was the scent of flowers. I looked down—my arms were filled with masses of red roses. Terry stood beside me, his hand holding mine, and the audience stood at our feet.

We made our way off the stage and downstairs through the crowds, to change into evening clothes. In my tiny dressing room, the quiet seemed deafening. I sat before the mirror and looked at the face reflected there: Katherine Sloane Lawrence, Broadway star. It was a beautiful face, I noted objectively, as dark-lashed eyes gazed back hugely from the small face. The lips were red, the cheeks flushed, the chestnut hair gleaming. This was the face of a young woman who had what she wanted, a face that seemed hardened now, almost jaded. Stunned, I watched as tears poured down my cheeks. Oh, Nick, I cried out silently, why aren't you here on this of all nights?

There was a knock on the door, interrupting my reverie. It was Lester, telling me to hurry; the carriages were waiting to take us to our party at Delmonico's. I slipped into a daring black dress, decolleté, the neck lined with glittering jet beads. I pinned a circlet of black feathers around my chignon, and put on Nick's diamonds. One more glance into the mirror—I was glamorous and mature and every inch a star. I felt happy again. Lester waited in the hallway.

"Did you hear the applause?" I asked. "Wasn't it wonderful?"

"Sounded good, Kate, but the reviews will tell the tale."

"They'll be good, don't you think?"

"Who can predict New York critics? Come, come. We'll soon know. Terry's already in the carriage. Here's your cape. Come."

I followed him up the stairs to the stage door, where he turned to me, his hand on the knob.

"And Kate, I heard what you did to find Terry last night. Thanks. Whatever the critics say, you're my shining star." He mopped his brow and opened the door, his first speech of the night completed.

The principals were seated at a large round table in the center of Delmonico's, the elegant restaurant rented by Lester for our party, and filled with the glittering and influential of New York. It seemed that half the city passed by our table to offer congratulations, and I sopped up compliments like a sponge. There was no need for wine; the praise was heady enough for me.

When the first editions of the papers arrived, the room seemed to hold its breath while Lester, with shaking hands, rattled through the pages of the *Herald* to the column of the man who was possibly the most powerful dramatic critic in New York. He cleared his throat, did not even bother to wipe his damp brow, and began to read.

"A dazzling first-night audience turned out at the 14th Street Theater last evening, for a play that will take its place alongside *East Lynne,* languishing in that particular kind of melodrama that some find appealing. To this theater-goer, *The Gypsy and the Soldier-Count* smacks of sentimentality, false emotionalism, and triviality."

I felt a cold chill attack my bones, but then Lester continued, "For that very reason I predict—" here his voice took on a sudden burst of life— "that Lester Markan's latest will run for months!"

At that, we all let go our breaths and began to relax.

"Although the play is of a genre that offers little of lasting value to the theater, the production is vital and lively, and stars the most attractive couple seen on Broadway in recent memory."

Now the cheering and clapping began, and Lester climbed onto a chair to shout over the din, "Terry O'Neill, the fine Irish actor, turns in a bravura performance: strong, yet gentle and believable; powerful, but never overshadowing his co-star. Miss Kate Lawrence, a name you will hear again and again, is not only beautiful in the extreme, but is possessed of a brilliant talent. Here is a woman who is fiery, tender, loving, vengeful. Here is a woman—"

I heard no more. We were a hit! I floated on a cloud of dreams and fantasies that had all come true. Sasha had given me the words; Lester, the direction and faith; Terry, the talented partnership; and Nick, the love and encouragement. Through the men in my life, I had become an actress and a star.

The other reviews were similar, except that some received the play itself more favorably, expressing great hope for future works by the neophyte Monsieur Deschamps. Somehow, clutching all the New York papers,

I got back to Clara's—alone. Terry had been determined to share his success with all the rest of New York, and he left at about three in the morning (with Drew as his bodyguard) for a nearby pub. Heeding Lester's reminder that we had a performance the next night too, I stepped out of my dress and petticoats into a hot bath, and from there, after a warm glass of milk, up the stairs to bed.

We sailed through December. Barney got his exclusive interview. I sent a stack of clippings home to Courtney. Christmas came ˉand went—another Christmas away from my family. Lester raised my salary and I began, for the first time, to know the security and power of money and fame. And I was famous! The fashionable ready-to-wear stores had begun showing "Katerina scarves"—inexpensive copies of Nadja's scarf, which I used in my dance. I enjoyed the notoriety and acclaim that came with success, enjoyed the turned heads and whispered admiration.

And of course, Terry ate it all up. Pictures of us filled the gossip pages of the weeklies. One—which I did not send home—showed us leaving a cafe after a midnight supper, with the caption, "Real-Life Lovers." We were lovers, but more than that, we were friends, and as our friendship grew, our affair lost its initial passion. Terry's talent and his zest for life drew me to him. I could not deny my fascination with his many-faceted personality, but more than this, he needed me. I had seen the pain and suffering in his heart, and I was to learn that there was more.

I attended my second ball at the Players' Club. My mind went back to last year when, innocent and carefree, I had tucked two pale pink camellias in my hair and gone off with such anticipation to the December ball where I had first danced with Nick, first kissed him, first held his body to me and foolishly hoped the moment would last forever. Over six months had passed since I had heard from Nick, and I knew I must begin, at last, to build a life without him. But as Terry and I

left for the dance, almost as an afterthought, I picked a
pink camellia from a bowl on the hall table and tucked
it in my hair.

It was in January that Terry missed his first performance. He did not arrive for the usual half-hour call, and
fifteen minutes before curtain, he still had not appeared. Time was too short for us to search the Irish
saloons again. Lester sent Charlie and the call-boy for a
quick check of the neighborhood pubs, but they found
no trace of the elusive Terry O'Neill. Drew changed
hurriedly from his own costume into that of the Soldier-
Count, and came into my dressing room.

"Don't look so terrified, Kate. I know the lines."

"Darling, of course you do." I moved to him, arms
outstretched. "I'm afraid I was still thinking of Terry,
when this is your night. Do forgive me." I kissed his
cheek.

"Maybe Terry just decided to let me have a go at the
part," he laughed.

"Maybe. And quite a go you'll have; you know the
words, so just let them flow."

"I will, Kate, and I don't need to worry, because you
can carry the play without me."

But I didn't have to. Drew was marvelous. Once I
thought he might have forgotten his lines, but he recovered quickly, and we sailed right through. Of course,
some of the audience was disappointed that Terry
O'Neill had not appeared, but they knew they'd seen a
fine performance.

Terry showed up the next afternoon, unshaven,
shaken, and, as I expected, contrite, reeking of cheap
perfume and bad whiskey. I was more disappointed
than angry, and refused to listen to his explanations. I
knew the pattern now: he was afraid of failure, but
more than that, he was afraid of success. And I was
powerless against the black Irish demon that rode him
so hard, rode him, sometimes, to the ground. But we
did talk about it finally in February when he disappeared again, this time for two days.

The second night that Drew played for Terry, I received a note backstage at intermission, requesting my company at a late dinner, and signed "J. Carlyle Wharton"—the attractive older man who had led the reel with me at Thelma's party. I'd had to help prepare Drew for the performance, and with my remaining energy, would have to help Terry when he returned. The time had come for me to have a boost, and Carlyle Wharton was just the tonic I needed.

When I joined him in the green room, I was glad I had accepted the invitation. He was as attractive as I remembered, and while he knew my beginnings, he also knew how far I had come from the little Southern girl who so desperately wanted to act. I was gaining a reputation as a wise and witty woman, an image I worked hard to maintain, reading all the newspapers and magazines—*Harper's, Leslie's Illustrated, The Ledger*—and attending late-night dinners several times a week with New York's literary and artistic crowd, as well as Lester's acquaintances from the business world. But in spite of this, I was not yet twenty, and there was much I could glean from a man like Carlyle.

He took me to Arnado's, a new restaurant off Madison Square. Since I had been there only once before, I was pleased that the maitre d' remembered me; Carlyle did not miss the exchange between us.

"I wasn't aware of your widespread fame, Katherine."

I laughed. "Dino just remembers me from another evening."

"I believe there is more. You're becoming a celebrity and, my dear, I must tell you how I too enjoyed your performance tonight." He spoke knowledgeably about the play and the cast and other theater he had seen. He asked about Monsieur Deschamps, and I gave him a little background, adding that I had recently received a letter from Sasha, who was in Rome, saying that he was thrilled at our success and was busy working on a new play based on Roman mythology. I did not mention the rest of the letter, in which Sasha swore his undying love and immediately added that he was in Italy at the villa of Count and Contessa Marpose, who were "sponsoring" him. The count, I imagined, was very old and La Contessa very lovely . . . No, Carlyle did not need to be told everything! Nor, when he asked about Terry, did I mention the reason for his missing two performances. I wanted the evening to be free of any tension, and I could not speak of Terry without being faced with it.

After asking permission, Carlyle ordered for me: a sparkling wine and an aperitif of tiny oysters, followed by pasta, veal, and finally *zuppa inglese* for dessert. I felt pampered, a feeling I adored, especially tonight, when my mind was full of Terry and the play. With Carlyle, there was none of the wild desperation of my life with Terry, none of the fighting or the torment. I seemed to have stepped out of a turbulent wind into a cool, dry shelter. A storm continued to rage outside, but here there was comfort.

"Have you traveled in Italy?" I asked, after he had placed the order in Italian with our ever-attentive waiter.

"Frequently. Business takes me throughout Europe and the East." He knew that I had traveled to England and France and assured me, "You would love Italy, and Greece too. Of course, business trips can be gruelling, but I travel for pleasure as well. I don't know if my cousin in Deaton told you, but I'm building a town house here in New York, and on my trips I search for interesting art. I am primarily intrigued with painting and tapestry, but recently, in Athens, I found a lovely statue—first century B.C., or so I was told—of the young goddess, Diana. Above the perfectly proportioned body, her marble head is tilted at a most intriguing angle and her features are quite beguiling. I was forced to pay an outrageous price, but I wanted her. When I want something that much, I won't be denied." He looked at me with pale gray eyes, causing me inadvertently to lower my gaze. Then he added lightly, "Would you like to see the statue?"

"I would love to."

"You will be among my first guests when the house is completed," he said, raising his glass in toast.

I touched my glass to his. As we smiled at each other, I also smiled to myself, remembering Courtney's attitude toward Carlyle. He was an older man, yes, but with his years had come success and wealth, as well as a confidence younger men lacked.

"Would you be offended if I asked what you were thinking, Katherine? You seem so far away."

"Forgive me. I was thinking of Deaton and my family," I half-lied with a blush.

He did not seem to notice, and even found something to interest him in my remark, asking, "And what do you think of Courtney's impending marriage?"

Both Courtney and Laurel Ann had written about the June wedding, which had come as no surprise. "Courtney seems truly in love with the boy," I said. "Of course, they are very young, but she's determined. I believe she's doing what is best for her."

"I am amused, Katherine, when, at your age, you speak of youth in others." After a pause, he added, "Yet there is a maturity about you that almost makes me forget my own years. I noticed that in Deaton. You took my breath away there, my dear. You were like an exotic orchid among pale lilies. But I suppose you know that."

"A woman never tires of compliments, Carlyle."

Just then, dinner was served, and we continued our conversation about New York, London, music and art and literature. He knew so much more than I, but I held my own.

The hours flew, and it was after two in the morning when he dropped me at Clara's, with a kiss to my gloved hand and a promise to see me again when business brought him once more to New York.

As soon as I opened Clara's front door, I knew I was not alone. I walked down the hall and into the parlor, where Terry was asleep on the sofa. As I entered the room, he awoke.

"Well, Kitty, I see you finally decided to come home." He was sober, at least.

"Oh, Terry, where have you been? You missed two performances. Even Lester is going to lose patience."

"Bugger Lester. There are other plays—"

"Other plays!" Now I was angry. "We've committed ourselves to a full season, and the audiences want you; they want to see Terry O'Neill."

He rose from the sofa and crossed to me. "You never answered. Where have you been?"

"That's a question *you* should be answering. I performed tonight; you didn't."

"Everyone needs a night off," he said.

Unable to bear his nonchalance, I felt myself losing control, losing my temper—just as, I suspected, he wanted me to.

Through clenched teeth, I said, "The rest of us work every night except Sunday. Every night. We're not driven by some demon that demands perfection, and if we lack great talent, we at least try to do our best. But you! You're such a fine actor, why must you throw it all over for drinking and fighting and God knows what else?"

He was silent, though his face was flushed, so I plunged insensitively ahead. "Terry, you don't have to fear success. It's yours; no one will take it away."

His red face grew crimson. "I'm sick and tired of your half-baked ideas about me being afraid of success. I'm not afraid of anything, and what I do or don't do on the stage is between Lester and me, do you hear? Now, where were you?" He had grabbed my shoulders and was shaking me. "Who were you with?"

I shouted back to get his attention, "I was with a man from Carolina. A family friend, that's all. Oh, Terry, I didn't desert you, darling."

He pulled me to him, kissing me, holding me. "Jesus, I'm so sorry I shouted at you. I know I'm a damn fool, but I can't lose you. I need you, Kitty."

"You haven't lost me, Terry. Come to bed now. I'm tired, and I know you are."

He followed me upstairs where, together in bed, I held him to my breast and listened to him at last, as I had refused to do before. He wouldn't tell me all that had happened, but my suspicions had been that the Clan-na-Gael was partially responsible for his disappearance, and I was right. Since Terry had first mentioned the group, I had learned a little more about it from Barney. No one knew much. The society had begun eight or nine years before, and was dedicated to a violent course in Ireland. Terry himself had told me the money they raised was being used to arm the Fenians. He cursed them while, at the same time, he supported them financially. He said he despised the hopeless dreams of freedom for Ireland, but he returned to these people again and again. Where I had once thought he was drawn by the warm feeling of being with his own people, I now knew there was more.

His spree had begun, he told me, innocently enough, with dinner at Ryan's two nights before. There had been the usual talk of money, arms, the Fenians— He couldn't remember now. "Too many whiskies," he said, "too much useless chatter." From Ryan's, he joined other pals and put the Clan-na-Gael behind him at least for a time, as he drank his way from saloon to saloon and, no doubt, from woman to woman. In the saloons he was just another Paddy. He did not have to be clever and amusing; he did not have to be on stage. Nothing was expected of him, and there was no myth to live up to. I wondered, as he told me his innermost thoughts in the night, whether I would ever understand this lusty, brawling, complicated man.

After we talked, he slept, his head still resting against me. I ran my hands through the wild red hair and thought about the daily battle he must be fighting with the darkness inside him. I knew I had become stronger during my time with Terry, but was my strength enough for him to hold onto? Was I powerful enough to fight his twisted memories of the past and his black fears of the future? It could not matter. Our fates were intertwined.

During the night, Terry promised me that the brawling and drinking were over, and that he would finish the run without missing another performance. He was as good as his word. He appeared every night, and each performance was perfection, amazing me anew with its freshness and vitality.

In April, Lester announced that we would complete the New York run and travel abroad in May for a two-month tour of London and Dublin. I was afraid Terry would be thrown into another black mood over the thought of appearing first before the hated British, and then before his own people. I held my breath. The storm did not come. For myself, I was overjoyed at the prospect of returning to England, and wrote Sasha immediately, hoping he would be able to see me in his play at last.

To add to the euphoria, my friends returned all at once to New York—the Piersons, Clara, Johnny—all back from tour. Clara reclaimed her house, and although I was invited to stay, I took a small flat nearby for the last month of the American run. Not only had I grown used to having my freedom, but with Terry a frequent guest, I needed to be on my own. I hired a young Irish girl, Mary O'Donnell, as a maid. She lived somewhere in Manhattan with an enormous family, to whom she returned each evening at seven, as I left for the theater. She was a pretty girl with shiny brown hair, blue eyes, and freckles, and was very eager to please. She and Terry got on famously, and he teased her unmercifully about her lingering Irish brogue. She handled him as if he were an older brother, impressed neither with his fame nor his tall tales.

Clara looked wonderful. While on tour, she had met a New England businessman, who had been able to visit her in several of the stops. She glowed—and glittered, with diamond bobs in her ears and a huge ruby ring.

"Of course, he's older, Kate, but still quite charming and terribly wealthy. And so unhappy, poor dear. His wife is a virtual invalid, which makes him very appreciative of my, umm—" she paused, looking for the right word— "vitality."

I fell back, laughing, onto the bed. "Clara, you are priceless. How I have missed you."

"But I notice you haven't pined away. Now tell me all. And I don't mean about the play; I'll see it tomorrow. Besides, William insisted on reading every word of every review aloud. He and Glenna consider you their own special discovery. Of course, they're very worried."

"Worried? Why ever—"

"Over the men in your life, what else? Nick was difficult enough for Glenna to accept, but Terry O'Neill— the last of the Irish rovers! Personally, I adore the man. Tell me, is he everything they say?"

I laughed. "I'm not quite sure what that means, but I would say he's everything—and more. He can be wildly exciting or deeply melancholy. And I never know which to expect."

"That sounds terrible."

"Men like Terry are never easy to understand, and even less so to love."

"Then don't tell me any more; I can't stand to be depressed. Besides, I'm sure he'll be charming when all the crowd gets together tonight. Oh, by the way, Gideon has gone abroad to write, but Johnny is philosophical over the desertion, as you will see. Now let's find something elegant for me to wear to dinner. This red with the jet beads? No, too showy. Hmm, maybe the green . . ."

Our last two weeks were a round of parties, capped off by the grandest of all: Lester's soirée after our final performance, held on the stage of the theater, with everything set up while the actors were below changing.

The caterers had arrived before the end of the play, and the minute the curtain fell for a last time, they rushed out to spread a long buffet table with smoked oysters, shrimp, lobster Newburgh, stuffed mushrooms, and, as centerpieces, sculptured birds of caviar and paté. The orchestra pit was banked with flowers, and in the center aisle, champagne flowed from an artificial fountain. Guests—and again, all of New York seemed to be here—mingled with the actors, sipping wine or settling into front-row seats, their plates heaped high with delicacies. The cast sat at small, candlelit tables placed downstage from the buffet. Seated on the apron of the stage, Manolo played his guitar, and the music drifted over us in waves of love. This was a party that New York would talk about for months.

I wished that my family could be here to share the evening. But Jamie would not leave the farm, and of course Laurel Ann would never come without him. And Courtney—I was probably the last thought in her mind, which was crowded now with plans for the wedding. Maybe someday the boys would make the trip North to see their aunt perform.

Whenever I lifted my glass, it was filled again with champagne. The bubbles sailed to my head, but I didn't care; this was my night, and I meant to enjoy it. One by one, we were called upon to make a speech about the end—and the new beginning—of the production. Lester went on and on, while Terry was brief and expectedly witty, and Evan serious and scholarly. When my turn came, I hesitated, not knowing where to begin. Then I spied Manolo. I gestured to him, and a murmur went through the crowd as they discerned my plan.

"I am neither as clever as Terry nor as long-winded as Lester—" The audience roared. "But I dance better than either!"

Terry objected strenuously to this, but I ignored him as Manolo began to play. That is, I tried to ignore him, but very soon he was beside me, dancing with abandon, if not skill. Drew joined us too, and Boris. Finally I pulled Lester into the circle. Then, one by one, they moved away, and I was alone. Dancing had always been an important part of my life, and I danced my thanks that night to thundering applause, which meant everything to me, for I was being recognized by my peers, by my own.

The evening continued with more champagne, more dancing, and even another speech or two. At four o'clock, I could go on no longer, and shared a hanson with Clara, since Terry's night had obviously just begun. I was tipsy myself when Clara let me off at my flat, but pleasantly so, and still on top of the world as I undressed and prepared for bed. I had just finished brushing my hair when I heard a tapping on the door. At this hour, that could only be Terry. I let him in, grimacing to see that not only was he drunk, but he had a bottle of whiskey in his hand.

"Terry, it's almost morning."

"What did the Bard say? 'Our little life is rounded with a sleep.' And I say, life is too short to sleep away, so let's talk, Kitty."

"Tomorrow, darling. Not while you're drinking—"

"Oh, yes, especially while I'm drinking. Have you a glass? No, you won't fetch it? Then you won't mind if I do."

Terry followed me into the bedroom, a whiskey-filled glass in his hand, and settled in a chair. He drank silently for a time. The earlier glow had left his face, to be replaced with something else, a new kind of sadness.

"You know what you mean to me, do you not, love?"

He was going to get maudlin, but there was nothing I could do now except listen.

"I think so. But I also think I know what's bothering you. It's Ireland, isn't it?"

The trip had long been on his mind. His drinking tonight had simply opened the tap of his feelings. He was wary of facing his own people in Dublin, more even than of facing the hated British.

"It's not just returning home. It's Sian."

This was the first time he had mentioned his wife since the night at Clara's so many weeks before. I had avoided the subject too, not wanting to face my role in the confusing triangle that was further complicated by the presence of a child.

"I don't worry so much about Maeve," he said as if reading my mind. "She's a strong child, and she'll survive. But I've hurt Sian, and I never meant to. Kate, she brings out the worst in me, just as you bring out the best. Or try to, God bless you." He almost smiled, but the sadness prevailed. "I don't know what to do about her bloody cause. I want to help, but I know she's wrong. And all the while she hates me because I left, because I chose the stage. She hates me even more because I've made a success with my career, while she's doomed to fail in that terrible fight for Ireland." Again he was silent. But he had put the bottle away. "How can I face her, Kate?"

"You'll face her. I'll help you to." I moved beside him and held his head against me. He pulled me to him, and I slipped my arm across his shoulders. "I'll be with you in England, and Ireland too. Look, darling, the sun is rising. This is a new day, Terry, a new day for us."

I felt him relax against me as we sat together, the only two people in the world, watching the sun's golden rays spread over Manhattan. A new day, I had told Terry. But suddenly, I too was afraid, and I didn't know why.

Chapter 4

This time, the crossing to England was a difficult one. Even though we were well into spring, a North Atlantic storm caused our Cunard liner to heave and rock and sway, until most of the passengers were forced to take to their cabins. An uneasiness developed between Terry and me almost as soon as we had reached the open sea, an uneasiness I put down to poor weather and seasickness, but I knew there was more. I had promised to help, and I would, for I cared deeply about this man. But I was anxious for myself as well. I would be returning to England in a starring role, and the press, which had treated me kindly before, might not be so tolerant this time.

Finally, after three days, the skies cleared, and we clambered onto the deck for a look at the sun. Terry and I found chairs somewhat protected from the wind and lay back, wrapped in our warm steamer rugs. Fragmented sunlight scattered like diamond buckshot across the surface of the water as, overhead, soft clouds raced toward the horizon. Terry snuggled down in his Astrakhan coat, the brim of his black felt hat half-covering his face. He looked every inch the actor, and from the passengers strolling by, he drew admiring stares which he acknowledged with an occasional sweep of his hat. His bright eyes shining, his red hair flying in the wind, he was both regal and untamed. Members of our troupe appeared on the deck among the other passengers: Evan, in deep conversation with Boris, and bundled heavily to avoid chilblains; Aurora Spence, a bit unsteady in high French heels; Drew, wearing neither coat nor hat, bent over his playbook; Manolo, all smiles, his guitar bouncing on his shoulder.

Expectedly, Madame had declined to make the trip, and had been replaced by the fine character actress, Sylvia Montenegro. She was traveling with her granddaughter, combining the trip to England with an educational tour for the child. As the two passed, Terry stood and bowed gallantly, drawing blushes and giggles from little Maria, who clearly worshiped him. When Aurora passed a second time, her gait was steadier, for she was now arm in arm with Drew, recently her constant companion. His playbook was nowhere to be seen. Terry beckoned them to join us.

"Come and take a seat. Too much exercise is terrible for actors," he said with groundless authority.

Aurora was as cool as Drew was warm and friendly. They were total opposites, even down to their looks—his starkly blonde, hers dramatically brunette. Drew had told me seriously that he believed Aurora chose him for his coloring. "I make her look beautiful," he had laughed. They *were* a striking couple, and although I found Aurora rather shallow, I envied the ease with which they strolled through their affair, making the path that Terry and I traversed seem so much more torturous.

As we huddled together in our deck chairs, chatting against the wind, Terry visibly derived energy from their avid attention and began to outline his plans for showing us the real, not the tourist, side of London.

"We'll go to Gray's Inn Lane to have a look at the fire-eaters, and then to Leicester Street to see a Punch and Judy show."

I evidenced little enthusiasm for fire-eaters, and Aurora said, "I absolutely hate Punch and Judy—all that hitting and slapping."

Laughing but clearly undaunted, Terry continued, "In the evening, we'll go to a music hall. They're not as fancy as the Sloane Square theaters, but they're far more entertaining, not to say energetic. Members of the audience often jump up on the stage to get into the act. We'll depend on Drew to keep that tradition going."

Drew looked askance and said he'd rather see Henry Irving.

"Of course," Terry went on, "there'll be no need for dining in restaurants when we can take our meals from the street vendors. My mouth waters just thinking about their offerings: meat pies, hot cabbages, whelks and onions, broiled eel—"

Aurora and I wailed in unison, and Terry threw up his hands in mock despair. I was glad to see him happy, even if the happiness seemed forced.

My own laughter did not quite ring true, either, as I was clearly preoccupied with thoughts of the future. I knew that I would continue to act, for even without success and fame, the stage was my life. Yet I was somehow uneasy, because I also knew there was more. Clara's experiences had shown me well enough the course of an affair with a married man, and somewhere inside me was a longing for home, family, husband. This could not be, if I continued my present direction. But how would I change my course, and when the time came for change, would I know and choose wisely? Clearly, when I had first left New York and Nick to travel to London, I had made a choice, but I had not understood its importance until too late. I knew, and Clara often reiterated, that there was no advantage in worrying over the "what ifs" of life: what if I had stayed in New York; what if I had been with Nick when tragedy struck; what if I had returned home as soon as I had received his letter? But these were questions I must ask myself so that I would not make wrong decisions again. I wanted desperately to understand my choices. I wanted to control my destiny, when now I only seemed able to act out the days of my life, waiting until a choice was presented to me.

So I reluctantly put thoughts of the future from my mind as Terry did from his, and soon we were in London, billeted not in a small, side-street hotel, but at the very elegant St. James. I had a large suite of rooms, to which fresh flowers and fruit were delivered daily. Advance publicity for the play had been handled well by Lester's London agent, and box-office business was brisk. We were to play at the Royal, an exquisite jewel-box of a theater, and five days of strenuous rehearsal lay before us. With Evan as touring director, new blocking and stage business had to be set up and perfected.

During my free hours, I showed Drew and Aurora all that I remembered of London, my favorite sights and walks. Terry did try to enter into the spirit of adventure and led us, as he had promised, to his haunts off the beaten track. We even ate from a street vendor's cart, graciously declining eel, and followed Terry in and out of pubs along the Thames, where we drank warm, dark beer from heavy mugs, cheered his hopelessly bad dart games, and listened attentively as, with his pipe clenched between his teeth, he wove a new web of tall tales.

The press stirred up great anticipation over the opening, labeling the play "sensual melodrama," and some of the livelier newspapers speculated on the romance between the playwright and myself. One determined reporter even dredged up the old story about Christina Sabine's confrontation with me over Sasha. That article I tore out and sent to Sasha; the others I saved for Courtney's scrapbook. Surprisingly—and thankfully—the press here did not seem aware of any special relationship between Terry and me. His return had been greeted with enthusiasm, and he, like the rest of the cast, had been deluged with invitations.

Flowers overflowed the foyer of my suite, and calling cards piled up on the front hall table, the majority from men. Actresses, especially unmarried ones, could not expect to be invited into Victorian England's finest homes. Sir Giles, a widower who set his own standards and tastes, was an exception, with his lifelong devotion to the theater. All of the principals dined at his Belgravia town house before the play opened, and he was making elaborate plans for a final-night party at the St. James.

I also received flowers and a visit from a distinguished member of the House of Lords whom I had last seen, pink buttocks exposed, atop Clara in the meadow near Thornfield Keep—Clara's beau, Julian Sandusky. Well, I thought, as I arranged my hair before the mirror when I heard his knock, he's clearly in pursuit of a replacement, but if I remembered the mildly bumbling middle-aged Englishman correctly, I knew he could be handled easily.

"Julian, darling, you're looking well."

We grasped hands and then touched cheeks, barely, in an imitation embrace.

He gave his mustache a twist and eyed me wickedly. "Last year, Kate, I thought you were a very pretty little thing. Now you are a sophisticated woman. Quite irresistible."

"Thank you, Lord Sandusky," I said with a curtsy. "I love to hear the words, even though you are a terrible flatterer. Now, will you have some tea or perhaps a whiskey?"

"Always a whiskey." He followed me to the sideboard. "Just a bit more. Little more. Ah, that's fine. Now, tell me about yourself—and Clara."

So he was still interested!

"Clara is doing well. She has just returned from a successful tour and is back in New York, healthy and happy." No need to mention Clara's new love to the old.

"Always meant to write. Just never got around to it. Thought I'd get over to America this year, but—

Clara's a fine woman," he mused. "Do miss her." Julian
never quite got around to completing his sentences.

As we sat and talked in my elegant suite, all horsehair and red velvet and marble, I tried with difficulty to
dismiss my last glimpse of Julian in the meadow.

"I say, Katherine, you pulled a cropper on us. Running off. Yes."

When I had sorted out Julian's words, I realized that
he too was thinking of last summer. "Was there a mass
confusion after I left?"

"Hardly. Hardly. Giles calmed everyone down, and
we had quite a nice lunch. Quail, if I remember. Christina secluded herself for a day, then went off somewhere."

"Where is she now?" I knew Christina was not acting
this season, at least not on the London stage.

"She had quite a success in France last fall, I hear.
While there, she met a so-called Russian prince. Ran
off to Petersburg with him, they say. She's used rather
to those types. Pseudo-royalty and what have you. But a
Russian. Humph." Julian poured himself another whiskey, and I saw his eyes cut toward the bedroom door
and then back to me, with an admiring glance over my
figure. "What ever became of the Deschamps fellow?"
he asked.

"I've had postal cards from all over Europe, but he
seems settled now in Rome, working on a new play. I've
been half expecting him to appear."

"Frenchmen are entirely too unpredictable. Not like
us. Always know what's on an Englishman's mind."

When I smiled off his insinuations, he shrugged and
changed the subject. "See here, I want to have a dinner
party opening night. You and this Irish chap and old
Evan. Whoever else. Like you to meet some friends.
Hmmm. What do you say?"

"I think that would be charming. At your home?"

"Sly wench. And put my wife in a frenzy? At my
club, don't you know. Handle things quite nicely there.
Elaborate and all that."

"It sounds divine, Julian, and I'm sure all of us would love to attend."

I finally bid him goodbye at the door, and I do believe he managed to pinch the chambermaid as they passed in the hall. I certainly didn't need to be concerned about Lord Sandusky; my problem now lay with Terry. His wife would be arriving in London soon, and our relationship was slowly changing. We were seeing less of each other, and his dependency on me did not seem so great during the days of rehearsal. But I still slept with him when he wanted me. I meant to stop, but could not. After opening night, I told myself, we must agree to let this affair run its course. After opening night. Later, when Sian arrived, perhaps they could work out their problems, and the play could have a good run in Dublin. I could not think any further ahead than Dublin.

The night before *The Gypsy and the Soldier-Count* opened, Terry came to my rooms, as he often did. I sat before the vanity brushing my hair, and he flopped into a chair across the room. Neither of us talked. I broke the silence first.

"Are you worried about the opening?"

He nodded. When that was his only response, I continued, "I'm nervous, too. I suppose there's no way to prevent opening night butterflies."

"But they're not waiting to crucify *you*."

"Terry, darling, don't be foolish." I moved over and sat on his lap. "Your acting will bring the British audiences to their feet. Oh, Terry, Terry, I have such faith in your talent. When you are on the stage, lightning seems to flash all around us. You mustn't torment yourself so."

"I'm just in the doldrums. There's so much on my mind."

I thought I knew what he meant, but I did not know all, and I could not find the emotional strength to delve into his problems tonight. Instead, I led Terry to my bed and, through our lovemaking, tried to comfort him.

His body felt the same on mine, his pale skin freckled and muscular, his lips warm and demanding, his hands wild and seeking. But somehow, I was different. I could feel myself moving back, separating, detaching. Terry and I had gone as far as we could, and now we must turn back.

The next day, we plunged into dress rehearsal, with all its inherent problems: torn costumes, mishandled scenery, misplaced props. Just when everything seemed under control, a gas jet was knocked over, starting a fire backstage. It was quickly extinguished, with no damage except to our nerves, but the afternoon was so hectic that the performance itself was a relief.

I knew from the first scene that this would be our greatest night. Terry seemed to create a whirlwind of excitement, and we were all caught up in the magnificent force of his performance. I did not need to hear the applause when the curtain fell to know that we had won London—that Terry had won London, and all his fears had been groundless.

I fought my way through the crowd to my dressing room, where a maid was waiting to help me change. I had chosen an expensive new gown, silvery and shining, designed in Paris and sold on Regent Street. The material was gathered into a waterfall bustle and train that elegantly swept the floor. I piled my hair up and stepped into high-heeled silver slippers, to give me extra height. I was pleased with the way Kate Lawrence looked tonight. Opening night was over, and during the rest of the run, I intended to enjoy myself. If Terry wanted to engage in black moods, he could do so alone. I was the toast of London, and I planned to enjoy playing that role as well as the role I played on stage. Terry and I had come this far together. The time had come to stand apart.

From the flurry of the crowded green room, full of friends and fans, we were escorted out to carriages for the drive to Julian's club. He had arranged that the members of the cast be scattered, with careful planning on his part, I felt sure, at tables with the other guests.

Terry seemed miffed that he and I would not be seated together, but I was somewhat relieved.

I saw him take his place at a table with Sir Giles, bewhiskered and beaming, who turned to introduce Terry to a beautiful young woman across the table. She, as I later found out, was a well-known artists' model. Julian had obviously guessed at our Irish actor's reputation. The woman's eyes did not leave Terry as he took his seat and threw an expression of helplessness in my direction. Perhaps this would be a first step in untangling the skeins of our life together.

At my table were seated Julian, a British acting couple whom I knew slightly, a rather vacuous-looking woman with brightly painted lips, and to my right, a fair-headed young man named George Simpson. Only well into the meal did I learn that this unassuming young man was also Lord Haversham, heir to a vast publishing empire in England. Across the table, the red-lipped woman was batting her eyes at Julian with consummate skill and great success. Well, I had certainly misjudged Julian's intentions toward me. The woman was obviously his mistress! Why, then, I wondered, had he so conspicuously seated me at this table? I gazed toward Lord Haversham on my left. Could he be the reason? Surely not.

The meal was elegant, rich, and heavy. Course after course, each with accompanying wine, was set before us, and I found that I was wildly hungry. My attack of nerves had passed, and although I wanted the critics to like us, I was not concerned about the reviews that would be in the papers the following morning. Our success was already assured. Terry and I were a team, at least on stage, second to none. Between interruptions by well-wishers stopping at the table, thoughts of the future pushed into my unreceptive mind. I imagined us together again, perhaps playing Shakespeare, but the image was cloudy and vague. I knew that if we could work out our personal lives, our future on the stage would be unlimited, yet I still could not seem to see that future clearly.

When the constant stream of visitors was at an ebb, Lord Haversham attempted to engage me in conversation. He spoke so quietly that, over the din, I was sometimes unable to catch his words, but he was obviously a lover of the theater and especially of my performances, not only tonight but last year in *Rip* and *The Octoroon*. As he spoke, I realized to my amazement that, indeed, it was precisely because of Lord Haversham that Julian had seated me at this table. Of course, nothing makes a man so attractive to a woman as his continued interest in her, and when he invited me for luncheon and a drive in Hyde Park two days hence, I accepted. In a short time, the London press would unearth the truth about Terry and me. With Sian's imminent arrival, Lord Haversham would be a diversion for the reporters. Besides, how often did a girl from Deaton, South Carolina, have the opportunity to be escorted by a peer of the realm?

The party over, we all made our way, somewhat tipsily, back to the St. James, where I collapsed into bed and slept soundly until I heard the loud thump of the morning papers against my door. I ordered a big breakfast and sank comfortably into the red velvet sofa, the papers spread before me. Drew rushed in with hardly a knock, more papers under his arm, and a huge smile on his face. The reviews were splendid, he shouted; the critics loved us! Evan joined us shortly, followed by Boris and then Aurora and Sylvia, until most of the cast was gathered in my suite, ordering more breakfast, laughing, reading the reviews aloud. All of us had been mentioned in glowing terms, and the London critics were enthusiastic about Sasha's talent. We could not have asked for more.

Just as we finished composing a telegram to Lester, Terry entered. I had expected him to be as elated as the rest of us, especially after his spectacular performance, but he was very subdued and thoughtful, and would remain so for many days. He looked through the papers almost disinterestedly, and when Evan, always thinking ahead to the next challenge, asked about Dublin, I answered for Terry.

"If the British have accepted this Irishman as—and I quote—'one of the finest actors on the boards today,' what won't the Irish say?"

Terry looked up then, and shrugged his shoulders. "Who knows about the Irish, crazy as they are? They'll either laud me or lambast me. But they'll love Kitty, that's for sure. Irishmen appreciate a beautiful woman." He glanced quickly at me. "Not like the cold-blooded British."

I realized that he had not been oblivious to my long conversation with Lord Haversham, but I was too elated to be brought down by a lovers' quarrel today. I turned to Evan and asked about the theaters in Dublin.

"They have very fine theater houses. Henry Irving has appeared frequently in Dublin in recent years, but so has our own Boris."

"There's no better audience than in Dublin," Boris said. "They're infatuated with the spoken word, as we all know." He directed that comment, with a smile, toward Terry, who remained strangely silent. "There have been a number of fine Irish playwrights," Boris added, "and because of their gift for words, I expect many more to emerge."

We continued to talk about our trip to Ireland. All of us were looking forward to playing The Queen's Theater in Dublin and enjoying the hospitality of the Irish people. But long before we scattered for luncheon, Terry had silently gone alone to his room.

That night, his performance was good but not inspired. Something seemed to have gone out of him, and as I held him—my soldier-count—in my arms and made my final speech over his dying body, I was flooded by very real emotion. In many ways, Terry was lost to me, for we were torn apart, not by death but by circumstances.

The days flew by. Terry and I continued to act out our lives on the stage, but away from the theater we saw less and less of each other as we both inwardly prepared for Sian's arrival. We still occasionally lunched with Drew and Aurora, and once or twice Terry joined some of the cast for sightseeing, but we talked only briefly, and he did not come to my room. A quiet sort of fury seemed to be eating away at Terry, but I refused to be consumed by it. Instead, I had my first luncheon with Lord Haversham, then another and another.

On our second outing, Lord Haversham confided that he did not wish to keep secrets from me, because he wanted our friendship to be an open one. When I agreed, he proceeded to tell me about his nickname. As he was quite serious, I tried to contain my amusement. He had been, he told me, called "Bunny" as a boy, because of his somewhat prominent teeth, and the name had followed him through school. So many of his friends continued to call him Bunny that he had rather gotten used to the name over the years, and if I wished, he said, I might call him Bunny also. I replied that I would be delighted. This secret off his chest, he then went on to the real subject of our little talk: he was betrothed. A blush colored his pale cheeks as he told me about the girl, now eighteen and on the Continent, traveling with her aunt. From the time they had been thirteen and seven, he and Minna had been prepared to marry. Their families expected it. As I listened and responded with understanding to this confession, he insisted upon telling me more of his personal life. He, like many young men of his set, had carried on brief liaisons with other women—shopgirls, bored wives, an actress . . .

I looked at him coolly at these words, no longer amused. "Was that the purpose of Julian Sandusky's introduction, Bunny? To supply you with a mistress until you marry?"

"No, Katherine, no, good heavens, no," he stumbled on, before recovering sufficiently to add, "I just wanted to meet you. I was amazed that you agreed to have luncheon with me, and a drive. You are so beautiful and famous. I'm not that handsome or debonair, and I'm terribly pedantic, what with my books and stamps."

"You are not at all pedantic, Bunny. You're charming and kind and, yes, you are quite debonair."

He looked flustered at this compliment. "I'm proud that you will be seen with me, when you—that is, when the papers say that you—" His voice, always very soft, trailed off completely.

"Don't believe all that the papers say. Sasha Deschamps was a good friend, but no nicer than you, Bunny."

"And O'Neill?" he almost whispered.

"He is a very exciting man, and I care deeply for him, but I don't love him. In fact, I'm beginning to believe that the theater is the one true love of my life. It has never let me down or deserted me."

His pale hair and mustache grew even paler with each blush, and he blushed now at my confession, which revealed more than even I had realized. When he had collected himself, he said, "Katherine, I would be most pleased if I could show you London these next weeks. Of course, if you'd be bored, please say so."

"Bunny, you fool, I'd adore to see London with you. Nothing would give me more pleasure." So I promised to spend Sunday, my only free day, with Bunny. I knew Terry would sulk, but I didn't expect that he would be alone. The model whom Julian had seated at his table after the opening had begun to appear nightly in the green room.

Because Sunday was windy and cold, the kind of London day I had encountered on my last visit, we were forced inside and could not walk about Mayfair or Piccadilly as I would have liked. We went instead to an art show in Park Lane, at a lovely Regency house which had recently been converted into a gallery. The works of a popular English painter were being shown. Having heard how, as a child, I rode bareback through the cornfields, Bunny thought that I would enjoy the paintings. I was intrigued by the lifelike quality of the work, but despite my youthful escapades, after the first dozen or so pictures, I began to tire of horses at the hunt at the stables, at auction, at Ascot. I soon drifted away and began to observe the crowd, which was infinitely more interesting and less repetitive than the paintings.

Thus I was standing by the front entrance, when a very peculiar little man entered with a flourish that captured my attention completely. He wore an unusually high silk hat which, when removed, revealed a very small man, hardly taller than myself. He carried a long, narrow walking stick and wore bright yellow gloves, which he removed with great meticulousness. He glanced disinterestedly around, and then made his way into the front room with a quick gait, his chin protruding ahead. He stopped only once to remove his monocle, blow daintily onto the glass, and wipe it carefully before replacing it to view the painting before him. He was obviously not pleased with what he saw, and moved away quickly, with a touch to his drooping mustache and a stroke to his curly hair. I could not seem to take my eyes from him, and only hoped that he did not notice my unladylike stare. Suddenly, to my amazement, Bunny appeared in the room, glimpsed the little man, and crossed immediately to his side. They talked rather animatedly for a long time while I watched in wonder. Unable to resist any longer, I headed toward the two men.

"Katherine," Bunny said, seeing me approach. "I wondered what had become of you."

I answered that I had grown rather tired of looking at the paintings, as each one seemed much like the other. At this, the little man gave a hooting laugh, which caused the others in the room to turn and stare.

Bunny blushed and said softly, "Katherine, I would like to introduce you to Mr. James McNeill Whistler. Mr. Whistler is a most prominent artist who has seen you on the stage and asked to meet you. Jimmy," he said, turning to his friend, "May I present Miss Katherine Lawrence?"

Mr. Whistler stepped back with an exaggerated motion after kissing my hand, and, below his dark brows, viewed me from all angles, removing and replacing his monocle several times. Then he said, in a rather squeaky voice, "You are a symphony in color!"

I looked at Bunny questioningly, but it was Mr.

Whistler who answered my question. He wanted to paint me. He admired me as a great actress and a great beauty, and was especially interested to find that I was from the South. He was also an American, although now an expatriate, and his family had been Southern sympathizers. Mr. Whistler went on, in his funny voice, eulogizing me in glowing phrases and dismissing all the popular artists in disparaging terms, saying that he was the obvious choice to paint me.

I stood mesmerized, answering occasionally in mono-syllables, while he made arrangements for my sitting. As he left, handing me his card without a further glance at the paintings he had come to view, I realized that I had agreed to sit for him on my return from Ireland, assuming that Lester had no immediate plans for me in New York.

"Bunny," I said later as we left the show and climbed into his carriage, "what was the meaning of that scene with the strange little man?"

Bunny stammered for a moment until I assured him that I had not been offended and that I did want to have my portrait painted, but also wanted to know something about the painter.

"Whistler is a well-known artist," he said, relieved, "and although some of his work has been controversial, he is rather famous, especially for 'The Little Girl in White,' which is a lovely portrait of Jo, his mistress."

I looked dubious, and he added, "No, no, Katherine, no, there is not a suggestion of anything like that. Good heavens." He blushed and then went on more seriously, "It is quite the rage to have one's portrait painted and, I must add, to be the artist who discovers the next emerging beauty. Perhaps Jimmy is nominating you for such an honor."

"Dear me, do I want to become an emerging beauty?"

"Probably it would do no harm to your career."

I nodded. "Now, are you saying that one is discovered by an artist, painted, and then becomes an emerging beauty?"

"Well, yes, if one is, in the first place, a beauty. Otherwise, that wouldn't quite happen, would it?"

I laughed gaily, eliciting a toothy smile from Bunny.

"The phenomenon is rather strange, I must admit. Last year, Mrs. Lillie Langtry was suddenly discovered. She was the wife of—well, I'm not quite sure what old Langtry was, but she was seen at a fashionable dinner, and within the year, eleven artists had painted her portrait."

"Eleven?"

"Yes, isn't that odd? Well, she is rather lovely, but not nearly as lovely as you, Katherine, with your dark hair and eyes," he added, almost as if he were embarrassed at having noticed.

I smiled my thanks and then asked, "What happened to Mrs. Langtry?"

"She was last seen riding in the park with the Prince of Wales."

We laughed together and, in gay spirits, arrived at the dining room of Claridge's, which was, as Bunny explained, the finest hotel in London. From the street it was not at all prepossessing, just a half-dozen houses joined into one. Its fame came from visiting royalty and the resident French chef. During dinner, I learned more about Bunny. Like most wealthy and titled Englishmen, he had no need to work for a living. His time was spent pursuing hobbies like his renowned stamp collection. He admitted to owning a string of race horses— "abysmally slow, most of them"—and a yacht which he shared with two others.

"How different from my life," I challenged. "I must work for a living, but fortunately my work is what I love best. The theater is my hobby *and* my life."

"But you have so much more; you have a vibrancy and a zest for life that is sadly lacking in the women of my set. I respect you, Katherine. I'm proud to be your friend."

"And I'm proud that we are friends, Bunny, but don't put me on a pedestal. I have learned that caring too much, thinking too much of someone, can be a mistake."

"This is no mistake. No, Katherine, don't stop me or I shall never find the nerve to speak again. I want to say only one thing more, and then we shall talk of other matters. If—if at any time—that is, if you ever need me, please know that I am here."

Tears came to my eyes as I thought how kind he was to accept me on such blind faith. His family would be scandalized that Lord Haversham was dining in public with an actress when he was betrothed to an heiress, yet he offered me his protection, and asked that I give him only friendship in return. Perhaps, with Bunny's friendship, I would be able to endure the storm that was sure to accompany Sian's arrival.

Each evening, Bunny succeeded in entertaining me, even when I was too exhausted to do more than return to a hotel, where he joined me for a glass of port. He was not an exciting man. Beside Terry he seemed meek and mild. But he was kind and thoughtful, and even amusing, in his way. One night when I felt especially lively, he suggested that the time had come for a surprise. Around midnight, Bunny directed his driver to take us to the Palace Theater.

"I've never heard of the Palace. Who is playing there?"

"Rather *what* is playing there, Katherine. The Palace is a music hall, not a legitimate theater."

"A music hall!" I remembered Terry's description on the ship. "Oh, no, will I have to get up on the stage and perform?"

Bunny laughed. "Then you've heard about our music halls? No, I guarantee that you will not have to participate, although you may well want to stand up and applaud before the evening is over. But wait, you'll see."

When we arrived, Bunny maneuvered us through the crowds into our seats. The theater was large and well-appointed, with comfortable upholstered seats, and gaslights reflecting off gilded pilasters. However, the audience was more rowdy than at the Royal, more of a working-class element, eating and drinking with abandon as they milled about, much as audiences must have done, I imagined, at Shakespeare's Globe Theater.

An orchestra appeared in the pit and struck up a tune familiar to everyone around me. ("The Jumbo March," Bunny whispered.) Finally, the review began: performers sang in cockney accents and wore clothing studded with metal; comedians told jokes, again in cockney accents that I could hardly understand; jugglers, balancing acts, and acrobats followed one after the other. A circuslike atmosphere prevailed, which mixed all elements of showmanship, from slapstick to spectacle, with the talents of the individual performers. I laughed as heartily and applauded as loudly as my neighbors. After all, this was theater too, perhaps the earliest kind of theater.

"I love this, Bunny," I whispered. "How clever of you to bring me here."

"Just wait. Just wait," Bunny answered, literally jumping about with anticipation. And finally I knew why. The lights dimmed and a lone guitar began a plaintive strain, slightly out of tune but immediately familiar, as a half-naked girl placed a card on the easel at stage left: *The Gypsy and the Soldier-Sweep*. They were doing a parody of our play!

"Imitation is the sincerest form of flattery, Katherine. When I heard of this, I knew we must see it. Rather jolly, what?"

"Rather," I answered in my most British tone.

The skit was indeed amusing. Katerina was played by a large, buxom wench who whirled about the stage with much abandon. Her lover, a lonely chimney sweep, was spindle-legged and barely half her size. The hunters were costumed as English bobbies, and their horses consisted of two men under a blanket—one the head, another the unsteady tail. In a corner, three witches right out of *Macbeth* stirred up a wicked brew and sang terrible prophecies. The scene ended with Katerina falling on her sweep and causing his demise. Like the rest of the audience, I stood and cheered the remarkable performance.

As the theater cleared, I told Bunny that I must go backstage. Katerina—a strawberry-blonde without her gypsy wig—was delighted by my appearance. She said she had been playing music halls for twenty years and was always thrilled when a famous star came backstage. A famous star! On that, I literally floated home and was riding high on a wave of ebullience as Bunny took me to my door. But when we stepped into the suite, I came crashing back to earth.

"Terry!"

He got up from the chair where he'd been sprawled, and came toward us. As he moved, he reached for a table to steady himself. His weight caused it to shake precariously, and he almost fell. Bunny cried out, assuming Terry was hurt. I knew better.

"Oh, God," I said, without stopping to think, "you've been drinking." The words were a challenge, but it was too late to retract them.

"You're damn right," he shouted. "But you must realize that I've been drinking with the ordinary folk while you've been screwing the gentry."

Bunny moved forward without an inkling of what to do, but wanting desperately to protect my honor. "I say, O'Neill!" He tried unsuccessfully to raise his own voice. "That's no way to speak to a lady."

"Lady!" Suddenly Terry's expression changed, and he gave Bunny a shy smile. "You know what I call her, George, old thing?" he asked in his most British tones. I felt Bunny relax beside me. He thought Terry was being friendly. Again, I knew better. "I call her Kitty," he shouted out, "because she has the morals of an alley cat."

"Now, I won't let this go on," Bunny said with new-found authority.

Terry pushed him aside with one arm, much as if he were weightless and moved toward a tray of liquor set out on a sideboard. He spoke with his back to me, seemingly disinterested, but the meaning of his words was very clear. "Get him out of here, Kitty, if you know what's good for him."

Bunny moved toward Terry with his fists raised in a brave, futile gesture. Terry did not turn around. I stepped in front of Bunny and gently took his hands in mine. "Please, I won't allow a fracas. Terry and I are colleagues, and whatever is upsetting him has nothing to do with you, Bunny. If you leave now, everything will be all right."

"I would prefer to stay with you until this is settled."

"No, that's not at all necessary. I'll be fine, believe me." I took his arm and guided him to the door. As he picked up his gloves and top hat, I saw him hesitate once again. "Truly, Bunny, I'll be all right."

"I'll stop by early tomorrow," he said firmly.

"I'll look forward to seeing you. Good night." I stood on tiptoe and placed a kiss on his cheek. As I closed the door, I turned to Terry. "Why?" I shouted desperately. "Why, when you hold London in your hands, must you start drinking again?"

"None of that's important."

"Not important! You were talking, before we opened, about being crucified by the British. You were terrified to face opening night. Now that they worship you, it's not important. Oh, God, I just don't understand."

"There's more, Kitty, there's so much more."

"There's always more, always another excuse."

"Why would I need an excuse, when I have reasons enough to last a lifetime? Sian's coming in two days, and I'm driven almost to madness just thinking about her. And all the while you're out with that—that—pasty-faced British hypocrite."

"And what about your beautiful model? She's in the green room every night, so don't tell me you haven't been taking her out."

"Yes! I've taken her out. I've even taken her to bed." I felt my stomach churn. "I was expected to, obviously. Don't blame me. That idiot Sandusky's *your* friend."

"That's hardly a reason to—"

"Oh, Kitty, for God's sake, she meant no more to me than a Bowery whore. You turn away from me, and this woman throws herself at me. I'm a man, for God's sake, Kitty." He drained his glass. "But never mind. After a taste of the actor, she's gone back to her artist. Meanwhile, I've lost you, haven't I? Sian's coming with all her mad ideas, and I've lost you to this pompous bastard, Lord Bunny!" He laughed long and hard, but there was nothing amusing in the sound. "I might as well give it all up now. The play too. Why bother to go on?"

He walked to the sideboard and poured another tumbler of whiskey, which he raised to his lips, but before he could swallow it down, I acted.

"Damn it, Terry, I won't let you do this." As I spoke, I flung my hand out, knocking the glass away. Brown liquid splashed against the white wall, and a thousand pieces of crystal danced across the parquet floor. I grabbed his hands and held him.

"You aren't going to give up anything, do you hear me? You're a fine actor, a great actor. I haven't made you great. That happened long before me, and will go on long after. I care for you, Terry. If we can no longer be lovers, we can still be friends, and we can appear together on the stage. But if you walk out now, if you throw away your career because some harmless Englishman takes me to the theater, then you're not much of a man after all, Terry O'Neill."

He pulled away and stood glaring down at me from his great height. For a moment I almost feared for my life. How easily those hugh hands could curl about my neck. But he did not attack me. Instead he turned, crossed the room, and flung open the door. I sagged down against the sofa. He was gone, but where? And would he be back? Wearily, I prepared for bed. But just before putting out the lamp, I pulled on a robe and went down the hall to Drew's room to prepare him. If, indeed, Terry did not return, Drew would have to go on for him.

There was no sign of Terry the next day, and Drew, with mixed feelings of delight at the opportunity and concern over Terry, ran through the play with me. My own feelings were not mixed. There was only anger— anger at Terry for running away from situations he could not control. Of all those he hurt, he hurt himself the most. Even good-hearted producers like Lester would be increasingly wary of Terry as he became less and less dependable.

While I sat at my dressing room table, beginning my makeup for the evening, I thought that perhaps I should have been kinder, but in being kind, I would have had to be dishonest, and the time had come for Terry to face the truth. I glanced at the vase of flowers on the table. Bunny had sent roses both to the hotel and to the theater, after visiting me early that morning. I had explained Terry's behavior away casually. After all, weren't all actors slightly mad? Still, I was appreciative of Bunny's gesture. He really cared what happened to me.

I was sure that the knock on the door was my dresser, but when I turned, I saw a disheveled Terry. Disheveled but not drunk. I could tell by his eyes and the way he stood, and I went to him at once, reaching up to enfold him in my arms.

"Terry. How glad I am to see you."

He held me tightly for a moment, and when he spoke, his voice was low. "You are right, Kitty. Walking out is not the answer, nor is drinking. I love the theater. Sometimes I think that's all I have."

I almost wept at his words, because I had begun to feel the same about myself.

"I can't lose the theater, not now, not since I've lost you," he said.

"You haven't lost me, Terry. We'll be together where we are the best—on the stage. Some nights you light the stage with your talent, and no other light but yours makes me look so good."

He ran his hand down the side of my face, and I

could almost feel the heat of his warm blue eyes, which seemed to be committing my face to memory. I felt myself go weak under the intensity of those eyes.

"And I shall never stop loving you," he whispered, "but even a stubborn Irishman knows when to pull back." He gave me a quick kiss. "And now I must tell Drew to take off Maurice's costume. The star has returned."

Chapter 5

We were a team again that night, and the next, but I awoke Sunday morning knowing that everything was different. Sian would arrive today. Terry had decided to meet the ferry from Ireland at Holyhead. The eight-hour train trip would necessitate his leaving at dawn and spending most of the day either on the train or waiting for connections at the stations. They would not arrive back in London until early Monday morning, but Terry was determined to make the long trip for her sake.

"I hope to bring her back to a home and hearth," he had told me before he left, "and away from that terrible cause of hers. That's my dream for us now. I don't believe I love her; I believe I love you. But she's my wife and Maeve is my child, and I must try. But oh, Kitty, sometimes I have such a fear—not of her, but of that undying, unyielding devotion she has to Ireland; she could make trouble for us all." Then he said the strangest thing. He said that often the innocent are the ones

349

who suffer in complicated political situations, simply
because they *are* innocent. "Perhaps Ireland's troubles
are mine," he added, "but not yours. Never yours. I
don't want you involved."

I laughed and said that I was not political and had no
intention of getting involved. But his remarks had confused me, and I would think back to them many times
in the next days, and confront him with them again before we left for Dublin.

With Terry on his way to face the challenge of Sian, I
spent another Sunday with Bunny. I made a great effort
not to seem preoccupied, but he sensed that something
was wrong. Although he did not question me, he put all
of his charm and quiet humor into our outing, and I
was silently grateful to him.

Sian and I never met, but a few nights later, I
chanced to see her briefly. As I was leaving the St.
James dining room, she and Terry entered. Unaware of
my presence, they made their way quickly to a table in
the rear. Sian was not what I had expected. She was
slight, as slim as myself, though somewhat taller, and
pale—so pale I imagined that I could see the blue veins
beneath her skin. Almost as pale as her skin was her
hair, of the faintest red. Her face was dominated by
eyes that were green and deep, and glowed with an inner light. I knew I was looking at a woman who dared
to dream great dreams, a woman who was afraid of
nothing. From the few moments that I observed her
talking with Terry, I became aware of a deep intensity
about her, as if, beneath the pale skin, her movements
were controlled not by muscle and sinew, but by tightly
strung wires which vibrated at the slightest touch. This
intensity seemed to encompass the whole room, and
gained its force, I was to learn, from a deep fanaticism.

As our London tour neared its end, I put Sian and
Terry from my mind as much as possible, and filled my
free hours with Bunny and his crowd. He was a help in
the shopping into which I threw myself, purchasing a
new frock at the slightest excuse and buying countless
gifts to take home to friends and family. During these

shopping trips, Bunny scurried along beside me, his
arms laden with packages, delighted with each new purchase, happy to wait patiently at the dressmaker's or at
Murphy's Millinery, where his suggestion of a different
feather for my new toque caused Mrs. Murphy to clap
with joy at the perfection achieved. His taste was impeccable, and he happily accompanied me on my search
for Courtney's wedding gift, a search that occupied two
long afternoons. As soon as I had arrived in London, I
had sent her beautiful Belgian lace for her veil, and all
sorts of powders, soaps, and scents to pamper herself.
But I, who had encouraged her to follow her heart,
would not be there to see the couple exchange their
vows, so I wanted to buy her a special wedding gift.
This time Bunny's suggestions were of little help, since I
found it impossible to explain to him that in their new
home—a tenant house on the farm—a Georgian silver
service would not be appropriate! At last, in a shop off
Regent Street, we found a pair of eighteenth-century
candlesticks. Extremely ornate and far too expensive,
Bunny pronounced them the ideal gift, and I agreed
without explaining their added practicality—if Bufe
and Courtney could just afford candles, they would at
least have light in their cabin.

Bunny had also chosen the beautiful summery frock
and matching parasol I was to wear to the most special
outing of my London stay—the opening of Royal Ascot
Week. The day was particularly important for him,
since he had a runner, a two-year-old colt named Arundel, and he was beside himself with excitement as we
began the drive out from London toward Ascot, he in
morning costume and high hat, I in billows of frothy
white lace and ruffles.

Unlike others of their class, Bunny's parents were not
interested in horses, either in the race or the hunt, and
thus his stables were his own. He ran them with the
enthusiasm of a delighted schoolboy, but with far more
seriousness than I had at first suspected. Up before
dawn many spring mornings, Bunny had watched, along
with his trainer, all of Arundel's workouts, and it was

he who had made the final decision to let the horse have a go at Ascot. As eager as he was to have the pleasure of standing for the first time in the winner's circle with a Haversham Stables colt, Bunny was more interested in proving himself and turning what had begun as a pleasant hobby into a profitable business venture.

We followed the early races from Bunny's box, and then excitedly walked down the chute to the paddock to watch the saddling-up. The day was warm and sunny, the turf lush and green, the flowers in resplendent full bloom. Ascot in June! A dream I had never dreamed in my barefoot, bareback South Carolina summers.

I was impressed with the finery of the rich leather tack and rustling silks, no less than with the horse beneath these trappings. Arundel was a fine-looking colt, I noted as Bunny delightedly pointed out the strength of his lines to me, pleased with my understanding of the animal's conformation. I met Tim, the jockey who would be up today, a slight young boy full of smiles and high hopes.

"He's run well in his other outings," Tim told me, "but he's yet to win a big one."

I ventured that this would be the day, and gave Tim my handkerchief to wear in his sleeve for luck. Then I noticed the white patch on Arundel's right front fetlock.

"Where I come from," I said postively, "that is the mark of speed."

Bunny laughed and said that was one he'd never heard, but he was willing to believe in anything today. I lingered a moment, before we left, to give Arundel a careless hug, inhaling that wonderful conglomeration of odors that every horse-lover could identify instantly: hoof oil, liniment, saddle soap, cresol, and new-mown hay. He blew softly on my ungloved hand and gave me a nuzzle with his head.

"He's definitely a winner, Bunny," I laughed, as we made our way back, with one more stop to place bets under the colorful umbrella of a bookmaker's stand. Feeling confident, I put five pounds on Arundel to win.

Then we just had time for a glass of champagne in the clubhouse before the seventh race was called.

The pounding of hooves on manicured turf is no different from the pounding of hooves on dusty South Carolina back roads. It is not the sound that is different at Ascot, but the lack of sound. The minute the horses left the starting gate, I was on my feet, cheering madly for Arundel, while in the grandstand and other boxes, and no doubt within the royal enclosure could be heard, barely, the polite clapping of gloved hands.

The field stayed bunched together to the quarter-mile post, when one horse pulled ahead to set the pace. Through Bunny's powerful field glasses, I searched in vain for the purple and white silks of Haversham Stables. Then, as the pack rounded the far turn, a second horse pulled out. It was Arundel, with Tim bent low over his neck. I could almost hear his words of encouragement as the two lead horses left the rest of the field far behind and raced toward the backstretch. Tim did not lift his whip. He didn't have to. Smooth muscles rippled under glistening flesh as Arundel moved ahead, crossing the finish line with an easy three-length lead. He had won!

The day was Bunny's, and he made the most of it, red-faced and stiffly dignified as he posed for photographs with Tim and Arundel in the winner's circle; more relaxed but still red-faced as he accepted congratulations at his club's tent; full of unrestrained glee, his normal color at last restored, as we drove back later to London. We had supper in town before I returned to the St. James to change for the theater—for, in spite of the excitement of the day, I still had to perform that night—and Bunny went on to a round of Ascot parties.

When he left me at the hotel, he kissed me for the first time, not a kiss of passion or desire, but a warm kiss, a comforting kiss, a kiss that clearly thanked me for sharing this fine day with him. Perhaps, I thought as I entered the suite and closed the door behind me, you are growing up, Kate, and for once not jumping headlong into an affair, but enjoying instead an uncompli-

cated friendship with a man. Still, I could not help but
wonder whether that warmth and comfort could ever
develop into anything more.

As I took off my Ascot finery, I tried to imagine
making love to Bunny. I stood naked before the mirror
and conjured him up beside me, his thin frame exposed,
his soft, pink skin touching mine. I looked deep into the
mirror and imagined him there. He turned to me; our
loins touched; his lips found mine as we embraced—
Then the mirror's image grew faint, fluttered, and disappeared from view. No, the scene was quite impossible! I was sure it could never be played. Bunny and I
would remain friends, each making an unspoken bar-
gain with the other. As the debonair man-about-town
who was the escort of Katherine Lawrence, Bunny
gained status in the eyes of his contemporaries, and I
visited the best restaurants and clubs of London, met
the cream of society, glimpsed the Prince of Wales at
parties, and enjoyed myself thoroughly. Bunny was a
calming effect in the maelstrom that surrounded Terry
O'Neill . . .

Terry's plans for renewing his life with Sian were obviously not working. Oh, his performances were as fine
as ever, but underneath, I could see the naked edge of
erratic behavior beginning to emerge. I had to wait for
days for an opportunity to discuss Sian with Terry. My
chance came just before the end of the run, when we
both arrived early at the theater and sat down in my
dressing room for a cup of tea.

"What a long time since we've had a chance to relax
and talk together."

"I know, Kitty, dear; it seems like months, rather
than a few weeks."

"How have things been with Sian?"

His answer came slowly, and was carefully worded.
"We're existing in an armed truce, cordial, almost
friendly, but there seems to be little chance of restoring
a life. The best I can hope to do now is prevent real
danger."

I remembered how he had spoken, before she had

arrived, about revolutionary acts. The words still struck me as melodramatic until I remembered something else: Sian's face and the intensity I had seen there.

"Is she involved in something dangerous?" I asked.

"She's always surrounded by danger. I'm sympathetic to her cause, for Ireland deserves to be free, but the underground group here in London—"

For some reason, a shiver of apprehension went through my body. "Oh, Terry, please don't get involved."

"No, no, I won't. I was afraid for a while, I don't mind telling you. But it's all right now. Sian's a strong woman, but I think she still loves me, and I think I can change her mind. I'm sure I can."

I should have questioned him further, but I did not. Perhaps I didn't believe that the revolutionary acts he alluded to could be so terrible. Or perhaps I didn't want to know.

"Terry, promise me you'll keep safe," was all I could ask.

"Of course, my darlin'. And will you promise something for me?" I nodded. "Promise that you won't give yourself to Lord Bunny."

We both laughed, but he was serious. "I know that we can't be together, but I can't bear the thought of you with him."

I wanted to respond in a way that would be honest, yet would not hurt Terry. "Bunny and I are friends," I admitted, "and I like him, Terry. But we are not lovers, nor will we be."

"Bless you, Kitty, that helps." He kissed me lightly on the forehead. "Now, watch that second act curtain. You're coming in late." With a wink, he was gone.

When Bunny and I were having a late supper after the performance, I thought again about Sian, and I asked Bunny questions about the political situation that I had not been able to ask Terry.

"The Irish, Katherine, are always up in arms over something. Not a very bright people, or so it seems. I understand, now, that they've given up all this shooting and bombing and are going to work through Parliament. They call themselves the Home Rule Party, and there's one chap—Parnell is the name, I believe—who seems to be taking the lead." Bunny took a sip of wine and then, as if he'd just remembered, added, "Right now, Her Majesty, Disraeli, the Foreign Secretary, and the others are too involved in this Russo-Turkish thing to waste time and energy with a rag-taggle of potato-eaters. Forgive me, Katherine, if I sound cruel, but the Irish question simply isn't important when compared with the possibility of war with Russia."

"Why doesn't the Queen just give them what they want? Give them their country back?"

"Well, I daresay things are a bit more complicated, Katherine, but under no circumstances would the British Empire willingly give up its possessions. You Yanks had to fight for your freedom." He spoke that last quietly, and not without a blush.

"That may be why I'm sympathetic, even though I'm not political."

Something in my head clicked when I made that statement, and for a moment I thought of what Terry had said about the innocent being hurt, but as Bunny responded, I dismissed the memory of Terry's words.

"Soon you'll be sounding like a member of the Irish Republican Brotherhood. Ireland is a part of England, and that's that. They are the ones causing trouble—seizing ammunition, ambushing soldiers, blowing up depots. Did you know they tried to blow up Prince Albert's statue in Phoenix Park?"

"Oh, Bunny, I don't know whether to laugh or cry—at the English, at the Irish, at Victoria, at the underground. I guess I admire the rebels for their hopeless fight. At least they're committed to a dream."

"But the dream is destructive and illegal, Katherine."

"From your viewpoint, Bunny, not from theirs. Oh, I don't want to argue with you, dear."

"No, no, Katherine, certainly not," he stammered. "Come now, let's talk of something more pleasant."

Bunny could not tolerate anything approaching contention, and I, too, was just as willing not to discuss the Irish, but I continued to think about their plight, and somehow I felt a secret connection with Sian because of my own commitment to the stage and to my dream, even if that dream was of much less heroic proportions than hers. Whatever she might do here in London, I applauded her courage, not knowing, then, that her acts would affect my future and bring drastic changes into my life.

Two days later, we closed in London. All preparations had been made for our Dublin venture. The scenery and props would be packed up and shipped ahead after the final performance, and the troupe would follow in three days' time, sailing from Holyhead on the overnight ferry across the Irish Sea.

All during our last week, I had been receiving intriguing bits of mail penned in a bold hand. Poems, letters, short notes, all were from a young student, a poet and playwright he called himself, who promised to attend the final performance with a claque from Magdalene, his college at Oxford. The young man, whose name was Oscar Wilde, described himself as my most dedicated fan, having seen *The Gypsy and the Soldier-Count* five times, and having, just last week, lovingly removed my picture from the theater lobby to place it where, he said, God surely intended—in his own rooms, above his bed. All of his correspondence began, "Priestess of Beauty," and went on to laud me in such terms that I was embarrassed to show anyone the letters. But something told me to keep the poems, and I placed them carefully inside the worn front cover of my cherished book, *The Memoirs of Mrs. Siddons*, where they remained for many years.

My appearance on closing night was greeted by overwhelming applause, which I gathered to be Mr. Wilde and his friends. Terry met the challenge by raising the level of his performance, and thus inspired us all. The final curtain calls were endless. Now, I thought, if only Dublin were half as accepting.

I greeted friends and fans briefly in the green room

before Terry, Drew, Aurora, and I made our way to the
stage door, where a carriage was waiting to take us to
Sir Giles's farewell party at the St. James. Drew pushed
open the heavy stage door, and when I stepped out onto
the street, a deafening cry went up: "Katerina! Katerina!"

Stunned, I looked out on a sea of faces, as a young
man emerged from the crowd and made his way toward
me, holding a single red rose. He bowed low over my
hand, presented the flower, looked dreamily up at me
through heavy-lidded eyes, and sang out, "Oscar Wilde,
at the service of the Priestess of Beauty whose carriage
awaits."

I decided to play the role he had chosen for me.
"Monsieur Wilde, enchanté."

He made a sweeping gesture toward the carriage, but
before I could take a step, he had removed his evening
cape and flung it onto the street before me. I placed one
foot on the satin lining and then boldly walked over the
cloak to the open carriage. He handed me up the step,
but before seating me, he called out, "Gentlemen, Miss
Lawrence has no flowers. Shame on you."

Like rain from the sky, I was deluged with flowers of
every color and kind, pouring over me and falling into
the carriage. As Drew and Terry watched openmouthed, I took my seat upon a bed of flowers.

"But Mr. Wilde," I laughed, "this carriage is not
going anywhere. There are no horses."

The amazing Mr. Wilde raised his hand, and six of
his husky peers stepped forward, lifted the carriage
rods, and moved off easily in the direction of the St.
James, with the rest of the students forming a phalanx
on either side as, like Cleopatra, I was drawn through
the still-crowded streets of London. The exhilaration of
the moment reached me and, to Mr. Wilde's delight, I
came to my feet, my arms filled with flowers, the wind
blowing my cloak and hair. I scattered blossoms into
the night air and watched them fall into the laughing,
applauding crowds. I reveled in my youth, my beauty,
my happiness. I was riding in a carriage to the future,

where anything was possible. I would conquer Dublin, I would play Shakespeare, I would be reunited with Nick. I was a star. Anything was possible.

The distance from the heights of euphoria into the depths of hell is great, but the fall from one to the other takes but an instant. Sometimes I look back and try to reconstruct those events in Ireland. I am able to put them in order but not in perspective, and even now I don't understand. I will never understand.

The passage across was uneventful. We boarded the ferry at Holyhead and disembarked at Kingston, the port town a short distance from Dublin. Sian did not, as we had expected, accompany us, but stayed behind for another week in London—a strange decision, but one that filled me with relief, although even without Sian, Terry seemed tense and nervous, quick-tempered and morose by turns. Since he was not willing to talk, I avoided him, and so avoided conflict.

We docked in the predawn hours. Through the darkness I was barely able to make out the shoreline, and as we entered the harbor, fog enveloped us completely. The air was cold and damp, and the mist settled with clammy fingers on my skin. There would be no sight of rolling green hills or smell of heather this night.

We were greeted by uniformed officials and asked to wait in a large, barnlike structure, while our baggage was checked by customs. There had been a few other passengers on the ferry besides our troupe, but they were quickly cleared while we waited, a handful of bedraggled actors huddled in the corner of the cavernous, drafty building while custom officials moved aimlessly among our belongings, examining trunks and checking name tags, but making no attempt to open anything. The sharp sound of their boots on the stone floor echoed eerily off the distant walls. Terry paced and cursed under his breath.

"The fucking blighters, what the hell are they doing?"

"Looks like they're waiting for someone," Evan said.

Just as he spoke, the doors were flung open and five men, officers of the local English regiment, entered.

"What is this?" Evan asked, stepping forward with great dignity to face the soldiers.

"Pardon me, sir," one of the officers answered. "I'm Captain Townsend, and we have orders to inspect your baggage."

"I'll be damned if you will."

Terry moved away from the group toward the trunks piled helter-skelter in the middle of the floor. "This is an American company, and we demand—"

"In point of fact, Mr. O'Neill," the captain interrupted, "you are not an American citizen. You were born in County Galway, Ireland, and are therefore a citizen of the United Kingdom."

We did not have time to wonder how the officer knew Terry, much less his birthplace, because his next words were so outrageous. "We have papers here entitling us to search for contraband weapons."

"Oh, Good Lord," Evan exclaimed, "we're actors, not revolutionaries, and we are most certainly not carrying weapons."

His words were backed up by a murmuring of dissent from the rest of the cast. The captain ignored our protests.

"If we may proceed. Men?" He gestured to the soldiers, who began to rummage through the trunks until they found what they were looking for.

"Here's O'Neill's, sir."

"Go ahead," Terry jibed. "You'll see what bloody fools you are."

I moved to stand beside Terry and prevent, I hoped, further antagonizing outbursts.

As we watched, the soldiers bent over Terry's trunk. "Locked, sir," a young sergeant reported.

"May I have the key, O'Neill?"

"I'll see you in hell first," was Terry's answer.

"Come now, Terry," Evan pleaded. "We'll put an end to this foolishness sooner if we cooperate."

"Never."

Captain Townsend shrugged and nodded to one of the men, who lifted his rifle and brought the wooden butt down sharply against the lock. It sprang open; the top was lifted: clothes, only clothes.

"Check the woman's," came the order, and the men moved toward my trunks. Terry lunged forward, but was restrained by Evan and Drew.

"Go ahead, Captain." That was my voice, cool and clear. "I have nothing to hide. Two trunks are mine: this large one with personal belongings, and the smaller trunk with costumes and makeup. The keys are on this ring."

"No, Kate." Terry's voice sounded strangled. "Don't give them the satisfaction."

But I had already handed over my keys. Quickly and thoroughly, the soldiers looked through my clothes in the first trunk, and then turned to the other, but as the key was fitted into the lock, Terry broke from Evan and Drew and flung himself at one of the soldiers, knocking him aside.

"She had nothing to do with it, believe me!" he yelled. "I planned it all—" The soldier steadied himself, leveled his rifle, and Terry froze.

"Terry, what are you saying?"

As I spoke, the trunk was opened and, instead of the costumes I expected, rifles spilled onto the floor with a sickening clatter. One of the soldiers lunged forward and grabbed me, holding my arms behind my back. When Terry saw that, he let out a terrible roar, knocked away the gun that was held on him, and threw himself at my captor, his fist crunching into the soldier's face. Terry's eyes blazed as he bent toward me.

"Get in touch with Bunny," he said. "You'll be all right." With that, he scooped up a rifle from the pile on the floor and pounded across the stone floor, through the open door, and into the pale dawn.

For a fleeting moment, no one moved. Then the captain yelled out an order, and two of the soldiers raced after Terry. I followed, with Aurora's hysterical screams ringing in my ears.

I heard the cry to halt behind me, but I kept going, desperately, after Terry. I ran across the narrow street that separated customs from the docks, and up rickety wooden steps. Unable to see into the distance, I rushed blindly straight ahead. I heard the faint moan of a boat horn. I heard my own breathing. I heard my footsteps and those of the soldier behind me. Then a dim light broke through the sky and reflected on the water ahead. I stopped and looked around frantically. I was at the end of a pier. I turned in every direction. There was no way out. Through the mist I saw a uniform. The soldier was coming toward me, walking now, his rifle held casually by his side.

"All right, miss, just come along with me."

Over his voice, shots rang out, dozens of them in rapid succession. I turned toward the sound, to see Terry across the slip at the edge of the next pier. He was outlined for an instant against the rising sun, then he toppled over the edge. I stared in horror at the gurgling water, red with Terry's blood. The sun rose, and I began to scream.

Somehow I was led back to the building, where I listened to explanations of what had happened. I heard the words, "The prisoner was killed trying to escape." They echoed over and over in my brain, but I could not believe. All was a dream—a nightmare from which I would soon wake. But I did not wake. Aurora was sobbing; Sylvia stood motionless, her arms around little Maria; Drew was talking furiously with the captain.

"The prisoner was killed trying to escape," the captain said to him again. "And this woman is the only one who can explain where the guns came from and why they were in her possession. Sergeant, escort Miss Lawrence to the carriage." He turned back to Drew, who was still shouting at him uncontrollably. "We expect you, and the rest of these people, to continue to your hotel and remain there until our investigation is complete."

Over Drew's voice, Evan tried to be calm as he said, "You cannot do this. Miss Lawrence is an American citizen. You have shot our companion in cold blood, and now you are taking her away. I shall not tolerate it. I shall contact the American embassy immediately."

"Do as you wish; Miss Lawrence comes with us."

Quickly, I was led into the carriage. Numb with shock, I could neither act nor react as I asked, "Where am I being taken?"

"To Dublin Castle, ma'am."

I sat silent and motionless, not even daring to think, until I was hurried into Dublin Castle, down dreary corridors to the basement. I was seated in a straight chair. The air was thick and dank and filled with terrible odors. A major talked to me next. I never knew his name. He kept asking me over and over about Terry, Sian, the guns, the underground, and I kept answering, "I don't know, I don't know." But I could not make him believe me.

Captain Townsend stood quietly aside, watching. Desperately, I turned to him for help. "Captain, I gave you the keys myself, you remember! How could I have known? I didn't know, I didn't know!" The captain only looked at me cynically as the major continued his questions.

Sometimes the two officers would talk to each other, whispered conversations in the corner. I was able to make out only a few words. "Must break her—time is short . . ." Then the questioning would begin anew. Terry. The guns. Sian. Was I Terry's mistress? How long had we been lovers? Did I know of the IRB? What of the Fenians? Was I a supporter of the Clan-na-Gael? Had I brought over the money that had been used to buy the weapons?

I could only answer those questions about Terry and myself. Yes, we had been lovers, yes, yes! But no more . . . I asked for water. They refused. The questions continued, hour after hour.

"You've made a mistake," I whispered, "a terrible mistake. I know nothing. Nothing!"

At last I heard the captain say, "It's almost noon. Put

her in a cell for a few hours. Let her think about what's ahead. And no food."

The major nodded and called for the guard, a burly fat man with keys dangling from his bulging waist and a look of dissatisfaction on his gray face. Beside him was a slim young guard who remained silent.

The heavy man spoke. "She'll have to leave her outer garments here, Major."

I had not even noticed that I still wore my green velvet cloak and my hat, and clutched my reticule in one hand. I handed them over as instructed, along with the jacket to my dress, but I was suddenly chilly, and asked if I might keep the jacket. The fat man shook his head as he led me to the door.

"Remember, Larson," the major said, "no food or water."

I walked between the two guards, along dirt floors through more narrow halls, to a tiny cell containing a cot, a table, a basin, and one chair. Across the bed lay a drab gray article of clothing made of rough fabric.

"Put that on," Larson ordered. When I did not respond, he grabbed my arm. "Put it on, I said."

"No, I won't. My friends will be here soon, and I prefer to wear my own clothes."

"Put it on, you bitch, or I'll do it for you."

I knew I must control my anger at the ugly words which oozed from his mouth—that fat, horrible depository of filth. I knew I must avoid further confrontation until Evan arrived to take me away from here. I agreed to change my clothes. "If you'll please leave the room," I added as politely as possible.

"Leave the room! Hear that, Tibbet?" he asked the other guard. "The slut wants her privacy—like she wasn't used to taking off her clothes in front of men."

I lost control. The anger I had been carrying with me since early morning erupted as I sprang at Larson, my nails digging deep into the fat, grinning face before he was able to reach out and hold me away.

"Let me go, you pig!" I screamed.

He began to laugh loudly, spraying me with his spittle. "Pig! Don't confuse me with that whoremaster of yours; there's a pig for you—Irish pig."

"He's a hundred times the man you are."

He kept on laughing, his mouth like an open wound across his face. "Except that he's dead!" He pushed me toward the other guard. "Hold her, Tibbet, while I teach the bitch a lesson." His puffy hand found the top of my bodice, and with a great rip he tore the dress off. His eyes raked over me with dreadful certainty, and beneath the fat rolls of his stomach, I saw the pulsating evidence of his desire.

Resigned, I shrank back and spoke in a wooden voice: "Give me the dress. I'll put it on."

He hesitated before throwing me the garment, which I quickly slipped over my head.

"Just remember who's in charge around here," he snorted. "It's me, J. P. Larson." With the back of his hand, he wiped away the blood that I had drawn from his face. "And don't you ever forget again," he said. "Come on, Tibbet, let's get some grub." Then to me, "We'll be back."

I remained standing in the middle of the room long after they had gone. The nightmare had become a reality. Certainly, Evan was working even now to secure my release, but suppose he had to return to London? That could take days. Suppose the authorities were skeptical? I could be here for weeks, or—if I were not proven innocent—even years! No! Evan would find a way. He would go to Bunny, and I would be freed. But would the freedom come soon enough?

They did return, Larson and Tibbet, to take me to the interrogation room, where I faced more of the same questions, on and on, always the same.

Soon I stopped listening, repeating "yes" or "no" as if by rote, and shaking my head when there was no answer to give. My stomach churned and my lips were parched and my eyelids were leaden.

Finally, as my eyes fell shut and my head began to swim, I heard Larson say, "Better get some food in her, Major, before she's worse than useless."

I was led away to my cell, and Larson brought a meal of thin soup and hard bread. I wolfed down every morsel and longed for more, but Larson had disappeared. Thinking I might have a chance to rest before they came back, I lay on the cot and closed my eyes, but suddenly there were rats everywhere—crawling over the floor, pouring from holes in the wall, scurrying back and forth in search of a way to reach me, a way up onto the cot where I lay. I sat up frantically, my eyes open wide, as wide as only horror could force them.

There were no rats—only the tiny cell, filthy but bare. Yet from somewhere within the thick walls of Dublin Castle, I heard sounds—scratching, rooting, groveling sounds that were the unmistakable noise of rodents struggling, like prisoners themselves, to break free. I gathered the dingy gray skirt around me tightly, away from the edge of the cot. And I did not close my eyes again until, in despair, they closed involuntarily against the sight of Larson standing outside my cell. I heard the rattle of keys as he unlocked the door. He was alone. I looked around, and he answered my look.

"Tibbet's off tonight."

As I sat up, ready to return to my interrogation, he spoke again. "Major had to caulk off, too. Can't be expected to do his job without sleep." Panic began to build slowly within me, growing, growing like a huge mushroom in my brain. Before he spoke again, I knew what was going to happen, and I knew, with the same certainty, that there was nothing I could do.

"I'm off tonight too," he said with a leer. He sat down on the cot beside me, settling his great bulk with difficulty. There was no way to avoid the hellish descent into the dark abyss of human lust that awaited me, for he would have his way, ultimately, no matter how I fought, and my earlier fighting had only aroused him. I would not think of what was happening, and when it was over, I would forget. I meant to ease the pain and degradation by remaining calm and passive, but as soon as he touched my bare skin under the course fabric of my gown, I screamed. His hand clamped over my mouth, but then he took it away.

"You won't rouse nobody in these dungeons with your noise," he said as he bent over me, his foul breath and rank sweat enveloping me.

I closed my eyes and let my own breath come out in short spurts, through my mouth, to avoid the stench as I forced my limbs to relax. But what was happening was too horrible, a thousand times worse than anything I could have imagined. His fingers, with their dirty broken nails, spread my legs apart, searching frantically and then plunging inside me, digging and tearing, preparing the way for his manhood. Tiny, stiff, and loathsome, it would not damage me, but his fingers had already drawn blood and searing pain. I wanted to faint, but I could only lie there and be used in the vilest way until finally it was over and he rolled off me, pulling his trousers up over his fat belly.

"Cold bitch, ain't you?"

I turned my face to the wall and wished for death. I had always fought for life, but now I wanted only to die.

Hours later, Tibbet came for me. I didn't ask where he was taking me, but only followed docilely in the opposite direction from the interrogation room, down winding halls—the same halls, I realized, that I had traversed when they had brought me here. Then we began to climb, up familiar stairs. Possibly—

"Katherine, thank God!"

Evan's voice, and Drew was with him. I ran to them, holding on, crying now for the first time. Drew held me tightly in his arms, comforting me. "Everything is all right, Kate. We're taking you home. Here, we have your cloak. They can't seem to find the dress."

"I don't care. Just get me out of here."

They took me to Dublin, to a clean, comfortable hotel, and I was able to bathe away all evidence of what had happened, and to bathe away the memory as well. That memory was already fading and would soon disappear; then I could believe that it had never happened. I could never share it with anyone. Ever.

Later the same day, as we waited to board the ferry back to England, Evan and Drew told me how they had arranged my freedom. Evan had telegraphed Bunny, who had immediately contacted the Foreign Secretary and the Prime Minister. Official telegrams had been sent to the Dublin authorities, and I was freed.

"Terry?—" I started to ask.

"Evan will stay for the funeral," Drew answered quickly. "I'll get you back to London and then home, if that's what you wish."

"Just get me away from Ireland."

I clung to him for dear life. He continued to talk to me, calmly and soothingly, as we crossed the Irish Sea. Bunny was waiting in Holyhead. He had commandeered a private railroad car in which we traveled comfortably to London. I knew that Bunny, through his official channels, must have learned the details of the aborted Irish plot, and I urged him to share what he knew with me, so that I could purge my mind of the horror.

Drew moved away at the first mention of Terry. We would speak of him later, alone, but for now, although Drew had been my bulwark, he could not bear to listen.

Hesitantly, Bunny told me what he knew. Sian had placed the rifles in my trunk, apparently with Terry's cooperation, since she would not have had access to the theater. Why the rifles hadn't been shipped earlier with the sets, no one seemed to understand. I knew the reason: until the last moment, Terry had hoped to change Sian's mind. According to government sources, Terry had been involved in the plot for months, and had brought Clan-na-Gael money from America to buy the rifles. That had caused the anguish that I had assumed was due to worry over the play. Someone, probably a traitor in the revolutionary group, had warned the British, and now Terry was dead—a useless death, pitiful, and yet, ironically, right. Terry had been doomed, like so many other Irishmen who search for another life and find themselves irrevocably bound to their homeland. Zara had seen Terry's death in my hand. I had known, yet I could not stop the inevitable winding out of fate.

Bunny urged me to stay in London, where I would be able to rest and regain my strength, but I could not. The time had come to leave Europe behind and return to my family and friends. I kissed Bunny goodbye as I stepped onto the deck of my steamship at Dover. I knew that he had again pulled strings to book passage for Drew and me, but I did not need to proffer thanks. He understood.

Each night aboard ship, the sleep I longed for stretched out like a peaceful valley in my mind. I closed my eyes and climbed to the crest of a hill and saw soft, fluffy clouds hanging over a lush green valley below, and I felt as if I could just slide down the other side of the hill, tumble down and reach that wonderful sleep. But just as I started toward the valley, Terry appeared— Terry laughing and joking, Terry drunk and angry, Terry covered with blood—keeping me from sleep, making me think at last about what had happened to bring me to this place . . .

In my waking sleep, I searched for something that would make me accept his death, accept it and understand, and I clung to one thought: he had been a tortured man, and now he was at peace. I clung, but the thought was not enough. I was afraid he had died for nothing, for Sian's cause, not his own. He knew the rifles were in my trunk; he had probably placed them there. Why? Because I had asked him to face Sian, and she had asked him to face his destiny. I could only hope, but I could never be sure, that in the end he *had* died for a reason, for the land he loved. That hope would have to be enough to carry me through the rest of my own life. For a brief moment we had soared together, and I did not mean ever to forget him.

Drew and I ate alone at a table in the corner of the dining room, walked the decks in the warm June sun, and finally spoke of Terry. I told him of my sleepless nights and of my attempt to understand; I shared my feelings of guilt and found that he felt them too.

"We all did, Kate. We all remember times when we could have helped, could have understood, maybe could have prevented what happened. So don't blame yourself."

"No, I shan't. I believe, now, that Terry had to live out his fate, and none of us could have prevented what happened. I survived that terrible instant when I saw him die. I believe I can survive anything now."

"Kate, I want to finish what he began with you. Your careers were intertwined, and so much lay ahead. I know I can never take his place, but I want to try—for myself and for him. Do you think that's possible?"

"Oh, yes, Drew, yes!" I put my arms around him and held him close. Our faces were wet with each other's tears. "But let's remember Terry with laughter; that's what he would have wanted."

And so we remembered the good times. We talked about his fine performances and his tall tales, and we docked in New York carrying the essence of Terry in our hearts.

There they were to greet us—William, Glenna, Clara, even Lester. I was whisked off to the Piersons', wrapped in their love. They were kind about Terry, not asking too many questions, but comforting. I shared my thoughts with them, but my time in prison I refused to discuss at all.

That night, I slept soundly at last, and although I awoke early, I was rested. I lay in bed, wondering whether to get up and risk awakening the Piersons, when I heard their voices. I pulled on a robe and padded quietly down the hall to have an early-morning cup of coffee with them.

Just as I was about to push open the swinging doors to the kitchen, I heard Glenna say a name, the name that was my life, my all—Nick.

Unashamedly, I listened. "We can't tell her now, William. The child has been through too much. We must wait."

"She'll find out sooner or later, Glenna, and she should hear it from us rather than from the tabloids. After all, Nick—"

I could wait no longer. I swung open the doors.

"After all, Nick *what*, William? Is he back? Has he come home?"

Glenna moved to me and took me in her arms. "Darling, I wish that were true. Oh, how I wish it."

My heart, like an anvil, plummeted downward and began to pound madly. "What has happened, Glenna? Tell me, for God's sake."

"I can't. I can't. William, please," she said imploringly.

I knew he was going to tell me something dreadful, something I did not want to hear, yet something I must know. I turned and looked into William's eyes. They were sad and empty.

"Kate," he said, "we just learned that Nick is dead. He died in the Brazilian jungle and was buried there."

Those were the last words I heard before all went black about me.

ACT IV

"We know what we are, but know not what we may be."

Hamlet, Act 4, Scene 5

Chapter 1

The North Carolina mountains lay slumbering deep in September heat. By night the air was cooler, but during midday, Indian summer stretched, drowsy and inert, over the hills. I sat in the dark green shade cast by the pendulous branches of a towering pine, hoping to catch an occasional tremor of breeze. Looking across the sloping green yard, I could see the stone building that was both my sanctuary and my prison. It was called Aesclepion: place of healing, place of nurture, place of rest.

Of all the twists and turns taken by the tributaries of my fate, this was the most shattering. I looked down at my skirt, made of soft cotton delicately trimmed with lace, the tips of the patent shoes barely showing beneath the hem. A newly acquired cynical humor caused me to imagine that a stranger, coming upon me through the trees or across the lawn, would not even suspect. He would see a pretty young woman—beautiful, many had said—seated beside a giant tree, a large-brimmed hat shading her face from the rays of sun that sneaked through gaps in the pine's lustrous needles. Only when the stranger stepped closer would he see that the young woman was seated in a wheelchair, and her legs were useless. Lifeless and helpless. Kate Lawrence, who once danced as the winds dance through a field of wildflowers, would never dance again. Nor walk. She was a cripple, an object of pity, more to be avoided than wept over.

I clenched my fists against the arms of the wheelchair in angry desperation. Aesclepion and Dr. Meyer, its director, were my last chance. If there was no help here, then the course of my life was charted. I would return to Deaton to spend the rest of my years in this hated chair, hated even though its mobility offered my only semblance of freedom.

"Miz Kate, you about ready to go back?"

The voice cut softly into my reverie, and I looked up. "Yes, Jesse, push me back."

Although I could maneuver my chair in the corridors of Aesclepion and on the flagstone walkways, I needed strong arms to push me up the grassy hill to the building. Jesse, his bald head gleaming above his smiling ebony face, effortlessly swung my chair around and headed me back. He did not leave me at the walkway today, but pushed the wheelchair across the wide porch, through the lobby, and down a side hall which led, circuitously, to my room. Out of sight of supervisors, he guided me with abandon as we raced down the deserted hallway. I leaned back and laughed, an almost believable laugh, but not yet believable enough to fool Jesse.

"Lord, Miz Kate," he said as he brought the chair to a halt at my door, "I'm gonna make you laugh for real one of these days."

Jesse wheeled me into my room and left me there beside the bed. He had taught me to help myself, and by leaving me alone, forced me to do so. I slipped off my shoes and, with difficulty, lifted myself into bed, feeling no sense of accomplishment. I was no closer to walking, no closer to dancing. I lay back against the pillows and slipped involuntarily into my reverie again, a reverie in which memory wore a skeletal face.

At the news of Nick's death, I had fallen into a deep faint and then into an almost convulsive state. Terrible nightmares filled every corner of my tortured mind: Nick in the throes of death, deep in a jungle that I had never seen, but which was frighteningly real in my visions. I saw him writhing in pain, saw him set upon by hordes of gigantic insects, devoured by monstrous snakes, eaten alive by hyenas dripping bloody froth from mouths as large as the jungle. I heard him scream in agony and felt the pain myself. I could not have known how he died. William's words had told me nothing.

"He died in the Brazilian jungle and was buried there . . ."

But in my nightmares I saw him die a thousand deaths. I suffered all of these deaths with him until I finally awoke, days later, unable to move my legs. When Nick died, my will to live died with him. Yet I lived on. Alone.

Almost a week had passed since Laurel Ann's departure, and I had talked to no one except Jesse. I could have taken my meals and treatment with the patients, or sat with them in the solarium, but as consuming as my loneliness was, I preferred that to being with the others—men and women sunken in melancholy as deep as a grave.

I sighed audibly and turned myself in the bed, thinking of the first doctor who had examined me in New York after I had regained consciousness. I remembered his equivocation, the nervous gestures with which he punctuated each hesitant sentence. He had told Glenna and William that I was apparently suffering from brain fever for which various treatments were recommended, all ineffectual. Alarmed, the Piersons had called in more physicians—an internist and a neurologist. Neither could find a cause for the paralysis. Without a cause, there was no cure.

More doctors moved through the haze of the next

week and the next—more tests, more glum faces, more
evasive answers to my fevered questions. Then, one
day, Jamie had arrived.

"I'm taking you home, Kate," he said. "All you need
is your family around you and plenty of rest." The trip
in the sizzling heat of August was grueling, changing
trains a nightmare, with Jamie carrying me from car to
car, sweat soaking his shirt.

Jamie had been wrong; home did not help. I still
could not walk. I could only lie in bed, perspiring in the
waves of heat that seeped into the room through curtains closed against the sun, unobjecting as Laurel Ann
massaged my legs, as if the strength in her hands could
be transferred to me.

Letters arrived daily from New York, letters of encouragement from the Piersons, Clara, and Johnny, and
from abroad. Somehow Bunny and even Sasha had
been notified of my illness and had written words of
hope and love. But hope was not enough, nor was love.

Drew and Lester plied me with manuscripts of plays
for the spring season, Drew's accompanied by remind-
ers of our future together. I answered the letters briefly.
The plays remained untouched. Not only was I
swamped with mail, but visitors came and went from
the house in Deaton, and I imagined their whispered
comments as they descended the stairway near my
room.

"Kate Lawrence was always so lively. Now look at
her."

"Kate Lawrence lived fast and loose. She danced to
the piper and now she must pay."

I did not hear the words, but spoken or unspoken,
they were in the air. I must pay with pain for the kind
of life I had led. There was no other reason. There was
no other answer.

With Thelma in tow, the loquacious Martha Goodwin had called almost daily, and it was she who told
Laurel Ann about Aesclepion. Her cousins, Irene and
Carlyle Wharton, mentioned the sanitorium often and
with respect, she assured Laurel Ann, for the director

was said to have cured "hopeless" cases: a man who had been blinded, a woman who had lost the ability to speak. The stories might be exaggerations or outright lies, but Laurel Ann and Jamie were willing to grasp at any straw. I was noncommittal. Taking my silence for acquiescence, they had brought me to Aesclepion. Laurel Ann stayed with me for two days. I did not feel homesick when she left; I had been home, and home had not helped.

Here at Aesclepion, a program had been arranged for me that included exercise, massage, mineral baths, and a special diet, all of which I followed dutifully, for every moment filled was a moment free of memories. But though I threw myself into the program, and though a healthy color soon tinged my cheeks and skin, I remained a hopeless cripple. Nor could I stop the darkness from falling, bringing tortured nights filled with terrible, unremembered dreams.

Today the regimen would be expanded to include sessions with Dr. Meyer. Jamie and Laurel Ann had met with him when they brought me to Aesclepion, but I had yet even to see the redoubtable doctor, and I wondered what the sessions would be like. More examinations and useless treatment, I supposed.

A shadow crossed my bed, rousing me from my thoughts, and the curtains began to flutter crazily in the sudden wind. I looked out the window at the blackening sky. Autumn was approaching. Soon, if I remained at Aesclepion, the air would be too cool to sit outside, and I would be confined absolutely to my chair and my room. Jesse scampered in to close the windows.

"Rest period's over, Miz Kate. Time to see the doctor."

Five physicians in New York, two from the Medical College in Charleston who had examined me while I was at home, and now Dr. Meyer; would he be just another in the long line of experts without answers? And yet a flicker of hope darted unwittingly across my heart, causing me to feel suddenly afraid, afraid of the pain that would come when, once more, the hope proved groundless.

I lifted myself into the chair while Jesse watched proudly. "You're my best patient, Miz Kate. I'm sure gonna miss you when you get well and leave us."

He had no doubts. Just a matter of time, Jesse kept repeating; the doctor can work miracles when his patients have the will. Though Jesse did not believe my laughter, he had never seen my tears. I had kept from him my deepest feelings of despondency, and in doing so, helped to keep them from myself.

When we reached the doctor's study, Jesse knocked softly, pushed open the door, and let me wheel myself in. I knew his face was beaming at the director from behind my chair. Dr. Meyer came around his desk to greet me, a huge mountain of a man in his fifties, dressed in a rumpled frock coat, dark trousers, and a cravat that was decidedly askew. He was certainly not the forebidding presence I had expected.

There was to be no treatment, I soon realized; in fact, the doctor did not even examine me as all the others had. He returned to the oversized chair behind his desk, sat down, and began to talk with me as a friend would, easy conversation, touching on many subjects that were close to me. He told me about himself, speaking in a voice slightly accented with a European inflection. His conversation answered many of the questions that had been churning in my mind since my arrival at Aesclepion.

Gustav Meyer had been born in Austria, and had come as a young doctor to America with his bride. After practicing for several years in New York, he and his family—there were four Meyer sons—had moved South to open a sanitorium in the hills of North Carolina. Dr. Meyer was a warm man, an easy, friendly man who made me relax, even laugh. If his intent was to win me over, he succeeded admirably. I saw no possibility that these talks, which were to continue day after day, would have any effect on my paralysis, but they did help to cure my loneliness. From time to time, as he spoke, Dr. Meyer glanced at an old-fashioned watch which dangled on a heavy gold chain across his broad abdomen.

"My grandfather's," he explained. "It is large and cumbersome, but—" He shrugged.

"It's important because it was in your family," I finished for him.

"Yes, Miss Lawrence, exactly." He beamed at me, soft, gentle eyes alight above his dark brown beard. I could not help thinking of a stuffed animal I had had as a child—a big brown bear which lay comfortably for many years among the pillows on my bed, and this thought, too, pleased me.

"Now, Miss Lawrence, we shall talk about you. How have you been feeling?" He looked at me over the rimless spectacles that perched precariously on his nose.

No! I did not want to talk about myself! I wanted to continue in this pleasant, easy vein. I looked away, not answering, and then I tried to change the subject as I asked about the leatherbound volumes that lined the wall of his study.

He frowned and leaned toward me. "You have a deep sadness, Miss Lawrence. Will you tell me about it?"

All at once, almost against my will, everything came out in a painful gush, as if a dam of heartache had at last given way within me. I told him about Nick during that first session—and the second—and the next. Tears flowed as I spoke, but I ignored them. The tears were just an outward sign of my inner sadness, and neither concerned nor embarrassed me. I realized that I had not talked to anyone about Nick since I had learned of his death. My friends and family had avoided mention of him, not wanting to upset me further; the subject was too painful, they thought, and so did I. But we were all wrong. Talking about him helped me live with the awful truth. Nick was dead. All my tears could not bring him back. He was dead.

"I shall never forget him, Dr. Meyer," I vowed.

"I know that, Katherine, but as time passes, the pain

will grow less. Though it may leave a scar, the wound will heal."

"I feel as though when Nick died he took part of me with him. I can live without him, but I can never be complete without him." I cried out then the dreaded thought that was always with me. "I will never walk again!"

"Yes, you will, Katherine, if you want to."

"Want to? Of course I do."

"Why do you think you're paralyzed?"

I knew why, but I could not answer. As at our first meeting, I looked away.

"I want to hear what you think, Katherine."

The pain I carried was personal and shameful. I had long thought I would never be able to share it with another soul, but when I looked into Dr. Meyer's eyes, I saw there a trust so absolute that I could hold back no longer. "I think I deserve what happened to me."

His expression did not change as I unburdened my guilt over the life I'd led. I told him about Terry, relived the dreadful night, the soldiers, the shooting. If I had cared enough to listen when Terry needed so desperately to talk, I confessed to the doctor, Terry would have told me about the guns, and the Irish Sea would not have run red with his blood. And if I had cared more for Nick than for my career, I would never have gone to London, I would have stayed in New York. But they were both dead now—the gypsy's prophecy proven true, twice over. On and on I went, mired in self-castigation and guilt. Dr. Meyer let me talk until there were no more words, just as, before, he had let me vent all my tears.

"This may be difficult for you to believe now, Katherine, but you are not to blame. I can help you to understand this, and I can help you to walk again. I can, Katherine. I can cure you."

His words echoed in my brain, and while my brain refused to believe, my heart longed to, and my own response was almost a plea. "How could this be possible?"

"Have you ever heard of hypnotism?"

"Yes. I've seen hypnotists perform—in theaters and sideshows."

"There are other uses. Medical uses. Amazing results have been achieved with illnesses like yours."

"Through hypnotism?"

"Yes. By hypnotizing the patient, we have found that we can cure illnesses that somehow respond to no other treatment. I would like to use hypnotism as part of your treatment, Katherine."

I was confused by this new possibility, and not at all sure I wished to submit myself to something that seemed more like magic than medicine.

"I must have time to think, Dr. Meyer."

"Naturally. I would not want it any other way."

Between interviews, I still followed the regimen mapped out by Dr. Meyer. The weather cleared, and I bathed daily in the thermal springs of mineral water, continued the exercise and massage. Late one afternoon, sitting in the solarium, I began to think seriously about the treatment Dr. Meyer had suggested. His thoughtful words about hypnotism vied with images of craggy carnival performers shrouded in long black cloaks, who mesmerized members of the audience into states where they crowed like roosters or barked like dogs. The idea of being helpless under another's control was unacceptable to me; yet I knew that I could trust Dr. Meyer.

Jesse appeared at the door of the solarium and crossed toward me, a smile on his face. He was holding an envelope, which he handed to me with a flourish. The note within was written on expensive cream stationery, with one sentence scrawled in blue ink across the page:

Katherine, I must see you right away.
                              J. Carlyle Wharton

Carlyle? I could not see him, not this sophisticated man by whom I had been feted as the belle of the ball, the toast of New York. To be visited by Laurel Ann's friends in Deaton had been bad enough, knowing what thoughts about me filled their heads, but to be visited by Carlyle was unthinkable.

"Tell him, no, Jesse. Tell him I am too ill."

"Yes, ma'am, Miz Kate."

In a few moments, Jesse was back. "The gentleman says he ain't leaving, Miz Kate. I guess you better see him, 'cause he says he's gonna sit there until you do."

"Oh, all right," I sighed. "But Jesse, can you fetch me my mirror and a brush?"

Jesse beamed. He returned in a flash, and quickly, with shaking hands, I brushed the fringe of curls about my face and pinched some added color into my cheeks. Obviously, J. Carlyle Wharton would not be put off until he accomplished his mission—one of mercy and pity, I surmised—so I might as well face him with a smile as with a frown.

He entered the solarium, his stylishly loose lounge coat cut to perfection, his high collar softly starched, an aura of impeccable grandness surrounding him as always. He reached out to me, taking my hands.

"My dearest Katherine. I would have come sooner if I had known."

If he had known of my paralysis? My lifeless legs? My wheelchair? My smile faded.

"Carlyle, please, I don't want your pity."

"Pity?" He took a seat beside me and, reluctantly it seemed, released my hands. "Why pity, Katherine? You are still the most beautiful creature I have ever known."

My look of disbelief caused him to continue, "I thought you lovely in Deaton, lovelier in New York, and exquisite now."

"I am a cripple, Carlyle."

"You are simply wounded, a beautiful, wounded bird who will soon fly again."

"I think not."

"There are doctors."

"I've seen seven physicians, and am now under the care of an eighth. You see the results." I indicated the despised wheelchair. My depression was heightened ten-fold in the presence of Carlyle, a healthy outsider who had known me when I was whole.

"There are doctors in Europe, fine doctors. If you are not progressing here, I would like to help. As your friend and a friend of your family, please allow me to."

"Carlyle, don't let your pity for me—"

"Why must you continue to use that word, Katherine? Can't you see I want to help because of my feelings for you, none of which includes pity."

I managed to smile again as I took his hand. "My doctor here, Gustav Meyer, says he can cure me."

"Yes, I have just spoken with Meyer, and I expect that, because of my casual mention of the man, Martha Goodwin convinced your family to bring you here. Rather than relying on Aesclepion's reputation, I would have taken the time to thoroughly investigate the director's credentials; therefore, I do feel some responsibility. In the month that you have been here, has any progress been made?"

"We have talked."

"Talked?" There was a hint of contempt in Carlyle's repetition of the word.

Suddenly our roles were reversed, and I began to feel protective of Dr. Meyer—if not of his abilities, then of the man himself, of his warm, gentle kindness. "He wants to hypnotize me," I said, unsure of the reaction this would bring.

"Hypnotism? What about electric therapy—faradization?"

I was unfamiliar with the term and could only shrug.

"Well," he went on, "I shall speak further with Meyer tomorrow. But for now, he has agreed that you may leave the sanitorium and have dinner at my chalet this evening. My sister expects you, and I shan't be refused."

I felt momentarily rebellious against Carlyle's manipulation, but then I realized that such direction and strength could be just what I, in my confusion, needed. I had barely nodded in agreement when he swung my chair around and headed me toward the lobby. He insisted on lifting me from the walkway into the waiting carriage, repeating the procedure in reverse when we arrived at Schloss Wald, his chalet near Asheville. The house loomed above us, massive against the darkening sky, and once inside, I was aware of a heavy spaciousness. Decorated in a style that was at once orderly and casual, it was almost too well-planned for the feeling of comfort that was obviously intended. High ceilings were beamed with dark wood, and a huge fireplace was flanked by heads of animals, shot, I presumed, by Carlyle.

There was an illusion surrounding my first evening at Schloss Wald, that I was here in the North Carolina mountains to rest and take the waters. No mention was made of my illness; the wheelchair was quickly put aside, and I joined Irene on the large divan, with Carlyle seated opposite us. The Whartons entertained me with stories of their trip to Paris, the state of the French theater—the Comedie Français and Bernhardt's latest triumph—and the ever-worsening manners of the Parisians. Not until after midnight, when Carlyle left me at the door of Aesclepion in Jesse's care, was the reality of my situation mentioned again.

"I believe your appointment with Dr. Meyer is at eleven in the morning," he said, and before I could answer, he added, "I'll be there."

"Carlyle, no, please—" I protested.

"But I shall, of course, dear child. If Meyer cannot help you within a reasonable time, then we shall simply find someone who can. As I said, I bear some responsibility in this. Until tomorrow." And he was gone.

"Seems like a mighty high-handed gentleman," Jesse mumbled.

"He's just used to getting his way, Jesse," I answered. But I laughed to myself, for Carlyle was indeed highhanded. He had not become a master financier because he took no for an answer; nor did I intend to refuse his decisions made on my behalf, when I so desperately needed someone to help.

The next morning, I warned the doctor of Carlyle's plan, which did not in the least perturb him. He only smiled and said, "I am glad that you had a pleasant time and that you have a friend nearby who cares."

When Carlyle arrived, promptly at eleven, Dr. Meyer showed the same equanimity as he told us about the sanitorium.

"Our hospital was named after those ancient sites dedicated to the god of healing, Aesclepius. There was an Aesclepion at both Cos and Epidaurus. There, the ill could find physical and emotional rest; here, we try to minister to those same needs of our patients."

"I understand your use of mineral baths and the related massage and exercise programs, but hypnotism?" Carlyle's voice was cooly inquisitive.

"To fully answer your question, allow me to go back in time," Dr. Meyer said. His voice, in contrast to Carlyle's, was warm and thoughtful. "I took my degree in neurology at the Medical School of Berlin, but I learned very early that treatment of the nerves and tissues of the body is not always adequate to achieve cure. My subsequent studies with Dr. Auguste Ambrose Liebeault in Nancy, France, and Dr. Josef Breuer in Vienna, introduced me to the use of hypnotism with cases of conversion hysteria."

"Hysteria?" I said. I did not like the sound of that.

"Don't worry, Katherine. What matters is the cure, not the label of your disease. Mr. Wharton," he said, turning once more to Carlyle, "since you are a friend of Katherine's family, I would like to tell you specifically what I believe to be the cause of her illness. She has experienced several severe traumas, more than even the strongest mind could handle. To escape the accompanying pain, she has turned her psychic anguish into a physical illness: her body has accepted her mind's suggestion that she is paralyzed, helpless, unable to face the world, a woman only half alive."

"But Dr. Meyer," I interrupted again, "this is no 'suggestion.' I *want* to move."

"Of course you do, and through hypnotism, I can

give you suggestions that you càn move. There may even be other frightening experiences that you will relate to me in hypnosis, which you may not now remember."

"You mean—"

"What, Katherine?"

"My dreams." I had told Dr. Meyer nothing of the dreams, but his eyes did not scold; rather, I saw understanding there, as if he knew of my fears and my reluctance to voice them.

I turned to Carlyle. "I would like to begin hypnosis," I said, adding with certainty, "I trust Dr. Meyer."

Carlyle seemed satisfied with the doctor's plan of treatment, which we would pursue for a month. However, Carlyle later assured me that if I were not improved in that time, he would contact other physicians.

I felt secure. Each man's strength—displayed in Dr. Meyer's confidence and Carlyle's determination—would be used to fight my illness. I put myself in their capable hands. They also agreed that I should continue to spend evenings at Schloss Wald, and I did not argue with this decision.

I was an easy subject for hypnotism. Dr. Meyer began by having me center my gaze on his gold watch. His voice urged me to concentrate on the watch as he held it up, letting it swing idly on the chain.

"Your lids are growing heavy, Katherine. You are feeling sleepy—sleepy. Your eyes are closing. You are sleeping; you are at peace. Relax, Katherine, relax." His voice washed over me as the ocean washes over shells on the shore, cleansing them until they lie exposed in the sunlight, nestled shiny and bright in the sand. So his voice cleansed my mind of all thoughts, loosening the tension that clung to me and washing it away. He became only a voice, which held me to him by the gossamer thread of my concentration. From far away the voice spoke softly to me: "Now, Katherine, raise your hand." Seemingly without volition, my hand rose, touched my cheek, and then returned to my lap. "Katherine, you will remember everything that we discuss. Everything."

And from far away, my own voice answered, "Yes, doctor."

"Fine. Now I want you to listen to me, and to believe. Nick is dead, but you are alive. You cannot atone for his lost life by giving up part of your own, nor can you hide from life because of your despair that the man you love is dead while you live on. You are not being punished. You could have done nothing to save Nick, or Terry. They were responsible for their lives, you for yours . . ." On and on the voice spoke, assuring me, encouraging me. "Now, when I count to three, you will awaken refreshed, with a zest for life, a will to get better, a desire to live. One . . . two . . . three . . ."

I was wide awake, and I remembered everything.

That first session made me relaxed and confident. Subsequent sessions broadened these feelings and added yet another—hope.

In the next week, the bud of hope began to blossom into the flower of reality as Dr. Meyer made suggestions to me, while I was in a hypnotized state, that I could move my limbs. First it was only my feet. I found, upon awakening, the slightest tingle of feeling. But this was a beginning—I could move! Tears of joy coursed down my cheeks. I wanted Dr. Meyer to hurry, to cure me all at once, to have me walking, but he would not. He insisted that we proceed slowly. As more feeling came to my feet and legs, he intensified the exercise and massage program in those areas. I wrote to my family, telling them about my progress; I wrote to my friends, telling them that I would be in New York by Christmas. I was sure, now, that I would be. And I told Carlyle.

He and Irene arranged a celebration dinner and toasted me with champagne. Carlyle was now convinced that Dr. Meyer could cure me, and was satisfied. As we returned to Aesclepion, there was something more I knew I must say to Carlyle.

"I wish that I could have brought more joy to you and Irene these past weeks. Now that my spirits are high, I want to apologize for the problems I have caused."

"I won't hear that, Katherine. You are always a joy, but in your illness, I think you became an even more precious treasure, too precious and beautiful to lose."

"I wonder that any man could have thought me beautiful in a wheelchair surrounded by so much sadness."

"I do not know about *any* man, Katherine. I can only speak for myself. I find you irresistible, and I want you very much." He leaned forward and kissed me tenderly on the lips, causing tears to well in my eyes. "Dear Katherine, don't cry."

"These are tears of gratitude, Carlyle, for your affection and friendship."

"Friendship? Perhaps for now, Katherine. But I shall want more than friendship from you."

I understood what his words meant, words that would remain in my mind over the next days.

Gradually I was able to lift my legs and bend my knees, and triumph lost its illusion of inaccessibility forever when I heard Dr. Meyer's voice saying, "Stand up now, Katherine. Lean toward me slowly, and push yourself up."

His voice alone moved me forward in the chair; his voice alone lifted me to my feet. When he brought me out of hypnosis, I was again seated opposite him.

"Whenever you are ready, Katherine, you will walk." His tone was conversational.

"Yes, I know." I remembered my earlier talk with Carlyle; his words were with me still. "As I learn to walk again, might I not also learn to care again—for Carlyle?"

"He seems devoted to you, Katherine."

"He speaks of more than devotion. He may love me, want to marry me."

"And you?"

"I don't know. From the moment I first realized that I could be healed, I began thinking again of the future, which seemed lost to me for so long. I don't want to drift as I once did, from one man to another, losing each to tragedy. I could not bear to return to that life, and yet I want to act again—and to love again."

"I'm proud of you, Katherine."

I smiled, but could not smile away my past. "One question persists, Dr. Meyer. If Carlyle does wish to marry me, what would he think if he knew about—my love affairs?"

"You must ask him, Katherine. Only then will you know."

I dressed with special care that evening, berating myself all the while for having left my glamorous dresses at home, but I managed to find something of the old Kate Lawrence magic under the patina of despair that had so long covered me. The ride to Schloss Wald was especially beautiful as I gazed from the window of the carriage that Carlyle had sent for me. The trees, which were just beginning to turn, flashed scarlet and gold and russet for a breathtaking instant just before the flaming sun settled behind the rocky face of a mountain peak, and the first star of evening blinked dimly in the suddenly darkened sky. On this star I said my final farewells to Nick, who would always be a part of me, but from whom, tonight, I would be released to a new life.

Something in my manner must have spoken to Irene's romantic nature, for she made her excuses and retired shortly after dinner, leaving us together before the roaring fire.

"You are looking lovely tonight, Katherine," Carlyle said. "In fact, lovelier than before, if perfection can be improved upon. Is your treatment progressing well?"

I tried to keep from smiling, but could not.

He saw the look, and he guessed. "Katherine—"

"No, please, stay there. I want to walk to you." I had not come to this, my most exciting performance, unprepared. Alone in my room after seeing Dr. Meyer, I had taken my first tentative steps, rested and tried again, until I was sure my legs would have the strength to carry me the short distance I had planned—the distance from the divan where Carlyle always seated me to his own chair beside the fire. Placing my hands on the table before me, I rose to my feet. The look on Carlyle's face was glorious as I slowly moved one foot, then the other—three steps, four, never taking my eyes from him. Just as I reached him, he opened his arms and I collapsed with shaky legs against him. After he settled me on his lap in the comfortable leather chair, I related each detail of my progress. Dr. Meyer had assured me that by November I would be able to return to Deaton, and shortly thereafter to resume my career.

"You plan to act again?"

"Acting is my life, Carlyle."

"Is there nothing else?" he asked, and although I understood the meaning of his words, I could not answer.

"Katherine, you have seen how I care for you. Even if you had never walked again, I still would have wanted you—just as I do now. I can give you so much, my dear. Please let me. Please say that you care for me, too."

"Yes, Carlyle. How could I not? But I hope you will understand that I must have my career."

"My sweet Katherine, you may have everything that you want. During the theater season we can live in New York; we can travel the remainder of the year. I want to show you Rome, Paris, Vienna, St. Petersburg. I want to give you the world. Marry me, Katherine, and I will make up for all that you have suffered." He drew me to him and kissed me with a gentle passion.

"I want to say yes, Carlyle, but I don't want to enter into a marriage without complete honesty." Quickly I told him of my love for Nick, of Terry and Sasha, and even of that first youthful experience with Drew.

A shadow passed over his face, and I thought I had lost him until, after a long moment, he turned to me.

"What courage you have, Katherine, to tell me these things. You are a beautiful woman, and I cannot deceive myself that other men have not loved you, but they are in the past. From now on, there is only the future. But you must be true only to me. Will you be faithful, Katherine?"

"Yes, oh, yes, my dearest."

Carlyle rode back to Aesclepion with me, again kissing me warmly as he left me at the door.

Now it begins, Kate, I told myself. You can have it all: happiness, a career, a man who loves you and will not leave you. The evening star had dimmed and was barely visible in the heavens.

"Goodbye, Nick, darling," I whispered.

My happiness was marred that night by the same terrible dream from which I had so often awakened, recoiling but unremembering. Tonight I remembered. I was in a tiny room, dark and dingy, from which there was no escape, and everywhere there were rats crawling across the floor, their fat, ugly bodies waddling from side to side, and every rat had a horrible human face, a face I had seen rise above me on a forgotten night . . .

"Have you dreamed this before?" Dr. Meyer asked when next we talked.

"I think so, but I can't be sure. I have had terrible dreams ever since Ireland. I wanted to tell you about them, but I knew you might help me to remember, and somehow I was afraid to remember."

"Under hypnotism, you will remember what your mind has blotted out. Are you afraid now?" I shook my head. "Then come, Katherine, for one final time. Look at my watch, concentrate. You feel your eyes becoming heavy . . ."

Dr. Meyer's voice led me back to Ireland, back to Terry's death, back to Dublin Castle. I saw the vile rats again, and I recognized the human face that masked each one: the face of the guard, Larson. I felt his filthy hands on me, I knew again his defilement of me. I remembered everything.

When Dr. Meyer woke me, I felt free at last of the bonds that had encircled my unquestioning mind and filled my nights with despair.

"Will I continue to dream about it?" I asked fearfully.

"I think not. Now that you have told me, you will not have to relive it in your dreams. But you must also tell

me, and honestly, whether you are frightened now of
having relationships with men." When I looked blankly
at him, he prodded, "Sexual relations, Katherine."

"No, I don't think so. Love has always been a glowing experience for me. Larson was a perversion which
will be wiped away by my life with Carlyle. I am not
afraid of Carlyle, doctor. He is refined and gentle and
kind. All I want now is to please Carlyle and care for
him as he cares for me."

And that he cared was obvious in so many ways during the last month I spent in North Carolina. Although
I remained at Aesclepion and continued my regimen, I
spent most of my time at Schloss Wald, sharing lazy
days with Carlyle, taking long rides and walking in the
autumn-painted hills behind the chalet. Irene's kindness
matched his. She was a rather reserved woman who, at
forty-one, had never married and was devoted to her
brother, but—according to Carlyle—was completely
charmed by me.

When business took him to New York, I continued to
visit the chalet daily. Irene wrote to Laurel Ann about
plans for the wedding, which would take place at the
Wharton family home in Savannah just after Christmas.
Of course, I wrote Laurel Ann too, almost every day,
and all my other friends as well—everyone I could
think of—to tell the news.

Delayed by inclement weather, Carlyle telegraphed
that he would arrive at Schloss Wald just before I was
to travel home to Deaton. Dr. Meyer cheerfully released
me early from the hospital, so that I could spend my
last two days at the chalet.

The first light snow of the season had begun to fall
when Carlyle arrived, his arms laden with packages
bearing the names of New York's finest stores.

"Carlyle!" I cried, "Good heavens!" and all semblance of sophistication fled as, like a child, I dived into
the boxes.

In one was a cloak of cloud-soft Russian sable, and
in the others were a magenta satin robe, a gold bracelet
molded to form a coiled serpent, and Italian leather

boots. Carlyle teasingly held onto the last box, a small square one, and my heart skipped a beat as I realized what it held. At last he placed the box in my trembling hands, and I opened it with a delightful gasp. An emerald ring, green as the ocean depths, surrounded by a circlet of perfect diamonds on a wide platinum band! Carlyle slipped the ring on my finger.

"There is no other like it in the world, Katherine, just as there is no other woman like you." He touched my cheek with a propietary air. "And soon you will be mine."

I sat curled up beside him on the divan until late into the night, and we talked quietly of our future and of my new role as his wife. Languidly, I lifted my hand to see dancing flames reflected in the emerald. Green fire. How like Carlyle to think of a ring at once exotic and elegant. I stole a glance at his aristocratic profile, silhouetted against the golden light, and felt a flickering of desire rise within me. Could we not celebrate our engagement by making love now, in this perfect setting? No—I dismissed the thought from my mind. Ours would be a traditional betrothal, our love consummated only after exchanging the solemn vows that would make us man and wife. Then would follow a lifetime of love. Across the room, the windowpanes were beginning to cloud with the gathering snow, but I was warm and safe at last.

Chapter 2

The days between Thanksgiving and Christmas fused together into one long holiday—my first in three years—among my family, with Laurel Ann happily taking charge. She had at last accepted the reality of Courtney's marriage, and was looking forward to the birth of her first grandchild. Jamie was slower to come to grips with his only daughter's new life, and he flinched markedly whenever his gaze fell on her blossoming figure, but the holiday spirit pushed cares into the background. We all ignored Jamie's scowling face, and soon he had no alternative but to brighten along with the rest of us. And for him and Laurel Ann, my engagement was true cause for celebration. Forgotten by both were my travels to New York and Europe and my success as a star on Broadway, unremembered too the horror of Ireland and my subsequent illness. I was about to achieve the ultimate status in their eyes: married life with a wealthy and distinguished man of good family.

The almost daily arrival of the delivery wagon from the depot was accompanied by the well-timed descent of a hoard of Laurel Ann's friends to cluck over my trousseau. Not only had I used catalogues to order from New York stores, but Glenna and Clara had shopped extensively for me. All bills were sent to Carlyle, who insisted that the trousseau be part of his wedding gift. But he was not entirely satisfied with gifts purchased for me by others, or even with the quantity of presents he had brought me from New York. He would not be content until I had received the one final, perfect token of his love . . .

One evening when I had just begun to recover, I wore Nick's necklace to dinner at the chalet. Carlyle casually asked who had given it to me, and when I answered truthfully, he made no response; in fact, the response did not come until weeks later, when I had returned home to Deaton. Late one afternoon, I was alone at Magnolias when the package arrived from New York: a Tiffany case containing a diamond pendant inset with Oriental rubies. Holding the opened case in my hands, I climbed the stairs in the fading sunlight. The house was unusually quiet as I went into my room. In the back of my top bureau drawer was the narrow silk-lined box that held Nick's diamond necklace. I picked it up and pressed the cool, almond-shaped diamonds for a moment against my cheek, then I slipped them back into the box and closed the drawer. The Tiffany case holding Carlyle's pendant I left open among my other presents on the table for the perusal of Laurel Ann's friends.

Courtney alone voiced skepticism over my approaching nuptials. She was now into her fifth month and, I thought, looked pale and drawn. However, she insisted that she had never felt better and, caught up in her determination, I agreed—almost. She was the first to see the pendant, which she held gingerly and in awe, but with a complete lack of envy. These were trappings that would never be hers, nor did she have any desire for them. In the same vein, she helped me sort through the lingerie that I had collected.

"Gracious, Kate, you have shifts and gowns and chemises in every color. Why, this set is the shade of a peach just before picking time," she said, conjuring up a color that only a country girl could know. She let the piles of fragile lingerie sift like a diaphanous rainbow through her fingers until she burst out with a mood-breaking cry. "Oh, Kate, he's so old! Why, he's over forty. How can you?"

In spite of her seriousness, I could not help but laugh. "Darling, I never think of Carlyle as old, but to be honest, he's not just over forty; he's nearly fifty!" I laughed again as she moaned.

"His age doesn't matter anyway. You just couldn't love him," she responded with all the knowledge of a new bride.

"But I do, Courtney. There are many different kinds of love." I held up my hand to stop the words that were forming on her lips. "I know what you're going to say, and I *don't* feel about him the way you feel about Buford, but that's first love and, well, first love is special. This is a different kind of love, Courtney, a wiser and, for me, more mature love. When I needed him, Carlyle was there. I owe my recovery as much to him as to Dr. Meyer, because Carlyle believed in me and encouraged me and loved me—yes, loved me. We will have a wonderful life together, a perfect life. A life we share completely." I moved beside her to sit as we often had since childhood, side by side on the bed. "At last I have someone who is always there, someone with whom I can share a home and a family. I've missed these things, Courtney. Now I can have them as well as my career, and I can do so much for everyone—for you and the boys and the baby."

She was not entirely appeased, but the serious look on her face was replaced with a mischievous one as she said, "Tell me at least that he's a good lover, and I'll stop pestering you."

My eyes must have shown wonder at her question.

"Now, Kate, I'm a married lady and know all about bedroom ways; can't you tell?" she said, pulling her dress across her expanding abdomen.

I laughed. "Remember that conversation we had last fall when I came back from France? Yes, I must admit, my innocent little Courtney has grown up!"

She nodded in agreement. "But that doesn't answer my question, and don't play the blushing bride with me, Auntie Kate. I read those clippings from New York and London—even some you didn't send yourself. I know about Terry O'Neill and that Frenchman—"

I threw up my hands. "So I am found out."

"I'm not sure what Mama and Papa know—probably everything—but they always pretend ignorance when they don't approve. I don't pretend, so tell me, *is* he a good lover?"

"Well," I answered slowly, choosing my words, "he is kind and considerate and gentle—"

"You haven't! Why, you haven't—"

"You little minx, I'm going no further with this conversation! Your Auntie Kate is a respectable woman now, who plans not just an old-fashioned wedding but an old-fashioned engagement as well, as her future husband expects. But," I said with a giggle, "I'll tell everything after the honeymoon!" We ended the conversation in laughter; still, she did not understand why I had accepted Carlyle. Married or not, Courtney was a child in so many ways, and even though we were close in age, in experience we were worlds apart, and I could not make her understand that to come at last to the end of my search for someone who would bring peace as well as love to my life was, more than anything, a relief. No, I could not explain this to Courtney. She would never understand, and I—I had no more use for the past.

Christmas week was an unending feast of good food and good spirits for everyone. Carlyle and Irene came to Magnolias for the holidays, and although our wealth could not compare with the Wharton's, I was proud of my family. Their warmth and love, their hospitality and charm, filled every corner of the house. Days were spent before a roaring fire, and nights under piles of eiderdown as the weather turned—for South Carolina—unusually cold.

The day after Christmas, sunlight broke through low-hanging clouds to warm us for the trip to Savannah, which we completed in a leisurely fashion, stopping overnight at the home of Carlyle's cousin, Nell Carson, and continuing on early the next morning, our numbers now enlarged by five—Cousin Nell and her children. Also converging on the Wharton home at Lafayette Square in Savannah would be other cousins, aunts, uncles, and more distant relations of Carlyle's from as far south as New Orleans. The one family member missing would be his daughter Augusta, who was studying abroad. Carlyle took great care explaining to me that he could not ask Augusta to interrupt her classes and travel all the way home just for a twenty-minute ceremony, and I did not disagree, although I suspected that he had not told all of the truth. Augusta was nineteen years old, and far more than miles separated her from the woman who, barely two years her senior, was about to become her stepmother. I doubted that she was ready yet to bridge an ocean and stand beside her father as he took me for his bride. I could not blame her. The winning of Augusta would take time.

For now, I turned my attention toward the Savannah guests and the luncheons, parties, and tea dances which would fill the remaining two days before our wedding. We would be married on December 30th and leave immediately for our honeymoon on Carlyle's yacht, now lying at anchor in the Savannah River; we would celebrate New Year's Eve as we sailed north toward New York. The beginning of a year; the beginning of our lives together. I held onto that thought, banishing all others.

Doubts nagged at me—the same doubts, I imagined, that have nagged at every bride through the centuries—as I was gathered up in the wedding festivities, all of which I seemed to be viewing through a curtain made of billowing lace and silk, of floral bouquets and colorful gift wrappings.

On our way to the parties, I did try to grasp as much of Savannah as possible, but even that was a veiled, storybook view. Cobblestones gleamed as white and smooth as polished marble; elegant homes rose from streets lined with palms and palmettos; charming parks and squares were bright green even in winter. The city of my wedding welcomed me. I was pleased that we would be visiting here often, although we would make our home in the mansion that was now being completed in New York, and spend holidays aboard the yacht or in the Asheville retreat.

As the view of my surroundings was dreamlike, so were the conversations I held with a myriad of relatives, conversations that danced in my head along with the laughter, the smiles, a whispered word from Carlyle, a touch. Some of the older ladies did manage to take me aside for down-to-earth intimate chats, remembrances they had of Carlyle and Irene as children, hints of Augusta's rebellion—a nice child, they told me, but rather spoiled—and assurances that I would capture her heart in time, as I had theirs. One of the ladies, Virginia Moody, Carlyle's ancient great-aunt, assured me that he was a "remarkable man."

"I know that, Aunt Virginia."

"But that's not all, honey. Did you know that it wasn't until a few years ago that he was able to get back the old Wharton Place on Lafayette Square? They lost it after the war," she confided. "He paid an incredible price, and I do mean incredible, to buy it back." Aunt Virginia lowered her voice to the barest whisper and leaned conspiratorily toward me, her wrinkled hands grasping the top of her cane for support. "The folks who lived there did not want to sell, but Carlyle—well, he got his way."

Laughing, I agreed as I looked down at the sparkling ring on my finger. "He usually does."

"Carlyle says everyone has his price, and I suppose he's right. Lord knows, he's worked hard enough, what-

ever else they say about him, with his banking, stocks,
shipping, land speculation, and I don't know what all. I
heard—" she leaned toward me once more— "that he
invested heavily in railroads, too. Practically everyone
of wealth has, though, don't you suspect?"

I nodded, her mention of railroads causing an instant
of pain as a memory tried to part the illusory veil
through which I had so far viewed my wedding festivities. Carlyle's investments had turned to gold while
Nick's had turned to dust, changing the course of my
life. Dust to dust . . .

"My dear, what is the matter?" Her aged voice trembled as she asked the question.

"Why, nothing at all, Aunt Virginia." I closed my
eyes and forced the memory of Nick away. "I just want
to find Carlyle. It's time I danced with my husband-to-
be, don't you think?" I flung myself into the dance, and
the comforting curtain closed about me to part only
once more, briefly, but with a terrible clarity, the next
morning as I dressed for my wedding.

Laurel Ann was helping me, and we were both chatting happily when the memory returned. The curtain
was torn back and an image of Nick appeared before
me. I saw him as clearly as I saw Laurel Ann. Had I
allowed myself to reach out, I felt sure I could have
touched him. When she saw the expression on my face,
Laurel Ann stopped in mid-sentence, and although she
could not have known what was happening, she took
me in her arms as if she did know. She held my head
against her bosom and so averted my eyes from the
image on which they had been locked.

"What is the matter, Kate?"

"Nothing. Just premarital nerves," I lied, trying to
tell myself that Nick was gone, and I must let his memory go too.

"Don't worry, darling," she said, smiling softly. "I
know you must have doubts, but we all had them—even
Courtney, deny it as she will. Just remember, Katherine,
that Carlyle's going to take care of you and make you
happy. Nothing else matters."

When I stepped back and opened my eyes, Nick's image had disappeared, and with it my doubts. I smiled, too, and bent down so that Laurel Ann could lift my wedding dress over my head and arrange the folds of candlelight silk as they billowed into place. Chosen and purchased by a man with great wealth and taste—Carlyle himself—the dress combined fine fabric and detail with simplicity of line. My hair was piled high, and Laurel Ann covered it with the veil of Brussels lace I had sent only six months before to Courtney. Laurel Ann stood back for one last approving look. Then, with a quick kiss, blinking back tears of joy, she left me to join the wedding guests.

I passed from the bedroom into the hall to meet Jamie at the head of the great stairway I would descend to become Mrs. Joseph Carlyle Wharton. Through the open doors of the parlor below, I could see the guests assembled. At the front of the room, Irene, my only attendant, stood in relaxed anticipation, her dark coloring beautifully set off by a dress of deep claret velvet. Beside her stood Carlyle in morning coat and gray striped trousers, perfectly composed. The wide sweep of the graceful stairway, each polished mahogany step banded in shining brass, seemed to beckon to me as the string music began and we started down the stairs.

As with many important occasions in my life, my wedding day became a blur of which I remembered only snatches: the rough fabric of Jamie's morning coat beneath my hand as we approached the minister; the smell of burning candles mingled with the fragrance of the flowers banked against the marble fireplace; the tears which spilled at last down Laurel Ann's cheeks; the serious demeanor of Courtney and Bufe; the still-damp hair and bright faces of Phillip and John. I heard my voice and Carlyle's repeating slowly the marriage vows; I felt his kiss, cool and light after the final blessing: "Those whom God hath joined together, let no man put asunder."

There was a sumptuous spread of food on the long Sheraton table in the dining room, but I don't remember eating at all, and even as I tried to be a part of my own wedding, I still felt, in my abstraction, no more than a spectator.

"Is all of this really happening?" I asked Laurel Ann when she and I were once more alone in the upstairs bedroom.

"Yes, darling, it is. You're just too excited to take everything in, but, goodness, you'll remember in years to come."

I nodded my head as I finished buttoning the jacket of my going-away outfit of bronze taffeta and velvet, also designed in New York at Carlyle's request. There was a knock on the door, and there stood Jamie and Carlyle. The time had come to leave. I pinned on the absurd little hat of feathers and ribbons that completed my outfit, gave Jamie and Laurel Ann a hug, and then took Carlyle's arm once more to descend the stairway, this time amidst a shower of rice and good wishes.

Our carriage rolled through the gathering twilight toward the river, and Carlyle, with an understanding that seemed to anticipate my own nervousness, drew me tenderly to him. The gossamer veil that had covered my wedding day lifted, and I saw everything clearly at last. The curtain had risen, and Carlyle and I were together on the stage. Our lives stretched before us.

Carlyle's tastes, however grand, had not prepared me for the palatial comfort of his yacht, the *Augusta*. It had five well-appointed cabins, a paneled dining room, luxuriously furnished with a heavy oak table and chairs of Spanish origin, a large Regency salon, and a small, austere study for Carlyle, as well as living space for the numerous servants and crewmembers, who were so quiet and efficient that I was aware of them only when they arrived, as if automatically, to attend to our needs.

To my surprise, Carlyle and I were not sharing the main cabin, my trunks having been placed instead in an adjoining stateroom.

Carlyle answered my questioning look: "Knowing the immense wardrobe and all the paraphernalia you glamorous women travel with, I suspected you would need space to spread out, but my dear, I am just here—" he indicated a heavy oak door— "if you need me." As usual, he had thought first of my comfort.

We stood together, watching through the portholes as the shoreline grew dim and the *Augusta* picked up steam, its screw propellers cutting efficiently through the water. Then Carlyle left me, and without help from the maid, whom I sent away, I unpacked my clothes for the voyage. For dinner—our first as husband and wife—I chose my favorite dress, a mauve cashmere which softly molded the outlines of my breasts, waist, and hips. It was sophisticated enough for Carlyle's tastes, yet more seductive than anything he had yet seen me wear. For my wedding night, I unpacked a lovely pale yellow gown, silken soft, with a matching peignoir trimmed in ostrich feathers. As I touched the airy feathers, a tremor of excitement ran through me. I realized how passionately I ached for the intimacy of our marriage bed, yet how glad I was that we had waited until we were man and wife for this night. Our discovery of each other would be heightened by our rising anticipation. What kind of lover would Carlyle be? I mused. He would not be like Terry, savage one moment, and childlike the next; nor like my Sasha, a greedy sensualist; nor would he set my very being aflame—no man could be Nick. He would be gentle, kind and thoughtful, bringing to our lovemaking the very traits I had witnessed so often in him, but he would be passionate as well, for he too had waited long. And I would be totally loving and giving, putting all other men from my mind and heart. This I had vowed and this pledge I intended to honor: "Until death do us part." I savored once again the total commitment of those words.

Our wedding dinner was a feast of Russian caviar on toast, juicy lobster, thin-sliced roast beef, jellied fruits, and flaky pastries. And I was ravenous—so ravenous, in fact, that Carlyle teased me unmercifully about my appetite. As I took the last exquisite bite of custard tart, I answered that I was simply making up for an entire

day during which I had purposefully avoided eating anything because of my nervousness.

"But you are nervous no longer, are you, Katherine?"

"Absolutely not! I've never felt more relaxed and
content," I said, placing my hand on his arm. I sat beside him at the formal table in the dining room. My
place had originally been set opposite Carlyle at the far
end of the long table, but as soon as the waiter had left,
we quickly rearranged the seating plan.

"There are some formalities that simply do not apply
on one's wedding night," Carlyle said. "And now that
we are both relaxed and content, let us toast ourselves
with champagne."

He reached into the brass-and-mahogany bucket beside the table and extracted a chilled bottle of champagne. Cubes of ice clattered deliciously as he replaced
the bottle with another.

"So as not to be disturbed by my steward, I had him
set out a large supply in advance."

We both laughed and sipped the sparkling wine as we
discussed our future plans. As soon as we had arrived in
New York and were settled in the Brevoort, I would go
at once to begin supervising the decoration of our town
house at Park Avenue and Forty-eighth Street. While
we discussed each detail, my thoughts occasionally
raced ahead to the night before us, but I was enjoying
myself so that even my desire for my husband was
muted by the exciting ideas we were sharing, ideas that
brimmed over in my mind and left room for little else. I
had seen many fine houses, not only in Savannah and
New York, but in England and France as well, from
which to glean decorating possibilities for our new
home.

"I've never had a home of my own, Carlyle, never. I
love Magnolias, but that is Jamie's. Otherwise, I've
lived in rented rooms and hotels and borrowed flats. I
want our home to be special."

"And so it will be; we will see to that together." He
asked about my friends in New York, and I lovingly

described Clara and Johnny, Lester and the Piersons, but without lingering on theatrical topics. He seemed relieved that I would occupy my time when we reached New York as his wife, not as an actress, but he did hasten to assure me that I could act again when the time was right.

"Somehow, at this moment, I can't imagine myself on the stage." I took his hand. "I can only imagine myself in your arms."

He saw the look of desire in my eyes, and I knew his own feeling imitiated mine, although his face, as always, revealed nothing. However, as midnight approached, he quickly drained the last of the champagne from his glass, and we rose from the table where we had sat, through many hours passed unnoticed, to walk arm in arm into the passageway.

My heart began to pound at the mere closeness of him. Too long had I been alone, sharing my bed with no man; now, there would be one man and one only— my husband. At the door of my stateroom, he took me in his arms, as I knew he would, and his lips joined mine in a long kiss. My mouth opened under his searching tongue.

"Katherine, I do love you so. I am the most fortunate man in the world that you belong to me at last."

His words, although spoken calmly, had a desperate ring that prompted me to assure him, "You're no more fortunate than I, darling, and certainly no happier."

He left me then, with one more tender kiss, going into his stateroom to change and leaving me to attend to my own toilette. I did not need to be clothed in the seductive trapings of my trousseau to give myself to my husband, but I knew he would wish our initial union to be perfectly conventional. After attiring himself—in a silk-and-velvet dressing gown, I imagined—he would come to me. Well, I would be ready.

With mounting excitement, I pulled off my clothes and slipped into the gown without bothering to put on the peignoir. I loosened my hair, letting it fall in rich, dark coils to my shoulders, and then I turned back the

satin coverlet on the bed and propped myself on two
fluffy pillows to wait. My eyes felt heavy, and my head
spun from an evening of champagne. I would just lie
back and close my eyes for a moment . . .

When I awoke, the tiny ormolu clock on my bedside
table showed three o'clock. I had fallen asleep, champagne the culprit. Carlyle must have come in, seen me
sleeping, and returned to his cabin, unwilling to disturb
me. Quickly, I ran to the adjoining door and opened it.
In the semidarkness, I could make out his sleeping
form. So he too, exhausted by the day's events and
lulled by the wine, had drifted off. I smiled to myself as
I crossed to the bed and quietly slipped under the sheets
beside him. I longed to wake him, to slowly remove his
sleeping garments and my own, to feel my bare skin
against his, to place my hand against his manhood and
feel him come alive at my touch. But again I forebore.
Although we were now man and wife, I must allow my
husband to be the aggressor. Later, when we had been
together and understood each other's ways, perhaps I
would be more bold, and perhaps he would delight in
my boldness. But for now, I would wait and surprise
him by my presence when he awoke to find me snuggled beside him in the morning.

But the morning no more satisfied my expectations
than had the evening before. When I awoke, Carlyle
had already left his bed, to reappear shortly with a
breakfast tray for me.

"Good morning, my love." He placed the tray carefully across my lap. "You were sleeping so soundly I
did not want to waken you. And Katherine," he added
seriously, "allow me to ask your forgiveness for last
evening. I must have dozed off."

My laughter interrupted him. "Don't apologize, because I fell asleep myself! We shall just have to see that
tonight is different."

Since Carlyle was already dressed, I realized that he
would give no thought to lovemaking while the sun was
high. I had learned that lovers need not be covered by a
blanket of darkness to give themselves to each other,

but I knew better than to display my wiles in the art of lovemaking to my husband who, although he knew of the men who had come before him, would not want to be reminded of them again. So I finished by breakfast while he sat with me and shared a cup of steaming coffee. Then I asked about the day's activities, which, as I had expected, were carefully planned.

First, we took a quick turn about the deck. Because we were in the Atlantic heading north, we had to bundle up warmly against the biting wind, and soon had to take refuge in the glassed solarium on the aft deck, where the cues were already set out for a game of shuffleboard. Although I possessed some athletic ability and a good eye, try as I might, I could not capture a single game from Carlyle, and he showed no inclination to give me a handicap.

"This is serious business," he called out, as his disk drove mine off the board. The words were spoken in jest, but I suspected that, even at play, Carlyle could not bear to be a loser.

After lunch, we took a grand tour of the *Augusta*, sleek and shining from bow to stern. How proud Carlyle was of her—as he was of all his possessions. If the weather worsened, he informed me that we would put into shore and continue our journey by rail. I knew this would not be a pleasant alternative for him, since Carlyle did not easily tolerate changing his plans. Teasingly, I told him that he could not rule the elements as he ruled his financial empire.

"And what about my wife?" he teased back.

"I cannot imagine that we would ever find ourselves at cross-purposes, Carlyle. We seem so well-suited."

"My beautiful, beautiful Katherine, you so gladden my life." His kiss was a promise of the future.

The late afternoon hours were more leisurely. We passed our time in the salon, drinking hot tea, reading, and writing letters. I glanced at my husband, sitting across from me and still dressed in sporting clothes. With one hand, he occasionally brushed back his thick hair. His gray eyes were just the color of the crest of a midwinter wave at sundown. Even casually dressed, he would as easily have graced the drawing rooms of Europe as the deck of his yacht. I took pleasure from his presence and from thinking that this was what a married life should be; this was a good life, one in which we would live as promised in our marriage service, "in perfect love and peace together."

To celebrate New Year's Eve, we planned a late dinner in the salon, where our food would be served buffet-style. I pondered at length over what to wear. Something elegant would be expected, but I had always preferred the unexpected, and so far that was exactly what our honeymoon had been; therefore, I chose one of my bridal nightgowns, black satin with lace insets over the breasts and shoulders. As with all my gowns, a matching peignoir completed the ensemble, but once more I chose to do without the added frills. When I moved across my stateroom toward the door, the luxurious satin caressed my stomach and thighs with a touch as light as a lover's hands, rousing me to a state of tension that I knew could have but one release.

Carlyle, dressed to perfection in evening clothes, was at first surprised by my attire, but immediately covered that emotion with an undisguised smile.

"Katherine, you are amazing."

"Well, as an actress, I always like to catch my audience unawares," I teased. "Besides, we *are* alone, and you *are* my husband, so . . ." I looked at him challengingly, and he raised his glass in silent understanding. I returned the toast, careful this time to sip my wine with restraint through the evening.

As the new year approached, I moved to sit on my husband's lap. As I had hoped, his arms tightened around me. My lips sought his, and he responded with intensity; I could hear my heart pound and my breathing become heavy. A soft moan escaped my lips. I did want him; I did want to be a complete wife to my husband. I stood up, my hand extended, to lead him to his cabin. Whether my bold eroticism shocked him or not, tonight would be different; I could wait no longer.

I helped Carlyle off with his jacket and tie, and had begun to unbutton the studs of his shirtfront, when he motioned me away and stepped into the adjoining bath. Moments later, he emerged in his dressing gown, just as I had imagined. I noticed the sinewy firmness of his legs, the gray hairs curling on his chest, and my need intensified. In a swift movement, I drew off my gown. It dropped like a black shadow at my feet. I knew by Carlyle's sharp intake of breath that he found me desirable.

"You are beautiful, Katherine, as beautiful as a Greek goddess. Your skin is like alabaster—"

"Touch me, Carlyle, feel me. I am not a statue. I am your wife."

I lay back provocatively on the bed until, at last, he moved to me and threw off his robe. As his body touched mine, I hungrily drew him down to me. I returned his kisses with a lust intensified by months of waiting, of longing, and of heated desire. His lips moved to my breasts, kissing them, caressing my eager nipples.

"Darling," I whispered, "you are wonderful, wonderful—"

I touched his chest and moved my hands down across his flat stomach to his manhood, which I expected to find hard and throbbing. But instead—

In his cry was the agony of a wounded animal. "It's no use, Katherine."

My mind raced like lightning, shattering my brain with questions. Had I been too wanton, too eager to please myself? Yes, I was at fault, but I must not show my alarm. I must arouse him slowly.

"Darling, don't worry. Please."

While Carlyle lay as if he were dead, I moved my lips across his bare skin. Then I felt his breath quicken. Everything would be all right. At last I touched his flaccid member with my lips, gently kissing him, tasting him with my tongue, taking him in my eager mouth. Nothing. Frantically, I continued, willing him to come to life and attain the male hardness which would penetrate my yearning softness. Nothing!

Carlyle suddenly moved to the side of the bed and sat

up. "It's no use, Katherine. Don't humiliate yourself any longer."

"Humiliate? Carlyle, you are my husband and I am your wife. I want us to be joined together, my darling, in every way."

"Katherine, I am sorry. I should have told you."

"You mean that you knew, Carlyle? This has happened before?"

The unfulfilled desire that raged within me was replaced instantly by a seething anger, but he did not seem even to hear my question as he reached for his dressing gown and, with reassumed dignity, tied the sash at his waist before speaking.

"You are so beautiful. I am obsessed with you, Katherine. I thought that would make a difference."

"Carlyle, what do you mean?"

Barely able to control myself, I stood at the very edge of fury. That he should have waited until we were married to reveal—what?

"There are tendencies, Katherine, vagaries in my nature which have always been with me. I am not to blame for them, nor do I feel guilt over them. My tastes are different; they are what, in your wide experience, you would be prompted to call unusual."

"What are you saying, Carlyle? I don't understand!"

"Just this. There is a way, unusual as I have said, but not at all difficult, that I can be aroused enough to satisfy a woman, to satisfy you, my dear Katherine, so that we can be joined together as we both so fervently wish. For, let me assure you, I wish it as you do, my dear."

"Carlyle, for God's sake, if there is a way, then I shall do it." There was desperation in my voice now, but there was also hope.

"Do you mean that, Katherine?" His cool demeanor was immediately replaced by a look of love and gratitude. I felt suddenly relieved. He pulled me toward him, and we held each other almost frantically, trying to reinforce the desire that had been in the room earlier.

"Yes, Carlyle, I mean it," I heard myself say. "You are my husband. I will do anything for you."

He turned up one of the shaded gas lamps near the
bed and moved to his chest of drawers. When he came
back to stand beside me, I saw the narrow strap of
leather in his hand. My sudden intake of breath all but
blotted out his words.

"Katherine, I know that I have deceived you, but if
you will punish me, whip me as I deserve, I can make it
up to you. Beat me, Katherine!"

"No!" I screamed so loud that the sound must have
reverberated throughout the yacht. Fearful of arousing
Carlyle's wrath, I clasped my hand over my mouth so
that I would not cry out again, but he had not moved.
The leather strap dangled from his motionless hands. I
forced myself to meet his gaze, only to find in his eyes a
look of pleading. Very softly, I repeated, "No, Carlyle,
you must not ask such a thing of me. I cannot do it!"

He reached out to touch me, but I drew back instinctively.

"Katherine, please, don't hate me. Pity me if you
must, but don't hate me." He sank beside me on the
bed. "I want you to listen to me, and I believe then that
you will be able to do as I ask."

I almost cried out again, but his words stopped me.

"I have never known the kind of lovemaking which is
regarded by others as normal."

There was such a tremor in his voice that I was
stunned. This was not the cool and unshakable Carlyle
that the world—and I—had come to know. I reached
out and took his hand in mine, forcing myself to listen
to his terrible words. As he spoke, my loathing subsided
and turned finally to a kind of understanding . . .

Punished severely as a small child by a high-strung
mother who followed beatings of his buttocks with cud-
dling and caresses, often taking the child into bed with
her, his earliest memories of pain were confused with
feelings of love. Irene was not born until Carlyle was
nine years old, so his boyhood was spent in the company of a nursemaid, with visits from his unstable
mother and rare appearances by his father. The nurse's
name was Nellie.

"We used to play together with my toys on the floor. I laughed frequently, as children will, over nothing, but sometimes my joy seemed to upset her, and she would hit me. I remember being surprised the first time she struck me, and confused as well, because I didn't know what I had done wrong. But I also remember that, although her blows hurt, I knew—somehow—I deserved the pain. And afterwards she always took me in her arms to comfort me. Often she kissed me. I loved her very much." He looked over at me, and his eyes were empty. "I don't know what happened. I only know that I grew up with pain and love somehow irrevocably mixed."

When he achieved young manhood, he attended boarding school in Charleston and visited the brothels with his classmates, only to find that he could not satisfy a woman without first being whipped. "Punished," he called the experience.

"I did not even know, until I heard the other boys talking of their adventures, that my own needs were any different. And then I felt disgusted, guilty, but I could not change. I have never been able to change."

But he had married in time, and even his wife, I learned, had succumbed to his demands.

"Olivia was hardly more than a child when we married; she knew nothing of life. Although she realized that these tendencies of mine were not normal, she was too shy and inexperienced to reveal her true feelings."

After Augusta's birth Olivia had become ill, and their intimate relationship had ended. Since that time he had, in the brothels of New York, New Orleans, and Paris, been able to buy the kind of woman he needed, but even these experiences had been infrequent in recent years.

"Don't you see, Katherine, that our relationship has so many facets, and this is only one of them. It should not change the way we feel toward each other."

But even as he spoke, he must have understood how different were my own feelings, because he continued with hardly a pause, "I had hoped that for you, who are so young and passionate and beautiful, I could be a real man, a potent man, the kind of man you thought you married. But I cannot be that man, so I must beg you to do this for me. For us."

He placed the strap in my hands, and I nodded. Had I any other choice? I wondered, as before my glazed eyes, he removed his robe and stretched spread-eagle on the bed, his buttocks, chalky white, exposed to me.

"Punish me," he moaned. "Hit me; beat me; hurt me."

A stream of profanities issued from his lips, and his wild excitement reached me. If I hit him, he would become a man, hard and probing; he would take me—full of pain and fury, yes—but he *would* take me. He would ease this need within and make me his. I raised the strap above my head. I needed only to bring it down across his buttocks, once, twice, three times. I could almost see the welts, red and raw, erupt on his white flesh. Once, twice, and then—

My arm froze in midair. I could not do this! If I did, I would be as sick as Carlyle, as this man stretched out before me, spewing forth words tinged not with love but with filth, begging to be beaten. There had to be another way! I threw down the strap and, with a sob, ran to my room. The metallic sound of the lock dropping into place emphasized the finality of my decision; he knew this as well as I, and did not come after me. At last I crawled into bed, where I lay awake through the night, searching my heart and my mind for an answer.

By morning, I knew what I must do. I responded to the soft knock on my door to find, not Carlyle, but a young steward with my breakfast tray. I drank a few sips of coffee and dressed quickly, oblivious to my appearance, which was of little consequence when we had looked last night upon each other's inner nakedness. But while my hair was disheveled, and my face revealed the dark circles and swollen eyes of a tortured night, I was stunned by Carlyle's appearance when I confronted him in his study. He was, if anything, more impeccable than usual in dress and demeanor. Nor did his words

reveal that he had suffered any of the turmoil which
had filled my night.

"Good morning, Katherine," he said with accustomed
calm. "I'm glad to see you up and about, my dear. Have
you had breakfast?"

"Only coffee. I'm not hungry." Suddenly angered by
his obvious nonchalance, I added, "After last night."

"Did you not sleep well?" He glanced up from the
column of figures on the desk before him. "You seem
distraught. You mustn't let yourself become upset so
soon after your illness."

I dropped into the chair beside his desk, and looked
at him in amazement. I had entered the room with an
open mind, determined to save what already seemed the
shambles of this fledgling marriage, but he was equally
determined to dismiss last night entirely. For a fleeting
moment, I wanted to be part of that subterfuge, to pretend that his sickness did not exist, to go on living together as we had begun, to present a pretty picture for
the world. But no, I could not live a lie. I had tried to
withdraw from life once before and had learned that
the only way to live my life was to confront it head on.

"Carlyle," I said slowly, choosing my words, "we
can't pretend that last night didn't happen. We must
talk this over."

I met his gaze straight on, and he looked away
briefly, caught off-guard for a split-second.

"Whatever you might believe to the contrary," he
said finally, "I do not feel the need to justify my behavior."

Amazed at his words, I tried to interrupt.

"No, let me finish. I am what I am. I cannot change.
Nor, on the other hand, can I change my feelings for
you. I treasure you above all else. Ordinarily I am not a
patient man, but I am willing to wait as long as necessary for you to accept my ways."

"Never!"

He looked up sharply. There was no hurt in his eyes
now, but I had seen it there once, and knew the pain
which lay beneath.

"There is no need, Carlyle, for you to wait and hope. I will not—I cannot—give in to your demands, but I can do more. I can give you the help you once gave me. You must consult a doctor, Carlyle."

When I saw the look on his face, I insisted, "Dr. Meyer will know someone in New York, someone who can help you as he helped me. And I will face this with you; I will be beside you."

He did not speak for a time, but he had pushed aside the work on his desk and was looking at me thoughtfully.

"God knows, I would do anything to keep you, Katherine. Anything. You are too precious to lose. I have never felt the need to ask for medical opinions, but seeing how important this is to you, and because I value our marriage above all else, I shall do as you wish. I shall consult a doctor in New York. But—" and here his eyes narrowed— "you must also make a promise. Last night, because of my longing for you, I told you things I have never told another soul. You must swear not to reveal my secret. And you must forget my words."

I had unwillingly discovered the chink in his armor, and he was desperately afraid it would be revealed. But he was my husband; I would keep his secret. Nothing would ever be the same—or even as I had imagined— but we still had a chance, a good chance, as long as we were true to each other. The marriage vows I had taken only a few days before had been severely tested, but they had held fast. Now I must be as strong as those vows.

My husband opened his arms, and I went to him.

ACT V

"The wheel is come full circle, I am here."
King Lear, Act 5, Scene 3

Chapter 1

New York. As always, the city brought me to life, cheered me, gave me hope. Even as the icy winds of January swept the avenues, I was revived. Once back in the city I loved, the tension I had felt between my husband and myself lifted. I was filled with optimism and eager to plunge into my life as Mrs. J. Carlyle Wharton. Certainly, Carlyle and I gave the appearance of a happily married couple, an illusion we came almost to believe ourselves in those first carefree weeks while we awaited the completion of our town house. We entertained at the Brevoort, attended concerts, danced at parties and balls, and shared the final planning for our home.

Sometimes I slipped away, when Carlyle was busy in his office and I could find a moment to myself, to visit Clara. The streets, crowded even in the cold, beckoned to me as never before, and the cobblestones echoed their welcome as I lifted my skirts to step onto a waiting horsecar. The clank of my coin in the box, the friendly

greeting of the blanketed driver high up on his wooden
seat, the jostling, knee-to-knee proximity of the other
passengers, reassured me as, with a great hug, I was
taken into the city's arms.

Yet, in another sense, I was homesick. To be so near
the theater, but not be a part of it, tore at me. I plied
Clara for details of her rehearsals, and listened to
Johnny despair. He had finished a short and entirely
unsuccessful run in a revival of Love for Love at another theater, and was chomping at the bit to be back in
Lester's familiar ranks.

"Though he will probably spurn me," Johnny added
dejectedly. "Lester said I was a fool to go into the Con-
greve, and of course he was right, but there was nothing
for me with Markan Tours last fall, so what was I to
do? If I don't work, I turn to stone."

We laughed at Johnny's words, but I understood just
how he felt. I ached to be back. And clearly I knew
why. Carlyle was generous and complimentary and gracious, but we lacked the special intimacy that I knew
could exist between a man and woman. This was the
void I needed to fill, knowing all the while that I could
not now—at the shaky beginning of my marriage—
return to the stage. So I closed up the void that was
within me, sealed it with Lester's words of assurance
that an opening would always be available in the Markan Company, and turned my attentions to our townhouse.

In fact, our new home was not just a town house, but
a mansion to join the others that were beginning to line
the avenues above Thirty-fifth Street, no longer the
northern limit of fashionable homes, as society moved
uptown, following the lead of the mode-setting Vander-
bilts. I would have difficulty in the future, the thought
occurred to me, dismissing our carriage and liveried
driver to take the horsecar shopping or visiting. The
mistress of a house that occupied a full block and was
imitative of an Italian palazzo—all gray stone and marble with narrow, arched windows rising like sentinels
above Fifth Avenue—traveled in style. I smiled to my-

self, fully aware that I was not about to give up all my
pleasures. As a newcomer, I would be forgiven an occasional lapse! I wondered, however, about my ability to
handle the decorating task before me. I had learned that
New York's wealthy furnished their own homes by
stripping the grand estates of Europe, and Carlyle was
no exception. He too had his agents abroad, and crates
arrived almost weekly with furnishings ranging from ba-
roque Spanish and Italian Renaissance to French Empire and English Regency. Throughout the house, there
seemed to be no unifying theme, and I would need,
without benefit of experience or training, to bring everything together tastefully with such good judgment as I
possessed. The prospect was awesome, but Clara, for
one, found my protestations unfounded.

"Come now, honey, you've hobnobbed with dukes
and counts and lords all over Europe. Just order a few
tapestries like the ones at Thornfield Keep, throw in a
suit of armor, and presto! You're all the rage."

Clara's words were not meant entirely to amuse. I did
have a flair for colors and styles, and Carlyle certainly
had the financial resources from which to draw. There
was no reason why the shining star of Broadway
couldn't shine as brightly on upper Fifth Avenue. With
more courage than capability, I decided that our home
would be the grandest in the city. When the decorating
was completed, we would give a splendid dinner party.
Carlyle was enthusiastic about a party to christen our
home, but insisted that it should be a small gathering of
his closest associates, as befitted his position and his determination to avoid the limelight. As for my friends
from the theater, it would be more suitable, he insisted,
if we entertained them separately, at a later date.

That my friends were more amusing and charming
than his colleagues from the world of finance was not
the question, he assured me. "The two groups simply
would not mix, my dear."

As far as he was concerned, the matter was closed,
and as my desire was to please him, I did not belabor
his decision.

Long days were now spent at the house, ordering painters and carpenters about, arguing with drapery hangers, talking to tradesmen, haranguing plumbers to work more quickly. This role as overseer was an unfamiliar one which I took on eagerly and in good spirit, to find that a spontaneous gaiety was my reward, a gaiety that did not hamper the work.

With Carlyle's arrival, however, laughter dimmed. My husband was a perfectionist, meticulous in detail, demanding the best. If a craftsman's work was not turned out properly or to his liking, Carlyle did not chastise, but rather disciplined with sarcasm and ridicule, later taking his criticism to the supervisor, pointing out, with his gold-tipped cane, the man who did not please.

In the evenings his mood was more relaxed, as we sat in our parlor at the Brevoort before a roaring fire, sipping hot toddies for extra warmth. Comfortably settled, with the house plans before us on the floor, we discussed the day's progress, inspected fabric swatches or paint samples, worried over the exact placement of a piece of furniture, made final decisions only to change our minds, and laughed at our capriciousness. When at last we put the plans away, I longed for Carlyle to follow me into my bedroom and make me truly his wife. But he did not.

"Be patient, Katherine," he once whispered as he kissed me lightly, and so I learned to wait, hopeful that the doctors would find an answer for us, or at least open a door that might lead eventually to an answer.

In late February, we finally moved in. The city honored us with a snowstorm, but I was still able to supervise our recently hired servants as they transferred personal belongings from the Brevoort to Forty-eighth Street. I was home. My first home. My final home. There was splendor here, but there was warmth here, too, and love. If there was not yet satisfaction in that love, it would come in time. Carlyle's statue of Diana, her head tilted back, a fountain spraying her alabaster skin with fine mist, smiled up at me as I climbed the

stairs to my suite on the second floor. I rang for Alicia
to draw my bath and lazily perused my bedroom. I had
chosen well here. I smiled to myself. Carlyle and I had
chosen well. It was he who had insisted that the suite be
furnished in Louis Quinze, a period when the furniture
was delicately curved and feminine—more ornamental
than I would have wished, or so I thought, but Carlyle
had been right. The rooms suited me perfectly. He had
insisted that I choose the colors and had complimented
me on the combination, which, when the bedroom was
finally completed, I was relieved to see blended as I had
hoped. The walls were covered in palest lilac Scala-
mandre silk, with a darker shade of faintly patterned
damask for the tiered draperies; the chaise longe and
armchairs were of subdued Venetian red; the Savon-
nerie rug was of soft taupe, with a hint of the moss
green that dominated the bed's delicate canopy. The final touches—paintings, porcelain figurines, china toilet
articles—were Carlyle's, and complimented without
cluttering.

I moved into the bathroom, turned off the flowing
gilded faucets, stepped into warm, scented water, and
relaxed in pink marble splendor for over an hour. At
last I stood up and, for the first time in my life, let a
servant towel me dry. Both of us giggled. Alicia was a
young girl, and this was her first position as a personal
maid. We would learn together.

I slipped into my rustling taffeta robe, and passed
through the sitting room across the hall to Carlyle's
bedroom, which I had not seen since its completion. I
was stunned by its sheer opulence; yet on looking again,
I saw that he had chosen correctly, if not to my particular taste. The room was a symphony played upon a single theme of dark polished wood and plush velvet, the
heavy Jacobean and Spanish furniture lacking even the
suggestion of a curve, with table and chair legs straight,
and, though carved, not ornately so. It was a precise
room, if a ponderous one.

Back in my dressing room, I heard Carlyle across the
hall, giving instructions to his valet. I would dress care-

fully for our inaugural dinner, knowing that Carlyle would look me over with a critical eye, and wanting to make sure that it was an approving one as well.

Dinner by candlelight was perfect—almost. The silverware gleamed on the table, reflecting sharply in Baccarat crystal and bone-white china emblazoned with a dramatic *W*. I had not expected service this first night to be faultless, but indeed it was nearly so, until one of the waiters, unused to the heavy doors separating pantry and kitchen, dropped a tray of plates. Noiselessly the debris was cleaned up, but Carlyle's lips had already tightened.

"Darling, he's nervous," I reminded my husband.

"The servants are your responsibility, Katherine. I cannot countenance inefficiency."

"I'll see that this doesn't happen again," I said boldly, not at all sure that I, any more than the servants, could perform miracles in just one night, but knowing full well that the young waiter must not err another time. Carlyle might forgive one mistake, but never two. On this fine evening, however, he was too pleased with himself, with me, and with his home, to linger on the episode.

As we crossed the grand foyer after dinner, Carlyle led me to the fountain, where he took my face in both of his hands and gently turned my head in what I realized was the exact pose of the statue. A shiver raced through me, and I moved away casually so he would not suspect how his gesture had disturbed me.

"Remember, Katherine," he was saying, "when I first spoke to you of Diana? I did not exaggerate. Notice the purity of her lines, how they flow, and see the absolutely correct tilt of her head, the position of her hands. Is she not faultless?"

"Yes," I answered weakly, bothered not so much by the presence of the statue, which was certainly a work of art, but by the obvious comparsion Carlyle was making, which he emphasized with his next words.

"Now I have you both, side by side; both beautiful, both perfect."

"You mustn't compare me to her, Carlyle, because I am not perfect."

"But of course you are. Have you not achieved perfection with this house, and are you not perfectly attired? Certainly your great beauty is nothing less than perfect."

"I am also a human being," I added.

"Which makes your perfection all the more astounding," he said, laughing.

But I was more disturbed than amused, knowing that to meet with his disapproval would be to destroy his image of me. Well, I would make mistakes; he would just have to face that. I refused to be put upon a pedestal like this inanimate object, beautiful as she was. He would have to love me with my faults, as I loved him with his.

Climbing the curved stairway by his side, I was prompted to ask Carlyle about his progress with the doctor. He expressed optimism, while reminding me that results would be slow.

"Maybe I should come with you on the next visit, darling," I said when we reached my door. "Don't you think that might be helpful?"

"I shouldn't think so at all," was his curt reply.

"Well, perhaps this is too soon," I said trying not to show that I had been stung by his tone of voice, "but mightn't we at least be together? Stay in my room tonight, Carlyle, and in the warmth of my bed we can talk and share our thoughts."

I imagined, but did not voice, the tenderness that could be between us as we relaxed and pleased each other with our hands, peacefully and in harmony, with no thought of his illness. We could begin, tonight, a voyage toward understanding leading to the shores of an all-encompassing love, which could reinforce the doctor's treatment and bring about recovery.

Carlyle's voice interrupted my thoughts, and his words put an end to them completely. "I don't believe that would be helpful, Katherine. Perhaps in time."

Again the admonishment that I must wait, but tonight I was to receive more than a tender kiss as my consolation. While I remained in the sitting room, Carlyle crossed the hall, to return in a moment with a tiny silver box, which he opened for me. Inside were diamond and ruby earbobs.

"I had them made to match the necklace which was your wedding gift. I hope you will wear the set for me at dinner tomorrow. The rubies will go especially well with your green velvet dress," he said.

"Yes," I agreed, "they will." How many more presents, I wondered, would I receive before he gave me the final gift of his love?

The next weeks, during which Carlyle was more attentive than ever, were pleasant ones. He returned early from his office to have sherry with me and talk over the day's events. There were no further problems with the servants, and, except for a certain tendency to make decisions for me, especially regarding how I should dress on important occasions, Carlyle was kind and considerate. We breakfasted together each morning, sharing the *Times* and discussing the topics that were in the news during that late winter of 1878. I was particularly intrigued by the confusion over Commodore Vanderbilt's estate, which, though the commodore had been dead nearly a year, was still not settled, at least to his son, Cornelius J.'s, satisfaction. One witness in the case commented that the old man had simply "never expected to die!" I had great fun reading reports of New York's juicier scandals aloud to Carlyle, who always chuckled over my renditions. He was not, however, amused to hear that the Ways and Means Committee in Washington was considering a bill that would put a tax on income, so I skipped articles touching on that subject. But I could not resist the gory details of the death of Mme. Restel, who had grown rich by what the *Times* euphemistically described as "the practice of nefarious business." She cut her own throat from ear to ear in the bathtub; however, the next day there were widespread reports (which the *Times* printed, but with haughty disbelief) that the body found in the blood-filled tub

was another woman, and Mme. Restel had left the city
for Canada! Before long, I became the official reporter
at the breakfast table, and Carlyle rarely even picked up
the paper. This was our most pleasant time of the day.
But on those mornings when he did not join me or when
he came down late, I found myself skimming over the
rest of the paper to get to news of the theater in the
"amusements" column. I gobbled the words up and
ruminated over them for the rest of the day, unable to
satisfy my hunger for the stage.

One rainy morning in March, a few days prior to our
party, I awakened quite early for some reason and was
in the breakfast room well before the usual hour. I
poured myself a cup of strong black coffee and had just
taken the first sip, when the butler appeared in the
doorway.

"A telegram, ma'am. Just delivered."

My heart leapt. This would be news about Courtney,
whose child was due later in the month. The baby must
have arrived ahead of time, I thought as I tore into the
envelope. The words stunned me. I read them again,
unbelieving.

Courtney died last night in childbirth. Her daughter
survives. Funeral Thursday.

Jamie.

"Carlyle!" I screamed, bringing him down the stairs in
a rush.

"What is the matter, Katherine?"

I thrust the telegram at him and sank back in my
chair. My eyes focused on the cup of coffee before me,
and I could not draw my gaze away. My mind was
empty of thoughts.

"My dear, I am so sorry," I heard Carlyle say. "She
was very young." He drew up a chair beside me. "I
know you must be dreadfully upset."

"I loved her. She was like a sister," I whispered. I
turned my head at last to look at him. My own shock

somehow obscured the lack of emotion in his face.

He pulled a heavy gold watch from his pocket, snapped open the lid, and consulted it thoughtfully. "You certainly would not be able to make the morning train, so I don't see how you can get to Deaton by Thursday."

"I must try. Laurel Ann will need me, and Jamie and the boys—"

"They have each other, Katherine, and you cannot help Courtney now. Do I need to remind you that Thursday is also the day of our dinner party? If you must go, why not wait and leave Friday morning?"

"If I must go?" Anger joined the sadness churning within me. "Of course I am going. I will do my best to get to Deaton for Courtney's funeral, and as for the party, we will simply have to cancel."

"Please calm down, Katherine, before you make yourself quite ill."

He attempted to pour me a fresh cup of coffee, but I shook my head adamantly. He poured some for himself, and calmly stirred in a lump of sugar while I watched in disbelief, wondering how, in the face of this terrible news, he could remain so detached. After taking a sip, he added a second lump of sugar. Then he spoke, but not of Courtney.

"My dear, the guests have already accepted."

"I will send the footman with notes immediately, and I will make the morning train as well. After all, I am going to a funeral, and will hardly need to worry over appropriate clothes."

"Such sarcasm does not become you at all, Katherine, but I accept that this is a trying time. I suppose if the guests receive their letters today, that will be proper. As for catching the train, I will have Jerris order a carriage for an hour from now. I will also send a boy for the tickets."

"Thank you," I answered more calmly. "And please forgive my outburst, but this has been a tremendous shock."

"I understand perfectly, my dear. I wish I could accompany you. Business will not allow me to leave town now; however, I could possibly make the journey over the weekend."

"That's very kind, Carlyle. I hope that you will be able to."

The trip to Deaton was a nightmare. I did arrive in time to hold the tiny baby named for Courtney in my arms as her mother was buried in the red soil of South Carolina. Bufe disappeared after the funeral, walking away in search of solitude in his agony.

During the next days, Jamie became an old man before my eyes, but Laurel Ann endured. She cared for the baby, consoled the boys, received endless visitors, and somehow managed to get meals to the table on time. I tried to help, but I was almost as useless as the others in my grief. I made excuses for Carlyle, pleading a business crisis. Under normal circumstances, Jamie and Laurel Ann might have questioned his absence, but not now. Letters arrived from Carlyle to all of us, properly sympathetic with our loss. Added to my note was his regret that he would not be able to get away as he had hoped. I had not expected him to come.

I stayed on for two long, painful weeks, during which time I had hoped to see the boys and Jamie return to a sort of normalcy. But they did not. I had hoped, as well, that Laurel Ann would shed the tears she was so stoically holding back, but she did not. Nor did Bufe return. I could wait no longer. As much as I wanted to stay, I had responsibilities at home.

The skies were inky dark when I stepped off the ferry from New Jersey, and there was a feeling of snow in the air. I had not let Carlyle know the time of my arrival. I could have telegraphed him, but I had put off doing so until too late, for reasons I did not understand myself. I may have been thinking that I needed to be alone for a while before facing him, but as my cab rolled across town before turning up Fifth Avenue, I knew my real reason.

"Stop at the next corner in front of the theater,

please," I called up to the driver. Once, not so long ago, I had been the independent and vital Kate Lawrence, star actress. I needed to be her again, now more than ever. I needed to see Lester. I asked the driver to wait, agreed with his prediction of snow, but told him I would not be long, and stepped out in front of the 14th Street Theater. The marquee was dark, but through the door panes I could see a lamp flickering in Lester's office, and another in the green room. Rehearsals were over; the players had gone home or to a nearby restaurant for a late dinner, which would last well into the night and would be peppered liberally with theater gossip. How well I remembered.

An elderly man whom I did not recognize came from the green room, a mop in his hand, to open the door. "Theater's dark this month, ma'am."

I smiled. "Yes, I know," I said and was just about to answer that I had come to see Mr. Markan, when Lester appeared from his office.

"Kate, you baggage, come on in here."

Nothing in the room had changed; there was simply a lot more of everything, and as usual, no place to sit down. He found a chair from which he emptied a pile of scripts onto the floor, gave the cane bottom a cursory dusting with his handkerchief, and gestured for me to sit down.

"You really need an amanuensis," I said.

Lester mumbled and made his way back to his own small space behind the desk. He knew I was not here to tell him to hire a secretary.

"I want to come back, Lester."

"Do you know," he said, almost as if he hadn't heard me, "that I didn't cast Drew in the play we're rehearsing now?"

I nodded. The Piersons had told me that Drew was in California visiting his family.

"Nope," Lester went on, "I didn't cast him. Just sent him home and said come back when you get my telegram, and don't take work with another company. Didn't give him a reason, either."

"Why, Lester?"

"Because I'm superstitious, like most theater people. I didn't want to jinx my plan. Oh, he knew the reason, Kate, and you know it too. Drew's next part is going to be opposite Kate Lawrence."

I can't say I was surprised to hear those words, because I had hoped for them—even expected them—but I let out a squeal of joy just the same, the first real display of happiness I had been able to muster in a long time.

"In what, Lester?" I asked.

"Shakespeare. Oh, don't look so surprised. You're not going straight into *Macbeth* or *Othello*, but since you seem to have an affinity for Kate-named parts, I thought—"

"*The Taming of the Shrew*!" I almost shouted.

Lester went on as if I hadn't spoken. "Boris is free, and he will make a fine Baptista. Since Clara is tied up with this tour, I thought Aurora would do as Bianca, and Johnny will get a chance to use his comedy skills as Gremio. And of course, Drew will play Petruchio." Lester's voice dropped and for a moment he seemed to be talking to himself. "Not as passionately as Terry, but a Terry O'Neill comes along once in a lifetime."

I reached across the desk and caught his hand to bring him back.

"Well, yes, Drew will be fine," he said, "I'll have most of my family together in this one, Kate."

"Yes, Lester." As I rose to leave, I hugged him impulsively.

"Dear Kate," he said, "I was so sorry to hear about the loss you suffered. What a terrible trip that must have been for you. Are you all right now?"

"I'm fine. Fine. Just anxious to get back to work, that's all."

He walked me to the front door, and the old man with his mop came out to unlock for us.

"Thanks, Jimmy," Lester said, and then remembered how long I had been away. "Oh, Jimmy, this is Miss

Kate Lawrence, one of our stars. She's come back to play *The Taming of the Shrew*."

"I'll look forward to that one, Mr. Markan, I sure will. She's a mighty pretty lady."

"Yes, she is," Lester agreed. He walked out to the waiting cab with me. Then, with a tenderness so suggestive of his nature, at least to those who knew him well, he patted my hand shyly. "You've had success with the Markan Company, Kate, but you've had tragedy with us too. That's going to change. I promise good times in this theater, but you have to promise something, too. Take care of yourself, Kate, and make sure that new husband treats you right."

I reached out to hug Lester once more and buried my face against his chest so he would not see my tears. Sometimes he was too preceptive, and I didn't want to be tempted by his concern to tell him the truth.

Mr. Wharton, Jerris told me when I reached Forty-eighth Street, was at his club, but would be returning within the hour. After taking my cloak and sending the footman to the cab for my baggage, he asked, "Would you be wanting dinner, ma'am?"

"No, thank you. I'm not at all hungry. But do see that Alicia prepares my bath and have some sherry brought up to my sitting room, please. Oh, and Jerris, bring up brandy as well. I expect Mr. Wharton will want a nightcap when he returns."

I remained standing in the entranceway, feeling so small, so alone in this house that I had given my heart to, and which now seemed alien, as if I were a stranger and my home a foreign land. The fault, I knew, lay as much with me as with my husband, but now that I was returning to the theater, I would be my old self again. We would still have time for parties and evenings out, for late suppers after the performances. I would still share Carlyle's life and friends, and now he would be able to share mine as well. Once, for a brief moment, there had been warmth in our home, and there would be again. I would find gaiety and bring it back to this house, find happiness and let it fill the rooms. And I would find love as well.

I dressed carefully for Carlyle in my purple velvet robe, a startling and almost unfashionably bright color which he had chosen. A band of intricate embroidery was set in the front, and wide pleats fell gracefully to the floor in back. I applied a touch of perfume to my hair and wrists, and smiled into the mirror, pleased.

"You're the only woman in the world beautiful enough to wear that color."

Carlyle moved into the reflection behind me. I turned and, with two steps, was in his arms, holding tight, my kisses filled with hope.

"My precious Katherine, when you're away from me, I forget how beautiful you are. I've missed you."

"Oh, Carlyle, I am so glad to hear those words. I wondered if you'd be angry because I stayed away so long."

"Of course not. You owed that time to your family. You had no choice, just as I had no choice but to remain in New York and take care of my business."

I nodded as convincingly as possible.

"I knew you would understand," he said, smiling. "Now let's go into the sitting room and have a nice long talk. I see you had the fire lit."

"Yes, and put out your favorite brandy."

His smile was genuine, but it faded when I told him about my plans to return to the theater.

"I realized that you would wish to return in time, but I had hoped that you would wait until I could produce a play for you."

"I know, darling, and I want you to, but I must not let this opportunity slip by. You know how I've longed to play Shakespeare. Lester has no plans for a tour, so we won't be separated."

He still looked tight-lipped and unconvinced.

"Rehearsals are a week away," I added, hoping to recapture his earlier smile. "I'll have ample time to arrange our dinner party."

He didn't seem to be listening. "Dowd will co-star?"

"Yes," I answered. "We work well together."

"In that case, I'm somewhat perturbed, Katherine. Wasn't this Dowd once very attracted to you?"

I was too amazed to answer. On the night at Schloss Wald when I had told Carlyle the truth about my life, I had attempted to be completely honest. But I had never expected him to use my confession against me, especially when he knew full well that I felt only friendship for Drew now. Yet he persisted.

"I don't like the thought of sharing you, dear girl, when you have such a tendency to become, shall we say, involved with your co-stars." The saccharine tone of his voice did not sweeten the bitterness of his words.

"Drew is a friend," I countered. "He's not like Terry." My face was hot with anger. "Not at all!"

"Control yourself, my dear, or your voice will carry to the servants." My husband sat calmly before me, watching my rage build up inside me, until I was forced to move and stand beside the fireplace with my back to him. My hand closed around one of the china figures on the mantel.

"Surely you don't plan to throw that exquisite Meissen piece, Katherine?" I heard him say.

I loosened my grip on the figure. Yes, I had been tempted to hurl it at him—or the actress in me had been tempted. Well, I could also play the opposite part, that of the perfect wife who would not think of disturbing the decorum of her home. I moved back to sit beside Carlyle, my facade as calm now as his. He smiled his approval.

"As your husband, Katherine, I have a right to be interested in your activities."

"Certainly you do, and I want you to be a part of my life, Carlyle," I went on in my most rational tone, "as I am a part of yours. I've shared your interest in our home; now won't you share my interest in the theater, which means so much to me?"

"Dear Katherine, I would not forbid you to return to Markan. I made that promise long ago."

"But I'm asking for more, Carlyle; I want your support and encouragement."

He lifted his eyebrows without replying.

"You've come this far with me, you've helped me when I felt I could not go on, you've offered love, marriage, and security. Go the rest of the way with me now."

"Sweet, funny little Katherine. Haven't I always told you that you can have anything you desire? Is this what you want most—your toy, your play, your *Shrew*? Then you shall have it. That does not alter my belief, however, that your place is by my side. I shall give my permission, but don't expect my approval. Now, try to get some rest. You've been through a difficult time."

I had won an empty victory, but at least I would act again. Carlyle would not be able to escape the happiness that would come with my return to the theater, a happiness he would share in time, as, in time, he would share my love.

Chapter 2

The air that hangs over a dark stage, especially in a theater that has been closed for weeks to the outside world, is musty, close, and heavy, and yet, to me, it is fresher than the air of a Carolina meadow after the rain, for it renews me. From it I breathe new life, and with each breath, my spirit is freed of weighty problems, and my mind is diverted from painful memories.

I would play Kate for Courtney. Of all the plays I had read aloud in the bedroom we had shared as children or performed in our rickety shed, *The Taming of the Shrew* had been her favorite. Courtney, who had so little of the shrew in her, seemed to delight that the willful Kate was tamed at last by love. Often, Courtney had played Bianca to my Kate, and now, as I spoke Shakespeare's lines, painful memories of those long-gone days did at times return, but they were sweet memories as well.

Kate was a demanding part, as was Petruchio, and the nuances with which we shaded our readings would

be as important as the words themselves. Several days
before rehearsal formally began, Drew and I worked together, usually with Lester present, sharing ideas about
the roles. Kate should be played as fiery, stubborn, and
tempestuous, and not as a coarse, abrasive harridan.
She should be exasperating, but still sympathetic. There
were similar problems with Petruchio. He needed to be
arrogant but not cold, masterful but not cruel. As director, Lester would be able to bring out the sense of humor that was needed in each character.

These rehearsals lasted one or two hours a day at
most, and were usually conducted in the early afternoon, when Carlyle was certain to be busy downtown.
As full rehearsals began, I continued to adjust my hours
to my husband's. When darkness fell outside the theater, I began to squirm until Lester released me, and I
was able to return to Forty-eighth Street. Carlyle liked
for me to sit opposite him at the dinner table at eight
o'clock sharp, and he liked, as well, for me to dress, not
in the street clothes I wore to rehearsal, but in an evening gown, low-cut and flattering, showing off the glow
of my skin in the candlelight. Our dinner party had
been a great success, and we were deluged with invitations. Often we joined Carlyle's business associates for
dinner and an evening at the opera or a concert at the
Academy of Music.

As the weeks passed and my rehearsals intensified, I
could see that Carlyle was not pleased. Although he
said nothing, I sensed that he was waiting for me to
make a mistake—a mistake so grave that he would be
left with but one choice: to demand that I quit. I was
confident that I could avoid that mistake. As long as I
continued to handle one or two engagements each week
without overtaxing myself, as long as my spirits were
high—which they were—and I was by his side on every
important occasion, a charming and beautiful hostess,
he could not object. Nor could he have reason to be
jealous, when I came straight home in the carriage he
sent to the theater each evening.

I judged him correctly in all else but his jealousy.

There came an evening when Lester was not able to stop the rehearsal—or even my part in it—at the usual time, without destroying the flow that his direction depended upon. I was forced to dismiss my carriage and driver, knowing that I would be several more hours at the theater. At last we broke up and poured out into the chilly April night as the church clock across the street was striking ten. A hack pulled up, its harness rattling, the horse's breath steaming into the dark. Drew rushed to open the door for me, but before the hack moved away, Aurora and Johnny and Charlie, the stage manager, had also piled in.

Laughter sang in my ears all the way uptown. We knew that the play had begun to take shape tonight at last, and we were all pleased with ourselves, Drew and I especially, since we had polished the most difficult scene in which Katharina and Petruchio meet for the first time. The lines are fast and furious, following each other with hardly a beat or a breath between, and we sang them out again as we dropped the others off on the way to Forty-eighth Street.

When the hack bumped to a final halt, Drew and I looked out to find ourselves at my house, with everyone else long gone and our own scene just coming to an end. Drew paid the driver with a flourish, shouted out his last line—"I must and will have Katharina to my wife"—and swept me into his arms and up the stairs to the front door. Over Drew's shoulder, I saw the astonished driver, immobile, his whip poised in one hand, staring after us. By the time Jerris opened the door, Drew had deposited me on my feet, but we were still laughing. The door swung open to a cold marble silence. Drew caught his breath. This was the first time he had seen the house. We moved slowly into the vast hall, leaving our laughter behind.

"It's so—so quiet," Drew whispered.

"Somehow," I answered, "that is not the description I expected."

"Oh, it's beautiful too, Kate. I'm just astonished by the silence."

Then, boldly, he gave voice to the strident braying noise he had decided to use in response to the line spoken by me, as the shrew, "Asses are made to bear, and so are you." The bray echoed around the hall, stirred up the air, and brought back our laughter. The noticeably shocked look on Jerris's face turned immediately to one of forced nonchalance as he took my coat and disappeared. I took Drew's hand and led him toward the salon.

"Come, as soon as Jerris recovers, I'll ring for brandy."

"No need, my dear." The voice came from above, and we both turned, dropping hands.

Dressed in a wine-colored smoking jacket, Carlyle stood at the top of the stairs. One hand rested on the balustrade. From where I stood, I could almost make out the flawless press of his pearl-gray trousers. He spoke again as he started down the stairs.

"Allow your husband to attend your guest, my dear. Or is this a private rehearsal?" The words were not unpleasant, but the implication was chilling.

"Darling," I said as I went to meet him, "do join us, please. Rehearsal was prolonged tonight, but we made great progress, and Lester promises not to keep me so long again."

I knew I was overdoing my explanation, but I felt I must pacify Carlyle so that Drew would not see the disapproval that was wrapped around every mention of the theater, especially tonight when we were so late. Carlyle's kiss on my brow had the warmth of one of his expensive jewels. Nor was there any warmth in the words, however cordial, that he spoke to Drew.

"Come along, Dowd, brandy is set out in the library, and there's a warm fire. You'll need to fortify yourself before the ride home."

Drew almost acquiesced. Then I saw his eyes change as he reversed the decision. "Thanks, Wharton," he said easily, "but it's late, and I'm very tired. Sorry to keep your wife away for so long. Good night, Kate. I'll see you at rehearsal tomorrow." He turned quickly, crossed the hall, and let himself out the front door.

"I'm tired too, Carlyle," I said, but he was not looking at me. He was gazing after Drew, or, rather, at the door through which Drew had departed.

"Will I see you in the morning?" I continued.

He turned to me then. "Certainly, but do you have no time for me tonight?"

"I assumed you were working upstairs and wanted to get back."

"I haven't seen as much of you recently as I would like, Katherine," he went on, ignoring my observation.

"I know, darling, but the play is finally taking shape, and from now on—"

"Would you give it up if I asked, Katherine?"

I had been waiting for that, but I had not expected it so soon. I was also surprised that his words came in the form of a question, rather than a demand.

"I am your wife, Carlyle," I answered, "and I want to please you, but acting is a part of my life, as I told you long ago."

"I promised that you would act, Katherine, and I still want you to, but not under circumstances like these—with someone else producing, with Dowd co-starring—" He looked back toward the closed door, as if Drew had just gone out. His eyes narrowed, and I understood.

"Carlyle, you can't possibly be jealous when I've told you so often that we are friends only."

"Young friends," he said. "Beautiful and handsome young friends. No one could blame you if you were attracted to him, and certainly no one could blame Dowd for wanting you—again." That last word sounded with the surprise of a rustling program in an already quieted theater.

"We are only friends," I repeated wearily, unwilling to discuss the matter further. "I'm very tired now, and I must go up to bed. Will you excuse me?"

"Always, Katherine. Good night."

I did not sleep well that night, and Carlyle's unpleasant words played their discordant theme on my mind for the next days, until one afternoon when they reverberated clearly and with uncanny accuracy.

Rehearsal had ended quite early, so Drew and I stayed on alone to go over the wedding scene in which Petruchio intends to bring his shrewish wife to heel. I wanted to appear submissive, yet let Petruchio, my lord and master, know that Kate was tamed only because she wanted to be tamed. At last we were almost satisfied, and agreed to stop before the reading grew stale and uninteresting. Drew carefully turned out all the gas jets as we left the stage. Now only one flame burned, over our heads above the stage door. Our shadows danced like lanky puppets against the wall. Drew slipped my cape, the elegant gift of sable from my husband, around my shoulders.

"We make a good team, don't we, Kate?" Carefully, as though performing an act of great importance, he tucked in my scarf and buttoned the cape high at my throat, as he went on, "I've known that for a long time."

"Have you?" I asked lightly.

"I loved you long ago, Kate—"

"Drew, please."

"No, let me say this. I loved you when you were young, when you were a pretty girl, fresh and unspoiled. The freshness is still there, Kate. You haven't been hardened by all that has happened. But there's wisdom there now, and beauty. Such great beauty."

The light from the single jet flickered across Drew's face. I moved away, not wishing to see the deep feelings reflected in his eyes. When I turned, he caught my hand and made me stay. His hat and cape lay on the chair by the door; he made no move to pick them up.

"I won't let you go until I've said everything that must be said. I loved the pretty girl you once were; I love the beautiful woman you are now. I know I'm speaking out of turn, but something tells me I have more right to speak now than in the past, when I was quiet because of Terry. I understood when you chose

him, Kate. There was an excitement about Terry that
was magnetic. Men loved him too. I loved him."

"I know."

"More than that, I wanted to *be* Terry, to have his
talent and his zest, to have everything of his. Even
you."

"He never owned me, Drew."

"Of course he didn't. Nor will any man—least of all
the man you've married." Drew held onto my hand. "I
haven't spoken before because I wanted what you
wanted, Kate. But you're not happy. Something is
wrong in that marriage."

"Don't be ridiculous, Drew."

"Look at me, Kate. Tell me that you love J. Carlyle
Wharton, the financial barracuda. Look at me and say
you love him."

I looked straight into his eyes as I spoke the words,
"Yes, I love him." But my voice betrayed me with its
quiver.

Drew pulled me to him exultantly. "I knew it!" He
held me so close that I could feel his heart pounding.
"And if you don't love me, at least you care for me. I
have enough love for us both. 'Kiss me, Kate,' " he said.
His voice was the voice of Petruchio, but when I turned
my face away, he stopped acting. His lips followed
mine, and the words he spoke were his own. "Kiss me,
Kate. Kiss me."

I kissed him, again and again. His lips were soft,
warm, tender. Not demanding, simply asking, hoping. I
felt myself respond to that hope, wrapped in his intense
passion. Sasha's words rang in my mind—"You're a
woman made for loving, Katerina"—while Drew's arms
tightened about me. I knew I should break away before
his desire became reckless, leaving no room for second
thoughts. I would break away, but first—first, let me
kiss him, let me hold him, just for a moment! Finally, I
leaned back against the door, closed my eyes, and
caught my breath; it was over.

But Drew did not know my thoughts as he pressed
against me, his body hard with his need. His lips

touched my ear. "We can go to my dressing room, Kate. This time won't be like before. You know that."

One thing was very clear now: I mustn't let Drew know how much I needed the love and warmth he offered. I shook my head. "I can't, Drew. I'm sorry I clung to you that way when my commitment is to Carlyle. I have no taste for adultery."

"You're committed, even if you suffer?"

"I am not suffering, Drew. Marriage is complex and complicated. I'm sorry this happened tonight. I'm entirely to blame, and I'm very sorry."

I touched his cheek with all the tenderness that was within me. I could have shared his love; I could have satisfied my longing, but that would have been selfish and unfair to both Drew and Carlyle.

"This must not happen again, Drew." I pushed open the door and stepped into the night air.

"I can't stop loving or wanting you, Kate." Drew's voice echoed in the empty alley.

I took his arm as we walked toward the street. Stars filled the immense sky. "Perhaps you can't, for a while. But you're young and handsome, and someone will soon mend your broken heart."

"Don't tease me, Kate. I do love you."

"I know that, and I don't mean to tease. But you and I both know this cannot be, that we must stop before we are both sorry."

"If I didn't know better, I'd say you've become a prude, Katherine Lawrence."

"Mrs. J. Carlyle Wharton," I corrected.

"We would be good together, Kate, this time."

"Please, Drew, let's not talk about it anymore."

He agreed with a smile, the enchanting, boyish smile I had come to depend on. "I won't pine for you, Kate." Then, more seriously, "But if you are unhappy, and if you ever need to talk to someone, talk to me. Let me at least be Clara while she's gone."

I laughed. "You have my word. But everything's going to be all right. Here's my carriage. Can I give you a ride?"

"No. Boris and I are meeting on Hudson Street for dinner. I may even walk over. See you tomorrow."

That night, taking his cue from my special efforts, Carlyle relaxed, and his former easy charm emerged. After dinner, I sat beside him in the library, which had become our favorite room. His arm encircling me, he talked of a trip we planned for the future—to Venice, Rome, Florence.

"That does sound marvelous, dear," I said, resting my head on his shoulder.

"I'm glad you like the idea. You know how I want to give you pleasure. I want to buy the world for you, but you must let me."

"And so I do. Look at this house and my jewels and gowns—"

"Yet you still insist on working."

"You knew that before we married."

"I envisioned my own role differently; nor did I realize how the theater would consume you."

"I'm going to reform, darling, just as I promised. We've had a lovely evening together, and there will be many more. Now tell me again about Piazza San Marco."

The next day dawned sweet and clear, with more than a taste of long-awaited spring, and with no hint of what was to come. I arrived a few minutes late at the theater, and as I climbed the iron stairs to the wings, I knew immediately that something was terribly wrong. A pall of sadness hung in the air. I pushed through the side curtain and looked out over the stage. Lester stood on the apron, the cast members huddled in front of him.

"What's happened?"

Lester heard my whispered words. "Terrible news, Kate. Terrible."

I looked around quickly as he spoke. Drew was not there! "Drew?" I cried out. "Is he—" I could not bear to speak the word. *Not again!*

"No, Kate, he's not dead, but he is hurt, although not as badly as Boris."

"Boris! What—"

"Last night, as they left a bistro on Hudson Street, they were attacked by thugs. Drew's arm is broken. Apparently, he was hit by a metal pipe. His face—well, they seemed to concentrate on his face."

I felt suddenly sick. Johnny reached out to support me, and I leaned against him.

"Boris is in critical condition. The back of his skull was crushed, and he's still unconscious. The doctors aren't sure he's going to live."

"Where are they?" someone asked.

"In St. Anne's, a private hospital near the river. The nuns who run it are excellent nurses."

"I must go at once—" I heard myself say.

"Let me finish my announcement, Kate. Ladies and gentlemen, I've decided not to continue with rehearsals for *Shrew*. Fred was to understudy Drew, but I feel an obligation to Drew—and Kate—and all of you—to delay the opening until we have our Petruchio back. That won't be long, I'm told. No more than a month. As for Boris—" The words strangled in his throat, and he used his wrinkled handkerchief to wipe his eyes. "We'll just have to wait and see about Boris."

Tears filled my own eyes as Lester continued, "You'll all stay on full rehearsal salary for the next two weeks. By then we should have a clear idea of the new schedule—so don't any of you join up with Daly or Booth while you're waiting." Lester didn't even try to force a smile at this weak joke. "All right," he said finally, "I'll be in touch within a fortnight. That's all."

I went immediately to St. Anne's, having arranged to stay at the hospital until Aurora arrived in midafternoon. Johnny would take her place in the evening with other cast members filling in the next days so Drew would not have to be alone. There was nothing any of us could do for Boris. He had not regained consciousness. No visitors were allowed.

Drew was awake, propped up on starched white pillows. Vivid bruises splashed like a violent rainbow across a face twice its normal size. His head was bound in gauze; one eye was swollen shut. "Kate," he said through cracked lips, "will you kiss me now?"

"You fool," I answered, trying to cover my tears with laughter as I bent to touch my lips to his raw cheek. We talked only briefly, as the nurse had just given Drew an injection to help him sleep, but there was time for him to go over the horror of the night before. I had not meant to hear the details, but he seemed to want to tell me. So with sickened heart, I listened.

The night had grown misty after he and Boris had dined, and quiet, without even the far-off grating of carriage wheels against the cobblestones. As they left the restaurant and began to walk in search of a cab, they passed a dark alley, unnoticing. There were many such alleys tucked away along Hudson, and it was impossible to avoid them. But here three men slipped from the shadows, hardly more than shadows themselves. Drew had only an impression of his assailant—dark clothes and gloves, a knitted cap pulled low, and—caught for an instant in a sliver of pale moonlight—a lead pipe raised with cunning purpose. Drew had used his arm to protect his head, but after knocking him down, two of the men had bashed his face with their fists. "I'm told my beauty is not permanently marred," Drew said with a painful smile. Apparently, Boris had been struck on the back of the head before he had had time to protect himself. "Is he still unconscious?" Drew asked, and I nodded. Drew told me that he had been able to crawl into the street and attract passersby, who brought the police. No money had been taken, he added thickly, just before falling into a heavy sleep. I sat beside him until Aurora arrived, leaving me with no excuse but to return home. I left the building through scrubbed white halls along which the nuns hastened, their habits rustling, past Boris's room; there was no sound from behind the closed door.

Carlyle came into my suite as I was dressing for dinner.

"What has happened?" he asked when his eyes met my reflection in the mirror.

I looked at my own face for the first time that day, and I saw the strain there, the paleness, and the memory of Drew's pain. Carlyle sat beside me at the dressing table as I poured out the story.

"Terrible," he said, "and strange, too, that they weren't robbed. Well, that part of Hudson goes through a seamy section of town. We must do something for your friends." He moved to my bell pull and rang for Jerris. "Send the footman to Balducci's market. I want baskets of fresh fruits delivered to St. Anne's for Mr. Dowd and Mr. Golding. Oh, yes, and flowers too. The least we can do, Katherine," he said, turning to me as Jerris left. "Now finish dressing, darling. We have just time for a glass of sherry before dinner. I, too, have news—and of a more pleasant nature."

The sherry relaxed me somewhat, and the white wine with dinner a bit more, but I was still not adequately prepared for Carlyle's announcement, which he had postponed until dessert: Augusta was coming home. Apparently she could put off the day of her return no longer, as reason accumulated upon reason to bring her home: to see her adored father, to face me finally as his wife, to introduce the young man she had met abroad and planned to marry. My respite from the theater came at an appropriate time, Carlyle reminded me, for now I would have the opportunity to get to know my stepdaughter. I looked up with narrowed eyes at that remark but met only candor. My husband was not, as was I, still thinking of Drew and Boris in their hospital beds, but of his beloved daughter, the object now of all our immediate plans. She and the young man were to arrive on the *Amerique*, docking on the first of May. I began to feel almost gay as I thought ahead to their arrival. Augusta's beau would not be staying with us, but I expected that we would be entertaining him often, and with that in mind, I would need to rearrange our social calendar, and some of our menus as well. Coming from the Continent, he would no doubt appreciate the French culinary skills I had so carefully taught our cook. As for Augusta, there was no thought of my being a mother to her, but I determined then and there to be her friend.

My two lives merged, separated, and merged again in the days that followed, as I put the final touches on Augusta's suite of rooms, between trips to St. Anne's. Boris remained in a coma, but Drew at last left the hospital on the road to recovery. I knew my visits would soon have to cease as, inevitably, on the day that Augusta came home, Kate Lawrence would reluctantly fade into Mrs. J. Carlyle Wharton. But if the actress could be sublimated, her appearance could not be entirely altered. When the day arrived and Carlyle left for the docks, I tossed aside dress after dress before settling on a blue chambray with high neck and long sleeves. This would have to do, I told myself; I could not look motherly if I tried!

At the sound of a carriage and voices below, I started down the stairs. There they were—Carlyle, dark and debonair, his face filled with delight, and Augusta, pale and thin, dwarfed between the two men. Excitedly, I joined them. The other man was tall and lean, a hard man, I thought at a glance. His hair was unusually long and a mustache, like a pirate's, slashed darkly across his face. But there was something—something so familiar . . .

"Katherine, my love, here is my Augusta, and her fiance, Mr. Chapman." Carlyle smiled at me. "My wife Katherine."

Mr. Chapman raised his eyes to me in one long look, somehow pure, yet almost pitying. I heard the door close, Jerris's footsteps move away, the water in the fountain spilling lazily against the marble. These sounds magnified until I felt I could see them, and they were black and filled my eyes as I fainted.

I had fainted only twice in my life: once, when I learned of Nick's death, and today, when once again he stood before me. A warning must have sounded within me to cause the collapse which alone prevented my shouting out his name. Nick. Nick!

"Are you all right, Katherine?"

I opened my eyes to see Carlyle bending near and
Alicia hovering in the background.

"Are you all right?" he asked again.

"Yes," I answered, "and I certainly do feel foolish. I
expect Augusta must think me quite odd." My voice
was cool, calm, and gave no indication of how my mind
was racing ahead, spilling out thoughts, so personal
and intimate, of the moments of love Nick and I had
shared, that I had to turn my mind away and look
aside, for fear those thoughts would be revealed on my
face.

"I told Augusta that the excitement had no doubt
been too much. But is there anything else?"

"I didn't feel well today." The lie came as easily as
the words that had preceded it. "I avoided telling you
for fear of dampening your own excitement. But I feel
better now, Carlyle. I'll get up—"

"That's out of the question, my dear. You must rest
here in your room. Alicia will bring tea and toast."

Suddenly my calmness fled. Panic swept over me.
Nick might leave before I had a chance to see him
again! I tried to get up, but Carlyle restrained me.

"Katherine, my dear, what *is* the matter? Augusta
will be here with us for some time, and we will doubt-
less see a great deal of her young man as well. Believe
me, there is no urgency."

"Of course," I agreed. I forced a smile, which I managed convincingly to maintain until Carlyle and Alicia
had left and I was alone at last, my tea and toast untouched on a tray beside me.

I tried to clear my thoughts of all but the essentials,
and yet my mind raced ahead, stopped, and then raced
on again. I could not control it; my emotions took
flight, and every vision I had ever had of Nick melted
into one sensuous, pulsating form, to whom I saw myself joined as I had dreamed for so long—a dream at
once impossible, and yet now within my grasp. I did not
consider that he might have changed, that he might not
be the man I had once known, that he might not want
me as I wanted him. I did not ponder over what miracle

had brought him back, or why he had changed his name. It could not matter that he was engaged to my husband's daughter any more than that I myself was married.

And yet it did matter. The next morning's light brought cold reality. Nick had returned, but he belonged now to someone else, to my own stepdaughter. I allowed the questions that flooded my unwilling mind to surface at last, realizing that they must all be answered before I could know what lay ahead for any of us. First, I must find out about Nick; then I must endeavor to see him alone.

My attempt to learn something of the Nick who was now Stephen Chapman was almost thwarted by Augusta's reticence. She came to my room as I was finishing the breakfast Alicia had insisted I have in bed.

"I hope you are feeling better, Katherine." The voice was soft and well-modulated, with a touch of an accent which fell just short of being British. She was several inches taller than I, slender, with a long graceful neck. Her hair was soft brown, pulled high on her head. Her eyes were pale, very like her father's. I watched her as we talked, and she demonstrated with every move her ease of manner and perfect composure, also like her father. Her face was not beautiful, or even pretty, but she herself was regal, and a girl, I decided, who had always gotten what she wanted easily, without a struggle. She was not, as I was soon to find out, given to easy conversation. Yes, she admitted, the trip had been pleasant, but she was happy to be back in New York. Her father, she said, looked well. The house was quite nice. She hoped that we could get to know each other well. I saw an opening here, and took advantage of it.

"I hope so too, Augusta. Please, tell me about Europe. Or better still, tell me about your romance. I should think Mr. Chapman was very perplexed by what happened yesterday."

"No, he said very little."

I tried again. "Have you known your fiance long?"

"For a while." Silence. Inwardly I groaned, but then

she went on. "We met in Monte Carlo, and I saw him later in Venice and Paris. He's quite nice."

I chose my words with great care as I asked about his background and his line of business. She responded, I thought, just as carefully, before allowing a little animation to come into her face.

"He's in export-import. He came to Europe from Brazil. Brazil—can you imagine! At first I thought he was just like the others. Most of the men I met in Europe were fortune hunters," she clarified. "But Stephen—" a smile formed on her delicate lips— "Stephen has his own money."

"He's wealthy?" Augusta nodded her assent, and my heart plummeted as I thought of the accusations that had been made against Nick. But if they were true, then why, I wondered, had he come back?

"His business has all been in the foreign market," Augusta said. "I believe he wants to invest in his own country now."

"Well, when will I see this exciting Mr. Chapman again?"

"This afternoon, if you wish. He's coming for tea at four, and then we're going for a walk. Do you feel up to joining us for tea?"

"I'm completely recovered, and I would welcome the opportunity." My smile was genuine, but I trembled inside.

My hand was trembling too, as I held it out to him when he arrived promptly at four, but his was steady, as were his eyes. He started to speak; I interrupted; he began again. Then silence. I poured the tea with unexpected skill, although my own cup rattled in the saucer. I could not bring myself to look at him, and once I looked, I could not turn away. He was so much older, less polished now, tougher. I wondered what part of the Nick I had known still existed in this man.

"Augusta," he said (and I noticed that even his voice was different), "have you given Mrs. Wharton the gift we picked out in Venice? I'd like to see if we chose correctly."

"Oh, no, I forgot." Her face fell for a moment. "But I'll get it now."

"I was just going to suggest that." Nick stood up as she left. I too, rose from my chair and moved part of the way across the room. The door closed behind Augusta. I tried to speak, but could not even say his name. My lips were dry; my throat was parched.

"Don't say anything, Kate. Just listen to me, please. Coming here last night was not in the plan. I had asked to be dropped off at my flat, but your husband insisted. I could only hope you would not be so angry that you would give me away, reveal my identity."

"Give you away? I'd sooner sacrifice myself, don't you know that?"

He had moved toward me, and now stood so close I could have touched him, but I dared not. "I've changed, Kate. We've both changed. Nothing can be the same as before, but I want to talk to you, to explain. I'm staying in a flat on East Thirty-ninth. Here's the address. Can you come tomorrow?"

I nodded as I took the card and slipped it inside my sleeve. At that moment, the door opened and Augusta came in, bringing with her my gift, a leatherbound volume of opera librettos, including *La Traviata*, which I had first seen with Nick. It was because of him that I had come to love opera. I knew that he had chosen the gift for me.

We had planned a small dinner party the following night for Augusta and some of her school friends, but Carlyle expected me to spend the day with her as well. I knew better than to disappoint him, since his disappointment could often be devastating. But nothing would prevent my seeing Nick.

The weather turned out to be my strategist. I awoke to a fine spring day, which Jerris had allowed to fill the breakfast room by opening, for the first time, the windows onto our terrace. Cheered by the clear signs of spring, Carlyle did not dwell overlong on my plans for the day, and I was able to assure him only that I would take Augusta out for luncheon. After I kissed Carlyle goodbye at the door, I rushed to my room to dress, while Augusta still slept. With a parting word to Alicia that I had just remembered a final dress fitting and would return in time for lunch, I rushed from the house. There was a carriage waiting, but I dismissed it, preferring to walk the ten blocks to Nick's flat. My heart pounded my breath grew short. I saw nothing on the streets as shapes passed by, to my eyes neither women nor men, but only shadows. I had only one thought: with every step I am getting nearer to him. Nearer. Nearer.

At last I was there. I was climbing the steps . . . my hand was on the door . . . Nick was standing in the darkened hall. Beyond, in his room a fire was burning in the grate. He took my cape, and I turned to him, filled with a need to know that was, for an instant, as great as my passion.

"Why, Nick?" I cried, "Why?"

"You know why, Kate. The police wanted me; they still want me."

"But why didn't you write to me, give me some clue?"

"I had to make a decision, Kate. I did what I thought would be best for you."

I caught my breath in despair as he explained, "I didn't want you to wait for me when I might never return. I had nothing to offer you then. Or now. I'm sorry, Kate, but I thought it was best that way."

I had taken the chair that Nick offered. He stood in front of me, a few feet away. "Sorry?" I breathed an agonizing sigh. "When they told me you were dead, I wanted to die. But somehow I lived."

"I'm glad, Kate."

"And began a new life. Married Carlyle."

"Yes. And knowing that, I should never have asked you to come here today. But Kate——" he looked away, the muscles in his jaw tensing——" since that moment when I saw you again, I've thought only of how I wanted to hold you, to touch your hair, to taste your mouth once more——"

I don't know which of us moved first, took the first step toward the other, but the few feet that separated us were breached on an instant, and I was in his arms. As he pulled me close and kissed me, I was filled with all the wild desire of the past, yet with more; with a peace and gentleness that told me I had come home. Our endless kisses joined together spirit as well as flesh.

We made love before the fire, and the flames danced in my eyes and blotted out the world around. The four walls that had confined us divided, split, separated, until there was no room, no house, but only a glowing space in which we were one, joined in a union more holy than faith, more binding than marriage. I knew that all of the love I had given and had received in my whole life had been only to prepare me for this moment.

When did the walls come together again, the room surround us once more? I saw the sparks of fire recaptured behind the grate; I heard the crackling of the burning log, I heard Nick's voice.

"The day is too warm for a fire, but I lit it, hoping— hoping to see your skin glow golden in its light, the way I'd seen it glow so many times before." My hair had become loosened and fell like a dark veil half across Nick's face. "And to see those golden lights in your hair again."

I touched his cheek and looked into his remarkable eyes, at once gray and green and now, in the firelight—

"And your eyes are gold too," I whispered. But the skin that had once been gold was tarnished now, and scarred. My fingers lightly touched the marks on his face and chest. Tenderly, I bent to kiss each one.

"Oh, Nick, what have you been through to change you so?"

He smiled almost bitterly, and the look in his eyes was far away. "I'm no longer the dilettante you once knew, Kate. I've seen so much. Too much, I'm afraid. But you, Kate. You are as fresh and lovely as ever." He leaned up on one elbow and gazed at me with a look so deep and full of meaning that it took my breath away.

"Oh, God," he whispered, "I don't think I ever knew until this moment how much I ached for you, and—"

"And what?"

"And loved you, Kate, I love you with my whole heart now—now, when I can't have you."

"Nothing is impossible," I said softly.

Nick rolled away from me and began pulling on his clothes. "Kate, I need to tell you why I came back. I should have told you sooner. Here." He tossed me a shirt, which I slipped on. "Sit back and listen to me." He began to pace up and down. "I didn't steal the railroad money; I want you to·know that."

"Augusta said you were wealthy—"

"Money I made in Brazil, honestly, or as honestly as one can, there. I was framed in the railroad scandal, Kate, not by Monte Powell alone, but by someone higher up, a man whose name I saw once, a man I vowed to track down and bring to earth, no matter what. And now that I've found him . . . my God, I can't."

My head began to swim. I tried to swallow; my throat was dry. "Why?" I choked. The word lay sickeningly on my tongue.

"You know why, Kate. That man is your husband."

Had I known? And if so, *how* had I known? Somehow. Somehow. I sat for a full minute in stunned and horrified silence. But having begun, Nick continued, needing to get to the end of his story, and so free his mind of its terrible burden.

"I made a small fortune in Brazil. It was part of my plan for revenge, and then I went to Europe where chance threw Augusta into my arms."

"Do you—"

"Love Augusta? Lord, no. I haven't even made love to her. She was my only way—the only way I could see—to get close to him. She was my luck, Kate, and I badly needed some luck for a change. Augusta's a nice child, and, I'm glad to say, a tough one; I don't believe I've hurt her." Nick turned and stared into the fire, his hands gripping the mantelpiece. "What I·planned to do to her father was cruel enough. When I found you had married Wharton, married the man who had ruined me—" Nick had not turned to face me, but kept his eyes averted— "I still would have done what I planned, Kate. I still would have brought him to his knees. I knew I was taking a risk coming back with you here, but I meant to avoid you. As if I could have avoided you." A sigh seemed to rack his body. "Now, with you involved— I won't cause you any more pain, Kate."

He turned to look at me then, and saw the confusion in my eyes.

"To have done what we just did—" He seemed to be struggling to find the words he needed. "I *have* changed, Kate. The man I once was could never have said what I'm about to say, because he could never have felt what I felt just now for you, what I feel at this moment, when all the love I've ever known is there in your face. I know you feel the same way, and to have come back into your life and set us both on fire this way was wrong. What happened can't be undone, but it won't happen again."

"What do you mean?"

"I'll go away from here, Kate. I won't ever forget what Wharton did to me, but I'll let it rest. All at once, revenge does not seem so important, not at the cost of more pain for you. The world is wide. There is a place in it for Stephen Chapman."

That was all! That was all that held us apart. He only wanted to protect me, to preserve my marriage. My relief was so great that I almost laughed, but seeing Nick's face, I could not laugh.

"Nick, you must see how wrong this is, to go away, to give up the chase that has led you over thousands of miles, for fear of hurting me and destroying my marriage. Nick, my marriage is a farce, loveless and meaningless." He started to speak. "No, my darling, let me tell you what I've never told anyone, for fear of being disloyal to Carlyle." I shook my head in silent wonder. "Disloyal to the man who took you from me, ruined you. All that money—I suppose my house is paid for with that money, and my clothes."

"Kate, you didn't know."

"But I could have been more honest with myself. I knew I didn't love him when we married; the day after, I knew I could never love him."

I told Nick the whole story. I told him of Carlyle's unusual needs, of my humiliation and despair, and Nick watched my face, unblinking, as I spoke. When I finished, he dropped silently to his knees before me. There were tears in his eyes.

"My darling," he said at last, "come away with me. Wharton has torn us apart once; I won't let him do that again." He held me gently in his arms and smoothed my hair absently as he spoke. "We can go to South America. To Spain or the East." Then his face changed. "Hell, I can't ask you to give up acting. I know what the stage means to you."

"I've always said it was my life, but that's not true. You are my life, Nick."

We were silent for a long time, holding each other with such a tender familiarity that I could not believe we had ever been apart.

"I remember telling Courtney once— Oh, Nick, did you know she died?"

"My love, I'm so sorry. How—"

"Not now. I won't be drowned in sorrow again now." He held me even closer and I went on, "But she and I were talking once of love and men. Our men. I remember telling her that there was a darker side of love. Well, my darling, I have seen that darker side, and now I want to come back into the light, but not alone. With you."

"Then come with me now, tonight. Don't go back to him."

But even as he spoke, Nick knew that what he asked was not possible. "He'll follow us," he said. I nodded.

"Then we must plan carefully. I'll decide on our destination, and I'll book passage from Charleston. You must tell him you are going to visit your family. You'll have to be convincing."

Again, I gave my silent assent.

"Give me two days—no, three—to make the arrangements. Then get a train to South Carolina. I'll find you there."

"We must remember that he doesn't let go easily, Nick. I'm like one of his possessions, one of his beloved statues. Unless we're very careful, he'll find us and—" A convulsive shudder shook me.

"Don't be afraid, darling. Nothing will part us now."

I left almost joyfully just before lunch, arriving back at Forty-eighth Street to find Augusta waiting. We stepped right into the carriage and headed for our luncheon. The glow of Nick invaded my whole being; the memory of him was implanted upon me forever. We had spent the rest of the morning together, as we had so many times before. He had leaned back in his chair, lit a thin black cigar, and talked to me just as he used to. And he had laughed, his dimples cutting deeply into his tanned skin. He was the Nick I had known before. And loved. But never as I loved him now.

"Don't be afraid. Nothing will part us," he had said, and I believed him.

EPILOGUE

After Kate had left, Nick went back to the sofa and sat down. He stared, for how long he did not know, into the fire's dwindling flames. The flames sputtered and turned to glowing embers, and still he sat, all the time thinking only of her. She was everything to him now—all women, all life. She had given him the flame within her, and it would not die.

When Kate stepped into the carriage with Augusta, Nick was still sitting before the fire; when she returned to her house late that afternoon, his plans had been formulated, clearly and concisely, in a mind that never rested. He knew what must be done, and he moved to set his plans into action. After dressing quickly, he threw on a cape, picked up his hat from the hall table, and left the flat, locking the door carefully behind him. In three days he could arrange everything; in three days they would leave New York, separately. Within a week, they would be together. Forever.

For Kate, the time would not pass so easily. She could only wait.

"Isn't Mr. Chapman joining us for dinner?" Carlyle asked as a maid came in to clear away the tray of empty sherry glasses. Jerris had just announced the evening meal, and Carlyle offered one arm to each woman, his wife and his daughter, as they made their way toward the dining room.

Kate waited for Augusta to answer. "No, he has a business appointment."

Then Kate spoke, with a smile, as Carlyle seated her at the table: "Well, we shall try again tomorrow."

"What did you do today, my dear? Augusta says you were gone for quite a while." As Carlyle spoke, his daughter stared very obviously at the plate before her.

"I had a dress fitting, which I barely remembered in time. I left rather early, and Augusta was still asleep." She looked intently at her stepdaughter, whose eyes remained fixed on her dinner plate. "I shall not be so thoughtless tomorrow."

So that was to be the way, Kate mused. Augusta would report to Carlyle. Well, she would give the girl nothing to pass on. Nor did she.

The following day, the two women shopped, had tea, talked, lunched with the wives of Carlyle's closest associates, and attended a matinee at Daly's Theater. They dined out that evening, and again Nick did not join them. Augusta seemed to understand that he would need a few days to set his business affairs in motion; Kate knew he could not tempt fate by coming to the house. She tried to mimic his patience. And she managed through dinner, the ride home, a nightcap in the library; she managed while listening to the laughter and talk between father and daughter—evidence of their happiness at being together again.

But once in bed, Kate's patience waned. The moon rode high in the sky, and the window, cracked to let in the night air, also admitted the faintest whiff of spring. She could not sleep; how chould she, with her love only blocks away? Her practical side told her to stay; her impetuous side—the part of her that had given no thought to running away from home and joining an acting company or living with a band of gypsies or giving herself to a wild Irish actor—that side won, and soon she was dressed and moving stealthily down the stairs, across the hall, to the door. So filled was she with love, that once outside, she had no fear of being alone in the dark streets. But she had only gone a few yards when there was a touch on her arm. A scream lodged in her throat.

"Don't be afraid," the man said, "I work for Mr. Wharton."

"My husband?" she asked foolishly.

"Yes, ma'am. He's had a couple of us watching the house—in case of burglary, you understand."

"Yes," she acknowledged, and then lied lamely, "I wanted some air; I often walk out in the late evening."

"Allow me to accompany you, ma'am."

There she was, neatly trapped. To change her mind would appear more suspicious; she had no choice but to walk the block with her taciturn guard before returning to the house, where she remained awake for most of the night, her mind awhirl. Why had Carlyle not told her about the guards? Had he suspected her love for Nick? Did he know who Nick really was? By morning, her fear had reached fever pitch. There seemed no possibility that Carlyle could know yet, but if he did know, there was no time to waste. They would have to leave today—now—without plans. Just run. Leave the country. Go to Canada, to Mexico, anywhere, but go. Go today!

An excuse formed in her mind, one Augusta might doubt, but would have difficulty disproving. "Lester has sent word that I'm needed at the theater right away," Kate lied blatantly to her stepdaughter, and without waiting for a response, she left, heading straight to Nick's flat.

He was not there! She scribbled a note, saying she would return in the afternoon. But knowing she could not go home and unsure where to go, she remained standing by the locked door, frozen. At last she moved. There was one place to go and thereby make the deceit more palatable.

For a few hours, she gave herself to the one world that existed outside of Nick, a world she might never know after today; for a few hours, she sat in the back row of the 14th Street Theater and watched, silent and unseen, a rehearsal for the next Markan tour of Lester's amusing new version of *As You Like It*. As twilight fell, she returned to Nick's flat and saw that the note was not in the door. He was back.

"Nick, darling—" The door swung open and she heard a voice.

"Come in, Katherine."

Carlyle loomed before her, smiling, and across the room stood Nick, not moving. Why? And then she saw the gun in Carlyle's hand.

"Move to the chair, Katherine, and sit quietly. Your long-lost lover, Mr. Van Dyne, tried to take my weapon earlier, but I've convinced him of my firmness." Nick held his arm above the elbow, and thick red drops of blood spilled from his sleeve and down his fingers.

"Nick—"

"I'm all right, Kate, only sorry that you walked into this."

"I'm afraid that somehow I'm the cause—"

"How clever of you, my dear," Carlyle answered. "But you also should have guessed that I have long been suspicious of your activities. I hated the thought of you and Dowd together. You see, I never wanted to share any part of you with any man, my Katherine." He looked sadly at her, as if somehow the fault were hers. "I was sure that Dowd was taken care of; his little accident was easy to arrange." Kate caught her breath in helpless understanding. "Then I hoped you would grow tired of waiting for his recovery and give up your absurd theatrical endeavors."

"Drew is only a friend, Carlyle," Kate whispered uselessly.

"So I learned, too late. I became more suspicious

when you spent that long morning away from the house, away from Augusta. So I decided to have you followed. Last night, after your walk, my guard reported the activity to me. When, my dear Katherine, have you ever had occasion to take solitary walks in the dead of night?" he asked, not waiting for an answer, or expecting one. "Then, today," he went on, "my employee found your note here in the door. 'Dear Nick—' Nick. Of course! Something about Chapman did have me on edge from the beginning, but mine was a doubt that the happiness of Augusta's homecoming prevented me from following through. As you know, I am not usually so easily cuckolded." His mouth pursed with bitter revulsion.

"I don't know what you plan to do, Wharton, but let Kate go. Your quarrel is with me," Nick argued.

"Let Kate go? My dear Van Dyne, you are speaking of my wife. I will never let her go; she knows that. In fact, I can't let either of you go." Indeed, she knew he spoke the truth; he planned for them both to die in this room. Carlyle's next words were directed, in a voice she had grown to hate, toward his wife. "Van Dyne knows too much about my finances. He wasn't believed before; this time, I fear, he will be, and so I think I will have to simulate a lover's quarrel. Is that not good staging, Katherine? Perhaps I can let out to the press that you coveted my daughter's fiance, but he rejected you. You shot him and took your own life."

"You're mad, Carlyle!" Kate cried. "Sick and demented and twisted—"

"And you, my dear, are a little tramp. I should have known that your beauty was only a mask to cover a hideous ugliness."

To reason with him further was useless. She looked at Nick. He seemed unable to move, leaning against the mantle, a grimace on his face as he held his bloody arm. Then he caught her eye, and slowly his gaze dropped to her ungloved hand. She was nervously twisting the huge ring on her finger. Green fire, the emerald Carlyle had given her. Then another look crossed Nick's face, a

look Kate read as clearly as if he spoke the word: *wait.*
She loosened the ring as Nick began to talk to Carlyle,
pleading in words she could not understand, so soft and
unintelligible were they. Nor did Carlyle understand.
His eyes wavered; he took a hesitant step toward Nick.
It was then that she threw the ring, and it reached its
mark. Carlyle jerked back as the heavy platinum circle
hit him just below the eye. He raised the gun. Nick was
upon him, grappling. A shot rang out.

A nightmare erupted before her, a nightmare of vivid
colors splashed on a stark canvas. Her own face was
painted there, and it showed white terror, and on her
mouth a scream was forming.

And then Nick's voice assured her, "The horror is
over, Kate."

But they both knew it was just beginning.

January, 1880

A young woman sat in a closed carriage. Through the round side window could be seen, had there been anyone on that desolate hillside to see, a face flushed with anticipation. Dark eyes stared out at the falling snow, yet did not see the snowflakes at all, but only the gray, looming buildings beyond. Then a cry, tiny and muted, came from within the carriage—a child's cry, which grew stronger for a long moment before subsiding again.

Kate shifted in place and moved her baby easily into the experienced crook of her arm.

"Not much longer, little Sloane," she whispered as she pulled back a corner of the soft blanket and looked into her daughter's bright green eyes. She chucked the baby under her chin and was rewarded with a dribbling smile, which revealed two prominent lower teeth.

The day did not brighten; it merely grew colder, grayer, and more foreboding, but Kate did not notice. Soon Sloane fell asleep in her mother's comforting arms, and Kate, too, closed her eyes, not in sleep, but in the misty haze of memory.

What desperate promises they had made to each other, that spring afternoon almost two years before, while the dead body of a man she was sure now she had never known lay on the floor beyond them. She begged Nick to run, to run and take her with him. But he refused.

"I've killed a man, Kate. An evil man, yes, but the courts must have a chance to pass their judgment. This is the law we live under."

"Then marry me now, before the police are notified. We belong to each other in every way; let us be bound in marriage."

This time Nick wavered, but he did not give in. "Remember, Kate, when you once asked—a lifetime ago— why you would ever have to choose between me and the theater? 'I'll have both,' you said."

She did remember. "That *was* a lifetime ago, my darling. You'll never need to ask again, because I've already chosen. I want to be with you always."

"Kate, our 'always' is going to be a long time coming, and until then, I want you to go back to the theater, to play your *Shrew,* to have your finest hour. And then, when I'm free— Oh, Kate, Kate, how different my life will be then. I'll have to start all over, with no money, no career." Suddenly a smile flickered over his handsome features, a sad smile but not a bitter one. "I'll emerge as a man with a particularly unsavory reputation, and I can't even predict what my sentence will be. It is very liable to be harsh, so I ask you to withhold your commitment. I beg this of you, Kate. Wait until I'm free before you choose."

"My feeling will never change. I've never wanted anything but for us to be together."

"And so we shall be, if fate decrees it. But if, for some reason, we cannot be joined in this life— No, Kate, don't look at me like that. I'm not a religious man, or one who believes in an afterlife, but perhaps, in some other time, a man will look at a woman and see you, and they will love as we do."

"I'm not religious either, darling. I believe only in the finality of our love. I'll be waiting, Nick." She held him then, and kissed him again and again to fortify herself against the uncertain future that lay ahead.

He broke away at last and whispered, "We must go now, Kate."

"I know."

All of her friends were with her during the long trial. But it was Barney Helm who sustained her and kept up her spirits. She could see Nick from across half the width of the courtroom, and although she could meet his gaze and smile, she could not give him the hope she felt he needed. She wanted to testify in his behalf, but Nick's counsel doubted the wisdom of putting her on the stand. Nick himself was adamantly opposed to dragging Kate through the rigors of cross-examination, but she was persistent. Barney shared her belief that her testimony would be helpful. Barney was in court this time not as a reporter but as a friend, and his long experience in trial coverage was not lost on the defense counsel. Besides, Barney saw something in the girl that might help to sway the jury—an innocence and truthfulness that would not go unnoticed. And so, in spite of Nick's vehemence, the attorney agreed. And she *did* help, as Barney assured her again and again. But even Kate's believability could not make Nick a free man.

His name was cleared in the railroad scandal, in spite of his flight from justice, and the murder charge was reduced to manslaughter after copious evidence was heard regarding Carlyle's illegal activities and his role in the attack on Drew Dowd and Boris Golding. Nick was convicted on the manslaughter charge and sentenced to eighteen months in a work camp in upstate New York. Barney watched Kate's face as the judge pronounced sentence. She was prepared, but even Barney did not expect the stoic, tearless countenance with which she faced the photographers who rushed to load their plates before turning their huge cameras on her. They held their flash trays high, filling the courtroom with blue-white bursts of magnesium powder and clouds of acrid smoke. She was quite a girl—a woman now. He expected she had been a woman always; today it was proven and reinforced. He was proud of this strong and beautiful friend who had faced so much and for whom so much more lay ahead. He saw plainly on her face that she was not afraid to wait.

Yes, Barney had helped, and so had Lester, who brought her back into the comfort of the 14th Street Theater. Lester had held off, as he had promised, on *The Taming of the Shrew* until she and Drew were both ready. No time would ever be better than now. Boris had died after long, hopeless weeks in a coma. The company needed this show to bring them back to life; Kate needed it for her sanity's sake. Nor did she fail to realize that she would also need the money. Carlyle's estate had been divided among the three women—his wife, his daughter, and his sister. Augusta and Irene left for Europe almost immediately to avoid the press, the notoriety, and, Kate suspected, their own guilt in accepting these tainted funds. But she could not blame them; they had not known, and certainly their future lives would forever be colored by the knowledge of Carlyle's tragic flaw. Kate knew that neither woman, Augusta particularly, would soon return to the shores of America.

As for Kate, she turned over her share of the inheritance to Nick's attorney, with instructions to repay each investor in the Southwest & Rio Grande Railroad. To give herself and Nick a start on their new life, she saved every penny she could from Lester's very generous salary, and she sold all of her jewelry—except Nick's necklace. Never that. She would keep it always, whether or not she ever had occasion to wear it again.

And she moved to Clara's house, not only to cut back on expenses, but because she needed friends about her. Especially now. In July, the play opened to sell-out business, due no less to the allure of the notorious Kate

Lawrence than to the enthralling production, which surpassed even Lester's high standards. And by summer's
end, Kate's suspicions were confirmed; she was expecting a child.

"You must tell him, Kate," Clara said. "He deserves
to know."

"I'll wait until after the baby's born."

At Clara's disapproving look, Kate defended herself.
"Would it not be worse for him to know now, when he
has so long to wait, so long before he'll be able to see
his child?"

"I'm not sure that's your decision to make, but of
course you'll do as you wish." She laughed. "Have you
ever done otherwise? Just let me know what you decide."

Kate wondered over that last remark in the days
ahead, while she mulled over her decision and finally
wrote to Nick, as she had never doubted she would. Apparently Clara had no doubt either, for she and Lester
acted, immediately and on their own, to contact Nick's
attorney. Within ten days, he arrived for a conference
with Kate. The judge who had presided over the Van
Dyne trial, the attorney said, had passed sentence as
precedent required, but he had obviously done so with a
heavy heart, and he was delighted to allow Nick transit
to New York City for a few hours—just the time necessary for a marriage to be performed, if Kate were willing. If she were willing!

There were no flowers, no music, no lace dress or
curving stairway to descend. There were no wedding
guests; attendance was limited to the minister, elegant in
his frock coat, giving no indication that such a ceremony was not on his daily schedule, and two witnesses,
Clara and Lester. A uniformed guard stood inconspi-
cuously to one side. The look that passed between the
bride and groom said everything: they had always been
joined; today was but the formality.

Kate worked until October before returning to Deaton to await the birth of her baby. And when the time
came, a hurricane could not have caused the house to

tremble with more turmoil. Laurel Ann rushed about with stacks of clean sheets; Jamie and the boys stood up, sat down, prepared to pace, while Sassy boiled kettles of water.

But Katherine Sloane Van Dyne would have none of it. She made her way into the world before the third kettle had let out its shrill whistle, before Laurel Ann had reached the top of the stairs, and just as Jamie settled down for the tenth time with the evening newspaper.

"You're an impatient one, my girl," Kate muttered to the damp, howling bundle in her arms. "Let's just hope we both have the patience to wait out the long year ahead."

Kate and little Sloane opened their eyes at the same moment, as if God had made some unusual movement in his heaven. In the distance, the outer gates of Centerville prison swung open, and several figures could be seen through the gray mist. Kate saw only one. She tried to remain calm as she climbed down the two steps from the carriage.

You have a lifetime, she told herself, you and Nick and the baby, a lifetime of unknown wonder. Take care; there is no reason to run.

She lifted Sloane gently into her arms and settled the child securely against her breast. The tall man turned his steps through the snow toward them. She quickened her pace. He began to run. And then she ran too, her feet crunching over new-fallen snow, into his arms. The sky brightened above them, and at last the daylight broke through.

THE VAN RHYNE HERITAGE

BY LOUISA BRONTE

The family that became a railroad
dynasty, driven to greatness by daring
dreams and bold desires...
THE VAN RHYNES—

They began on a humble dirt farm and
became the millionaire titans of the
industrial age. A family like no other,
a law unto themselves, they would stop at
nothing to win the golden prizes of
ambition and desire.

With ruthless courage and pride, they
built an unshakable dynasty and forged
an American empire of passion and steel.

B12043105 $2.25

Available wherever paperbacks are sold

Second volume in
THE AMERICAN DYNASTY SERIES
launched by THE VALLETTE HERITAGE.

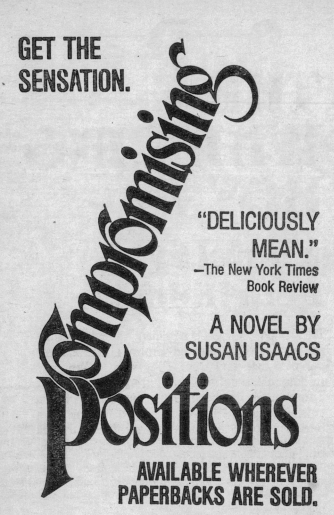

THE WHIPPING BOY

a novel by
Beth Holmes

THE WHIPPING BOY is a brilliant and often terrifying portrait of 12-year-old Timmy Lowell and his parents, Evie and Dan. They were a "model" middle class family—until they realized that Timmy, their first-born, was slowly turning into a psychotic killer. His father, locked into his own terrifying world, cannot help him; can't see the evil seed growing. Only Timmy's mother, Evie, can save him ... or become his next victim.

jove